Laura Preston

In Bonds

A Novel

Laura Preston

In Bonds
A Novel

ISBN/EAN: 9783337001827

Printed in Europe, USA, Canada, Australia, Japan

Cover: Foto ©Andreas Hilbeck / pixelio.de

More available books at **www.hansebooks.com**

IN BONDS.

A NOVEL.

BY

LAURA PRESTON.

"WITH CAUTION JUDGE OF PROBABILITY;
THINGS THOUGHT UNLIKELY, E'EN IMPOSSIBLE,
EXPERIENCE OFTEN SHOWS US TO BE TRUE."
Shakespeare.

A. ROMAN & COMPANY,

BOOKSELLERS, PUBLISHERS, AND IMPORTERS,

417 and 419 Montgomery St., San Francisco :

17 MERCER ST., NEW YORK.

1867.

IN BONDS.

CHAPTER I.

"In Love, if Love be Love, if Love be ours,
Faith and unfaith can ne'er be equal powers;
Unfaith in aught is want of faith in all."

"Trust me not at all or all in all."
Tennyson's "Vivian."

THE tide was coming in. Gently the swelling waves kissed the pebbly strand, as they yielded unto it their offerings of strangely-fashioned shells and clinging weeds. Gleaming in the last rays of the setting sun, they rolled murmuringly almost to the feet of a young girl who stood pensively watching their ebb and flow.

The scene was exceedingly wild and picturesque, and of it the fair wanderer formed a striking feature as she stood facing the ocean framed by gray, barren cliffs which rose abruptly upon each hand. Standing thus with the shadows of evening stealthily gathering over her face and enwrapping her form, and all surrounding it, she might have been fancied the very Genius of Solitude. She was of medium height, though she looked much taller as she stood, with her crimson shawl wrapped closely around her slender figure, gazing intently far over the waters. She was very pale—not purely white—but of that rich olive tint which dis-tinguishes beauties of the far South. Even her cheeks were unflushed by a tint of rose, yet were redeemed from sallowness by a glow of warmth which was diffused over her countenance, as if a sunbeam were prisoned there. Her hair was of purplish blackness, shining and wavy, brushed plainly back from the somewhat low forehead, and gathered in a large knot at the back of her well-formed head. A bow of crimson ribbon enhanced its blackness, and gave a tint of color to the cheek near which it floated. A shadow of deep thought—a faint trace of melancholy—seemed to settle upon her as she thus stood motionless, her full red lips compressed, and her white hands tightly clasped, as if in a mighty effort to restrain the impatience of her soul.

At last she started, and a smile of joy banished all gloom from her face as she heard the faint sound of a human voice break upon the stillness. Turning quickly she eagerly looked, first to the narrow, level beach on her left, and then up among the cliffs, upon a narrow path by which also the cove might be gained. On the summit of the highest cliff stood a young man, who waved his hand in token of recognition, and then began the descent of the precipitous path. The way was rugged and called into action all his agility and strength of muscle. His figure was tall and slender, but seemingly not fitted to endure much fatigue. His face was handsome, delicate in its outlines, and expressive of more pride than strength of character, its greatest charm resting in the gentle expression of the lips, the proud curves and lines of which seemed ever on the point of yielding to the joyous smile that betokens a benevolent soul. High-minded and good-natured, those who knew him best described Harold DeGrey to be. His was a character that needed no disguises, and affected none.

The young girl contemplated his descent with a smile of pleasure upon her lips, and sprang joyfully forward as he gained the flat beach and stood before her.

"La Guerita, I am most happy to find you here !" he exclaimed, clasping his arms around her and pressing a kiss upon her lips, smiling rapturously as she glanced at him shyly through her long curling lashes.

"My love," he continued, exultantly, "you know I promised you good news if you would meet me here, and did I ever deceive you, La Guerita ? "

"O no, Harold ! " she spoke eagerly ; yet she trembled and her lips grew pale.

"And I will not now, my own ! I have, indeed, good news for you ; or at least I shall be the most miserable of men if you do not find it so. I have seen Professor Harland. All is satisfactory. He consents to our union, and nothing now remains to serve as a barrier to our felicity."

"But, Harold, what did the Professor say ? " she spoke anxiously, as if scarcely satisfied with the manner in which her lover had spoken.

He instantly became grave, as he replied : "He said enough, my love, to allay all my —— your scruples. Mine your sweet face had long ago allayed."

"Did he tell you —— ? " she began eagerly.

"He told me very little, dearest, but what we knew before," interrupted DeGrey ; "and although, my love, it is indeed a pleasure to me to be confirmed in my ideas of the respectability of your birth, you will not, I am sure, believe that my affection for you could have been lessened even if your own foolish fears had been proven true."

She smiled a reply, and a little doubtfully, he thought, and coloring redly, he exclaimed : "Ah, La Guerita, you think it has not long been so, but I believe it has been the case for a much longer period than I am myself aware of."

"I am happy to believe it," she said unaffectedly, "but I would not have you blind to your own feelings or interests, Harold, or be so myself. I know that you are proud, and the mystery surrounding my birth must be a sore trial to you."

He did not speak, but the expression of his face showed that she was right. She stood at his side uneasily for a moment, then turning toward him with a quick, impatient gesture, asked, "What did Professor Harland say ? "

"Enough to satisfy me ! " returned DeGrey, ingenuously owning that his pride had long striven with his love, even as her own had done, but not so generously. "In the first place, La Guerita, he told me, as you know already, that Fabean and yourself were left in his care when mere infants by an elderly quakeress, and a gentleman of prepossessing and distinguished appearance. Professor Harland was at that time very poor, and in consideration of the princely sum offered him, readily consented to receive the two into his family, asking no questions, and receiving no information concerning them, save what the quakeress dropped in the few words, "God bless thee, for thou art saving two innocent babes a world of trouble. Thou hast a kind face; they will be safe with thee."

"I never heard of this quakeress before," cried La Guerita in amazement, "and her connection with me appears to destroy the theory that I am of foreign birth!"

"Not at all!" replied DeGrey, "for the Professor assures me that the gentleman spoke no English, and therefore he conversed with him only in Spanish. His knowledge of the language at that time was quite limited, yet he has now every reason to suppose that his conjecture as to the nativity of the stranger was correct. He believes, too, La Guerita, that Fabean and yourself are the offspring of a noble family—the liberal allowance yearly forwarded to you through Town & Forest, declares that you are supplied by no niggardly hand, while the noble bearing of both your brother and yourself, satisfies me that the proudest of the land might deem your alliance an honor."

The young girl had withdrawn from her lover's encircling arm, and looked at him as if to read his inmost soul, saying slowly, "Harold, have you no doubts? Are you indeed satisfied that I am worthy in all respects to be your wife?"

"More than worthy! Yes, more than worthy!" he cried excitedly, "I must have been mad to doubt it so long. None other ever questioned the purity of your origin; I would have stricken them to the earth had they dared to do so. The closest observers say there is about you an air of pride and conscious worth that low born people could never assume."

She smiled drearily, saying in a low voice, "I have such strange thoughts sometimes Harold. Occasionally in such hours as that preceding your coming, oftener still when I wake from a troublous dream; I so often wonder in what direction, over this waste of waters I must sail to reach my home, and those whom my birth should have made my friends."

"That is not after all a puzzling question," returned Harold DeGrey, "your very name is indicative of the place of your birth, 'La Guerita De-Cuba—the Fair Maid of Cuba.' Can you doubt that beneath the orange boughs of that sunny isle your eyes first saw the light?"

"Fabean believes that to be the case," said the young girl, musingly; adding after a few moments thought, "I myself have no cause to doubt it. I often wonder, Harold, that my brother thinks so lightly of our strange position; it does not seem to trouble him in the least, and indeed I thought but little of it myself until——"

"I troubled you with foolish questions," interrupted DeGrey. "My La Guerita," he continued, excitedly,

"I was ungenerous—ay, unmanly—I thank God my great love for you has made me strong! You know I was born and bred an aristocrat; by my high-born English mother—my peerless mother—I was taught from infancy to hold a stainless name of infinitely more value than all other possessions, and I do so still; the belief that was born with me will never die. But that your descent is as spotless as my own, thank God, I firmly believe."

"Else you would not be here!" she said disdainfully.

"Else, La Guerita, I had never loved you," he returned, gently. "Think you my heart would have sprung forth to claim as its mate one whose pulses throbbed with churlish blood. No, my very love is surety to me of your purity. Come to me, love! Come to me."

She sank into his arms, yielding to the love, that stronger than pride or duty, refused to aid her in condemning one who each moment uttered words that filled her soul with dread. "I am very weak," she sobbed; "I cannot say—'leave me ere it is too late;' yet I would rather that you should break my heart now, than live to know one pang of shame for me!"

"Leave you, La Guerita! Never!" exclaimed DeGrey passionately, aroused by his surprise from his usual calmness. "Have I not told you that I am convinced that some dark cloud envelopes, but stains not, a name as fair, and perhaps more noble than my own. Victor is assured of it, and even my mother; they long to embrace you. La Guerita, I love you; happen what may, I cannot leave you; never speak of it again. Have you not said that you love me?"

"I do! I do!" she returned, quickly and fervently. "That is why I tremble to look into the future. I would rather die than bring sorrow upon you. Ah, Harold! I have grown to be a strange coward of late."

"And needlessly, too, I am sure!" said DeGrey, caressingly, and soothing her fondly. Professor Harland showed me to-day the last letter he received concerning you. It was, as usual, written in Spanish, and signed "DeCuba." It contained instructions to the Professor, in case you should desire to marry. "The suitor must be of good family and spotless reputation," was explicitly said; and does not that alone clearly prove that you can lay claim to the same?"

She shook her head.

"Well! well!" he exclaimed, impatiently, yet fondly; "I cannot leave you, La Guerita. I am willing, for your sweet sake, to cast aside my usual caution, and take one leap in the dark. All the world will be light with you near me."

She received his caresses as if spellbound; she could not speak the words that hung heavily on her lips. The silence had become almost terrible to her, fraught, as it was, with so much of love and pain; when it was broken by a clear voice shouting forth a merry boating song.

"Ah! it is Fabean!" they simultaneously exclaimed; "and in good time, too. He has remembered what we had forgotten—that the tide rises high enough here to cut off all means of retreat by the shore. Had he not come we should have had to scale these cliffs to reach Fairview to-night.".

"Ah! Fabean is always thoughtful!" exclaimed La Guerita, gazing fondly and admiringly upon a young man who, with long and steady strokes, was guiding a small boat towards them.

"Make ready, there, to come aboard!" he shouted as he neared the shore, and looked laughingly upon his sister and her lover. "Pretty folks you are,' to make a tryst at such a place; you may thank your stars that I guessed something of it."

"I am inclined to think you a Yankee after all," said DeGrey, with a laugh, as the young man rested on his oars. "You are a veritable Jonathan for guessing, and there is nothing Spanish in your face, I am sure."

There was not, indeed. His countenance was of the purest Saxon type; his complexion remarkably clear and fair; his hair light-brown, and his eyes darkly blue. Both in face and figure he formed a striking contrast to his sister.

They sometimes deplored the difference, for they loved each other so deeply; they fain would have resembled each other, if only in person; for their dispositions were hopelessly at variance. La Guerita was often sad; while nothing ever clouded Fabean's brow. She delighted in intellectual pursuits; while he, at eighteen, still loved the sports of boyhood, and laughed all serious thoughts to scorn.

On that sunny afternoon his spirits were most exuberant, and 'ere they had long been seated in his boat, he had infected DeGrey with his mirthful humor. But La Guerita spoke and smiled but little; she seemed lost in thought. Her lover often attempted to laugh away the gloom that had settled upon her, and her brother laughingly rallied her upon her silence. At another time his jests would have aroused her from the deepest abstraction; but then they were powerless, and insensibly each became affected by her dejection, and fell into thought.

So many minutes passed; when suddenly La Guerita seemed oblivious of the presence of any one save her lover. She turned towards him abruptly, glancing at him with a troubled expression in her lustrous eyes, saying,

"I am doing very wrong. I know it; I know it."

"How is that possible?" exclaimed DeGrey.

"I feel that I am tempting Providence," she returned, in a low, thrilling voice. "I feel that I am tempting God to bring some great calamity upon me by consenting to marry you while this darkness is upon me."

"La Guerita!" rejoined her lover, somewhat sadly; "I have often noticed that God is to you a terrible and merciless Being—never the Christ who, in His tender mercy, came from heaven to save sinners."

She bowed her head, feeling keenly how clearly he had read her inmost soul.

They had reached a small dock, at the foot of an extensive lawn, and were about to land. La Guerita De-Cuba arose and silently gave her hand to DeGrey, and it was not until they were alone on the lawn that she ventured to speak to him.

"O, Harold!" she said then, as they stood together looking at Fabean, who was securing his boat, "I feel afraid to own, even to myself, my happiness; for, though filled with painful doubts, I am so happy to think I have one, besides Fabean, that I may love. Since I cast off the carelessness of childhood, I have often wept bitterly to think I had no claim upon the love or sympathy of any creature."

"La Guerita!" cried DeGrey, clasping her to his bosom, "you need never weep for that again. I love you, my darling, more than words can express. Let my actions prove it. Dearest, the Professor knows that you will shortly leave him, and approves my proposal, that on your seventeenth birthday you shall become my wife."

"What! within a month?" cried La Guerita.

"Yes, darling. What is to prevent?"

"'True, I have no ties elsewhere," she replied, with flushing cheeks and glistening eyes, "and I shall want none then. O, Harold, you will love me?"

"Ever—ever! my darling."

The promise, often as it had before been given, never had seemed so fraught with comfort as then. They walked on thoughtfully until they reached the house, which had been for nearly sixteen years the home of Fabean and La Guerita DeCuba. At the door the lovers spoke their parting words. La Guerita remembered them well and oft in future years.

"Harold!" she said, "whatever betides, you will never hate or forsake me?"

He held her in his arms, and looking steadfastly into her trustful eyes, replied: "As God lives, I will be true to you, my darling—my promised wife!"

CHAPTER II.

" There are two kinds of Love—that which yields all for the welfare of its object, whatever be its own pain; and that which claims all, caring nought for the weal or woe of the giver. Judge, ye, which is the noblest passion."

HAROLD DeGrey left his betrothed with the firm conviction that she was the scion of a race as noble as his own, and that she possessed principles as high as those which had for years rendered his name famous. Though by birth an American, he bore in his veins the proud blood of English parentage. Poor, but proud, had his father been in his youthful days, and as poor and proud the lady he chose for his wife. But loving each other ardently, they married, and sought in the New World the wealth denied them in the Old. It was soon found, but not long enjoyed; for the elder DeGrey, dying at the early age of forty, left a widow, who never ceased to mourn his loss; and two young sons, who, though in affluent circumstances, for many years most sadly needed his firm, yet gentle guardianship.

At the age of twenty-two, Harold was admitted to the bar, while Victor, his brother, younger by seven years, was preparing for college under the tutelage of Prof. Harland. It was during a visit to Victor that Harold first met La Guerita DeCuba. She was then scarcely fifteen years old, but gave promise of great beauty. Already had she attained her full stature and much of the grace of future years. Harold DeGrey forgot that she was still but a child, and from the first moment of their acquaintance felt that she was of all creatures the most beautiful—the most fitted to be loved. Greatly was he shocked to learn that her parentage was unknown —that she was educated and supported by a hidden hand.

"Thank God!" exclaimed DeGrey to himself upon receiving this information; "Thank God that I have discovered this so soon. I might perhaps have learned to love that girl; might even have desired to marry her, but for this disclosure."

And in spite of it, he soon discovered that he loved La Guerita DeCuba, and that his happiness depended upon his union with her. For many months the olden pride of the DeGreys held him back; then his mother's entreaties strongly influenced him; but he could not give her up. He knew that, even while he exclaimed in argument with himself, that he could not marry one of plebian birth, not even to secure life-long happiness.

Harold DeGrey had ever been noted for his practical and dispassionate mind. Never had he allowed his feelings to triumph over his judgment, and he was unwilling to do so even in this matter, wherein all his future joy was centered. For two years he loved her before he became satisfied that the mystery surrounding her had been cast there by other causes than shame and infamy, and spoke the words that were to La Guerita DeCuba the sweetest of all utterances.

He knew that she loved him, and

gloried in the blissful certainty. In his heart he humbled himself before her, as a subject smiled upon by a gracious queen. He felt himself strangely honored and blessed by her affection, and received those feelings as proofs of her nobility; and when he parted from her at the door of the Fairview Academy, he believed fully that his marriage would eventually add new lustre to his name, and give peace and joy to his restless, ambitious heart.

But it was with a mind filled with many forebodings, that La Guerita DeCuba watched him from the steps until he disappeared from her sight. Then she softly opened the door and entered the house, meeting in the hall a servant, who told her that a gentleman—Mr. Leveredge— was in the parlor, and had for some time been waiting to see her.

A look of pain, strangely mingled with horror, for a moment rested upon her face; but pausing a moment to subdue her emotions, she took off her shawl, and giving it to the servant, with a firm step entered the parlor.

As she opened the door a gentleman arose to greet her; but with a cold bow of recognition, and a slight wave of the hand, she motioned him back to the chair he had vacated, and seated herself on a sofa at some distance from him. Every motion of her body—every lineament of her face, expressed contempt and dislike; yet there was nothing in the appearance of Claude Leveredge to produce either.

His form and features were decidedly of true American mould. His tall, lithe frame his, piercing black eyes, and high cheek bones, were indicative of the red blood that tinged his veins. He gloried in those proofs of his descent from a warlike race, and was wont to say : "Virginians can find in North Carolina men born of a princess as pure and beautiful as was Pocahontas herself." Often had he told La Guerita the tale that for five generations had been cherished in his family ; how that a warrior of their name had saved an Indian girl from death, and afterwards married her. It was a simple tale enough, yet La Guerita had often listened to it shudderingly, feeling that the speaker was gaining from it a rule and guide for his own future.

"I have been waiting for you more than an hour," said the Carolinian. "May I ask what has so long detained you on the beach ? for there they told me you had gone. Surely the wild scenery you have looked upon daily for years had not power to charm you thus."

"I never weary of it," she answered simply ; "but it was not that, that detained me so long. I was talking to Fabean and Mr. DeGrey."

Mr. Leveredge smiled when he heard that Fabean had been of the party ; for he had feared that she had been alone with DeGrey, in whom he saw a powerful rival.

"And had you not one thought for me ?" he queried. "Fabean, at least, knew I was coming. Did he not mention it to you ?"

"No, Mr. Leveredge. In the importance of our conversation, he, probably, forgot the matter entirely."

For some moments Mr. Leveredge regarded her silently and most earnestly. Feeling the constraint of his manner most keenly, she arose and somewhat confusedly plead an engagement, and attempted to withdraw.

"You shall not until you have learned my errand here !" exclaimed her visitor, excitedly. "I know why you shun me ; it is because you know that you have deceived me."

"Deceived you ? Never !" cried La Guerita DeCuba, in tones of the most palpable surprise.

"You have ; you know that you have," retorted Leveredge, fiercely. "Have you not for years known my love for you ! When you were an infant, scarcely able to walk alone, it was I who guided your steps ; it was I who taught you to read ; I was your friend—the one your heart trusted, your hands caressed. I am he, whom, years ago, you vowed you would ever love."

"Claude !" There was a world of passionate reproach, entreaty, and sorrow in that single word, as La Guerita DeCuba uttered it, looking up with tearful, pleading eyes.

It appeared to soften the hearer's wayward mood, and with a face aglow with tenderness he approached and took her hand. She drew it from his grasp ; but not before he had whispered : "Dearest, you have not forgotten ?"

"I have forgotten nothing," she replied, in a low voice ; "I should be glad if I could."

"Ah, La Guerita !" he began ; "do not say that you wish to forget those days of long ago. We were both so happy then. I so joyful if I could have the privilege of defending you from insult or danger ; and you so proud to be so protected. La

Guerita, let the memory of the past be with you to-night. Let Claude Leveredge be the hero—*the lover*—he was in those early days."

"That is impossible," she murmured. "We have both changed so much since then."

"I have changed, La Guerita," he admitted, after a moment's thought; "or rather my true nature has perfected and revealed itself; but whatever changes have come over me, they have not affected my love for you."

She shuddered, turning nervously away to shun his burning gaze.

"You are afraid to look at me," he continued, excitedly. "Afraid to look at the man whom as a boy you loved and trusted. Ah, La Guerita DèCuba, when we parted, four years ago, little did I think I should see that look upon your face!"

"Do not speak of that time," she entreated; "I was but a child then, and you had always been kind to me. I——"

"I must speak of it!" he interrupted quickly; "I must speak of it! Do you not remember that, on the morning we parted, you promised to be my wife? La Guerita, I am here to claim the fulfillment of that promise."

She grew even paler than was natural to her; but her eyes flashed angrily as she returned scornfully:

"What was that promise? The thoughtless words of a child who, even while she spoke, feared more than she loved you."

"And why did you fear me? Had I not for years served you! Had I not protected you from infancy? O, La Guerita, have I served seven years by twice seven years for my Rachel in vain?"

By a passionate gesture she entreated him to say no more; but, unheeding the silent appeal, he continued:

"I would to God I had always remained with you; that I had never seen Europe. You are more to me than all the lands of tale and song. Yet, while I was wasting my precious hours amid faded grandeur, or that which must shortly fade, you were breaking the bonds I still cherished, and forswearing the vows I daily renewed."

His words seemed as daggers in the heart of La Guerita DeCuba! and in agonized tones she cried: "How can you speak such cruel words? O, Claude, I never deceived you. As soon as I fully understood the nature of the engagement I had so carelessly formed, I wrote to you, begging that it might be annulled. O, Claude! you were kind and generous then; be so now. You yielded to my wishes, and said that on your return I should be free to follow the dictates of my own heart."

"I believed that your desire, earnestly as it was expressed, was but a childish freak; but you loved me, and would do so whether bound or free. I did not dream that my innocent school-girl would so early have learned the lessons of a finished coquette!"

"You wrong me!" she replied, hastily; "I had not even seen Harold then."

The blood rushed to the dark cheeks of Claude Leveredge as he approached a step nearer the young girl.

"What, then !" he exclaimed, "you dare even to tell me that you love Harold DeGrey?"

"Yes!" she returned calmly, meeting unflinchingly his fiery gaze ; "I love him even as he loves me. I am to be his wife!"

CHAPTER III.

" Didst thou but know, as I do,
 The pangs and tortures of a slighted love,
 Thou wouldst not wonder at this sudden change ;
 For when ill-treated, it turns all to hate,
 And the then darling of our soul's revenge."

Powell.

TERRIBLE was the effect of this announcement upon Claude Leveredge. La Guerita was amazed and startled as she saw him turn the ghastly hue of death. His eye-sight seemed to fail him, and he sought a chair, with the slow, painful motion of one suddenly bereft of sight.

She thought of him then as he had been during the years he had passed at Fairview. Always impulsive and ungovernable in temper, he had been a very Goliath among the scholars ; feared and disliked by all, save La Guerita DeCuba, whose champion he had declared himself on the first day of his residence at Fairview. She had regarded him with a mixture of love and awe for many years, and when they were about to part felt that her best friend and protector was leaving her ; and so, amid sobs and tears, she yielded to his entreaties, and promised to become his wife.

She soon discovered the deep significance of her words. His letters were full of exacting, jealous love, terrifying her by its very earnestness. The chains he threw around her soon became to her too galling to bear. She was but a slave in his hand ; for

although three thousand miles of ocean lay between them, he still ruled almost as completely as before. From her childhood she had been accustomed to regard his frown as the most terrible of all calamities, and though long parted she could not forget her champion—her dauntless hero. Still he was to her the realization of her ideal of manly power and beauty, when his sudden return to Fairview dispelled the illusion that had for years deceived her.

With a fainting heart she saw that the independent boy had become a domineering churl ; the fearless champion had developed into a duelist, with the blood of an innocent youth upon his hand. Reports of his reckless career followed fast upon him, and it was with loathing that La Guerita put away from her the love that had once been her joy and hope.

For years he had been to her the noblest type of manhood ; but her idol was broken ; its hollowness betrayed. Dissipation had left deep traces upon his countenance, and the restless workings of his excitable mind distressed and repelled her. She had believed him strong in mind and principles ; but he had proved too weak to resist temptations, which ordinary men, with whom she had once seemed to compare him, would have passed lightly by. He had fallen where the frailest of his race had stood unflinchingly.

It was not until this failure of a glorious promise stood before her, and plead for the love she had given his youth, that La Guerita DeCuba fully realized the worth of Harold DeGrey. The comparisons she involuntarily made between the two left her no room to doubt which was the better man, or which she loved. With the threats and wild entreaties of a maniac, Claude Leveredge met her assurance that she would never renew the vows, happily broken three years before; and now, a month later, he had returned in a calmer mood to bid her reconsider her words.

When she said she was to be the wife of Harold DeGrey, he fully realized her feelings toward him. He was assured that if even a particle of her childish love had remained in her heart, to trouble and perplex her, she would never have engaged to marry another. He knew that he had fallen irrevocably in her estimation, and not even the self-esteem which had hitherto sustained him could whisper one assurance of success in the task to which he had applied himself.

"La Guerita DeCuba," he said at length, "you know not what you are doing. I shudder when I think of your future and mine! Can you hope for happiness?"

"Yes!" she replied, but very faintly. "Do not look at me so, I pray. You know I am alone in the world; my husband will be my all, and I must choose one worthy of my entire confidence and love."

"And you conceive Harold De-Grey alone to be the faultless being fitted to be your protector and guide?" said Leveredge, in tones of suppressed passion. "He is richer than I, perhaps, and with him the play of King Cophetua and the beggar girl may be more perfectly enacted."

La Guerita turned toward him, her slender figure and pale, expressive face quivering with anger and wounded pride, exclaiming : "He will at least protect me from your insults!"

Leveredge threw himself before her, as she turned to leave the room, and cried : "La Guerita DeCuba, be warned! Harold DeGrey comes of a proud race; he loves you; but do you suppose he would marry you if he believed you to be the offspring of shame? No, never! But I, La Guerita, were I a king, would take you from the very depths of degradation to make you queen."

"Let me go," pleaded La Guerita. "Say no more; my resolve is taken, and no earthly power can change it."

"Then you persist in your refusal to be my wife?" he asked, in a low voice, his accents thrilling with suppressed emotion.

"I shall marry Harold DeGrey," she said firmly.

He drew back from her, holding out his right hand and saying, with terrible and startling emphasis : "That hand, in a foolish, boyish quarrel, drew life-blood once, La Guerita De-Cuba, and it shall yet draw your heart's bitterest tears. I am not one to utter meaningless threats, and, remember, as surely as there is a God above us, you shall have bitter cause to rue the hour in which you have slighted and scorned Claude Leveredge. Ah !" he continued, solemnly and with strange pathos, "you would have been safe as my wife. No evil should have reached you; but now let it come; let it fall; let it *crush !*

"'Thou shalt love, and that love shall be thy curse;
Thou wilt need no heavier; thou shalt feel no worse.
I see the cloud and the tempest near;
The voice of the troubled tide I hear;

The torrent of sorrow—the sea of grief—
The rushing waves of a wretched life;
Thy bosom's bark on the surge I see,
And, maiden, no loved one is there with thee.'"

She raised her head with an imploring gesture, crying : "You threaten Harold ! If your vengeance must fall let it be upon me. Spare him !"

"I will spare neither," he said sternly. "Ah, you need not fear me now !" he continued, as she shrank in alarm from his outstretched hand. "See, I could rob my rival of his bride by one turn of this strong arm ; but you are safe ; my revenge shall be even deeper and sweeter than that !"

In his excitement he appeared to become quite oblivious of her presence. Turning from her, he slowly paced the length of the room, muttering, almost incoherently : "My first task shall be to discover the parentage of La Guerita DeCuba ; my next, to blast her happiness, whatever may be her origin ! You——" he turned towards the spot where La Guerita had stood ; but she was no longer there. Seizing the opportunity when he had turned his back upon her, she had crept silently from the room, and swiftly sought the shelter of her own apartment.

She stood for a few seconds in the center of the room, with her hands clasped over her heart, to stay its loud throbbings, while she eagerly listened for sounds from below. Soon she heard the hall door open ; then close with a sudden clang. Going, softly still and under the spell of fear, to her window, she saw Claude Leveredge descend the steps, pause for a moment, as if uncertain what course to pursue, and then walk hurriedly across the lawn to the water's edge. There he was soon joined by Fabean ;

and after a few moments conversation the two stepped into a small boat, and rowed slowly out of sight.

An hour later she received word that her brother wished to see her. After washing her flushed cheeks— for she had been weeping long and bitterly—she went down to the library, where she found him sitting near the table, with his face buried in his hands.

He looked up as she approached, and said : "I have just left Leveredge."

"I know it," she replied ; "I saw you enter the boat together. Had you an appointment with him ?"

"No. You know I am often on the dock on such bright nights as this. Leveredge knew my haunt, and sought me there. La Guerita, you will pardon me if I speak to you plainly. Are you quite sure that you have done right ?"

"Yes, Fabean ; quite sure. But did he send you here to question me ?"

"Did *he* send me ?" returned Fabean ; "No ; I came because I wanted to see you in your new character of heart-breaker. No, La Guerita," he added, with sudden seriousness ; "Claude Leveredge's last words of love or entreaty have been spoken." He arose and threw his arms tenderly around her. "You have awakened a demon, my darling, that will never sleep. I know you love DeGrey. I, myself, honor and revere him ; but I ask you again, my sister, have you done right in discarding Leveredge ?"

"You have never loved, or you would not ask me," she replied, in low, thrilling tones.

"After all our uncle may be able to conciliate Claude, by awarding him the hand of another niece," said Fabean ; "he may have a dozen in obscurity for all we know.".

"Fabean, I beg of you not to speak of our unknown supporter in that manner, or by that title !" she exclaimed, with some irritation in her voice and gesture ; "it is, indeed, very ridiculous."

"Ridiculous or not, I believe it to be the correct title to apply to him," persisted Fabean. "Well, well, my dear, it matters little who we are ; I will gain a name for us both. Ah, I forgot ; you are to take that of DeGrey, and will need no other."

La Guerita blushed, standing pensively before her brother for a few moments, then suddenly looking up, with a startled expression, saying, in a low voice : "O, Fabean, I wish we had even a name. I am terrified when I think I have not even that to give in exchange for all Harold will bestow upon me. I look with trembling, even though with joy, into this new life upon which I am about to enter."

"You should look into nothing more than a well-filled tea-cup to-night," interrupted Fabean, assuming his usual gaiety of manner, "and that you shall have an opportunity of doing in a few minutes ; so go to your room, and I'll order a cup of tea to be taken to you ; you need it to steady your nerves, which are like the chords of an eighteenth-century piano—all out of tune."

La Guerita gladly accepted this hint to retire, and as she ascended the stairs to her apartment, she heard Fabean whistling gaily, as if no thought of care had ever entered his mind, and as though the future lay as clear before him as the bright moonlight in which he stood.

"It is well that he can be so light-hearted," she murmured ; "Ah, would that I could be the same ; but the thought of trouble perplexes and saddens me, and the reality might madden !"

CHAPTER IV.

"An image was before mine eyes; there was silence, and I heard a voice." *Job.*

A WEEK later La Guerita DeCuba visited, for the first time, the home of her future husband. Invited thither by his mother, she went with fear and trembling, knowing well that the proud lady had given but a reluctant consent to her son's marriage, and that she bitterly deplored the sacrifice she believed him to be making.

But Mrs. DeGrey, though exceedingly proud, was duly appreciative of beauty and refinement, and was pleased to discover both in La Guerita, and before the close of the first day's acquaintance had decided that her son's choice was not to be wondered at, and but for the mystery of her birth would have been a most fortunate one.

With these sentiments rapidly clearing away her chagrin, Mrs. DeGrey strove by every means in her power to interest and please her young guest. No difficult task, for even the richness and beauty of her surroundings charmed the untutored mind of La Guerita, while she could not but be entertained by the unrestrained conversation of Mrs. DeGrey and her lover.

In the course of the afternoon he left the ladies to themselves, probably with the design of removing all restrictions from their intercourse, and that each might have the opportunity of judging the private character of the other. As the afternoon was warm, Mrs. DeGrey proposed that they should spend an hour in the garden ; and they, accordingly, proceeded thither. After walking for some time they entered an arbor, where Mrs. DeGrey left La Guerita, and went back to the house to give an order she had forgotten. Scarcely had she disappeared from view, when a shadow fell athwart the greensward that carpeted the bower. La Guerita looked up with a welcoming smile, expecting to see Harold DeGrey. To her surprise her gaze encountered that of a strange gentleman, who was standing rigidly erect in the entrance.

Her first impulse was to scream ; but a second glance at the cause of her alarm silenced her. " Doubtless," thought she, " he is an unfortunate friend of Mrs. DeGrey, accustomed to seek her here."

His appearance was prepossessing. He was middle-aged, tall, and handsome, with the air of a gentleman unmistakably about him. He attempted no apology for his intrusion, but gazed upon La Guerita with an intensity that both alarmed and displeased her.

" Do you wish to see Mrs DeGrey ?" she faltered, rising hastily, and contemplating immediate flight.

" Poor Dolores ! poor Dolores !" sighed the intruder.

Eyes so like Fabean's that they thrilled her to the heart, were looking wildly upon her, and thoroughly frightened, and with a feeling of certainty that the stranger was in some way connected with the mystery of her life, La Guerita cried, in great agitation,: " Who are you ? What do you wish with me ?"

For an instant she was struggling in his arms. Passionate kisses were rained upon her cheeks and brow. She uttered a piercing shriek, when, suddenly releasing her, the bold intruder rushed from the arbor, and dashing into a clump of shrubbery, was immediately lost to sight.

Alarmed at hearing the shriek, DeGrey, who was approaching the arbor, hastened on, and to his surprise and dismay found La Guerita, almost fainting from alarm, standing near the entrance to the arbor, looking wildly around her.

" My darling, what has frightened you ?" he exclaimed, springing to her side, and throwing his arms around her.

She clung to him with all the energy of fear and love, but for some moments could not sufficiently subdue her agitation to speak.

Mrs. DeGrey had now appeared and, much alarmed, demanded what had happened. " And what is this ?" she added, suddenly placing her hand upon the bosom of La Guerita.

With increased surprise the young girl beheld a magnificent gold chain which was about her neck, and from which depended a diamond cross of great value and beauty.

" *He* must have put it there !" she exclaimed, in bewilderment. " O, who can he be ?"

" He ! Whom do you mean ?" cried DeGrey and his mother simultaneously.

With as much coherence as her agitation would admit of, La Guerita related her startling adventures, elicing from Mrs. DeGrey many exclamations of surprise and dignified anger, and casting a heavy frown upon the face of her more phlegmatic son.

"It would be no use for us to do so," said Harold, in answer to a suggestion from Mrs. DeGrey that they should make a search of the grounds; "no doubt the man is far enough away by this time. Let us examine the cross; there may be something upon that to lead to his discovery."

It was accordingly inspected closely by Mrs. DeGrey and Harold, but no cipher or initial could be discovered. The size and brilliancy of the diamonds called forth many exclamations from the lady, who could not refrain from whispering to her son that she hoped the cross was but "a sample of what the wedding gifts would be."

But he was in no mood for such thoughts, and through the rest of the afternoon, though he endeavored to appear as usual before La Guerita, was both silent and thoughtful.

La Guerita was the same, and after bidding farewell to Mrs. DeGrey, whose admiration for her future daughter-in-law was most flatteringly apparent, she lapsed into a profound reverie, which lasted until the carriage stopped before the door of the Fairview Academy, and Fabean hastened forth to meet her; then she cried, eagerly:

"O, Fabean! Fabean! I have seen our father to-day!"

He uttered an exclamation, more expressive of joy than surprise, and cried: "And I, La Guerita, have seen our uncle!"

Professor Harland, who was standing near, turned toward them in sudden and great agitation, begging them to say no more there, but to follow him to the house. They did so, and were immediately ushered into his private study.

"What do you mean, La Guerita, by saying you have seen your father?" he asked, when he had closed and locked the door, the better to prevent intrusion.

"Ask Fabean about it," she returned, feeling quite unable to explain herself clearly, having scarcely recovered from the first shock her brother's words had given her. "Fabean, when did you see him?"

"Quite early this morning," he replied; "or, at least, just after you left for Greymont. I was sitting under the great willow, at the end of the lawn, considering the important question: 'To be, or not to be,' in relation to a perfect Greek lesson, when a gentleman—quite a fine looking one, too—walked up to me and said, most confidently: 'You are Fabean DeCuba.' 'Indeed!' said I, in a tone of great interest, 'I am happy to learn that that is an established fact.'

"He seemed amused, or rather, I should say, he looked like one that tried to be amused; then he looked at me very closely, and said something about the fineness of the day and the clearness of the water, admired my boat, and finally hinted that he should like to try her quality, as he had been quite a sailor in his youth, and had by no means lost all his interest in a fine boat.

"Upon that, I proposed to row

him a short distance in mine, as I well knew there was not a better boat on the coast. He accepted my invitation very readily, and we were soon on our way toward Ellisville. So interesting was our conversation, that I shot by that place without thinking of stopping; and I might still be rowing about the bay, answering his questions, which, I now remember, related almost entirely to family matters, had he not, to my great surprise, asked me to land him at a point nearly two miles below Ellisville. When I had done so he said, 'I have been here several times before, but I am a little at fault now. Can you tell me how far it is to Greymont?'

"I was so surprised at the question that I did not think of answering it until it was repeated; then I said it was about a mile, though I think now that it was at least three.

"'Thank you,' he said; 'and does the road lie over that hill? Ah, yes, of course it does. Are you going back to Fairview immediately?'

"'Are you going to Greymont?' I replied, giving question for question.'

"'Yes,' he answered, 'and be assured that the hour spent in forwarding me on my way shall not prove an unprofitable one to you.'

"I was surprised and indignant. The first, that he should have cajoled and deceived me into rendering him a service, when I would have done so had he simply asked me; and the second, that he should dare speak of reward, as if I had been a common ferryman. But before I could utter a word he wrung my hand fervently and leapt ashore. I watched him

for some moments; I had some thoughts of leaving the boat and following him, when he looked back, with an expression upon his face, such as has haunted my dreams for years. I shall never forget it! I had seen it before—long, long ago! It filled my mind with faint visions—my senses with faint odors. I saw, as through a vail, the face of a beautiful woman, dark and queenly. I think she wore upon her head a crown, or tiara; there was something—I cannot tell what; I was in a garden full of flowers, and in the distance stood a white cottage, embowered in vines. Nothing came before me distinctly—all was vague, intangible, dreamy! There were lights and shadows in strange confusion; there were strains of melody from soft voices, and enwoven with them all a moan—a heart-broken moan—which I know in reality once sounded in my ears! Ah, that dreadful moan! As it swelled upon my ears I shuddered, as with an ague, feeling as if the dead past had arisen before me!"

Never had La Guerita seen her brother so greatly moved; he clasped his brow with one hand, as if to collect his strange, wandering thoughts, while the other, which she held, was damp and cold as marble; his face was very pale, and he trembled violently. She knew that strange visions —faint memories—were haunting him like grim specters, in their weird and fanciful indistinctness.

"Strange! very strange!" muttered Professor Harland, "if—if that person has been here, that he has not visited me!"

"Oh, I forgot to mention my reward," said Fabean, awakened from his reverie by some question from DeGrey. "About ten minutes before your arrival a negro man came here, leading a fine bay horse, with a handsome saddle and bridle upon him, and delivered him to the groom, saying 'it was for Fabean DeCuba, from the gentleman he rowed to Ellisville in his boat this morning.' John was too much astonished to apprise me of my good fortune until the negro, whom he declares to be a stranger in the neighborhood, had disappeared. Friends, what are we to think? Are these gifts the effects of love, or of an uneasy conscience?"

He looked around for an answer, but none spoke; all were agitating his question in their hearts.

Some powerful, but undefinable, emotion induced Harold DeGrey to exclaim: "Professor Harland, I can endure no delay; La Guerita must immediately become my wife. La Guerita, remember, whatever happens, whoever you may be, you are to be my wife!"

"God bless you, DeGrey!" cried Fabean, clasping his hand; "God bless you, for now I *know* you love her!"

But La Guerita passed from the room without uttering a word, and, hastening to her room, cast herself upon her knees, and prayed with streaming tears that the great mystery of her life might be explained. Thus the night hours wore away, and the gray dawn, peeping in at her window, found her wan and haggard from her weary vigil, and revealed Fabean upon the lawn, trying his new horse, and gaily proclaiming him a beauty.

It was many days before La Gue-rita could entirely throw off her sadness; then she was shown a letter, signed DeCuba, which had reached them through an agent in Philadelphia, which not only approved of her marriage with DeGrey, but contained a check sufficiently large to procure a complete and elegant trousseau.

In preparations for her bridal, La Guerita DeCuba for a time forgot her cares, and in the increasing warmth of Harold's love felt no shadow of despondency or gloom.

CHAPTER V.

"Hear the mellow wedding bells—
Golden bells!"

WITH all the beauty of the summer, increased by a gorgeous tinting of its own, the first month of autumn had come. It was hailed with unclouded joy by Harold DeGrey, and with fearful, trembling happiness by La Guerita DeCuba, for in the tenth day of its pilgrimage they were to be united.

The sun that shone upon the marriage day had never smiled on one more fair and beautiful. The sky was cloudless, and the cool breezes that rippled the bosom of the bay, and of the ocean that lay like a lower sky in the distance, made sweet melody among the swaying trees, and filled the air with delicious fragrance from the autumn flowers, that flaunting in bright array, had succeeded the more fragile summer blossoms. Never over La Guerita had smiled a clearer sky, and never had the earth appeared so beautiful; still a cloud hung over her spirit, a gloom cast, even by that which was to her the most pure and lovely, as shadows are often thrown in clear waters by graceful willows that beautify their banks. She sighed and trembled when she thought of the intensity of Harold's love, which every day grew more apparent ; yet she knew that the world would be utterly dark to her were that love removed from her. Something of this feeling must have showed itself upon her countenance when they stood before the altar, for Harold whispered : " Darling, trust me."

Then the service commenced. There were many spectators, for both Harold and La Guerita were very widely known. The mystery enshrouding her had even lent an additional charm to the beauty and dignity of her person, and the high connection she was about to form was universally regarded with pleasure. Thus La Guerita DeCuba found herself no friendless bride on the morning that was to behold her a loved and honored wife.

Solemnly the aged minister had pronounced the opening passages of the marriage service, had put to De-Grey the usual question and received a ready answer, and turned to La Guerita with the query : "Wilt thou have this man to be thy wedded husband," when Harold saw her become deadly pale, and tremble from head to foot. She however recovered from her agitation sufficiently to give her answer in a low but distinct voice, and the ceremony proceeded without interruption. Harold received his bride from the hands of Professor Harland, who with great pride and satisfaction beheld his beautiful pupil, his much-loved foster daughter, united to the talented and wealthy DeGrey.

For a few moments after the conclusion of the wedding ceremony, a joyous confusion prevailed, but seizing her opportunity when her brother approached to offer his congratulations, La Guerita whispered to him : "Fabean, he——the gentleman who frightened us so, is here. I saw him in one of the side pews."

Hastily pressing a kiss upon her trembling lips, he bounded from her side and sought eagerly among the people assembled for the stranger ; but he was nowhere to be seen, and he was obliged, most reluctantly, to join the wedding train, without having caught even a passing glimpse of the mysterious visitant.

The wedding breakfast was given at Fairview, and a large number of distinguished guests honored it by their presence. In the excitement of the hour, La Guerita quite forgot the stranger until he was brought to mind by the sight of the magnificent gifts he had sent her. A large selection of elegant jewelry, diamonds, emeralds and pearls, bore testimony to the greatness of his wealth and taste, and fully realized the hopes of Mrs. DeGrey, which were expressed in the discovery of the diamond cross. Within one of the jewel cases was found a draft upon one of the Philadelphia banks for ten thousand dollars, but as no one in the company knew the exact sum for which it was drawn, its value was greatly magnified, and before the breakfast was over, it had reached in some active minds to a hundred thousand dollars or more.

Delight and astonishment for a moment rendered the young bride speechless, but Fabean exclaimed :

"Now, really this is very handsome of our respected relative! It is a pity that his excessive modesty prevents him from receiving in person the thanks he so richly deserves."

DeGrey said nothing, but thought "How great must be the wealth of which La Guerita has been defrauded, if this is a mere tithe paid as a wedding gift."

The same reflection crossed the mind of his lady mother, causing her to regard her beautiful daughter-in-law with increased complacency.

When most of the guests were collected around the table upon which the bridal gifts were displayed, dividing their attention equally between them and the bride and groom, to whom they had been presented, a servant entered the room, bearing on a salver a small oblong case, which he said had been left at the door by a colored servant. The initials of La Guerita DeCuba were engraved upon a silver plate on the top of the box, and greatly wondering from whom it came, she placed it upon the table before her, and opened it. The lid flew back, disclosing, to her horror and the amazement of all present, a small dagger, the blade of the finest steel, and the hilt of ebony inlaid with gold.

La Guerita turned deadly pale, and for a moment looked upon the gift as an ill omen, knowing well that it came from Claude Leveredge, but Harold DeGrey, although somewhat startled, and greatly annoyed, exclaimed with a loud laugh, "What a beautiful blade! Really it will make a splendid paper cutter," and passed it to one of the astonished guests, commenting on its beauties as if it were indeed a harmless cutter instead of the deadly weapon it in reality was.

That was the only incident that occurred to mar the joyousness of the wedding festivities. La Guerita could not look upon it lightly, though Fabean and DeGrey affected to laugh at the petty vengefulness shadowed forth in Claude Leveredge's gift. It was the only article in her house upon which she could not bear to look, when, after a short wedding tour, Harold took her to the beautiful cottage he had prepared for her reception. Though far less magnificent than the mansion occupied by Mrs. DeGrey and her son Victor, it was to La Guerita the most lovely and "the dearest spot on earth."

She called it Enola, fancifully transposing the word Alone. "For, dearest," she said to Harold, "I never am so happy as when alone with you in our own sweet home."

But Mrs. DeGrey had determined that her daughter-in-law should not be much alone, that her light should not be hidden under the bushel of domestic ties, and accordingly, during the winter succeeding her marriage, La Guerita was the belle—the life of society.

The season was passed in a round of gaieties of which, at last, even La Guerita grew weary, and was quite delighted when she heard that the last and most elegant party was to be given by Mrs. Leslie of Ellisville.

"I hope after that, I shall be allowed to pass a few weeks in quietness with you," she said to her husband as they entered Mrs. Leslie's parlors. Instantly La Guerita became, as usual, the center of attraction, and ere long the crowded rooms, the music, the hundred flashing lights, and above all, the deferential attentions of the most distinguished gentlemen present, charmed and exhilarated her, and, in the enjoyment of the hour she soon lost all thoughts of calmer and more precious moments.

She had been dancing with Victor DeGrey, a fine, handsome young man about twenty years old, and upon resuming her seat, asked him to bring her a glass of water. He left her, and immediately a group of gentlemen and ladies formed around her, and a lively conversation was commenced, in the course of which, one said : " For my part, I don't believe there is such a thing as true happiness in the world !"

" Why, all the people that are here to-night look happy enough, I'm sure !" exclaimed Mrs. Leslie.

"They *look* so, I grant," was the reply ; " but should you put to them, severally, the question whether they are really so, I am afraid you would receive many answers in the negative."

" I will try a few," replied the lady, "such a theory of yours is worth looking into, although it is such a gloomy one. I will begin with you Mrs. DeGrey, for you have the most joyous face in the room ; are not you perfectly happy ?"

La Guerita had been engaged in conversation with Fabean on a matter of some importance, and for the last few moments had paid but little attention to the remarks of those around her. She was a little startled at Mrs. Leslie's question, but answered readily : "O, yes, Mrs. Leslie, I am quite

happy ; there is no shadow on my path !"

She looked up gaily at the conclusion of this sentence, *and a shadow fell.* Claude Leveredge stood near the door, gazing intently upon her. He had overheard her words, and smiled mockingly.

Alarmed at her sudden pallor, Fabean asked the cause of it.

She turned toward him, and whispered : " Claude Leveredge is at the door ;" but when she looked again he had vanished. Fabean left her, with the intention of finding him, of whom she had spoken, and an instant later Victor stood before her, with a glass of water in his hand.

" I am not well," she said, in answer to his inquiring look ; " do try to find Harold, and ask him to come to me."

He left her, and she became aware that her hostess and her friend, Mrs. Ross, were speaking of her, in low, confidential tones.

" No wonder that she turned pale," said the first ; " I have heard that she jilted him most shamefully."

"Where has he been for so many months ?" queried Mrs. Ross ; "at home, in North Carolina ?"

" No ; he spent the fall and winter months in Cuba ; he has only been here two days. I met him in the street yesterday, and asked him to come here to-night, but he declined my invitation. I am surprised to see him, and still more so that he has not paid his respects to me."

He had spent the winter in Cuba ! The words rang in La Guerita's ears, and the thoughts excited by them made her sick and dizzy. " Has he discovered anything ?" was the first question that presented itself to her mind, but the answer: "No!" came readily, for she remembered well that the expression upon his face had been that of a tireless pursuer, not of a triumphant victor.

She was glad when Harold, who had been much alarmed by Victor's account of her disordered looks, came to her. Although she had entirely recovered her color and self-possession, she urged an immediate return home, waiting only to hear from Fabean, that Leveredge had entered his carriage, and been driven rapidly away, the moment after she had discovered him.

Harold was much surprised and annoyed on hearing of the strange conduct of his former rival. To him it was incomprehensible, for La Guerita had never told him of the terrible threats he had made just before her marriage.

All, however, were, on the following day, much pleased to learn that he had taken the cars for the South within an hour after leaving Mrs. Leslie's.

Fabean and Harold were both certain that he had made no discoveries, at least, of an unpleasant nature, as, they were well assured, he would disclose them; and as nothing was for some time heard or seen of him, he soon passed from their minds. But La Guerita often thought of it with terror and a nameless dread, feeling that the trail of a serpent was over the flower-gemmed path of her life.

CHAPTER VI.

"Vengeance has no foresight."
Napoleon I.

FIVE years had La Guerita De-Cuba been the wife of Harold De-

4

Grey, before aught else occurred to disturb the tranquility of her mind; and even then it was only a little thing, which only her great love and solicitude made of moment. One winter evening, after waiting long and patiently for her husband, a note had been sent her from the office, informing her that Mr. De-Grey had received *private* news of great importance, and had started for Philadelphia at a moment's notice.

Nearly two weeks had passed since then, without bringing her a line from the absent one, or any news of his whereabouts. La Guerita was daily becoming more uneasy, and even the calm lawyers, his partners, openly commented upon his strange absence, and spoke of making public inquiries for him. This his brother Victor strongly opposed, saying: "He told you when he left that he might not be back for a month, and that you might not hear from him within that time. Let Harold alone; he knows what he is about, I'll warrant you."

Even La Guerita, when spoken to, in effect gave the same answer, feeling assured it was the investigation of some important business that detained him and kept him silent; and with almost overpowering emotions she surmised that the business was connected with the mystery of her own life. She dared not say this even to Victor DeGrey. Perhaps if her brother Fabean had been near she might have gained relief for her troubled heart, by unburdening to him her fears; but he was far away. The winter before, Harold DeGrey had suffered much from general debility, and his physicians, perceiving in him signs of incipient consumption, advised him to spend the winter in a warmer climate. For many reasons, Cuba was selected as their sojourning place, and there Harold DeGrey, his wife, and son, passed three of the happiest months of their lives ; and thither Fabean soon went, having, with his usual levity, resigned his situation in the bank, and declared his intention of spending the ten thousand dollars, that had fallen to his lot on his twenty-first birthday, in travel. This resolution had been induced by letters from La Guerita, who had described, in glowing colors, the projected tour of the Burfords, an American family, who had long been residents in Havana. And soon after Fabean's arrival in Cuba the DeGreys had been greatly vexed to hear that Mr. Burford had begged him to travel with them as his secretary. Fabean eagerly accepted the position, quieting all opposition by the remark, that he "would be seeing the world and obtaining an insight of business at the same time."

That was undeniably true ; but that did not comfort his sister. Her objections to the tour were not created by thoughts of business, but by the existence of a young lady, the eldest of the five younger Burfords. She was a most charming girl— young, beautiful, refined ; the one of all others La Guerita thought most fitted to captivate the heart of her brother, and, alas ! to be captivated by him. Had La Guerita been at liberty to choose a wife for her brother—a sister for herself—Myrta Burford would have been the favored one ; but Fabean had already chosen for himself, after a six weeks' flirta-

tion ; and, to the dismay of all his friends, had engaged himself to a mere boarding-school Miss—the daughter of Mrs. Leslie, of Ellisville.

Carrie Leslie was a pretty, well educated girl, of unexceptionable family, and the sister of Thornton Leslie, the warmest friend both of Victor DeGrey and Fabean DeCuba. The brother was delighted with the match, and both Victor and Harold thought it excellent ; but La Guerita looked beneath the surface, and putting aside all worldly considerations, saw that Carrie Leslie was far too frivolous to awaken any deeper feeling than transient admiration in the heart of her brother.

She was speaking of that to Victor DeGrey, one afternoon, when he had called in, as usual, to say : "No news from Harold !" and to have a romp with his little nephew, and to kiss the delicate babe, that lay like a spotless lily upon its mother's breast. The little Harold, he found, had gone to his grand-mama's, but was shortly expected home ; so he drew a letter from his pocket, sank into an easy chair, and began reading, patiently awaiting his coming. Two weeks before he would have hesitated to read a long letter in his sister's presence, conceiving that the act would seem most ungracious to her ; but he was glad of any excuse to parry her anxious inquiries and conjectures concerning her husband, and eagerly caught at an expression in the letter he was reading to speak of her absent brother.

"I believe, after all, you were right," said he ; "I don't believe Fabean ever did love Carrie. There is not a word in this letter about her; on the contrary, it is full of praises of the incomparable Miss Burford. I suppose he thinks himself privileged to speak of her as an angel, because he thinks she is going to die and become one; but I don't think Carrie would like it. But there is one thing certain, she wouldn't break her heart about it. Have you heard of the flirtation she has had with Loring?"

"I have heard of a dozen flirtations within as many weeks," returned La Guerita, impatiently; "and, in spite of your jokes about them, Victor, they trouble me greatly. One love affair is enough in any woman's life."

"You did not always think so," retorted Victor, laughingly. "What do you think I heard two or three days ago?"

"That I had had a dozen before my marriage?"

"No; but that the single one that tormented you so was coming from France, to marry a country cousin, to whom he has been engaged for ten years or so; a sort of family arrangement, I believe. Just imagine the gallant Claude giving up his 'Donna Luisas' and 'Md'lles De St. Armands,' for a country cousin, with two or three thousand a year."

"I hope he will be happy," she said, seriously.

"So do I," said Victor, laughing ironically; "but I am not going to fret about it if I find he is not. I wish that boy of yours was come, it is raining like the mischief. I have missed all the fine weather in waiting for him, and now I am going home the shortest way, for I am quite sure

mother will not let him come home to-night; so you needn't expect him."

"But I should be so dreadfully lonely without him," she urged.

"Nonsense! you have Altie; she will be company enough for you, with the new novel I brought you yesterday; so good by!"

She had been but a few minutes alone, when she heard a carriage roll swiftly up the graveled paths. She saw, with much satisfaction, that it was her own, in which she had sent him to Mrs. DeGrey's. She turned to summon a servant, when, to her amazement, she beheld her old friend, Thornton Leslie, spring from the carriage, with her child in his arms. A moment later it was in her own, senseless, apparently dead.

"He has only fainted," cried Thornton reassuringly; "it is nothing to be alarmed about. Bring him to his senses, and I'll tell you all about it in two minutes."

All other feelings were lost in her alarm for the boy. La Guerita, ever calm in an emergency, turned to the servant, who had followed Leslie into the room, and bade him go for a doctor; he did so, and the women servants came in, only to be sent away after restoratives. La Guerita would not yield the child even to his nurse, and hastily began to disrobe him. A faint odor stole over her senses, and, with a scream, she recognized the peculiar aroma of chloroform. Around the neck of the child was found a handkerchief saturated with the subtle fluid. That being instantly removed, and the proper restoratives administered, after a few anxious moments the child was restored to consciousness. Thornton assisted eagerly in the work, and when he saw the mother warming her child's lips by passionate kisses, and bathing his cold brow with her hot tears, he said: "I can safely leave him now; but I pray you, Mrs. DeGrey, never let him out of your sight again."

"Where did you find him!" she asked eagerly; "was he not with his nurse? The faithless creature; I trusted her so implicitly."

"There is no fault to be found with her," returned Mr. Leslie. "I was riding on the road from Ellisville, and about midway between this and Mrs. DeGrey's I passed your carriage, in which sat the nurse, crying out for some one to save the child, and weeping and wringing her hands frantically, while the coachman was swearing like a madman, and trying in vain to quiet the restive horses.

"'What has happened?' I cried. Immediately the man recognized me, and begged me, for God's sake, to bring back your child; a gentleman had, a few moments before, stopped the carriage, and saying that he was an old friend of Mrs. DeGrey's, had taken the child upon his lap, though the nurse objected because of the rain; had fondled and kissed him; then wheeled suddenly into a narrow path, that leads through the cliffs to the sea, bearing the frightened child before him. I needed no urging, but putting spurs to my horse, dashed in to the narrow way, where it was impossible for the carriage to go, and, after a few seconds' hard riding, discovered a solitary horseman; I even saw the child in his arms, and heard his shrieks of fear. Then began the most exciting race I ever took part in. Both were well mounted; I, perhaps, the best; I at least had the advantage, in having no struggling child to manage; I was soon within a few feet of the fugitive. Little Harold saw me; 'Mr. Ledlie, he's hurtin' me! O, Mr. Ledlie! Mr. Ledlie!'

"If I had needed a fresh incentive to action, that pleading voice would have supplied it, though it lasted but for a moment, for the abductor threw a handkerchief over the child's mouth, and wound it about his neck. I thought the child was being murdered; I recognized the villain that held him, and, drawing a pistol from my pocket, cried: 'Release that child, or I'll kill you!'

"Mrs. DeGrey, that man and I were at school together for years; he knew that I never uttered a threat that was not followed by action, and that I seldom missed my aim, when a boy, and was not likely to do so now, when it was taken in defense of injured innocence; he hesitated for a moment, then glancing at his horse, seemed to comprehend that it could not bear him over the cliffs at a pace to secure him safety from my pistol ball, so, with a fearful oath, he took the child by the skirts, bent over, and dropped him on the road, and galloped off, swearing vengeance.

"I was rejoiced, upon picking up the boy, to find him uninjured, though unconscious; I passed the carriage on my way here, but would not trust the child out of my arms until I could place him in yours."

For some moments La Guerita could say nothing; she clasped her son convulsively to her bosom, kissing him again and again. The driver and nurse, who had by this time arrived, noisily repeated so much as they knew of what Mr. Leslie had said, but their mistress scarcely heard them, and motioned them from the room ; turning to Mr. Leslie, when they were alone, with the exclamation : "How can I ever thank you ? my heart is now too full ! I can only say, I would rather see my child in his grave than in the hands of Claude Leveredge."

Mr. Leslie flushed to the temples, stammering : "Mrs. DeGrey, I mentioned no names ; I would not have you suppose——"

"You need not attempt to deceive me !" she interrupted ; "I know that Claude Leveredge, who swore, when I married Harold, that he would make my life miserable, is keeping his word. God help me !"

"It is a pity I didn't give him a shot to-day," thought Leslie ; then said : "You need fear nothing in future, Mrs. DeGrey ; Victor and I will guard you well. It is quite providential that I had that pistol with me to-day, as I seldom carry one, except when I have a large sum of money with me. Your husband has often laughed at my scruples. By the way, where is he at present ?"

La Guerita colored deeply, dropping her eyes in confusion. "I can scarcely tell you," she stammered ; "he departed so suddenly ; I wish he were here to thank you as heartily as I do."

"So there's even a skeleton in this house," thought Leslie ; "what can be the mystery ; and where can De-Grey be gone ? None seems to have the least idea.

He sat down, and took Harold upon his knee, saying : "Now, my little man, tell me what the great black fellow said that wanted to take you away."

"Oh ! he muttered over me," returned the child, with a frightened look, "and he held me so tight that the buttons of his coat hurt me ; and, oh ! he looked so terrible ; just like the spook that nurse says carries off the bad boy ; but I looked for his horns, and couldn't see them ; I guess he draws them in, like the ugly snails in the garden."

"And did he say nothing to you?"

"Yes, he said be still you little devil, and said ever so many other naughty words ; and said he would kill me, when I screamed out to you."

"And was that all !"

"Yes," returned Harold, "but," suddenly clapping his hand on his pocket, with a look of great dismay, "he's tooked my new ball. Oh-h-h !"

He rushed from the room to acquaint his nurse with this fresh disaster. His mother for a few moments after he left gazed earnestly upon Mr. Leslie, as if from his frank, genial face, to gain courage to put into execution some half-formed resolve.

"What is it, Mrs. DeGrey?" he said at length, noticing her hesitation.

"Thornton," she said gravely, "we have been friends for years ; many times before you have served me, but to-day you have made me your debtor forever. Pray do not interrupt me, Thornton," as blushing ingenuously, the young man opened his lips to speak; "I say truly that you have made me your debtor forever. This is a painful subject to me, for I shudder with horror at the thought of my darling having, even for a moment, fallen into the power of Claude Leveredge; I never wish to speak of it again, but I hope at some time to show you the depth of a mother's gratitude."

"Any man would have done the same under the circumstances," interrupted Mr. Leslie.

La Guerita shook her head, remaining for a moment lost in reverie, and then exclaiming: "It is right; I will do it!"

Mr. Leslie was at a loss to know what to make of these broken sentences, especially when she turned to him, and remarked quietly: "We heard from Fabean yesterday."

Ah, indeed! So also did Carrie; does he speak of returning? Our Carrie is so shy, she will not give us a word of news; all engaged people are equally reticent, I suppose?"

He looked up with a smile, but there was none in answer upon the face of La Guerita. "O, Thornton," she exclaimed, "do you think they love each other so very much; do you indeed think so?"

He looked at her in great surprise, unable for some moments to make any reply. At last he asked, with some agitation: "Why do you ask me, Mrs. DeGrey, have you received any bad news from Fabean?"

"No! No!"

"Perhaps, then," he exclaimed excitedly, "he wearies of the engagement; and I assure you my sister has no occasion to force herself on any man!"

"You misunderstand me," cried La Guerita, "Fabean has never hinted such a thing to me; he may even hate me for what I am about to do— which is, to beg you to consider the matter deeply, before you permit your sister to link her life with one so overshadowed with mystery as is that of my poor brother. I pray you to reflect."

"You speak very strongly, Mrs. DeGrey."

"Because I feel strongly. O, Thornton, I have felt the curse of that mystery all my life; I feel it now a thousand times more than before, and it is for my husband's and my children's sake. Do you wish that Carrie should feel the same? I beg you not to allow her to marry my brother, until his parentage has been discovered."

Thornton looked at her in amazement; he saw that she was very much in earnest. Her face was paler even than its wont, and her eyes shone as if her very soul was concentrated in the glowing orbs.

"Tell me what you mean!" he said excitedly. "I never supposed before that you had any objection to this marriage! It cannot be that you dislike Carrie—your old friend and schoolfellow?"

"No; I love her very dearly, Thornton, and it is because I love her, and would save her from misery, that I now speak!"

"Let me understand you better, Mrs. De Grey."

"Thornton, for five years I have been a happy, happy wife; children have slept upon my bosom; my husband has shielded me from every ill, has given me ever the tenderest love;

and yet, I tell you now, that were I a girl again, I would never marry. No ; not if I loved more than woman ever did before, would I marry, until I knew the secret of my birth ! O, this mystery is to me a living death !"

She spoke rapidly, and in accents that penetrated with convincing power the heart of her listener. Yet it was long before he could understand the strong emotion which had induced her to speak upon a subject which for years she had not mentioned, even to her husband or Victor DeGrey.

"You amaze me !" he at length exclaimed ; "and I hope, and believe, you will pardon me for asking, whether you have heard anything which has led you to believe that an alliance with our family would not prove desirable ?"

"I have heard nothing," she replied ; "but I feel that the crisis of my life is near at hand. Fabean may escape the coming storm ; its fury may be expended upon me."

"I know that you speak in kindness," said Leslie, slowly ; "but your words are strange ; I scarcely know what to say. Your brother became engaged to my sister with the consent of all concerned, and it is very difficult for me to say that they shall not marry."

"Thornton, say nothing, unless he suddenly returns to claim his bride ; but pray that he may not come until this mystery is explained. I never wish another to bear the weight that is upon us ; it will make it none the lighter !"

"It grieves me, Mrs. DeGrey," began Leslie, "to see that you allow this matter to trouble you. Doubtless, Harold's danger has brought it to mind ; but you need fear no further trouble from Leveredge ; Victor and I will guard your house effectually until your husband's return, and it will only be necessary for you to keep your children in sight to secure their perfect safety."

"Thank you ! thank you !" returned La Guerita earnestly ; "and you will believe that I have your sister's welfare at heart, as well as my brother's ?"

"I cannot doubt it, Mrs. DeGrey, after witnessing the pain it has given you to speak ; I will remember all that you have said ; I will do all in my power to ward off the marriage ; not that I fear any revelation of crime or shame ; it is impossible that either can be connected with you."

La Guerita smiled dreamily, saying : "I hope so, indeed ! but I feel like one standing on the sea-shore, with wrecked vessels scattered around her, and seeing, at a great distance, a ship, ladened with precious souls, steering toward the rocks, upon which those others have been stranded ; and though the water may be deep, and no harm may ensue, can I resist shrieking that the rocks are there ! or that the waters may recede, and leave them dry on arid sands !"

"I know now what you mean," said Thornton gravely ; "my resolve is taken ; my sister's life shall not be wrecked upon the rocks of mystery. But we will speak of it no more now. Good-by ! Good-by !"

He wrung her hand and departed hastily, strongly moved and excited. "Poor woman !" he muttered, at length, as he galloped toward Greymont ; "she is beautiful and good, but strange—very strange !"

CHAPTER VII.

" And thou art dead, as young and fair
  As aught of mortal birth ;
  And forms so soft, and charms so rare,
  Too soon return'd to earth !
  Though earth receiv'd them in her bed,
  And o'er the spot the crowd may tread,
  In carelessness or mirth,
  There is an eye which could not brook
  A moment on that grave to look."

Byron.

To the sad wife at Enola the days of Harold DeGrey's absence passed drearily. Perhaps it was well for her that her children claimed the greater part of her thoughts, leading her mind, in spite of her great fear of some coming evil, to think of other subjects than that upon which she believed her husband had been called away.

From the moment that Thornton Leslie placed her little son in her arms, her jealous watchfulness never flagged ; she kept him constantly in sight. If he went to visit his grandmama, at Greymont, she held him in her arms thither and back ; if he played in the garden, she remained at his side, and would, even in the house, keep him in the room with her. At night, she had him removed from the nursery to her own room, and often awoke at night, startled by some fancied noise, to clasp him to her bosom in a transport of alarm.

Yet, while she felt for Harold's safety the most intense anxiety, her little daughter was not forgotten. The faithful nurse would seldom take her charge from the presence of her mother, so fearful was she that an attempt to abduct her would be made.

As Thornton Leslie had promised, her house was well guarded, and thus it happened that Victor DeGrey was one afternoon at Enola, making, in his turn, a thorough search through the house and grounds. At dusk he entered the parlor, where La Guerita and her children were sitting, and exclaimed :

"It is all right, La Guerita ; there is no stranger in sight to-night ; so Mr. Robber need not be expected to carry off one of our charges before morning."

"I am thankful for that !" was the low spoken reply.

"I would just like to see the fellow that tried to carry off my little prince !" cried Victor, catching Harold in his arms and swinging him to and fro, echoing the child's shouts of glee. "I suppose," he continued, addressing the child, "the fellow expected to obtain a large ransom for you. Did he turn you upside down, to see if you had any money in your pockets !"

"What nonsense you talk, Victor," exclaimed La Guerita, in order to detract his attention from the subject, as she had not even allowed Victor to know the name of the abductor, dreading much the scandal the knowledge would give rise to if known abroad.

"Well, I'll say something sensible now," retorted Victor ; "I hope the fellow, whoever he is, left town."

"But he has not," cried La Guerita, forgetting her caution ; "Thornton would have traced him if he had."

"I thought Thornton could remember nothing of his face and figure ; if I had known before that he could identify the fellow, I would have had him looked for ; I wish Harold would finish this confounded mysterious journey of his; he must be gone to the moon, I think, for we can find no trace of him. But, seriously, I wish he would come home; people are hinting queer things of him; they say, and I must say, I think it strange he has not given even his own family a clue to his whereabouts."

"Oh, I wish he would come home," sighed La Guerita, clasping her hands nervously; "his mind must be occupied by some dreadful thing, for he has not even remembered to write to his wife."

"Oh, it is not possible that he has neglected you so long!" returned Victor, with an incredulous smile; "his letters have, no doubt, miscarried, or else Harold has gone crazy. I have heard of some of our family being flighty. I am accused of being so myself sometimes."

La Guerita sank back in her seat, entreating him to say no more; his words affected her so horribly.

"A carriage has just entered the gates," exclaimed Victor; "who can it be at this hour?"

La Guerita looked out, and instantly arose with an expression of joy upon her face, yet trembling in every limb. "I believe he has come!" she exclaimed; "I am certain it was his hand upon the carriage door. Go and see; I can't."

She was indeed too much excited to move from the spot; but Victor rushed to the door, followed by little Harold, and the nurse took the babe from La Guerita's arms just as she saw her husband slowly descend from the carriage.

"He is ill!" she cried, as she caught sight of his face, and in a moment was beside him. With a face expressive of the greatest surprise and concern, Victor was assisting him up the steps, and motioned her back, saying: "Don't touch him now! he is faint."

"Thank God, I am home once more!" he said, as he stood in the hall and looked upon his wife.

. She fell upon his breast, moaning: "My darling! my husband! what has come upon us?"

"The worst!" he muttered despairingly. "O, my God, can it be so?"

"Harold! Harold! tell me what has happened!" she cried wildly; "I cannot bear this suspense; tell me—tell me!"

Yet even while she spoke she felt him sink beneath her, and in a moment beheld him in Victor's arms, as white and motionless as soulless clay.

He was borne to his chamber, and thither she followed him, saying to herself: "The worst has *not* come; he will die—he will die!"

"He has merely fainted," whispered Victor, soothingly; "we shall soon bring him to; I have sent for Doctor Marsh."

In a few moments he was at Enola, having, fortunately, been but a few paces distant when met by the messenger. Under his active measures DeGrey soon recovered from his swoon; but he awoke with the wild fever of delirium upon him, recognizing no one, and uttering nothing, save apparently meaningless words. For hours the physician remained beside him, but no change appeared in his condition. In vain La Guerita bent over him, with wild entreat-

5

ies and prayerful sobs; he only looked at her vacantly, once exclaiming wildly: "O, cursed love! take away this dagger!" striking his breast wildly, as if in a frenzy of despair.

Thornton Leslie was below, and Dr. Marsh went down to see him. "I am glad you are come," he said; "you have, for many years, been a friend of the family, stay here for an hour, I beg, and see that my directions are followed to the letter."

"I will, Doctor—I will; but tell me, what is the matter with DeGrey? The servants are too much frightened to tell me anything."

"And no wonder. I greatly fear the poor fellow has met his death-blow somewhere. Queer thing altogether, this journey of his, you know; brain fever will be the result, I strongly suspect."

They heard La Guerita upon the stairs. "I must go," cried the Doctor, starting up, "though only a case involving life and death could call me from here, and I've such an one on hand; besides, I can't bear to meet that poor creature's questions; my answers would kill her;" and he darted out of a side door, thus evading the scene he dreaded.

By these words Thornton Leslie knew that Dr. Marsh believed Harold DeGrey would die, as he was not one to create any unnecessary alarm, and with a shudder he turned to meet the almost frenzied La Guerita.

"Where is the Doctor?" she exclaimed; "Ah, cruel man, to go without giving me one word of comfort. What did he tell you, Thornton?"

"Simply that your husband has an attack of brain fever," he answered, in a trembling voice; "but, Mrs. DeGrey, I beg you to be calm; nothing can be gained by this excitement, and the effect upon your husband is much to be dreaded. Let me entreat you not to despair."

She left the room, turning a deaf ear to all his remonstrances and entreaties.

On her way up stairs she met her little son, who was standing in his night-dress, refusing to return to his little cot, and, with a startled expression in his dark eyes, piteously asking: "Why they cried so?"

Without heeding his questions, his mother took him in her arms and carried him into the room where his father lay. He clung to her shoulder with a scream of affright, as his eyes fell upon the ghastly face and wildly rolling eyes of the sufferer.

"Who's that?" he cried; "mamma—Uncle Vic, who is that?"

"Your papa; don't you know your own dear papa?" whispered Victor, as he took the frightened child in his arms and stood with him at the foot of the bed, hoping to gain some sign of recognition from his brother.

"No—no! that's not my papa!" cried Harold, shaking his head; "my papa is not white, like him; he looks like the men we saw in the big house, with no windows. Mamma—mamma, take me away; I's so afraid!"

She took him in her arms and left the room, feeling that she could not endure more of such a scene. After Harold was in his cot, she went, aimlessly, down to the silent parlors, where she found Mrs. DeGrey most anxiously awaiting her, though she, as yet, did not even dream the extent of the evil that had come upon her son.

"My poor girl!" she said, kissing La Guerita tenderly, "I know you must be dreadfully alarmed, and I suppose you are very much surprised to see me at so late an hour; but I couldn't stay away. The doctor stopped and told me all about it. I was dreadfully shocked to hear that our dear Harold has returned home delirious."

"O, mamma! not only delirious, but dying!"

Mrs. DeGrey looked startled, but replied, incredulously: "That, surely, cannot be, my dear. The doctor never hinted the possibility of such a thing to me; but I will go up stairs and see for myself how he is."

But she was met at the door of the bed-room by Victor, who gently, yet firmly, denied her admittance, while Thornton muttered, impatiently: "Those women will kill him!" Mrs. DeGrey overheard the words, and, as much offended as grieved, returned to the parlor, saying to La Guerita, as she entered:

"They won't let me into his room, so I can't just tell you how he is; but I am sure, my dear, you need not be so much alarmed. My husband once returned from a harassing journey with a fever, and was delirious two or three days; I was young and inexperienced then, as you are; but I learned afterwards that I had had no great cause for alarm; and I believe, and hope, it will prove the same now."

La Guerita made no reply, and Mrs. DeGrey remained silent, moving restlessly about the gloomy room.

At last she went to the nursery, where she found the children quietly sleeping.

"I am glad you have a light here," she said to the nurse; "I became quite nervous in those dark parlors, lighted only by the gas in the hall. Hadn't I better ring for lights to be taken there?"

"I think not, ma'am," answered the girl; "Mrs. DeGrey always likes quiet and darkness when anything troubles her; it seems to soothe her mind; I think she's best alone just now, ma'am."

And the girl was right; for in silence and obscurity La Guerita was, in a wild, erratic way, schooling herself to bear the great calamity which she plainly saw was about to fall upon her, and, as the hours passed, she grew slowly—not less despairing—but more calm.

When the doctor came she slipped noiselessly after him into her husband's room, and, unrecognized by him, took up her station at the head of the bed, half hidden by the flowing drapery. Mrs. DeGrey soon after entered the room, with her usual firm step and haughty air; but an expression of gloom and dismay slowly settled upon her face, as she gazed upon the ghastly countenance of her son.

"If he could but sleep, we might hope greatly," remarked Dr. Marsh, in a low tone aside to Thornton Leslie; "do you see that the narcotics are carefully administered? Poor Victor is almost crazy himself, though he looks so calm. I will be here again in an hour."

Mrs. DeGrey followed the doctor from the room, and, when, after an absence of ten minutes, she returned, La Guerita knew that she, too, had lost all hope.

None of the four could be induced to leave the room during the night, so anxiously were they to see some change in DeGrey. Doctor Marsh returned within the hour and joined in the vigil ; but even his quick eye could denote no alteration in the state of the patient.

"You will kill yourself," he whispered to La Guerita, as the gray dawn struggled in ; "you have not been out of the room, except once, when called to your babe, for the night ; go now, she is crying for you."

Her maternal instincts were aroused, and with a look of utter woe and despair, she went to the nursery and took the wailing babe to her bosom ; sinking upon the cot, utterly exhausted, she fell asleep, and for two short hours was oblivious of her misery.

She was awakened by little Harold's voice, and feeling that she could endure neither his fretful crying or boisterous play, she told the nurse to take him to Greymont, and watch him carefully. Thornton Leslie, she knew, would accompany them, so she had no fears for the child's safety ; and as little Althea could, upon the return of the nurse, be left entirely to her care, La Guerita felt some slight degree of comfort in knowing she would be free to stand beside her husband.

All through the long, weary day he remained delirious, recognizing no one, and at intervals breaking forth into invectives against some nameless person, or moaning, as if in very agony of spirit.

A celebrated physician from New York, had, by the advice of Doctor Marsh, been sent for, and he agreed with him in thinking that a long, quiet sleep would restore the mind of Harold DeGrey, and perhaps save his life. He also gave it as his opinion, that his disorder was owing entirely to some great mental excitement, and that in consequence he had not slept perhaps for weeks, and had lost his reason by the unbroken anxiety he had suffered.

On the third day of Harold De-Grey's return, a consultation of physicians was held. La Guerita felt while they were closeted together, as if the walls of the house were stifling her, and opening the window of the library in which she stood, stepped forth upon the lawn.

It was in the early days of the first month of Spring, and the air was filled with the faint perfume of opening buds. For some weeks there had been a great deal of rain, and the ground was sodden and cold, giving forth, to the excited imagination of La Guerita, a smell like that of a new-made grave, or freshly-opened vault. Even the graveled paths were wet and sunken, and gave but a dull echo to her slow, firm tread.

More hurriedly would she have gone had she known that from a clump of holly she was watched by dark, wild eyes, set in a face as pallid as her own.

She looked toward the setting sun as it dipped beneath the ocean waves, and wished that she too might sink to rest—to oblivion—and be unmissed, unwept, forgotten.

"But I shall not die !" she murmured ; "I feel that there is life, hateful life, in this bosom ;" and she clasped her hands above her heart as if she would gladly tear it from her bosom. "O, Harold, my darling! my love! You will die, and must I live?"

She sank upon the damp ground, for an hour or more remaining silent and motionless, then her misery found vent in such passionate words of direful meaning, that the face peering from the thicket behind her, grew livid in its paleness, as she cried aloud: "I curse him, as he has cursed me, with all my strength, and life, and soul! For I have no hope, no mercy, no God, to help or pity me! There cannot be a God of Love! There cannot be!"

She heard a rustling in the leaves behind her, but turning, saw nothing. A short, bitter laugh broke from her lips. "If I were seen people would call me nervous or perhaps worse," she murmured, "but I am not; no, no; my nerves are iron! They can quake no more; I know what is to come!"

These last words were spoken to herself, but appropriated by Dr. Marsh, who had quietly approached her.

"Of ourselves we can know nothing," he said gravely, taking her passive hand, and lifting her from the damp earth. "My daughter, we have done all that human wisdom can dictate; let us humbly and prayerfully leave the result with God!"

She cast away his hand, crying: "O, I can't bear it. I *cannot* bear it!"

"Child, sorrow must come to all," returned the kind hearted physician. "Give not your soul to despair, but remember that more will not be given you than you can endure, and that

God even tempers the wind to the shorn lamb!"

"Has he tempered it to me?" she cried. "Don't speak to me of resignation. I can never, never be resigned. Is he not taking my all—my life from me?"

"My dear Mrs DeGrey this is impious."

"Ah, yes; you expect me to bow and kiss the hand that smites me! What have I done that I should be punished thus. What crime have I committed that all the joy of my life should be taken from me."

"Be calm, my daughter, be calm; remember that many idols have been shattered before; many just women have been widowed and made childless, too, while you will still have your little ones left."

"Remember them! I do; but what joy can come upon the children of a mother with a curse upon her?"

The good doctor comprehended then the reason of her despair; for a moment he could say nothing, and stood before her in sad perplexity and grief. "I cannot comfort you," he said, at length; "I can only pray that God in mercy will."

And he knelt, with bowed head, beside her, holding the skirt of her robe, as he fervently prayed that the life of Harold DeGrey might be spared, or that strength to bear his loss might be given his young wife.

She listened with softened face, and pleading eyes, to the few sentences in which he entreated the life of her husband; but again the face grew hard as he prayed for her, and at last she exclaimed:

"Pray for his life! I care not for comfort if he is taken from me! Pray that he will spare my husband's life, or take mine also."

The good man arose from his knees, saying: "God's will be done," and taking the arm of La Guerita, led her into the house, away from the spectral face that peered after them from the depths of the shrubbery.

Victor DeGrey had already been told of the helpless condition in which his brother lay, and as Dr. Marsh and La Guerita entered the hall, he met them, with all the anguish of his soul depicted on his face. Unable to speak, he put his arms around his brother's wife, and pressed a kiss upon her brow. But she could not endure a token of sympathy, even from him, and put aside his arm almost sternly, and walked directly up stairs to her husband's room.

Thornton Leslie and Mrs. De-Grey were there. They drew aside when La Guerita entered, even the mother feeling that her grief was nothing in comparison to that of the young wife. With a thrill of joy they saw that Harold recognized her, though he was perfectly oblivious to the presence of all others. As she bent over him, he looked at her with pitying tenderness, and feebly placed his arm about her neck. They hoped that he would speak, but he made no effort to do so.

La Guerita laid down beside him, and pillowed his head on her breast, and to the amazement of all present, began to sing, in a low voice, more like an echo than a master tone, a simple lullaby—one with which her husband had loved to hear her soothe her children. Ere long they saw that a change was spreading over his countenance, a slumberous look crept into his eyes, and a lethargy was stealing over his frame. Mrs. DeGrey turned an inquiring gaze upon Dr. Marsh, but he made no sign of response, but with his finger upon the pulse of his patient, watched his face with intense anxiety, as he slowly sank into a profound and deathlike sleep.

"There is hope," murmured Mrs. De Grey.

But neither the Doctor, nor La Guerita heeded her words, and for hours both kept the positions they had taken, the doctor feeling that he could not drop the wrist in which life so faintly throbbed. But at ten o'clock he laid it down, and went into the parlor to take a short nap upon the sofa, and leaving his patient in the hands of Dr. Liston, his associate, telling Victor to call him if any change was apparent.

La Guerita had not for a moment ceased her wailing song, and it sounded through the still house like a funeral chant, as Dr. Marsh sleeplessly awaited his summons. At midnight it came. Victor entered the room, and said huskily: "He has awakened, and recognized us all. Dr. Liston thinks there is a hope! O, Doctor, can there be?"

"I cannot say; I will go up. I pray God his sleep came not too late."

When they entered the room, although DeGrey lay with his eyes wide open, gazing with a look of sad intelligence around, he had not yet spoken. He did so when the Doctor approached him, looking at his wife, and murmuring: "My love! My love!"

She tried to speak to him but could not. She knew that he was dying, and she could not, could not give him up.

"Bring the children in," he whispered.

His mother noiselessly left the room, and presently returned with the nurse and the two sleeping children. He signified that he did not wish them aroused, but kissing them fondly, had them laid where his eyes could fall upon them.

Then his mother bent over him, entreating him to speak to her. "God bless you! God bless you!" he said, as he kissed her. "Don't fret about me, mother, Victor will be left."

She drew back, sobbing bitterly.

"Victor," muttered the dying man, "Come here; close, close; you must hear; you must care for my wife when I am gone; and you, Thornton, and Fabean,—where are you all? No matter what happens, you must stand by my wife and the children. You'll not forget?"

"No, no!" answered both; and Thornton Leslie clasped the hand of Harold DeGrey, then left the room, quite overcome by his emotions. But Victor, impulsive still, bent over his brother, in an agony of grief, to hear his last farewell.

Tears come to women when trifles move them; but to most men, every tear is as a drop of life-blood wrested from the heart in agony. So were they to Victor, as his brother—his guide, his friend—pressed a kiss upon his lips, as if he were a child—the child of his fondest hopes, and then muttered, faintly: "Leave me with my wife. Good-by! Good-by."

Kissing her son's pale lips, Mrs. DeGrey left the room followed by all but La Guerita and the children.

For a time neither spoke, each breast was surcharged with feelings too deep for words. At last, he murmured: "Look up, my wife; let me see your eyes once more before I die."

"You *shall not* die, Harold. O, it is cruel—it is wicked—to take you from me."

"No, no, my darling, it is best! —it is best!"

"Why?" she cried. "O, tell me Harold what has happened?"

"My poor, poor child!" he whispered, soothingly caressing the damp black hair that had escaped from its fastenings, and lay wildly around her. "Poor little one! Trust in God."

She moaned bitterly, but said nothing. She could not wound him by giving utterance to her utter unbelief.

"O, if you could but live, my husband!" She sank upon his breast, and lay shuddering, clinging there, while she knew that he wrestled and pleaded for her with God—the God she rejected—with the strong desire of a trusting heart.

"Tell me what has come upon us," she entreated, when his lips ceased moving; "What called you away?"

"Is the letter gone?" he answered, in a tone that assured her that his mind was wandering. "Yes, yes, it is! You'll never know the secret." Then with a great effort he lifted himself, and strained her to his breast, saying: "Remember, I never ceased to love you—to love—"

She heard a stifled moan, and looking up, screamed with terror at the awful pallor of his face. She was heard by those without—they rushed in and found him lying in her arms, gazing upon her face. They stood in awe around, and for a few moments nothing was heard save a faint sob or moan. Once the tearless wife bent down and kissed his ashy lips. He smiled, and they saw a glorious light come into his raised eyes, then slowly fade; and they knew that Harold DeGrey was dead.

CHAPTER VIII.

> " Life leaves—dead, and brown, and sere,
> Round the threshold, lone and drear—
> Rustle in the autumn breeze.
> Raindrops slowly fall and freeze :
>   Soft lips hushed,
>   Young lives crushed,
>   Bright hopes scattered,
>   Harp strings shattered—
> Withered flowers, and vines, and tears,
> Cover graves of earlier years ! "

THREE suns had risen and set since the owner of Enola had lain as soulless clay where he had once ruled a master spirit. Their last rays were falling upon his grave when La Guerita entered the silent library with a packet in her hand—the letters he had imagined destroyed.

When he died, in spite of his half delirious words, she believed that it was still in existence. Even her agony did not induce her to forget what she believed contained the secret of her life. She sought and found it, thrust in the pocket of his coat, as if of no importance; he had, perhaps, in his distraction destroyed some other papers, but that mattered not : the secret was safe.

On their return from the funeral Mrs. DeGrey and Victor had entreated her to go with them to Greymont, but she refused to do so, saying she was better alone. So they left her, think-ing it was perhaps better, for her mind seemed dazed ; perfect solitude might restore it to activity again.

"They have taken even his body from me," she moaned, as they left her in her silent dwelling ; and again, like a refrain from far-off shores, came the strange words into her mind that had been surging through it through all the days of her widowhood :

> " Take the dead Christ to my chamber.
> *   *   *   *   *   *   *
> Bear him as in procession,
> And lay him solemnly
> Where through the weary night and morning
> He shall bear me company ! "

"They would call me sinful," she muttered ; "Sinful ! when he was all I had to love—my Priest and King, and more ! But now he is dead ! dead ! dead ! "

> " Bear him as in procession,
> And lay him solemnly
> Where through the weary night and morning
> He shall bear me company ! "

She spoke the words aloud, and their strange meaning, with the hollow sound of her own voice, startled her. She clasped her hands upon her heart, and felt there the packet she had found, and with jealous care placed where no hands might tear it from her.

"I will read it now," she muttered to herself ; "I will know why I was called La Guerita DeCuba, and why— why *he* died !"

The shadows of evening were fast filling the room where she sat. She remembered that a servant was lighting the gas in the library when she passed, and thither she went to learn her history, still with the strange words of the poem surging through her brain, like a slow, monotonous melody.

Noiselessly she glided down the

stairs, and over the thickly-carpeted hall. For a moment she stood at the door, fancying she heard a slight noise—a cat-like rustle.

"'Tis but the crackling of the fire," she said; and opening the door went in, but receded in alarm as a tall figure turned toward her, then sprang through the open window, and in an instant disappeared from view.

Her first impulse was to fly, but a second glance at the room caused her to enter it. Trembling, yet calm and determined, she turned on the gas, and by its steady light saw plainly what the glare of the fire had but imperfectly revealed. The window was wide open, and a tool lay upon the sill, with which the lock of the secretary had been forced open. The papers it had contained were scattered about the floor, but she neither cared nor looked to see whether any were missing, as she quietly gathered them up, and threw them into the drawers. She closed and barred the open window, calling no one to assist her, or follow the daring intruder; she had recognized him, and cared not that others should.

At last she seated herself in a low rocking chair, not swaying back and forth as she had often done when engaged in idle reverie, but remaining rigidly erect and still, watching the ashes as they slowly fell, and remembering how Harold had once said: "No cinders of care shall ever fall from the fire of my love to which the ashes of sorrow may cling." Alas! the fire of his love by death had been quenched, and she had heard the fearful words, "dust to dust, ashes to ashes," as they laid his form in the cold ground, to molder forever away.

For hours the packet lay unopened upon her lap, her nerveless hands clasped over it; but at last some slight movement caused it to slip down the sable folds of her dress, recalling her mind to the task she had pledged it to perform. She stooped and took it in her hand, took forth the closely-written sheets from the torn envelope, looked upon the well-known writing of him she had loved as a child, and, as a woman, feared.

She passed her hand over her eyes, to smooth away a strange heat and blindness that gathered there, and then calmly read the opening words of the letter, so expressive to her of deadly hate.

"To Harold DeGrey, from one who swore never to forgive or forget.

"Upon receiving this you will at once conjecture that the news I have to tell concerns the woman you took from me more than five years ago. I write to you because I hate you, and because I know that my words will blast all your hopes, and darken your whole life.

"Perhaps you are already acquainted with my history, but at anyrate it will not prove uninteresting to you when told by myself. I have nothing uncommon to reveal. The events that have marked my life have been ordinary enough; my passionate soul alone has invested them with that importance which renders them so different to those that befall thousands of mortals who live long years, and die at last in the belief that the world has dealt kindly by them. I thank Fate, or Providence, that no such passive soul was placed in this frame of mine; and it is because of that, I could not lay my hand upon

6

my heart and bow in resignation when you stood at the altar, and gained the bride that should have been mine. I am also thankful that a certain patience—the patience of the serpent when it coils for a deadly spring—was given to this fiery soul of mine, so that no blind, mad impulse led me to kill your body, but to calmly, deliberately bide the time when I might torture—ay, *kill* your soul.

"But this is a digression, no doubt wearisome to you, but perhaps of importance in giving you a complete comprehension of what is to follow.

"It is just thirty years since I, a weak, struggling babe, came into existence, taking from my mother the life that refused to sustain us both. None rejoiced when I came—all wept when she departed. I was taken as an ugly and unwelcome burden, and ungraciously cherished by the sable nurse that had carried my dead mother as a babe in her arms. But there is a tender spot in the heart of every woman, and before long I found that in old Elsie's, and struggled into boyhood in the sunshine of her love.

"Some fathers would have turned with adoration to the only child of a dead wife, or would have hated it as the instrument of her death. Mine did neither. When they took me to him, thinking that the sight of me would comfort him, he put me aside, not harshly, but as if I was some insensate thing, and they knew that I was to be cared for, but not in his sight or hearing. So the nursery my mother had so daintily fitted up for my reception was closed, and Aunt Elsie took me to a little cabin under wide spreading oaks, where neither my wailing or my mirth could reach the ears of the stern, silent man who lived in the closed house, a grim and cheerless hermit.

"I seldom saw him ; for once when he lifted me upon his knee, and looked in my face with his wild, dark eyes, I shrieked in affright, and he put me down, never again to lay hand upon me, or even glance my way.

"I remember well the strange feeling of awe, and yet of relief, with which I looked upon him as he lay dead in his coffin, and realized that the man whom for the ten years of my life I had regarded with almost superstitious fear would soon be hidden from my sight forever.

"O, how often that dead face has presented itself to my imagination within the last five years ! When I look in the glass I am startled to find it looking back at me, and I know that I am suffering torture like to that he so silently endured—and worse. His heart rebelled against the power of Death ; mine against the insolent act of man.

"During his lifetime my father, who had turned me over to the care of ignorant slaves, had been thought a fit guardian for me. But at his death a wonderful controversy arose between his relatives as to who should have the responsibility of educating and directing the morals of his heir.

"My uncle, Norton Holmes, the brother of my mother, was appointed one of my guardians, and by some unaccountable freak, as my relatives said, but which as I am now inclined to think was a judicious exercise of thought, a distant relative, one Acton Holmes, was appointed the other. This man had always been looked upon as a sort of autocrat by all the family, not so much for his wealth, extensive though it was, as because of the soundness of his judgment and the even dignity of his manners, which compelled admiration, awe, and esteem from even the most careless and irreverent. Perhaps the fact of his being unmarried, and the possessor of a large property, had something to do with his great and general popularity. Although he was but distantly related to me, the fact of his being appointed my guardian would have occasioned no remark, had it not been well known that he had not tolerated my father's eccentricities as others had done, and had even censured him severely for his neglect of me, and had not, indeed, for years set his foot upon the plantation, or looked upon my father's face until he lay dead. In view of these circumstances, it was with justice that it was thought somewhat singular that I, and what was much more important, my property, should be intrusted to his care. He seemed himself somewhat surprised and embarrassed at his position, and refrained from taking the part in the business which was natural and usual with him in anything in which he was concerned. My uncle settled the estate much as he pleased, and it was not until the final disposal of myself was arranged, that he said or did anything contrary to my uncle's will.

"He seemed to have settled the matter in his own mind beforehand, and my uncle was soon surprised out of his cherished plan of having me educated in his own family, and into a reluctant consent that I should be placed at school at the north. Acton Holmes chose Fairview for my residence, and thither I was sent.

"Perhaps you think that up to this point I have been unnecessarily diffuse, and that some of these pages might have been omitted. Read on, and at the end of this epistle you will know why I place so much importance upon these early events in my life's history.

"I was a little over eleven years old when I was placed at the Fairview Academy. I had never before, even for a day, been absent from the plantation upon which I was born. I had been a master from my birth; none ever dared oppose my will, for it had never clashed with that of my father, and the slaves he owned were trained to implicit obedience to all white people. When I went north all that was changed. Claude Leveredge was no longer the young *master*, judiciously feared and implicitly obeyed, but a *child*, who almost lost even his identity in a crowd of boisterous, fun-loving, caste-despising boys. The change at first disgusted me, but I soon found that a master spirit could rule in any place, and among all people. Before long my power of will, illustrated and enforced by my strong arm, had made me an autocrat among the pupils, and even the teachers, of Fairview.

"There were many there that feared me, and whispered often how they hated me; but there was one—an infant girl—who, twining her soft arms around my neck, said with truth: "Claude, I love you! I love you better than all the rest!"

"I don't know that I ever loved any one before; but from the day I entered Fairview my heart was centered in that little, winsome child. Her beauty was to me like that of a magnificent flower, daily disclosing more splendor and perfection. Her gentle arts and winning ways were to my fiery soul, my sensitive nature, my often wounded heart, like a soothing balm—a magic spell.

"All knew that I loved the child, for I caressed and protected her at all times, while to others I was a stern niggard of my favors; but none knew how early I said : 'I shall be a man soon, and La Guerita DeCuba shall be my wife.'

"Yet even in those early days pride kept me silent concerning her to all those who had a right to know of my associates. I think I never even spoke of her to Acton Holmes, who, during the vacations which I spent at the house of Norton Holmes, often questioned me. I could not bear that her origin should be questioned ; I believed that she was of the highest birth, and it would have maddened me had any one ever dared to have spoken of crime or shame in connection with the child I loved.

"DeGrey, you know all that happened in succeeding years: how I loved her ; how she promised to be mine ; how she wearied of her bonds ; how I broke them, fancying, vain fool that I was, that she would return and rivet them all the faster ; and how I returned and found her—O God ! another's.

"Perhaps your wife has laughingly told you how I once said I would unravel the mystery of her birth, and ruin her, whatever might be her origin. Her ruin meant that of the man who had defrauded me.

"I began my work very quietly. No foolish words, uttered in moments of madness, revealed the fixed purpose of my soul. Silence is the birthplace of thought ; thought the parent of action. I knew that truism well, and bound my once unruly member with the thongs of hatred and revenge.

"Until I had discovered the origin of La Guerita DeCuba, I could only blindly hope for vengeance. No plan for obtaining it presented itself to me. Naturally, my first act was to go to Cuba. For months I stayed there, stealthily working my way, going into the highest families, employing all sorts of characters to ferret out private histories, and expending thousands in a search that proved in vain.

"An insane desire to see La Guerita once more, and learn from her face whether she was happy or not, impelled me once to visit Ellisville. I think part of my desire for vengeance would have been satisfied had you wearied of your lovely bride, and proved to her that love was indeed the ephemeral thing that hers had been to me. But I knew by one glance into her eyes, by the few words she chanced to utter in my hearing, that your tenderness for her had never failed, and that the truest peace and happiness marked the life that had cursed mine.

"Yes, she was happy ; and I—? The misery at my heart—the madness of my brain drove me again to Cuba—to my unfinished task. But it daily grew heavier with sickening doubts and disappointments, and it was with a sigh of relief I received a message from Uncle Norton summoning me to the side of our dying cousin, Acton Holmes.

"Some words of his had once induced me to believe that he knew of my hopeless passion. But I made a confidant of no man, and that he could have aught to say to me upon the matter, never once entered my mind, even while I wondered at the urgent message that he had forwarded to me.

"Though I traveled with all speed, he died two days before I reached home. They told me he had died in an agony of mind at not seeing me, yet he left no message, even of farewell. I looked upon the still, dead face of my cousin, with more grief than I had ever felt before, for I knew that no other man had showed toward the neglected orphan, such tenderness as he.

"I went from the grave yard, where they laid him upon the very day of my arrival, to the house of Norton Holmes ; and as we sat alone after dinner, our conversation naturally turned on him who was silent forever.

" 'He was a genial man,' said I, after some desultory talk, ' 'tis strange that he never married.'

" 'Yes, truly,' answered my uncle with a laugh. 'There are not many men that would condemn themselves to perpetual celibacy for the sake of a handsome girl of the class one usually looks upon as without conscience as well as power.'

"I looked at him inquiringly, and perceiving my evident astonishment and ignorance, he said : 'I forgot you were but a child when the matter occurred, and even if you had not been, it is hardly probable that you would have heard of it, for Acton Holmes was not one to talk of his follies, or boast of his vices.'

" 'What do you know of his follies or vices, uncle,' said I, rather anxious to know more of the private life of one who had in public displayed unwavering uprightness and virtue. 'What do you know about either ; I supposed he was utterly free from them ?'

" 'And I might have thought so too,' he returned, ' but for a walk our respected aunt Matilda once took, and a discovery she made upon that occasion. The plantation of our deceased relative is, as you know, bounded on one side by the Y—— river, and on the banks of that stream. Aunt Matilda came upon a garden of choicest flowers, in the midst of which stood a lovely cottage, and upon the porch, with a little babe upon her bosom, stood a woman of queenly stature and wondrous beauty ; at her side sat Acton Holmes, with a boy upon his knee, whose face was the counterpart of his own.'

"DeGrey you know whom these children were.

[The paper dropped from the trembling fingers of La Guerita, and a low moan—"O God ! O God !" broke from her ashen lips. "But it *cannot*, cannot be !" she cried, and with lightning rapidity read on to the end of the fatal letter.]

"What was there in this history of my cousin's love to fill my brain with fire—my heart with ice ? for even then I could not entertain the supposition that rushed over me. But with strained ears that caught every intonation of his voice, I listened as my uncle continued :

" 'Our aunt Matilda being a prudent woman remained a silent spectator of the scene, and, justly fearing Acton's wrath, withdrew without discovering herself, and with the secret determination of keeping her own counsel for a time at least.

"'But such secrets do not remain sacred long, and, ere long, whisperings were heard that a beautiful quadroon had accompanied Acton Holmes from Cuba some years before, and was the mistress of that lovely cottage.

"'When the whisperings were loudest, Acton Holmes suddenly disappeared; for a year or more nothing was seen or heard of him, and as the cottage was empty it was generally supposed he had taken the woman and children with him; but before long she appeared at W——, with free papers in her hands. Beautiful still, but broken-hearted, people said, and they called her Dolores, though it is said her lover had ever named her La Guerita DeCuba—the fair one of Cuba.'

[She who read these lines seemed turned to stone, so awfully calm was she even when she read the bitter words of scorn that followed the history of her birth.]

"DeGrey you know all that I discovered, as my uncle dreamily told this bit of scandal, and moralized, as the living will, upon the career of the dead. I know not how I looked then, but fortunately the friendly dusk was there to hide me. I felt as if turned to stone; I could not speak or move, but only think—think that La Guerita DeCuba—she, whom I had loved—she, who had scorned me —she, a fancied princess, was the daughter of a bond-woman.

"I know you will not doubt what I have written, but if you seek proof, visit the place from which this is dated, and learn from a hundred lips,

from Norton Holmes, from a laundress—Dolores, the truth of what I have written.

"DeGrey, my revenge is sweet— sweeter than I ever dared hope it could be. Yet my task is not ended until the whole world shall point with shame and scorn to him who shares the fortunes of the slave-born woman, La Guerita DeCuba.

"CLAUDE LEVEREDGE."

Thus ended the strange epistle. La Guerita turned again to the beginning and read the date. "W——, N. Carolina, May 10th, 1859."

There, then, Harold had been. There where the story of her shame was known. There the cruel darts of scandal had pierced his heart.

She sat for hours before the slowly-dying fire, not thinking of her shattered hopes, her fallen aspirations, nor of him who had robbed her life of all its joys—but of her shame! That shame which had killed her husband, and would live in her innocent children. Some pages of the letter she read again. A needless task, for a pen of adamant could not have engraven words more deeply than were these upon her tortured brain. Yet she read them, again and again, bending over at last and fulfilling her husband's forgotten task— consigning to the flames the secret she should never have known.

Then she arose and left the room, feeling conscious that she would sink beneath the weight that had come upon her. She went up-stairs to her own room, and sunk upon the bed on which her husband had died. From that moment reason fled; she lay as upon surging billows, and sank down, down, down, into cold, slimy caves, where gleams from the eyes of ocean monsters threw rays of gold and crimson through the black depths. Out of the crevices of rocks and the bosoms of giant shells, and from under the floating arms of sea-weed, crept hideous demons toward her—gliding serpents, and scorpions swift as light. They floated and crept around her with horrible hisses and moanings, and eyes that glared with fury and hate. And she heard in the moanings and hisses the voice —and saw in serpents and scorpions the eyes—the basilisk eyes of Claude Leveredge.

CHAPTER IX.

" The outward, wayward life we see—
The hidden springs we may not know ;
Nor is it given us to discern
What threads the fatal sisters spun ;
Through what ancestral years has run
The sorrow with the woman born ;
What forged her cruel chain of moods—
What set her feet in solitudes ;
What held the love within her mute.

* * * * *

It is not ours to separate
The tangled skein of will and fate."

Whittier's "Snow Bound."

To La Guerita a lifetime seemed passed in those gloomy caves. Sometimes the waves parted, and for a moment she saw afar off forms of light and beauty ; when, again, the waters closing over her, even the remembrance of the light would fade from her mind, and the terrors of the horrible, in which she was immured, return, peopled with new and still more fantastic objects. At last came a time when the demons, and serpents, and slimy, creeping things, one by one, left her, and fitful gleams of sunshine darted into the loathsome caves, the dark walls of which slow-

ly took the semblance of a chamber at Enola. Gradually, and without any violent shock, consciousness returned to her ; and one day, opening her eyes, after a quiet sleep, she found herself in a darkened room, with Harold's mother leaning over her.

"Mother—dear mother," she said ; and that instant was clasped to the heart of Mrs. DeGrey, and greeted with tears and kisses, while a cry of joy burst from the lips of the only other occupant of the room—a beautiful young girl, with large, blue eyes, that shone with joy as she threw her long, fair curls back from her face, and bent to kiss the sufferer.

"Thank God, you are better," she whispered ; "this will be good news for Thornton, and for all. The time has seemed so long."

"How long have I been here ?" asked La Guerita, wearily.

"Ten days, my darling," answered Mrs. DeGrey ; "but hush, now, love ; you must not talk for a day or two."

"No—no ; I will not ; only tell me, are my children well ?"

Carrie Leslie turned aside her head, and Mrs. DeGrey, with difficulty, restrained some sudden emotion.

"What has happened?" cried La Guerita ; "tell me—tell me, is Harold gone?—is Harold gone?"

"No, dearest ! no !" returned Mrs. DeGrey, soothingly ; "little Harold is quite safe."

"And Althea ?"

"My daughter, the little one is dead."

"Dead ! dead !" It was all she said, yet the word was a very wail of agony.

"We were afraid to tell her," said Carrie Leslie to her brother, a few weeks later, "for Althea had seemed the best loved of her children; yet she never even wept for it; nor did she say: 'God's will be done!'"

"She could not," said Thornton, gravely; "she lives with an undying sorrow in her heart; these were Victor's last words to me as we parted at the gate, the night the will was read. Poor fellow! he is nearly heart-broken to see her so changed. It is dreadful, Carrie! Though Harold has been dead nearly six weeks, she has never mentioned his name or raised her head."

"Poor thing!" said Carrie; "and doesn't it seem a strange thing to be able to pity the proud Mrs. DeGrey? I had a note from her to-day, begging me to come to her; she would not see me the last time I was there."

"Don't fail to go," said her brother; "you must try to fill a sister's place toward her. I consider Harold's last charge to me gives a new duty to the whole family, while, of course, your relation to Fabean ——"

Carrie interrupted him, pettishly: "Don't harp upon that, Thornton; it is a ridiculous affair altogether. Consider your own duties, as one of Harold's guardians, as much as you please, and, pray, leave me to attend to mine."

Her brother turned upon her a searching glance. "Do you remember, Carrie, what I said to you a short time ago?" he asked.

She colored angrily, biting her lips, poutingly, as she replied: "Yes; I remember very well, and I consider, Thornton, that it was really cruel of you to place me in such a state of uncertainty; you all knew that there was some mystery about Fabean's birth when you were so eager for our engagement."

"I was a romantic boy then," said Thornton, sadly; "happy myself, and anxious that my friend and sister should be. You know I had no meaner thought; but, pshaw! 'tis wasting time to talk to you of that. Be a reasonable girl, Carrie, and remember that 'circumstances alter cases.'"

Carrie laughed scornfully. "Yes, the circumstance of his receiving but a paltry ten thousand dollars, and no hint of more, instead of a princely fortune upon attaining his majority, altered *this* case!" she cried.

"You are wrong," returned her brother, firmly; "and I tell you now, it is time for us all to lay aside romantic fancies, and especially for you to cast off the flimsy pretense of loving Fabean DeCuba."

"You are dreadfully cruel!" cried Carrie, bursting into tears; "you are actually insulting, sir! actually insulting!"

"It is two o'clock," said Thornton, quietly, glancing at his watch; "what time are you going to Mrs. DeGrey's, Caroline?".

"Now," she sobbed; "and I wish I could always stay there; I like Fabean DeCuba as well as you love ——"

Her brother put his hand on her mouth. "No, no, Carrie; I have your other confession, you know. Come, come, give me a kiss before you go; you know I always mean well. Pity it is that one has to speak to you harshly to convince you of it."

But she broke from him angrily,

and a few minutes later, still vexed and excited, entered the parlor of Enola.

La Guerita was there, for the first time in many weeks, and Carrie Leslie joyously uttered some pretty phrases of congratulation, wondering, at the same time, how such a beautiful young widow could wear such a "horrid, horrid cap!"

"You think I look very thin and pale, no doubt," said La Guerita, faintly, construing Carrie's glance into one of pity for her weak state, rather than her poor taste; "yes, yes; no doubt I am terrible to look upon; but it is no matter now—no matter."

"Oh, don't say that!" exclaimed Carrie; "you are only a little pale, and you never had much color, you know; I really think you look lovely, and the ruffles of that dress are sweet. I remember when I was in mourning; but I beg your pardon; I didn't mean to make you feel badly."

"It is nothing," said La Guerita, smoothing away the spasm that had contracted her brow; "but I am not strong, Carrie; yet, with all my weakness, I cannot die."

"Die! I should think not; why should you? Dear me, I should be very, very sorry, and so would Fabean and all the rest. Oh, dear me, yes!"

"Fabean, Fabean!" said La Guerita, softly; "O, Carrie, do you love poor Fabean?"

The question was totally unexpected, and, confused and annoyed, Carrie answered testily: "I declare, I don't know; I suppose so."

"And would it break your heart not to marry him?"

Carrie laughed with irrepressible amusement. "The idea!" she exclaimed; "what would mamma say to that! The idea of the heart of any well-regulated young lady being broken; but, indeed," she added, suddenly growing grave and haughty, "I cannot see what right you have to question me in that way. Has Fabean asked you to do so? Is he tired of me?"

"I cannot tell, Carrie; yet I almost hope so. But, Carrie, Carrie, even if he loves you with more than earthly devotion, I beg—I pray you not to marry him!"

She spoke in pleading accents; she—the proud woman—actually bent in suppliant form before that thoughtless young girl, and cried, again and again: "Promise me, Carrie, that you will not marry him."

The impulsive girl, awed and thrilled by the passionately spoken words, threw herself on her knees beside La Guerita, and cried:

"Why must I not marry Fabean? Who and what is he? I know that you can tell me."

"No, I will not tell you," she cried, shudderingly; "I cannot tell you."

"Oh, then you only ask me to resign your brother because you dislike me," retorted Carrie, with sudden willfulness; "I am not going to give up Fabean for any whim of yours; I will marry him."

"O, Carrie, you must not—you shall not!" exclaimed La Guerita; "you shall not be like the miserable creature you see before you to-day."

"Of course, I shall not be," interrupted Carrie; "do I look as if I should ever mope myself to death? No, indeed; I shall marry Fabean."

7

La Guerita caught her in her arms. "You are not worthy of my care," she exclaimed; "yet I love you—I will save you. Swear never to breathe to any mortal what I am about to say —swear and I will save you; swear, swear, for Fabean's sake—for your own!"

"I—I'd rather not," muttered Carrie, with ludicrous indecision; "somebody might ask me about it, and how could I help telling; yet I would like to know what your secret is."

"Four words would tell you. Oh, swear never to repeat them—never to breathe to mortal the secret they reveal."

Carrie Leslie was awed by the burning glances fixed upon her—by the rigid hand which held her own, and by the thrillingly spoken words.

"Indeed, I will swear," she said; "I will never, never let any one know what you are going to say to me."

La Guerita bent forward. "Listen!" she said; "hear all our shame—Fabean's and mine, Carrie; WE WERE BORN SLAVES!"

For once amazement held Carrie Leslie dumb. La Guerita repeated her words: "We were born slaves!"

Ah, what bitter meaning they had to her. If she could but have known how much lower were the emotions they aroused in the young girl that knelt beside her.

"I can't believe it," she said at first; "you are trying to humble me, Mrs. DeGrey. Do you suppose I could have married Fabean if he had been a slave? Ugh, the low-born creatures!"

"Alas! Carrie, it is true."

Carrie burst into tears of indignation. "Then, Mrs. DeGrey, I consider that we have all been shamefully imposed upon. The idea of you and Fabean having been born slaves, and, just as like as not, your father and mother not even married; and your brother having the presumption to want to marry me; it is shameful!"

La Guerita quailed before this girl's weak wrath and contempt, as if in her puny voice was concentrated all the contempt of millions. "I hear the voice of the world," she said, "and, O, Fabean, Fabean, I have given it into this girl's power to hurl such scorn at thee!"

She felt as if she could silence forever the indignant young beauty— the vain, pettish child she had, in her passionate eagerness, made her confidant. The next moment she felt the weak creature's arms around her, and her tears upon her cheek, while she sobbed out:

"Indeed, I am very, very sorry, though I couldn't help being a little angry at first. Of course, I can't marry Fabean, but you will forgive me for that, wont you. I hope he wont feel very badly, but, of course, he will see I couldn't carry out my engagement when he knows all."

"But he must never know," cried La Guerita, in affright; "you have given me your solemn oath not to disclose what I have said."

"And I never will, you may be quite sure," said Carrie, quite patronizingly. "Dear me, I am quite upset for the day; I never had such a shock before in all my life. What an escape I have had, to be sure; I feel so perturbed; I think, if you will excuse me, I will say my prayers; I remember that when anything used to fret me, mamma always used to tell me to say my prayers, and it used to do me so much good."

She left the room and entered the library. In a short time she reappeared, with traces of tears upon her cheeks, and said, very sweetly :

"I feel so much better. Dear me, it is such a comfort to be able to put off one's grief in that way; I really didn't think I could bear my burden, before I had laid it at the throne of God."

"He helps those who have but little to bear," answered La Guerita, gazing upon her with stony eyes.

"O, dear me, how can you say so !" exclaimed Carrie, as much shocked at what appeared to her most unrefined heresy as she could be at anything ; "don't you remember what Dr. Alston says every Sunday? Why, Mrs. DeGrey, I don't believe you trust in God, or that you have any faith !"

"I had once," returned the widow; "I used to think He would help me in time of trouble—that He would give me happiness ; I used to pray to Him, as you do ; but how has He answered me? Has He not pressed cups of gall and wormwood to my lips—taken from me all my pleasant things? My faith was in vain—my prayers have been fruitless ! He has given me darkness for light, and desolation for happiness !"

Carrie Leslie listened helplessly, feeling that the mind of her friend was in a most unhallowed state, yet knowing not how to make it better. She quoted some common-place phrases of advice and consolation, meaning well, but accomplishing nothing, and soon arose to depart. Then, as if again seized by sudden dread, La Guerita clasped her in her arms, and held her there until she had promised again and again never to reveal a word of what had been told her.

She was glad, at last, to escape ; and as she walked hurriedly down the garden path La Guerita looked after her with a bitter smile, saying to herself: "That girl is not a hypocrite ; that prayer she breathed comforted her. Ah, a thousand prayers would not comfort me. I know now what Christianity is ; what a belief in a *merciful* God is—a delusion to stay weak minds ! Nothing more ! nothing more !"

These words she bitterly repeated as she saw Carrie Leslie greet Victor DeGrey at the gate, and smile in answer to some remark, then place her hand upon his arm, and walk with him up the shady road.

Carrie Leslie had hastily resolved to keep her intention of breaking her engagement a secret until the deed was actually accomplished, but something impelled her then to make a confidant of Victor DeGrey, and with many blushes and a few tears she made the confession most adroitly, without ever meaning falsehood ; intimated that La Guerita had opposed the match, for her pride revolted from the idea of it being known to any one, that aught but her own free will had induced her to resign her lover. Yet she sought to impress upon the mind of Victor that she was performing a duty, not a fickle caprice ; and though surprised, and almost offended with the young girl for thus casting aside one whom he had for years loved as a brother, he was well satisfied that for once, at least, she acted from some deeper motives than mere impulse.

What it was he did not inquire. If he had, how much sorrow and tribulation might have been averted, for Carrie Leslie would not have kept her secret then. But, knowing nothing of the importance of his words, he only gravely said :

"Perhaps it is all for the best. It may be that you are not intended for each other." And in fancy Fabean stood before him, as he had once done in reality, with a tiny, delicate creature hanging upon his arm, and though her eyes were blue and her hair golden, they were not like those of Carrie Leslie.

Thornton met them at the gate of Mrs. Leslie's garden, and as the evening was fine, they strolled on. Neither of them felt in a lightsome mood ; and as they walked on the shore and watched the ebb and flow of the tide, they spoke of solemn things, and at last of the dead Harold DeGrey and his widow and child.

"After Mrs. DeGrey's severe illness," remarked Thornton, "I was surprised to hear she had so soon left her room. Dr. Marsh told me he thought for several days she would never rise from her bed again. Indeed, I know he had but little more hope for her than he had for Harold in his extremity."

"Harold's illness has always been a great mystery to me," said Victor ; "or rather, I may say, the result of it is a great mystery to me. It was mental, not physical, suffering that killed him ; of that I am convinced.

But what could have occasioned that suffering ? Oh, I would give the world to know !"

"Or so much of it as you possess," said Carrie, with a slight laugh, keeping the secret that she held only from a perverse feeling that, by doing so, she became at once superior in knowledge to her companions.

"Has it never occurred to you," said Thornton, reproving his sister's frivolity with a glance, and speaking with hesitation ; "Has it never occurred to you that Harold had obtained some knowledge of his wife's antecedents ? We have never been able to learn the object or direction of his last journey. Is it not probable that it was taken on La Guerita's account, and that he purposely baffled curiosity ? "

"It must be so," returned Victor, in perplexity ; "yet I must confess I never thought so before. It must be so ! Yet if Harold gained any painful secret, that in no way accounts for La Guerita's extreme melancholy, for he would not have imparted it to her. Poor creature, her grief seems almost to partake of the character of madness. I long for Fabean's arrival ; that may change the current of her thoughts."

"Poor fellow," sighed Carrie, "I fear he will not find Ellisville so pleasant as usual."

"Of course, he will not," ejaculated Thornton, impatiently, "his sister's dejection will render that impossible."

"I presume Miss Carrie alluded to something else," said Victor, slightly contemptuously.

Thornton Leslie turned toward his sister with a quick, nervous start, instantly divining the meaning of Victor's words.

"Yes," ejaculated Carrie, interpreting his searching glance, "I have decided to oblige you ;" adding, with a sudden perverse impulse, "But I have not done so to oblige you, Thornton, any more than you would be likely to give up *la belle* Southron to gratify me."

Thornton colored ; Victor whistled, and executed the expressive pantomime of putting a ring upon an imaginary finger and a cross upon the back of his friend, at the same time ejaculating "Caught !"

Thornton looked at his sister reproachfully, but she was in no mood to heed his frowns, and cried :

"It is all very well for you to stand there, signing for me to stop. But I wont do it. I'll say just what I please ; so that if her cousin does succeed in keeping you apart, everybody that cares about it may know that mine are not the only matrimonial plans that have miscarried."

"You are a very foolish girl, Carrie," said her brother, severely ; while Victor stood by, undecided whether to leave or attempt to reconcile the disputants.

"O, no doubt I am a foolish girl !" retorted Carrie, stamping her little foot into the yielding sand ; "I have been an obstinate girl lately, and a strange girl, too ; and now that I have become a yielding and an ordinary girl, I am, of course, a foolish girl." After which she proved herself at least an ordinary girl by bursting into tears and sobbing out that she wanted to do right, but she was not quite sure whether La Guerita even thought she had done so.

Hastening to his sister's side, Thornton soothed her as one might an ailing child. But though she wiped away her tears, her mood remained the same, and all were glad when the walk was ended.

Victor left the brother and sister at their door, and walked slowly in the direction of his own home, leaving Enola, in which a few lights already shone, some distance to the left, looking with troubled eyes to the upper windows, and saying to himself :

"There is a light in La Guerita's window, perhaps she is retiring ; I will not go in to-night—to-morrow will do as well. Poor girl ! poor girl ! She will never be the same again. O, good God ! what a trial has come upon us. If I could but know, as Harold did, what curse came with her into the family ! If I could even simply know the direction of his fatal journey, or even the name under which he traveled."

The last he would have known could he have looked upon the crumpled paper which La Guerita had found in a pocket-book, and that moment held in her hand. Upon it were written the words :

"Mr. Norton Holmes will call, according to request, upon Mr. Harry Grey at the R—— Hotel, M——, at ten o'clock on Wednesday morning.

"HOLMSFORD, N. Carolina,
"March 22d, 1859."

CHAPTER X.

"What were those fancies ? * * *
A wind arose and rushed upon the South,
And shook the songs, the whispers, and the shrieks
Of the wild woods together ; and a Voice
Went with it : 'Follow, follow, thou shalt win.'"
Tennyson.

IT would have been well if Victor DeGrey had not that night passed by the doors of Enola, but had entered in, and looked upon the grieving widow. Not for a moment would he have left her alone, had he guessed the wild thoughts and longings that filled her heart and brain as she sat in her dimly-lighted chamber, with the crumpled paper, the clue to her husband's wanderings, in her hands.

A sudden longing to visit her birth-place, and see her mother possessed her. A longing, born from no desire of sympathy or love, she was incapable then of wishing for either. She rather wished to probe deeper her wounded soul, to go where her husband had suffered for her even unto death.

She started to her feet and paced the room rapidly, sometimes pausing for a moment at the open window to gaze out into the night, as if with an uncontrollable impulse to fly into its darkness. Then, had she been placed upon a boundless desert, the dreary scene would have harmonized well with the wild thoughts that thronged her mind, while the incense starting upward from the garden, maddened her by its utter incongruity. Had she stood alone on the rocky shore of the sea, and looked over its waters, the solitude and grandeur might have given her peace, but the sight of lovelier things—the starlight shimmering over rustling tree and flower, even the calm face of her sleeping child seemed only mocking her despair. She wanted change, thunder, lightning, flood, anything terrible—anything more horrible than the passions which beset her soul.

Suddenly, the longing to behold her mother became a determination, and then came another thought so terrible that her very soul recoiled from it, and she sank to the floor as if struck by a heavy hand, shuddering from head to foot, yet calling back the terrible thought, clinging to it, and holding it in her heart, till it became the single hope of her soul.

The early hours of morning had come when she looked again from her window. The tardy moon was just rising from the sea, and faintly shining upon Enola. For a moment a tremor shook the woman's heart. She should never behold again the moonbeams shine upon her once-loved home, or upon the marble shaft that marked her husband's grave.

She could not go without beholding that—without a last farewell to his resting place. All was silent. Not a creature awake in the house—not a creature stirring in the roads. She looked around the room, caught a large cloak from the foot of the bed, and wrapping it around her, crept noiselessly down the stairs and through the hall. The bolts and lock of a side door readily yielded to her hand. She gained the garden, sped rapidly over the deserted roads, and soon sank exhausted upon her husband's grave.

There she burst in wild ejaculations of the atonement she would make, calling upon her husband's name, as if his dead form could rise and answer her. But she could not stay in the lonesome churchyard—she could not kneel beside her dead husband and child. Their eyes seemed to reproach her, a sense of guilt, a nameless terror, filled her soul. She staggered to her feet, and again sped over the lonesome roads, and, undiscovered, gained her chamber.

She had made a mad resolve to depart that night, and, without pausing to rest, prepared for flight. She dressed herself first in colored garments, over the mourning she wore, then unlocked a desk and took out a sum of money which she had laid by from time to time, and which she knew would never be missed. Then for a moment she paused and looked upon the sleeping child. "It is best," she said; "yes, it is best that he should share my fate. 'T will be an easy one for him. He will never know sorrow or shame as I have done ; I will save him from all that. Yes, yes, my child and I are one, we must make atonement together."

Tenderly she raised him from the bed, and without awakening him, dressed him in garments of a dark color, and then without one look around, rose up, and holding him close to her beating heart, left the room which had been for years her sanctuary.

She paused a moment at the door, then locked it, and put the key into the pocket of her dress. "That will give me a little time," she thought. There was a faint light burning in the hall ; she paused beneath it and looked at her watch—"half-past one."

Then she left her home, with fearful calmness—such, perhaps, as rested upon Hagar's brow when she led her son forth into the burning desert to meet his destiny. As one who goes to perform a direful penance, thinks more of the atonement he will make, than of the torture he will suffer, so went La Guerita into the darkness of the night—into the still darker future she had claimed for herself, and turned not back, nor

heeded the voices of Memory and Love which strove to detain her.

Four days later, her journey was over ; she was safe in the R—— Hotel, in M——, N. Carolina.

She herself could never tell by what ingenuity and cunning she had eluded the vigilance of the police, who, throughout the country, had been telegraphed of her disappearance ; how she had, a score of times, changed the identity of herself and child, and had arrived without hindrance at her destination. It seemed wonderful even to herself. She exulted over it, as a proof that her course was pre-ordained—that she was following out some mystical fate that no power could thwart.

She arrived at the hotel late in the night, and attracted the attention of neither the clerk or waiter, who, indeed, were too dull with sleepiness to notice whether the lady was young or old, dressed in mourning or in colors, or even if the child who accompanied her was a boy or a girl.

The landlord, however, the next morning looked at the name in his books with some curiosity, languidly wondering whether Mrs. H. Grey, was the wife of a gentleman of that name who had stayed at the house some weeks before.

It was late in the morning before he had an opportunity of knowing, for the servant who had taken up breakfast, had received her orders through the closed door, and had left the tray in the hall, whence it had been taken unseen.

This unusual proceeding, though as the landlord strove to assure himself might have arisen from a most trivial cause, served to increase his curiosity, and it was with alacrity that he obeyed a request from the lady that he would wait upon her.

Unconsciously he had in his own mind decided that his guest was the wife of the gentleman who had honored his house in the early spring time, and it was with surprise he noticed the mourning garments of the young widow.

His salutations were given somewhat confusedly, after which, La Guerita said quietly : "I am quite a stranger here, Mr. Sterling, and for certain reasons desire to remain one. Therefore, as I wish to learn some few particulars of certain persons here, and to do so privately, I beg that you will aid me to do so."

"Madam's recent affliction, no doubt——" began the landlord,

" Has entirely unfitted me for any excitement," interrupted La Guerita, and I beg of you during my short stay, to protect me from any publicity. Let one servant attend upon me, and let that be one who will not prate to others."

"I assure you, madam," said the really kind-hearted landlord, "everything shall be done to promote your comfort, and if in any way I can be of service to you, I pray you to command me." .

"Thank you," said La Guerita, gently. " It is only to have this note forwarded to Holmsford, that I need at present trouble you."

She held the note in her hand, looking at it doubtfully, as the landlord quickly exclaimed : "Ah, 'tis to be sent to Mr. Holmes, I presume. Certainly, ma'am, we know him well, he was a friend of Mr. Grey's I remember."

La Guerita shuddered from head to foot. "Speak not of him," she said, "I am his widow."

The landlord had conjectured as much from the moment he entered the room, yet at her words a feeling of awe came over him. He bowed silently, unable to speak, knowing that he could say nothing of condolence to her.

" Mr. Holmes will be much grieved," he said, at length. " Your note shall be sent immediately, madam. Perhaps there is some other friend you desire to communicate with ?"

" Yes," she answered boldly, and with a beating heart ; "there was another mentioned—Mr. Leveredge—Claude Leveredge. He lives somewhere in this neighborhood, I believe."

Suddenly the landlord's face darkened. "Thank God, no !" he said, with emphasis ; "thank God, the State is rid of him ! But I beg pardon, madam, he is a friend of yours ?"

" Not at all," answered La Guerita quietly, her heart beating wildly. "As he is not here, I am sorry to have excited you by mentioning him."

"No, no, madam, you don't excite me," returned the landlord, vainly endeavoring to appear calm ; "though God knows, some fathers would have murdered him for less evil than he has done me and mine. But enough of that, he is gone now."

" What, dead !" she almost shrieked the words.

" No, no, madam, such villains always run a long lease. I beg your pardon again, madam. He is not dead ; he has only left the country."

"Indeed !"

"Yes, ma'am, he sold all his negroes, and all his lands and houses, except the old homestead, and went cross seas more than a month ago."

"Strange! strange!" muttered La Guerita to herself.

"Yes, ma'am, it was," said the talkative landlord, considering himself addressed; "but, ma'am, if you know anything of them, you will remember the Leveredges always were a strange family. But—," growing excited again, "I never heard that any of them spent their lives in deceiving the innocent, squandering their fortunes at foreign gambling tables, and sacrificing even their old family servants to obtain means to live abroad in luxury."

"To *live* abroad?"

"Yes, ma'am, to *live* there. He has gone for good now. He came from the north about six weeks ago, and, as I have said, sold his plantations and slaves, swearing he would leave America for ever. I reckon there was nobody grieved much. There was almost murder every day on the place while he stayed there; he was absolutely mad with drink or some great excitement."

"Ah, I am surprised," remarked La Guerita indifferently. "I understood he was a remarkably dignified and reserved gentleman."

"Gentleman!" hissed the landlord between his teeth, and with all the contempt that could be concentrated upon one word. Then he laughed, as if in some slight triumph, saying: "You do not know the *gentleman;* few do, few do. But there is one I think that does."

La Guerita had just awakened to the impropriety, or at least strangeness of her long conversation with the garrulous landlord, but she lost all recollection of it at his words.

"Who," she said with sudden animation, "who can know this enigmatical gentleman—unless, indeed, after what you have told me, I should take him for a scoundrel?"

The landlord was rebuked; he felt how unguardedly he had spoken. "No, no, there are few that have that thought," he said in agitation. "She whom I spoke of has not that, yet she knows him well."

"And does not scorn him?" queried La Guerita, with a feeling at her heart she could not define.

"'Tis hard to say—'tis hard to say, ma'am," said the landlord gravely. "You see, ma'am, Miss Adela is a very superior person. Perhaps you know her, ma'am?"

"No."

"Oh, your husband's friends only. This Miss Adela, is Mr. Norton Holmes' eldest daughter; I've known her since she was a child, and a mighty pert little thing she was, but always different from most children. We country people, ma'am—though I say it myself—are apt to tell other people our business, and try to learn theirs; but Miss Adela never was that-a-way. She never took any notice of other people's affairs, nor ot what they thought of hers. She was always doing something that folks could'nt understand, and setting their curiosity agog; yet they always found out in the end that she meant well."

"You speak of the past. Has the young lady left this part of the country, then?"

"O dear no, ma'am, but she has stayed home far more than usual this

8

winter, and last summer she was north, and it was there they say the trouble first began."

"What trouble?"

"Sure enough, ma'am, I hav'nt told you. Why, that between Claude Leveredge and Miss Adela; they are cousins, you know, and folks say it was always intended that they should marry. 'Twas talked of when he was in Europe, years ago, and then, I fancy, Miss Adela was not averse to it; but she was only a child, and may have changed her notion; leastways, people have been looking in vain for the wedding these five years."

"What reason had people to suppose that Mr. Leveredge would marry his cousin?"

"A heap more to my mind than that she would marry him," replied the landlord, warmly. "Yes," he continued energetically, "people may say they're alike; that she's cold and haughty, and as unfathomable altogether as Claude Leveredge, but I grant them all that, and yet say she will never marry him."

"And why not?" asked La Guerita, greatly interested, knowing that the person spoken of might soon have almost unlimited control of her destiny.

"Because, ma'am, Miss Adela was not the woman to wait in a corner 'till it should please some one to take her out, and last summer, they do say, that she showed her cousin that."

"What, engaged herself to another?"

"Exactly, ma'am, and Mr. Leveredge was furious, and succeeded in breaking off the match, they say."

"Good God, what could he have done that for?" ejaculated La Guerita, startled from her wonted composure.

"In such cases, a gentleman's motives ain't hard to guess," returned the landlord. "Of course, he wanted Miss Adela himself, and it does my very heart and soul good to know he is foiled, whether Miss Adela acted out of revenge or not. There is no doubt, after dallying so long, he found when Miss Adela was about to marry, that he loved her to distraction, and that she scorned him. First of all, he broke off her marriage; then again he left Holmsford, after his cousin Acton's funeral, looking like a ghost; indeed a most horrible change had come over him. People said he had been discarded by Miss Adela—even his own servants said so. One of them told me that while he was at Holmsford, she saw him walking up and down a path in the garden, muttering the most horrible oaths, and that if he failed in his purpose, then he would leave the country for ever. Then he went north, and he was'nt gone a month before he came back, in a half frenzied state. Well, he never went near Holmsford. He sold off everything to the highest bidder—and bargains they made to be sure—and then left the State, swearing never to set foot on American soil again."

"I am almost interested in your local romance," said La Guerita, languidly. "And so he is gone—well, well. Mr. Holmes will be sufficient; you will please to remember to have the note sent to-day."

"Certainly, ma'am, certainly," said the landlord, taking the last words as a signal of dismissal. "And pray, madam, is there nothing else I can do ?"

"Nothing at present, I thank you, except to send me a good laundress, —some trusty woman. I fancy my husband particularly mentioned one connected with this hotel."

"No doubt, ma'am. We have the best; perhaps 'twas Caroline, or, yes—'twas Dode—or rather Dolores, a free woman, ma'am, that once belonged to a Mr. Holmes."

"Doubtless she is the same," said La Guerita faintly. "Send her to me."

"I will, ma'am, I will, early in the afternoon. But you look faint."

"It is nothing, nothing," she murmured, regaining her composure by a great effort : "Leave me, if you please, I am weary."

"Quite tired out with my talk," thought the landlord, as he wended his way down stairs. "Poor soul, no doubt she takes the death of her fine young husband hard. Well, no wonder ; and yet how attentively she listened to me. Shows at least that she, like most women, relishes a bit of gossip at any time. Jim, go to Dolores, and tell her she's wanted early this afternoon."

CHAPTER XI.

"Between the acting of a dreadful thing
And the first motion, the interim is
Like a phantasma, or a hideous dream."
Shakespeare.

LA GUERITA heard this order given in a loud, cheery voice, as she stood at her window, and shuddered as if it had been the announcement of some terrible fate. "Coward that I am," she muttered, bitterly ; "it must come, and now 'tis better than at any other time. What! shall I, who have rushed to meet the blow, be afraid to receive it ? No, no !"

Thus she muttered on ; sometimes of the past—oftener of the future, in which the names of her mother and Claude Leveredge were strangely mingled. Often she wondered that the former came not, and, frequently glancing at her watch, imagined moments never before moved by so slowly.

She felt a burning impatience seizing upon and mastering her—a wild, passionate longing for repose—for that repose the madman hopes for when meditating suicide ; she never for a moment dreamed of knowing happiness again, but she fancied that a deep repose—a dreamless lethargy, would come upon her after the fever and madness of the present were past. As one who, in the pain and frenzy of delirium, quaffs poisonous drugs and hopes for rest, so La Guerita DeCuba pressed to her lips a noxious cup, and craved oblivion.

It was strange that, amid these frenzied thoughts, she could fully realize her position, and force mind to contemplate it quietly. Point by point she considered the tale of the landlord. At the love of Claude Leveredge for his cousin she smiled, and accounted for his interference in her marriage to some freak altogether disconnected with her own history. For his subsequent actions —his agitation after the funeral of Acton Holmes—his sale of his property—his frenzy while attending to it —was all accounted for by the failure of his schemes for obtaining possession of little Harold, and, perhaps, a sudden remorse, brought upon him by the death of her husband.

"Yet it is strange that he left the country, after obtaining the object of his ambition," she murmured ; "for has he not for years lived only to see me plunged in misery, and now, that his hope is accomplished, he flies the scene. Strange, strange man ! Yet I see in him no free agent ; he is the sport of Fate ; his actions have been thus ruled that I may carry out my purpose—my holy purpose of atonement ! Every obstacle has been removed from my path ; the one which I most feared — Claude Leveredge — whose presence here would have utterly baffled me—would have even caused me to flee, as from a plague—no longer haunts the place to bar me from it. Appalled by the ruin he has wrought, he has fled the scene forever, and I am free ! free ! Free to call a woman of an accursed race, mother ! Free to pay the penalty to her folly ! "

Aroused and thrilled by the thoughts that crowded upon her, she at last arose, and with a quick, nervous step paced the floor, passing the open window, and even her child, without once lifting her eyes from the carpet ; once she laughed softly as she thought how she had fled from Enola and baffled pursuit.

The laugh, low and faint though it was, thrilled and startled her ; she suddenly paused in her walk, clasping her forehead, and asking herself, with horror, how she could laugh at such a time ; was she mad ?"

"No, not mad !" she answered herself, "and never shall be. Death will come before madness ; it did to Harold. No, no ; madness would not recompense his death : nought will but a long, long life of sanity preserved through torture. Ah, yes ! far worse than the bitterness of madness must be my atonement ! "

She looked at her child, as he stood by the window, restlessly gazing upon and longing to be in the garden below ; her heart yearned over the beautiful boy—her darling, her first-born ! Was the atonement demanded of him also ?"

The struggle in her heart was but for a moment ; she cast the question aside by another : "Was not the child a part of herself ?"

Alas ! that she did not ask : "Is not this Harold's child ?"

While she pondered the boy looked up, and filled with vague terror bowed his head and cried piteously ; then she caught him to her breast, showering kisses upon him, calling him a thousand endearing names, and, by the countless means that mothers know, quelled his restlessness and soothed him into quietness again ; even stilling his wailing cry : "O, mamma, let us go home ! Let us go to grand-ma and Uncle Vic ! "

"Hush, hush ! " she said, at last, in a low voice, a thousand times more sorrowful than his own ; "we are far, very far, from Enola."

"Oh, yes, mamma, but let us go back ; it is so hot and dusty here, and your little boy is so tired. O, mamma, I want to go home ! "

La Guerita put him from her, clasping her hands in agony, almost in remorse, as the child clung to her knees, repeating, again and again, amid sobs and tears, his piteous wail.

"Hush ! " said La Guerita, at

last, so sternly that for a moment his sobs were checked. "Listen to me, Harold; look at me; remember what I say; we are never going home again—never! Don't cry! Listen again! We are never going home; you must never speak of the place again."

"What, not of Enola, mamma—that pretty place, mamma! where papa used to be with us, before they carried him away to the church-yard?"

She groaned in anguish: "O child, child, be still! you must forget all that; never, never must you speak of it again. If you cannot forget it, you must tell every person that asks you questions that you have done so."

The boy drew back from her, his cheek slowly crimsoning and his eyes filling with amazement. "What!" he said, "must Harold tell a lie?"

"Ah, what have I done!" she cried, frantically; "I have put evil and falsehood into the mind of my child! But he will forget—he must forget that, and all the past! Yes, he shall forget," she continued, turning from the child as if to silence some stern antagonist; "he is so young, he will forget; he must—he shall!"

Then she turned to the child again, kissing and caressing him in a fierce, yet protecting way, telling herself that she was doing right to sacrifice him—feeling, in a vague way, that the spirit of her husband was pleased by the deed.

Thus the weary morning wore away. The early dinner was brought and sent back, almost untasted. Even the child could not eat; he was sick at heart with a longing for his home—its dear familiars, and its simple pleasures; he sighed for the fresh air and a romp in the garden; yet he dared not speak of either; and at last, overcome by the silence, the heat of the day, and that sickening languor, which even an infant can feel, he lay upon the floor and sobbed himself to sleep.

But he soon found a softer resting place; his mother lifted him in her arms, and pillowed his head upon her bosom. And so he slept, pressing his fair cheek upon her heaving breast, as unconscious of the tumult raging within, as a moss or flower that clings to a volcano's rocky side.

It seemed to La Guerita hours that she sat with her child in her arms. At last she was aroused by a firm footstep on the corridor. Her face blanched, her heart almost ceased to beat, as she heard a low tap at the door. She arose and laid the sleeping child upon the sofa. She strove to speak, but could not; she knew who came, and could not bid her enter.

The knock was repeated, a little more loudly than before. La Guerita, by a mighty effort, gained strength to totter forward and open the door.

There stood a tall, dark woman; strikingly handsome still, though her hair was gray, and half covered by a bandanna handkerchief, and her form clothed in homespun garments of coarse quality and the rudest make.

La Guerita noted all this, even in her agitation; she noted too how the salutation upon the woman's lips died away unspoken, as her eyes rested upon her face; how she gazed upon her as on one risen from the dead. She seemed fascinated, for some seconds she neither spoke nor moved : then she said, with a slightly foreign accent, the more perceptible perhaps from its tremulousness :

"I beg your pardon, ma'am, I don't know whenever I've been startled so. I——"

"Sit down," said La Guerita.

She seemed glad to avail herself of the permission, even though the lady remained standing. As she sank into a chair, she caught the image of herself and the young widow reflected in a large mirror. She shrieked aloud, starting to her feet, and pointing to the mirror, while she exclaimen : "Look, look, and tell me who you are. O God, it cannot be—!" She faced the mirror with frightful eagerness, drawing La Guerita to her side, and pointing to the images reflected. Then suddenly she said again : "For God's sake tell me who you are?"

"You know already," said La Guerita bitterly. "Stand back from me. I am your daughter—La Guerita DeCuba !"

For a moment the quadroon remained motionless, the words could not augment the shock the presence of her daughter had given her. The two women stood as if entranced. They looked at each other, but no word of love or welcome broke from the lips of either. The daughter looked upon the mother with eyes of accusing wrath, while she cowered before that gaze like one accursed, falling at last to the floor with a bitter moan, sobbing forth :

"My daughter ! my daughter, why are you here ?"

CHAPTER XII.

"What is the tale that I would tell ? Not one
Of strange adventure, but a common tale
Of woman's wretchedness; one to be read
Daily in many a young and blighted heart."
                              Miss Landon.

THESE words, huskily and faintly spoken by the prostrate woman, seemed to level the barrier that existed between mother and daughter. Suddenly they realized that they were mother and daughter, not mistress and menial. Neither spoke or in any way gave vent to her emotion. La Guerita sank into a chair ; Dolores slowly raised herself, and stood with downcast eyes before her daughter. 'Twas pitiful to see how stunned with shame and grief she was, how imploringly she lifted her hand, as if to entreat a moment's space for thought, saying, at length : "Wait one moment—only one ; I shall be able to hear you then."

This she said with trembling lips and voice, not as a mother welcoming back in hope and love a long lost child, but as one averting a threatened evil. La Guerita looked upon her with a countenance almost sublime in its accusing wrath and scornful pity, for in her very soul she spurned with contempt the fallen woman before her, and yet as deeply pitied the mother who feared to meet the gaze of her child.

Dolores Holmes saw that. She knew that a terrible sorrow had fallen upon her daughter's life, and that she was held accountable for it. She dropped her head upon her hands and groaned, and just then Harold awoke with a cry, and called his mother to his side.

The quadroon looked at him in

amazement; she had not noticed him until then. She drew near, she would have touched him, but La Guerita pushed her aside, as if her very presence were pollution. Humbly and sadly she turned away, forcing back the ready tears, and moving not again until La Guerita said calmly: "Are you ready to listen to me now?"

"Send the child away," she murmured; "Send him away before you speak."

"You are right," returned La Guerita; "'tis best that he should see nor hear nothing of what must pass between us."

So Harold, whose eyes seemed riveted upon the strange woman, was sent to the beautiful garden which he had all day longed to enter; and in a few moments the mother and daughter were alone, with the locked door between them and the outer world.

The silence that followed was short, for La Guerita felt that she had still a duty to perform, and with fresh impatience entered upon its accomplishment.

"The child is gone," she said; "The innocent child, before whom we could not speak of evil, and now I am ready to talk to you. I, your daughter—a woman in years and cares—am ready to learn of my mother why she cast me forth to the awful fate that has come upon me."

The mother cast an appealing glance upon her child, but saw no sign of yielding upon her rigid face.

"Don't look at me," she entreated. "Indeed I cannot bear it. What need have you to question me—to awaken memories long silent? You know I was born a slave, though white blood coursed through my veins. There! you can see it now, though years and toil have darkened me. It used to be my boast, that and my beauty. But oh, I have cursed it a thousand times; yet I blessed it when Acton Holmes for its sake loved me, and brought me from my Cuban home to be his mistress here."

"You dare say that to me!" cried La Guerita, with burning cheeks and flashing eyes.

"God knows I speak with shame," sighed Dolores Holmes, "But you have asked me for the truth; you have a right to hear it, and you shall if you still demand it of me."

"I do," returned La Guerita, still indignation in her tones; adding as she seated herself opposite her mother, "I will try to listen to you calmly, so tell me all, and especially how you, a mother, could put your infants from your breast. There, tell me that; I can ask no more."

"But I must tell you more," cried Dolores, eagerly, "and oh, perhaps your hate may turn to pity when you hear my tale."

"Don't speak of that," returned La Guerita, in the tone in which she might have said, "Don't hope for it;" and with a beating heart Dolores Holmes began the history of her life.

"You asked me a moment ago," she said, "how I dared to tell you that I gloried in my beauty when Acton Holmes brought me here to be the delight of his eyes, the idol of his heart!"

She spoke those words with passionate emphasis, as if by them to vindicate the conduct of the man who had wronged her, and with such intense feeling that all shame passed from her voice and mien. Then, startled and aroused, La Guerita knew that the life of her mother, like her own, had been blessed, then cúrsed by Love; then the first thrill of sympathy with her mother sprang into being. But she had sworn to let no tie of blood, or any womanly pity, debar her from judging Dolores Holmes aright, and without speaking she motioned her to continue.

"You are calm," said Dolores, "but I don't think I can be when I speak of those days. Oh, I loved him so! I loved him so! He was so handsome, so grand, so good! You smile. He was all that, and he loved me! Yes, he loved me; and if I had been the acknowledged daughter of Señor Alvarez, instead of a *slave*, he would have sought me as his wife with all the eagerness of the wild, ay, mad idolatry that filled his soul when first he beheld me.

"I had never been a favorite on the plantation. My mistress hated and my master shunned me. I think he was very glad when the young American proposed to buy me; and the happiest day of my life was that upon which I became the property of Acton Holmes.

"Why do you look at me so? God knows it was not strange that I should rejoice to escape from the tyranny of a jealous mistress, the coldness of an indifferent master, and the bitter servitude I had so long endured. How was I, an untutored child, to know my duty toward God, of whom I had seldom even heard? How was I to know that it was wrong for me to drink the cup of happiness which was held out to me—to take with joy the love so freely offered me? There

was no one to warn me from it; no one who cared to save me from a fate worse than slavery. I think Rosita, my master's daughter, would have done so had she been near, but she had lately married an American named Burford, and gone with him to spend the winter in New York."

"You mean Roland Burford, I suppose?" said La Guerita, in some surprise.

"Yes, that was his name," returned Dolores; "Can it be possible that you know him?"

"Fabean is now traveling with him in Europe. Continue; why do you pause?"

"To thank God that my son is safe!" she answered solemnly. "I feared to ask of him. But I pray you now to tell me is he prosperous?"

"Yes."

"And he has found a friend in Roland Burford?"

"A true and firm one, I trust," replied La Guerita, much affected by the mention of her brother.

"Ah!" murmured Dolores, musingly, "Roland Burford was a good man."

"And he is still," said La Guerita, somewhat emphatically; "but waste no time in talking of him now; speak of yourself, and, first of all, tell me how you gained such a complete knowledge of the English language?"

"Easily enough," answered Dolores; "my teacher was Acton Holmes. Ah! I have never forgotten the lessons he gave me, though later ones have faded from my mind. How could I forget anything that happened during the four years I lived in the cottage by the river—

those years, that were the only happy ones of my life?"

"It is needless for me to describe to you my daily life, save that for three years its peacefulness was unbroken. Until my boy was nearly two years old, not a thought of the future troubled me; my master was as kind as ever, and no pang of jealousy or distrust ever entered my heart, until I heard that a woman, who had lived as I was living, had been sold and sent far South, that her presence might not annoy her master's bride. She and her children had been sacrificed, why might not I be? Even then no thought of guilt troubled me; it was only fear that made me shudder; I could not believe that the man I loved—that loved me—would act so base a part; but he might die, and then what would become of me, and the child I had borne?"

"Then, too, I was soon to become, for a second time, a mother. Then I first learned to pray. Oh, how wildly I entreated that my child might never see the light, or that at least it might not be a girl to meet a fate like mine. Then, for the first time, I was moody and unhappy. I could only weep when my master caressed me, and answer with sobs, when he asked the cause of my dejection.

"In the early summer, my second child was born. I shrieked in agony and fainted when they told me it was a girl. There was a good, kind quakeress with me, who had known my master from his birth. Often had she reproved him for his sin, but she came to me in my hour of peril. By my subsequent dejection, not by

9

any words I spoke, she guessed why I had fainted at your birth. I think that Acton, too, must have gained some idea of the cause, for one day he came into my room, and said: 'Dolores, I am about to free you and the children.'

"My heart bounded with joy at the words; my fears all vanished; my soul was comforted, for I knew that Acton Holmes never retracted a promise.

"Yes, my soul was comforted for a time—for a time only. The good woman who had visited me in my need, did not turn from me—as a weaker woman would have done—when my bodily health was restored. She saw that my soul was weak, not naturally vile, so she would not leave me without an effort to save me. Ah, it was long before she could instill into my mind any knowledge of good or evil."

"But she succeeded at last?"

"Thank God, yes."

"What was the woman's name?"

"Asenith Bray. She is old and feeble now, and is called Aunt Sene by both black and white. She lives near Holmsford, in the little house in which she was born."

"I will find her. Go on with your story."

Dolores raised her eyes with a look of wonder.

"She can tell you nothing different," she said humbly; "I am giving you the truth, without seeking to exculpate myself. I know I deserve all your doubt and scorn, but——" her lips trembled for a few moments, she could say no more; then she continued bravely: "I think, perhaps, Asenith Bray could more easily feel charity and sympathy for the poor, ignorant slave, than you possibly can for the mother who has cast a stigma upon your being."

La Guerita interrupted her, impatiently. "Don't speak of charity or sympathy," she exclaimed, "I know not what they are."

Dolores sighed deeply, yet disdaining to reveal to La Guerita the effect of her words, continued firmly :

"I have told you that this woman —Asenith Bray—came to me after you were born. She told me, that though I was but a slave, my soul was as dear to God as that of my master ; and she told me that his soul, as well as mine, ran in danger of destruction.

"I told something of this to Acton, but he laughed and told me he could care for his own soul, and that he did not fear the vengeance of God for his conduct toward a woman he loved but could not marry.

"His answer silenced my apprehensions on that point. Then Asenith pointed to my children : 'They are to be free,' she said, 'but will they ever be happy ! They, the base-born children of a harlot. At least if you cannot redeem the past, make fair the future.'

"What did it matter ? There was negro blood in their veins, they could never rise in the world. My shame would not affect them. Yet for days Asenith's words rang in my ears, and then for the first time I realized fully that I had sinned.

"Again and again came Asenith Bray. Again and again she read passages from the bible which treated of my sin. At last a day came upon which I bowed my soul in anguish,

and craved the mercy of my insulted God. Oh, then—then it was hard to do what the law commanded ; to put the love of Acton Holmes from me, to entreat him to leave me and my children in peace. Ah, I never thought for a moment he would take my darlings from me, or I could not have spoken.

"I had time to weigh well my decision. My master went north that summer, and did not return until fall. Oh, how I dreaded his return. It seemed to me cruel that he hurried back, because he feared that I and my new-born child were ailing still. And in the midst of his kindness I had to tell him how I abhorred the life I had led, and to entreat him to put me away from him—to make me the lowest of his slaves—to sell me and my children at the block, rather than make me sin again.

"At first he did not understand me ; then he laughed, thinking some trifling annoyance had excited me. But when I burst into a flood of tears and with passionate emphasis repeated what Aunt Asenith had told me, he cursed her name, but I silenced him by pointing to my bible ; 'there,' said I, 'I learned my sin.'

"Bitterly then he upbraided me. 'I thought you loved me,' he said, and for that reason I have never looked upon you as a mere slave. But it cannot be possible that you have deceived me all these years— that you have ever feared and hated me.'

"'And I have not, I have not,' I cried ; 'Better far would it have been if I had done so. 'Oh, my master, I have loved you. I love you still ; but I hear the Lord saying

to me, as to the Magdalen of old—
'Go and sin no more.'

" I shall never forget the look he
gave me then—a look that said, ' I
have lost you for ever,' while he muttered : ' I taught her myself those
cursed letters—blind fool that I was.'

" Then he went from the house ;
I thought, I hoped, never to return.
Yet the very hope seemed death to
me, and I fell fainting to the floor.
That night, after the moon had risen,
Asenith Bray came to me ; she wept
over me, yet she rejoiced and com-
forted me.

" For three long months I saw no
creature but her. God only knows
what I suffered in that time, yet I
strove to reconcile myself to my fate.
What that was to be I never inquired
even of myself. I imagined dimly
that I was to live in that little cottage
for ever—I and my children, contented to know that Acton Holmes
was somewhere in the outer world,
caring for and protecting us. For
although he never came, or sent
any word to me, I placed in him the
simple faith with which an humble
Christian believes in and relies on
the God she cannot see."

Dolores paused, looking furtively
at La Guerita, who rose abruptly,
more touched by her mother's words
than she would own even to herself.
In a moment she returned to her seat
as if ashamed of her momentary
weakness, and impatiently motioned
her to proceed.

" He came to me in the early
spring," she began abruptly, yet in a
low, sad voice ; ' I was sitting upon
the steps with my baby in my arms,
and my beautiful blue-eyed boy playing at my feet, when the gate swung

back, and looking up, I saw my master standing in the path.

" I could neither speak nor move. I
think for the first moment I was overwhelmed with joy—the next with
fear. But Fabean rushed towards
him with a joyful cry. Then I sprang
forward and held him back ; but my
master bent down and caressed him,
then said : ' Send him away, Dolores, and let me look at the girl.'

" I obeyed, trembling with alter-
nations of heat and cold, as he took
you in his arms, looked at you gravely, kissed you again and again, and
said at length : ' Poor little one, she
is a tiny creature to leave her mother.'

" I was stunned by his words—
those cruel words ! I had never
thought he would take you from me.
As soon as I could speak, I entreated
him to spare me such a bitter pang,
crying out that I could not, *would*
not live without my children, that my
heart would break.

" I know he pitied me ; he could
not see my anguish and do otherwise.
He led me into the house, and endeavored to comfort me, and when I
became calmer, told me his plans.
They dazzled me, though at first I
would not yield to them. His children—*his*, he said—were not to feel
their mother's shame. He was pitiless, I thought then, as he went on
to say how, for their sakes, he had
yielded to my prayer, and that for
them he would vow himself to perpetual celibacy, that no legitimate
children might wean from them his
love.

" For a time I was madly jealous of
my babes : they were all in all—I,
nothing. Ah, since that, I have seen
wives bear the same pangs in silence,

and, ere long, I smothered mine, and listened with patience to his words.

"His plan was to free them, and place them where their birth would never be suspected. They could pass for white children, and an education and fortune should be given them.

"I cannot tell you what days and nights of bitterness I passed before I would yield my children up. Asenith Bray pleaded with me in vain; it was but the thought that your life, if passed in slavery, would be cursed like mine, that induced me at last to let them go.

"And so they took my children from me—Acton and Asenith. For years I never knew where they were; I only knew that they were safe, that they were never to know their mother —never to learn how low a thing she was."

Dolores paused, seemingly living again, in thought, the terrible hour that had left her childless. Her eyes blazed with fury and desperation, and her cheeks burned like live coals. La Guerita looked at her in amazement, until the light slowly faded from her eyes, and the crimson from her cheeks, and thought: "And thus her violent agony wore out; terrible but short-lived are the emotions of her race."

It seemed as if Dolores read her thoughts, for she said mournfully: "Acton Holmes came back to me and gave me the emancipation papers of my children and myself, but what were they to me? I had lost my children! Ah, have you ever missed a baby's head from your breast? Have you listened in vain for the

wailing cry or the happy murmur? Have you felt the turning of soft hair round your fingers, and baby lips pressing yours, and then awoke to find it all a dream? If so, you can pity me! For day and night have I passed like that since my children left me, broken-hearted, at that cottage door."

"Don't speak to me of that," muttered La Guerita huskily. "Calm yourself, and leave me; I can bear no more now. Let no one know that I have returned, and come to me again to-morrow."

She arose, and passed into her bedroom, fearing longer to trust herself in the presence of the woman whose tale had aroused the emotions of love and pity which she had fancied dead in her heart. She threw herself on the bed, pressing her hands upon her throbbing temples, and vainly striving to still the wild thoughts that crowded her brain. Ere long she started to her feet, aroused by the voice of Harold who rushed to her arms, exclaiming, with passionate sobs: "She did hurt me, mamma; she did hurt me."

"Who, my darling. Who dared to hurt you?"

"The woman who was with you, mamma; she saw me in the garden, and jumped towards me, and nearly killed me."

"How, my child?"

"Oh, she pressed me to her so hard, and kissed me, as if I was iron and couldn't be hurt; but I kicked her though," he added triumphantly, glancing at his dainty little boots, "and she soon let me go, and I know I hurt her, for she leant against a tree and cried awfully."

"Even this child repels her," thought La Guerita bitterly : "Even this child spurns the woman that bore me!"

CHAPTER XIII.

Is it madness or no!

THAT night the hours passed drearily to two persons, at least, in M——. They were filled to La Guerita, as they had ever been since her husband's death, with strange and exciting dreams ; and to Dolores they seemed fraught with bitter memories and wild apprehensions. She longed for the morning, that she might hasten to her daughter to learn why she had returned to awaken the buried past, to fill her heart with agony. Yet when the dawn came a sudden terror seized her, and hours passed before she dared to present herself before her daughter.

It was almost noon when she at last started to her feet, and hurried impetuously toward the hotel. As she turned into the street, she was arrested by the voice of the landlord, who had noted with much curiosity her long interview with his guest on the previous day.

"Stop a minute ! stop, Dolores !" he cried ; "Are you trying to overtake the steam cars? A mighty hot day this for such an experiment, I should think. Where are you going to at such a rate?"

"Only to the hotel, Mr. Sterling," she answered respectfully.

"Well, 'tisn't a running away, that I know of," he returned, with a laugh, "So you needn't go as if 'twas a racehorse, and you were forced to overtake it. Who do you suppose wants you at the hotel in such a hurry?"

Dolores well knew that the landlord had some object in putting these questions, and she shrewdly suspected that he wished to learn something of the widow and her son. She looked at him keenly, replying that she didn't suppose that anybody wanted her particularly, but that she had a heap of work to do and was in a hurry, for the widow lady had ordered her to go to her that morning.

"Ah, a very fine lady Mrs. Grey appears to be—a very fine lady indeed," remarked the landlord, "and her face seems quite familiar to me. I am sure I have seen her or her ghost before."

Dolores grew pale with alarm, and before the landlord could prevent her rushed past him, and entered the hotel. She ran up the stairs with a wildly beating heart, and knocked at the door of her daughter's room.

She was answered by a clear, ringing laugh, and the door was thrown open by Harold, who shrank back in alarm when he saw the dark, stern woman who had aroused his passion the day before.

La Guerita noticed his fear, and bade him go to the garden. With a flushed face Dolores stood by to let him pass, and then, locking the door, turned toward her daughter.

For a moment neither spoke. Dolores, indeed, forgot her errand ; she was too much lost in contemplation of the utter woe enstamped upon her daughter's countenance to remember that she had still to learn what had cast it there.

La Guerita first broke the silence. "I sent a messenger to Mr. Norton

Holmes last night," she said, "asking him to meet me here to-day. A gentleman has just driven up to the door; look from the window and tell me whether it is he."

Some fancied resemblance of the new comer to Claude Leveredge induced these words, therefore she was not surprised when Dolores answered in the affirmative.

She gazed at him listlessly as he sprang from his buggy, and stood for a moment giving directions to the negro servant who had accompanied him.

"I have come into town to see Mrs. Grey," she heard him say to the landlord, as he turned to enter the house. "Ah, little thought we, Sterling, when poor young Grey was here that we should see his widow so soon. But such is life. Send up, Sterling, and let her know I am here."

La Guerita met the messenger at the door, and sent him back with a request to Mr. Holmes that he would come up to her private parlor.

A few minutes later the servant announced, "Massa Norton Holmes."

- La Guerita advanced to meet him, with difficulty summoning words in which to thank him for his visit.

"I am only too happy to be of the slightest service to you, madam," returned Mr. Holmes, courteously, as he looked upon her with admiration and a perplexed gaze, which showed her face was familiar to him. Presently he nodded to Dolores, who had shrank into the darkest corner of the room, and then took the seat La Guerita offered.

Trembling from head to foot, she sank into a chair opposite him. She strove to command her voice, but it shook as she said : "You are doubtless curious to know why I have sent for you. I will explain."

She attempted to continue, but words failed her. She sprang to her feet, tore back the curtains from the window, and turned toward her wondering visitor, exclaiming : "Is my face familiar to you? Do you know me? Do you know me?"

Startled and disconcerted by her strange action and abrupt query, Mr. Holmes regarded her with amazement, knowing that her face *was* familiar, but totally unable to say where he had seen its like before.

"You are puzzled! Think, think, Mr. Holmes!"

Thus cried La Guerita, standing before him, trembling with excitement, dazzling his vision by her flashing eyes, her glowing cheeks. "Think! think! think!" she reiterated, each exclamation tending rather to baffle than accelerate his mind.

He began to imagine that he stood in the presence of a mad woman, and each moment grew more nervous and confused.

"What, does your memory fail you?" cried La Guerita. "Look! this will strengthen it," and with a grasp as strong as iron she caught the arm of the trembling quadroon, and drew her to her side.

"Good God!" ejaculated the planter, springing from his chair, "you are the daughter of Dolores Holmes!"

At his words all her mad excitement died out. She turned from her mother with a gesture of contempt, saying bitterly : "I am the daughter of Dolores Holmes!"

The poor woman burst into tears,

and threw herself at the feet of her pitiless daughter, entreating her to tell her why she had come back to publish her shame.

"I beg of you to say nothing, for a few minutes, at least," said Mr. Holmes, helplessly passing his hand over his brow, like one awakening from a perplexing dream, "I thought you called yourself the widow of Mr. Harry Grey."

She answered him composedly: "I am the widow of the man who was known to you by the name of Harry Grey. I was his proud and happy wife, until a villain stabbed him to the heart by revealing the story of my birth!"

She shrieked out the last words, adding frantically: "How could he live when he knew that his love, his honor had been given into the hands of a base-born slave?"

A deathly pallor overspread her face as she spoke these words. Not knowing what to say or do, Mr. Holmes entreated her to be calm, to seat herself, to cease speaking.

But she heeded not his words, but still standing, with her mother crouching at her feet, she told in disjointed, sometimes almost incoherent, sentences, the story of her woes.

She mentioned no names, yet she made the tale quite plain to the understanding of her hearers; and when it was ended Norton Holmes asked in amazement, as Dolores had done, why she had returned to acknowledge her origin.

Dolores hushed her sobs, and half raised herself to hear the answer.

Leaning across the table and looking the planter steadily in the face, La Guerita said, in low, thrilling tones:

"Norton Holmes, I have come to end my life as it began, to cast from me my false position. I have come to be a slave!"

For some moments Norton Holmes regarded her with a startled gaze, scarcely believing that he heard aright, and totally unable to grasp the full meaning of her words. Not so Dolores. She had instantly comprehended them, and cried:

"Alas, alas! she is mad! she is mad!"

"What was it you said?" he asked at length; "Was it that you had come here to be a slave?"

"Yes, *your* slave!"

"My slave? I have no claim upon you; you were freed years ago by Acton Holmes!"

"I know that you have no claim upon me," she said, "but I am free to give you one. I must—I will return to slavery! Freedom has been my curse! It has made me a desolate widow, without hope in the world or in God!"

"If you return to slavery that will not be changed," began Mr. Holmes, but she interrupted him, crying:

"It will be my atonement!"

"For what?" he demanded, in astonishment.

La Guerita laughed wildly. "For what? He asks me for what! He asks me for what I would render atonement! He asks that of the wife whose husband died for very shame of her."

Mr. Holmes gazed upon her for some moments in sad perplexity, saying at length in a voice of compassion: "Poor lady, poor lady! I pity you!"

"Then you will help me!" she

entreated, clasping her hands passionately together. "You think me mad, but I am not so ; I shall be if you deny my prayer ! I will not live if you send me back to that place where my husband lies buried !"

"You forget that I do not even know where it is," said Mr. Holmes, soothingly, "and indeed I would not send you back if I could. Become my guest ; your friends shall never take you to your home while it is hateful to you."

"No, no, no !" returned La Guerita, "I will never be a guest in any house. Make me your slave, and above all keep the secret I have given you inviolate ; let no one know who I am or whence I came."

"I will not, I will not !" exclaimed Mr. Holmes ; "Good God ! I know not what to do. If I might consult my lawyer."

"Do so," said La Guerita ; "Is he a man of honor, who can keep a a secret ?"

"Yes, indeed ; and in all things Ernest Gordon will advise us well."

Dolores had been listening in silent horror until these words were spoken, then she raised herself and cried entreatingly : "Don't speak to Ernest Gordon ; let it be any one but him !"

Mr. Holmes turned toward her frowningly, with a sharp reproof on his lips, which was, however, checked by a knock at the door.

O mamma !" exclaimed Harold, as it was opened, "Just see what beautiful flowers I've got ! Put a rose in your hair ; there, that pretty white rose."

He stopped suddenly upon seeing the strange gentleman, who indeed arrested his attention by placing his hand beneath the boy's chin, and raising it to meet his careful scrutiny.

"Ah," he muttered, "Acton Holmes can never be forgotten while that child lives."

"Child, what is your name ?"

"Harry Grey," he said, readily, glancing at his mother, as if for approbation for remembering so well the lesson she had given him.

Norton Holmes arose to depart. He was glad that the appearance of the child gave him an excuse for hurrying away ; he wanted to leave the presence of the beautiful young widow that he might ponder her words. He said something of this as he suffered the child to escape.

"You will remember that you are pledged to secrecy, and that your lawyer also must be," said La Guerita. "Send him to me and I will tell you all. Till to-morrow, good-by."

"She bade me farewell with the air of a princess," muttered Norton Holmes, as he descended the stairs. "How can she even dream of becoming a slave ? The idea is preposterous. Ah, I have it ; Dolores was right. The woman is mad !"

He paced the long piazza in a deep study, saying to himself at length, "I'll see the matter through ! I'll send Tom home with an excuse for my absence, and see Gordon this very day."

CHAPTER XIV.

"Think'st thou there are no serpents in the world
But those who glide along the grassy sod,
And sting the luckless foot that presses them ?
There are, who, in the path of social life,
Do bask their spotted skins in fortune's sun,
And sting the soul."
Joanna Baillie.

"ERNEST GORDON, Att'y-at-Law." So read the golden letters of a signboard, that had swung for more than twenty years before a small brick house, in the county-town of M——, in the State of North Carolina. It had attracted but little attention when first placed there by a poor and unknown young man, but in course of time it became the pride of every good citizen, being, indeed, to them the very symbol of wealth and respectability.

Early in his youth, Earnest Gordon had been called a "rising man," and ere his fiftieth year, he had, in the opinion of the people of M——, attained the very acme of human glory.

By a steady application to business, a thorough knowledge of his profession, and, it was said, a strictly honorable application of it, he had made himself master of a large fortune, and raised himself to a high and unmovable position; he held, it was said, the most cherished secrets of scores of families, and, therefore, his private as well as public influence was almost unlimited. Thrice had he represented the people in Congress, and was the acknowledged leader of public opinion in M——.

Lamentable, indeed, would have been considered the ignorance of any person who had ever been in M——, who confessed to not knowing Ernest Gordon, at least by sight, or to any doubt as to the whereabouts of his office. There it was that the sages and wits of M—— most did congregate; there the news of the day was canvassed; there the affairs of nations were discussed and settled.

This office was ever a pleasant place to a certain class in M——. To the idle, the ignorant, the ill-born, it

was unenterable, save on business; while to kindred spirits of its master its doors were ever open, and never so in vain.

The passer-by, early on a sultry afternoon in July, 1859, would have imagined it a club-room, rather than the office of a staid and venerated judge. A knot of gentlemen were gathered upon the shaded porch, sitting or standing in various attitudes, more expressive of ease than grace, and all indicative of southern life. Business hours were over, and the group of lawyers and merchants lazily abandoned themselves to the relaxation called for by the heat of the day.

But Ernest Gordon, ever active, ever vigilant, did not suffer the leisure hours passed in his office to be wholly unproductive. Local news first canvassed and dismissed, political discussions usually followed, and upon this afternoon promised to be of an unusually exciting character.

Ernest Gordon, as was his wont, said little, but listened most attentively to each opinion as it was advanced, smiling thoughtfully that day upon the estimates cast upon the characters of the candidates for the Presidency, and their chances of election.

"Democracy will not have the easy victory that you imagine," he said once; "the Republicans are strong—very strong. I tell you that slavery, the basis of our Southern Democracy, has of late been growing weak before its opponents; you know that—you, who have seen it reel before the puny blows of a novelist, and a mere compiler of statistics—you, who have witnessed the burning of a tissue of lies, called "Uncle Tom's Cabin," and the paltry book of Helper. We all know how the institution reels, when we even fear those frivolous missiles that have been hurled against it."

"They are not worth speaking of," said a pompous-looking gentleman, looking at Mr. Gordon with much surprise; "the deeds of Congress, sir—the works of the nation —those are what we must look to, not the highly-colored pictures of malicious individuals."

Mr. Gordon again smiled in his peculiar manner. "Those highly-colored pictures are what influence most the minds of the people," he said, gravely; "so 'tis in wisdom that we cast them into bonfires; there have been many of late. Yes, sir," he added, earnestly, "these isolated cases of the wrongs of slavery, which have of late years been brought before the public, have done more to make it abhorrent than a hundred years of legislation would have done."

"Ah!"

"Yes; and I tell you further, that were it possible to produce one incontestable case where slavery had been preferred to freedom, not only for its name—for much, indeed, is in a name—but for its strengthening and genial influence upon the mind, it would do more to reinstate slavery in the affections of the people than all the strength of our voices and force of our weapons can ever do."

"Perhaps so," admitted one; "but where can such an example be obtained. Negroes, though, without doubt, happier in slavery than in any other state, have not the strength of mind to acknowledge it. Were my own an exception I would gain you the wished-for example by freeing them all to-morrow; but, faith, I fear they are all such fools the smallest among them would cling to liberty, and I should be a penniless victim of misplaced confidence."

There was a general laugh at these words, in the midst of which Ernest Gordon rose to welcome a newcomer, who seemed well known to all, and whose appearance elicited exclamations of: "How'd you do, Squire? When did you come to town? All well?"

"All well, I thank you," returned the gentleman, as he shook hands with all in succession; "busy discussing politics, I hear. Well, well, I hope all will go right; these are troublous times. Gordon, excuse me, I am only in town for the day— can I have two words alone with you?"

He spoke hurriedly, and seemed under the influence of some great nervous excitement.

"Come into the office," said the lawyer; "I am always ready for business, you know."

He ushered his visitor into an inner room, and closed and locked the door.

"That's right, Gordon, that's right!" said Mr. Holmes; "no one must hear us; for, by Jove, I have a secret for you that will make your ears tingle!"

He spoke excitedly, yet with a certain childish delight almost pitiful to witness in a man—a man, too, of middle age, tall, and muscular in frame, and with a countenance that would have been sickeningly handsome, but for the lines around the mouth, that plainly indicated a vacillating mind.

The subtle lawyer knew his client well. He smiled at the sudden outbreak, and said, quietly : "No one can hear us, Mr. Holmes. Whatever your business is, you can safely intrust it to me, you know that?"

"I do, indeed!" said Mr. Holmes, almost gratefully ; "I shall never forget how well you managed John's affairs, and that sad fellow, Claude's."

"And, of course, he has been getting into trouble again," said the lawyer, impatiently.

"For once you are wrong ; he has been doing nothing of the sort," returned Mr. Holmes, laughing ; "and, in fact, he has nothing to do with the affair I have come to consult you upon. But the most extraordinary thing has happened."

"Pray explain!" exclaimed the lawyer, with more haste than courtesy ; "whom does the matter refer to!"

"Oh, to a dozen people, but mostly to Acton Holmes."

"To Acton Holmes!" exclaimed Gordon, in amazement ; "why, he has been dead six months or more ; his will is proved, and everything seemed correct ; what has turned up now?"

"His daughter!"

"My dear sir, I don't understand you," exclaimed the lawyer, blankly.

"I have actually puzzled a lawyer at last," said Mr. Holmes, laughing ; "why, Gordon, you don't mean to tell me you have been in M—— twenty years and not heard its choicest bit of gossip?"

"That can't well be" he returned, smiling ; "yet for the life of me I cannot tell what you mean. You tell me Acton's daughter is here ; he was never married ; how can I tell what you mean ?"

"I suppose you know Dolores Holmes?" was the reply.

"All the town does that," answered Gordon. "Oh, Oh! I see now," he added, his quick mind seizing upon the clue thrown toward him ; "I remember now—she was Acton's slave some years ago, I believe, and she had two or three children, that went no one knows where, hadn't she?"

"It appears that Acton knew where they were, and one of them has found her way back."

"What, to assert herself Acton's daughter?"

"Not at all! not at all! Good God, Gordon, it is wonderful—it is terrible ; she has come back to own herself Dolores' daughter—to reenter slavery!"

For a moment the lawyer, ordinarily calm under the most exciting circumstances, was overwhelmed with astonishment, then he burst into a laugh of uncontrollable delight. "Come back to slavery!" he almost shouted—"Come back! Here is a triumph for us! She is young! Is she pretty? Has she been supported well! Tell me all—tell me everything. This is a triumph, indeed!"

CHAPTER XV.

NORTON HOLMES looked at the lawyer in amazement. Until the cause of his hilarity was explained, he was inclined to think that he had taken leave of his senses.

"Your mirth is uncalled for," he said at length, "for I have passed my word that no one shall be made acquainted with her history. She, in some way, obliged me to do that."

"Obliged you! obliged you," exclaimed Mr. Gordon incredulously; "Why what sort of a woman is she to be able to do that!"

"You had better go and see her," returned Mr. Holmes, "for I confess myself totally unable to give you a just idea of her."

"I'll go," said the lawyer promptly.

"That would be best," observed Mr. Holmes doubtfully, "if she would consent to receive you."

Mr. Gordon laughed. "Receive me; why certainly she will. Amuse yourself with the papers for a short time, and I will prove it to you."

But nearly two hours elapsed before he re-entered the office.

"You are right," he said, "she is truly an extraordinary woman. I left you without first learning her history, that I might judge her character from hearing it from her own lips."

"And what conclusion have you arrived at?"

"None; positively none. She is a perfect enigma."

"There is no doubt that she is insane."

"Pardon me, I see nothing like insanity about her. We lawyers are in the habit of looking beneath the surface. That woman is either acting a part to obtain some hidden object, or she is blindly following the instinct of her race, who ever shrink from care, and joyfully accept slavery as a means of throwing the responsibilities of life upon another's shoulders."

"And you think that for that reason, Africans are happier in slavery than when free?"

"If in a civilized country, yes. And to prove that, I have long wished for the example which has now presented itself. But unfortunately we can at present make no use of it. Not only our pledge of secresy but the safety of the woman prevents that. If her tale is true, the slightest publicity would call her friends to her rescue."

"Which would certainly be the best thing that could happen," said Mr. Holmes. "I am sure I don't want her."

"Why she will be invaluable to you," exclaimed Mr. Gordon. Where will you find such a governess for your children. Ah, how happy should I be had she chosen me for her master."

"Adela would never consent to it," muttered Mr. Holmes.

The lawyer frowned. Miss Adela Holmes was one of the few ladies for whom he entertained any feeling but those of courteous indifference. But from her childhood she had been antagonistic to him. He admired her character, but could not sympathize with it, and silently determined that in that one case, at least, his will should triumph over hers.

"Let us put this business aside," said the lawyer suavely, "until after we have dined. I have no doubt but that your objections to La Guerita DeCuba's proposition will vanish when you consider it in all its points."

They left the office, and walked slowly down the shaded street.

"I utterly refuse to look at the matter in a political light," said Mr. Holmes. "I shall try to do what is best for the widow, and I am sure, if Adela were consulted, she would set us just right."

"Oh, without doubt," assented the lawyer, closing his lips determinedly, as he added in thought: "But she shall never have a chance to thwart me in this matter. Before this time to-morrow, that mad woman shall be a slave."

The lawyer's task was a difficult one, but he carried it forward without flinching. By the arts of persuasion he knew so well how to employ, he succeeded in a few hours, not only in satisfying Mr. Holmes that his duty lay in the enslavement of La Guerita DeCuba, but also in silencing the almost frantic mother, who, with prayers and tears, entreated him to save her child from the bonds she craved.

The next day all clients were denied admittance to Ernest Gordon. He devoted himself to Mr. Holmes, retaining him by his side while he examined various documents, and prepared others, going with him in the morning to visit La Guerita, who only begged that there might be no delay in the necessary formalities.

The lawyer courteously agreed to her demand for haste. Early in the afternoon a paper was ready for her signature, in which she voluntarily resigned her freedom, and chose Norton Holmes as her future master.

Mr. Gordon read it slowly and carefully, pausing at times to explain any doubtful passage. La Guerita listened with rapt attention.

"You have heard the terms of that document," said the lawyer, "are you ready to accede to them?"

"Quite ready," she answered firmly. "I have Mr. Holmes' verbal promise never to sell me, or part me from my child. That is all I require. I am ready to sign away my freedom."

"You will then deliver to me, as Mr. Holmes' attorney, your papers of emancipation."

"Certainly; they are in the hands of Dolores Holmes."

Mr. Gordon turned toward the quadroon: "You hear what your daughter says; give me the paper, Dolores."

"Never," she exclaimed, clasping her hands on her bosom. "She is mad, I tell you! She shall not sacrifice herself; she is mad!"

"I am not mad," said La Guerita in a voice of thrilling earnestness. "If you have a God, pray him to make me so, or else give me peace yourself. Let me make my atonement—I command you not to thwart me. Give me the paper."

Dolores drew the folded paper from her bosom, and started forward, as the lawyer took it from her hand and glanced over its contents.

"Now you may sign," he said.

Dolores covered her face and groaned, and Norton Holmes laid his hand upon the arm of La Guerita, saying loudly and in a voice of entreaty: "Consider the matter; consider it I beg. Do you know what that bond will make you?"

"I know what my freedom has made me," she cried. "It has made me a blight and a curse! It has made me a murderess! Stand back and let me sign!"

Mr. Gordon threw open the door, and the landlord and his brother entered. "These will be your witnesses," he said, placing the paper before her.

She seized the pen eagerly, and without a pause, in large, firm characters, signed the fatal deed. It was then signed by the witnesses, who, unconscious of the nature of the document, bowed, and withdrew.

Those who remained, expected to see La Guerita DeCuba swoon, or burst into tears after her desperate deed was done, but she sat down quietly taking her child upon her knees, and whispering softly over him that the anguish was passed, the atonement was begun.

They left her alone. Dolores rushed forth to her cabin to weep and pray, while Norton Holmes, feeling half guilty, as one who had blindly consented to the death of the innocent, walked slowly down the street, arm in arm with the triumphant lawyer, who, rubbing his hands delightedly together, exclaimed : "The best day's work I ever did in my life. Look back at your slave, Mr. Holmes, she is looking at her master from the window."

"Good God, it is dreadful," sighed the planter, "and what will Adela say ?"

The lawyer smiled, and glanced triumphantly back at the window where La Guerita still quietly sat. Oh, how madly she would have started from her repose had she known that the moment she signed the fatal bond, her brother Fabean stood at the door of Enola, and asked for his lost sister.

CHAPTER XVI.

" The past is spent and done with, and the future is uncertain."
Antoninus.

IT was arranged by Mr. Gordon, on the following day, that La Guerita should quietly leave the hotel, and, in order to baffle the curious, that she should take tickets for one of the southern towns, but leave the cars at R——, a station seven miles east of Holmsford. There Mr. Holmes, who had returned to his home, was to meet her, and conduct her to his estate.

She left the hotel without again seeing her mother ; she wished to forget all the past, and unconsciously shrank from the pain of meeting one who had been so intimately connected with it, for she could not yet forgive her, or palliate her sin.

Harold was delighted beyond measure to leave the rooms in which he had been almost constantly confined, and as they passed rapidly through the country, monotonous though it was, he found a thousand objects to arouse his wonder and delight. They were uncared for and unnoticed by his mother, who sat beside him unconscious of the wondering and admiring glances cast upon her, or of aught that was passing. It seemed to her a very long time before they reached the station at R——. They entered it at last, very slowly, and she regarded it with idle curiosity, dreaming not how valuable her scrutiny would one day prove.

She exchanged her seat in the cars for one in the carriage, in which Mr. Holmes had come to meet her, but felt not the slightest agitation or curiosity concerning the people she would shortly meet. During the long drive Mr. Holmes vainly endeavored to draw her into conversation, but he soon perceived that her thoughts were far away. She seemed, indeed, lost to the present, until Mr. Holmes, who had been talking with Harold, said :

"Look out of the window, Harry, and across the field, you will see a large white house ; that is Holmsford, where you are going to live."

Then La Guerita suddenly aroused herself. At first she saw nothing more than a large white house, half hidden by tall trees, and a long row of negro cabins, which, with numerous out-houses, almost formed the appearance of a small village. Upon approaching nearer, La Guerita perceived that the principal building was erected, after the fashion of many Southern houses, in two parts, which were connected and surrounded by piazzas, which were at that season festooned with flowering vines. Indeed, the house formed the center of a mass of shrubbery, that extended for some acres. The month of roses had passed, yet thousands were blooming still in the gardens of Holmsford, enchanting the eye and filling the air with fragrance.

"Adela has a passion for roses," remarked Mr. Holmes, as he assisted La Guerita from the carriage, and ushered her through the garden to a side door of the house, "and some taste, you will perceive, for other flowers as well."

That was readily apparent, if she had anything to do with the arrangement of the garden. Great was the variety of plants—nearly every species of native flowers and many exotics—all placed with such delicate regard to form and color that each attracted its due share of notice without in the least detracting from the claims of others. Before they reached the door by which she was to enter the house, La Guerita for an instant lost the remembrance of the Past in admiration of the beauty before her.

She did not notice the wondering eyes that from the kitchen and cabins watched her appearance, and, indeed, thought of nothing but the unexpected beauty of Holmsford, until Mr. Holmes, after leading her across a wide hall, opened a door and ushered her into a room, by the appearance of which La Guerita supposed herself to be in the common sitting-room of the house.

A young lady was standing near the window, so engrossed in thought that she did not notice their entrance until Mr. Holmes exclaimed : "Why, Adela, are you dreaming?"

In the moment's interval that preceded his words, La Guerita had marked the outline of a tall, graceful figure, arrayed in a softly flowing material of a delicate lavender color. She started as the name of Adela was pronounced, remembering that she had heard her likened to Claude Leveredge.

"You came in very softly, papa," she said, in a musical voice, "or I was lost in reverie ; I did not hear you."

Then for a moment there was silence, while the young lady looked at La Guerita with some slight surprise upon her countenance. Never in her life had La Guerita DeCuba found her expectations so much at fault; she had fancied Miss Holmes dark and stern; she was, on the contrary, remarkably fair, and wore a a gentle though firm expression rarely seen upon a woman's face. One would have imagined her naturally free from hauteur, but capable of readily assuming it. La Guerita was no ready translator of expressions, but she instantly detected one of latent hostility upon the face of Miss Holmes, and doubted not that she would, sooner or later, feel its effects. A slight frown contracted the forehead of the young lady, and arched the eyebrows, which were remarkable for their beauty, and the contrast of their dark-brown hue with the golden hair, which waved slightly back from the temples, and was coiled in a large knot at the back of her well-formed head.

The frown darkened on her delicate face, and her full red lips curled slightly, as Mr. Holmes said:

"This, Adela, is the—the person I was speaking to you about. Rita —I think we decided you should be called that?—this is my daughter, Miss Adela Holmes, whom I am sure you will find an indulgent mistress."

La Guerita started as the last words were pronounced, but looking in the calm, pale face before her, which was at that moment so strikingly expressive of a passionate and commanding nature, she felt that she was, indeed, in the presence of one who would rule as her mistress, not only in name, but in reality.

"She is younger than you led me to suppose," said Miss Holmes, turning to her father, "and scarcely looks as if she would be a fit teacher for Minna."

La Guerita was stung with a deep sense of inferiority by having her merits thus canvassed in her presence, much in the same way that one might argue the qualities of a bird or dog. Her cheeks burned and her head swam dizzily, and she felt at once the shame of her new position.

At that moment Miss Holmes caught sight of Harold, who had almost hidden himself under his mother's flowing mantle. She caught him eagerly by the arm, drawing him to her, as she exclaimed:

"Oh, the beautiful, beautiful child! O papa, how could she be so heartless—so wicked?"

"I am neither heartless nor wicked!" exclaimed La Guerita, clasping the child to her bosom as he fled to her, alarmed at Miss Holmes' impetuous manner; "I am kind; I am gentle; I am merciful; I have saved him from all the woes that I have known; his life will never be embittered as mine has been."

As she stood erect, yet trembling with excitement, her eyes flashing and her cheeks aflame, holding her child to her bosom with one strong arm, while the other was raised, expressive at once of love and defiance, Adela gazed upon her in unfeigned admiration, scarcely free from alarm, while Norton Holmes once more said within his mind: "She is mad!"

"I should advise you not to excite yourself," said Miss Holmes, after a moment's silence, in a tone of great sarcasm, which seemed to imply that she deemed the whole an excellent piece of acting.

"Where is your mother?" asked Mr. Holmes.

"In her room, papa, breaking her heart because Minna came home from the swamp an hour ago with a torn apron and wet feet."

Mr. Holmes smiled.

"Indeed, papa, mamma did not appear to consider the matter at all amusing; and I do hope this person will be able to keep the children in some sort of order; they are really enough to vex a saint."

"St. Adela!" returned Mr. Holmes, laughing, when the door opened and an elderly lady, followed by a little girl of seven, entered the room.

"Oh, dear Norton, I am so glad you have come!" languidly exclaimed the lady; "I have had *such* a fright this afternoon. Minnie came home from the swamp, where a thousand snakes *might* have bitten her, you know, with a torn apron, and *such* tears, *such* slits, *such* rents, as if she had climbed *every* tree in the place. and, O dear, with *such* wet feet! she *might* have caught her *death* of cold!"

"But I have n't though!" said the child, pertly, adding as her father caressed her: "Mamma said to-day that I should bring her gray hairs with sorrow to the grave. Now, I should like to know how I am to do that when every hair on her head is as yellow as Adela's?"

"Hush! hush!" said Mr. Holmes, warningly, and turning to his wife: "See, Myra, I have brought you a governess for the children; this is Rita—"

"And I am *very* glad she has come," said Mrs. Holmes, languidly, while Minna rushed from the room to convey the doleful tidings to her brothers. "Yes, I am *very* glad she has come," she repeated, deliberately surveying her new servant: "I *do* hope you *are* as accomplished as your master believes you. You know, Norton, these octoroons are often pretty, but seldom very sensible. Don't you think there is a queer look about this one's eyes? Can you play the piano, Rita?"

La Guerita was bewildered by her strange position; she had never for a moment imagined what her position or treatment as a slave would be; she seemed suddenly bereft of her identity; she was an automaton—a machine.

"She seems *very* stupid," commented Mrs. Holmes; "take her into the parlor, Adela, and let us hear what she can do."

Miss Holmes led the way across the hall into a large and handsomely furnished apartment. The sight of the piano aroused La Guerita's almost dormant faculties. She approached it eagerly, and seating herself, poured all the wild anguish of her soul into a voluntary of such exquisite pathos, that each note was the expression of some thought of love, or grief, or madness.

Adela stood entranced. Mrs. Holmes cried: "Divine! Where *did* you learn to play like that?"

"It was n't an hour ago that I shut and locked that piano," ejaculated a shrill female voice; "not one hour ago, and I thought I had the key safe in my pocket."

All started at these words, and La Guerita, with a deep sigh, awoke from the trance into which the melody had thrown her, and in which she had fancied herself in the parlor of Enola, with Harold bending over her.

11

She turned quickly as the shrill voice fell upon her ear, and, to her surprise, beheld an old lady standing in the door-way. She was at least seventy years old, and was arrayed in a short white gown, with a multiplicity of round capes, of all colors and all sizes. These, from the roundness of her shoulders and an habitual stoop, gave her the appearance of a hunchback, which was increased by the strange, vixenish expression of her wrinkled face, around which the deep borders of two caps vibrated tremblingly when she moved or spoke.

All this La Guerita noticed while the old lady's attention was fixed on Adela, who said, very quietly:

"I have a key of my own, aunt."

"Yes, that is always the way," she returned vehemently; "It's no use for me to try to save anything in this house. Everything here is going to *rack* and ruin. Dilsey has just broke another plate. Who's that?"

"A new girl papa has just bought," replied Miss Holmes.

"A new girl pa has just bought," ejaculated the old lady, looking La Guerita keenly in the face, flushing to the borders of her cap and throwing up her hands.

"What's the matter, aunt?" cried Minna, who had re-entered the room; "do you think that she is too pretty to teach us?"

"There's nothing the matter," she answered shortly, "and it don't make any difference what I think; but I know there's a nail sticking up in that carpet; it caught my gown and pulled me back. But that's the way with everything in this house; we should all die in the poor-house if

there was one in the county. Peggy's baby's got the measles; that'll die next, I suppose!"

They all laughed as she left the room, Miss Holmes saying: "Indeed, papa, the child is merely suffering from the heat; I saw it an hour ago. Aunt Matilda is always imagining something dreadful."

"Hush! here she is again," said Mr. Holmes, warningly, as a scuffle was heard in the hall, followed by a prolonged howl, and the words:

"Let me go! O Miss 'Tildy, just let ago my ear. Oh, Oh, Miss 'Tildy! O, Lud!"

"I'm just agoing to take you right in to your master," was the reply; "a pretty thing, I reckon, for you to be a sweepin' the yard with the new broom already."

Mr. Holmes stepped to the door and released the young culprit, a bright-looking negro boy, who, grimacing fearfully in an attempt to awaken his master's pity, protested his innocence.

"Well, Sam, what have you been doing now?" asked Mr. Holmes.

"I ha'nt been doin' nothin'," whimpered the boy.

"That's what he's always doing," snapped Miss Matilda.

"I mean, Mass'r, I warn't adoin' nothin' wrong; I was just a sweepin' the steps of old Aunt Libby's cabin with a new broom what Miss Addie gub me to do it wid."

"Why, Adela," exclaimed Mr. Holmes, turning to his daughter, "is it possible that you are going to put any one in that miserable place? Why there is not a hand on the plantation that will pass it after dark."

"It is the only vacant cabin, and Rita must occupy it," she replied, adding, as an expression of annoyance passed over her father's face : "Mamma was quite horrified at the idea of a servant occupying the governess' room ; were you not, mamma ? "

"Indeed, *yes*, my love," responded that lady, with some degree of animation ; "I couldn't endure the thought of it."

"A servant sleeps in your own room," said Mr. Holmes, angrily, and in Adela's, too, I believe."

"No, not in Adela's," returned Mrs. Holmes ; "Adela says she can't help feeling herself watched when one is in the room. Such nonsense! I am sure I couldn't do without one. Suppose I should need more covering or a drink in the night, or should be taken sick, you know. But that is a very different thing to having a servant in a distant part of the house, where she could be of no use to any one. I should never close my eyes in sleep, Norton, if I knew Rita was so close to me. Those octoroons are dangerous, you know. It was only *last* week that one attempted to poison a whole family in Lexington."

Mr. Holmes paced the room excitedly, biting his finger nails and glancing at La Guerita, who, with Harold upon her knee, was a silent listener to the conversation.

"I suppose you must do as you please, Adela," he said at length ; but I hope you have had the cabin made comfortable."

"Quite so, papa, and, if you please, I will take Rita there ; she looks tired."

"I hope she is not delicate," said Mrs. Holmes, querulously ; "Miss Fitzgerald was delicate, you *know*,

and the children *could* not be in school *half* of the time. It is *such* a relief to me to think that this governess can't leave us at a moment's notice. What a world of anxiety I should have been saved if you could have bought her before, though she does seem stupid—lost, in fact. Was *that* the reason your mistress sold you ? "

Before La Guerita could answer this perplexing question, Miss Holmes arose, and leaving the room, motioned to her to follow. She did so, passing Mrs. Holmes with a graceful inclination of the head, causing that lady to wonder "what would come next," and to prophesy that the world would soon come to an end.

Miss Matilda was standing on the piazza apostrophizing the wind for conveying the rose-leaves to that particular spot. She looked up as La Guerita passed her, and said sententiously : "Chickens come home to roost."

"And curses," thought La Guerita bitterly, knowing well that the keen-witted old lady had seen through the flimsy disguise which Norton Holmes had thrown over her identity, and with many conflicting emotions, she followed Miss Holmes across a lawn which lay at the back of the house, past a row of negro cabins from which she was watched by scores of eager eyes, until they stood before a hut somewhat detached from the others, but in no way differing in appearance. It was painted white, with green doors, with a blind of the same hue at the only window. A small garden surrounded it, which was then filled with weeds and the yellow stalks of last year's cabbages—the solitary remains of by-gone culture.

Miss Holmes took a bunch of keys from a small basket which she carried in her hand, and after trying several in the rusty lock—turned the key, and led the way into the cabin.

"I hope you like your future home," she remarked sarcastically, and with a mocking light in her eyes, as La Guerita looked around the single apartment. "There is a very good bed in the corner—we always allow our servants two pairs of blankets in the winter. Aunt Libby made that coverlet herself, and slept under it for twenty years, so I am sure it must be comfortable. That's a very good table in the corner though a little ricketty ; there are two chairs, and if you want another you can have it, and also a piece of rag carpet to patch that hole with. I shall expect to see it done to-morrow. You are looking at the chimney ; it does'nt smoke at all, and you see there are a good lot of cooking utensils in the hearth."

La Guerita knew why Adela Holmes had been likened to her cousin Claude as she listened to this cutting irony, but it did not anger her, she was too weary to become excited, and she answered patiently : "It is all good enough, Miss Holmes."

"'Taint half good enough !" ejaculated Minna, who at that instant appeared at the door, accompanied by her twin brothers, who were five years her seniors. 'Taint half so good, Miss Rita, as Celia has ; she's got white curtains to the window, has'nt she Alf. ? Ain't the new teacher pretty ?"

"She is that," acceded her brother warmly, "but she ain't Miss Rita—she ain't white you know."

"And I ain't going to mind her a bit," said his brother, "I ain't going to learn lessons for her."

"If you don't, I'll break every bone in your body," said Alf. threateningly, "I like her a heap better than I did Miss Fitzgerald already."

La Guerita thanked her champion with an eloquent glance of gratitude, and Alfred walked triumphantly away, followed by Rufus and Minna.

When they were again alone, Miss Holmes turned to La Guerita, saying sternly : "Do you realize the position in which you have placed yourself ? Do you realize what you are ?"

"I am a slave," she answered bitterly, stung with the shame that had haunted her since her entrance into Holmsford.

"Yes, *a slave*," repeated Miss Holmes with emphasis ; "a slave not only in *name* but in *reality*."

"I came here to be a slave in reality," she returned ; "I came here to forget that I ever was free."

"My father has told me your tale," said Miss Holmes scornfully, "a tale in which you would mention no names. I place as much faith in it as I would in an anonymous letter. I know not what your object was in coming here, but I believe it was to escape the consequences of some evil deed, or to perform one. But I warn you that Adela Holmes is not blind."

She opened the door and passed out, leaving La Guerita and her child alone in the little cabin which was thenceforth to be their home.

"Have I done so strange a thing," mused La Guerita, "in seeking to make reparation to another, and to find peace. for my own soul, that even the wisest deem me mad, or hopelessly depraved? O Harold, Harold, my dead love, you at least know my motives! O Harold, Harold!"

She sank upon a chair clasping her brow with her open hand, and crying aloud that she was "wretched, wretched, still!"

"I am very hungry, mamma," said Harold at length; "Why did they put us into this little dark house. It isn't pretty at all."

"But still we are to live here, Harry," said his mother calmly, "and you will learn to be very happy here. Are you very hungry, darling? Here is a biscuit I put in my pocket for you to-day."

He took it gladly, but before it was half eaten a young mulatto girl came to the door, and looking in, said: "Here is some supper Miss Addie sent you for Harry, and you'se to put him to bed just as soon as he's eat it, for Miss Addie says else he'll be tuckered clean out with a travelin so far, and Miss Addie she can't abide a sick nigger."

La Guerita felt stunned; she looked on helplessly as the girl placed the tray on the table and then sat down, familiarly continuing: "How awful white you is! Nigh as white's Miss Addie herself. Was your missus jealous o' yo, or what did she sell you for."

"I don't know," answered La Guerita, feeling the necessity of saying something to her *fellow-servant*, remembering with a sharp sting of wounded pride, that her caste was the same as that of the untutored girl.

"And after she had been and had you eddicated so; she must a been jealous," concluded the girl. "Well, I can't stop here a chattin', though I'd like to·mighty. There's Miss Tildy a screamin' to me to take the parrot in doors. I should'nt a bit wonder if he's a bit her finger agin. O, heddy, how riled she would be!"

And she left the cabin hastily, happy in the scene her imagination had conjured.

La Guerita was weary—very weary—and was glad to partake of a part of the supper which Miss Holmes had sent. She laid aside her bonnet and cloak, and unpinned the heavy braids of hair, that lay like leaden weights upon her burning head.

"How queer you look, mamma," laughed Harold; "just like that picture we had at home; don't you know: a mer—mer—what is it?—coming out of the sea; her hair was just as long and wavy as yours. I say, ain't this nice jelly? I like that lady—Miss Adela—ever so much, mamma, though she frightened me when she caught hold of me so tight. I thought that black man had come again to carry me away. But now I like her ever so much; but wasn't that other a funny old woman?" and he pulled his hair over his brow and shook his head, in grotesque imitation of Miss Matilda and her quivering laces.

So he prattled on, until his mother undressed him and laid him on the bed, standing by him until he had fallen asleep and the dusk of evening gathered around her.

It was insufferably warm, although

the window was open, and La Guerita threw open the back door, that
the night breeze might enter her little
dwelling. She sat upon the step—a
decaying log—and gazed upon the
scene that lay before her. Near at
hand was a field of cotton, but sparse-
ly grown, and beyond it a forest of
dark pines, that swayed solemnly in
the evening wind, filling the air with
a low, rushing sound as of running
waters. It soothed the excited mind
of the listener as no other music
could have done, seeming to whisper of wildernesses of shade and silence—boundless, fathomless—where
the echoes of the busy world could
never enter.

Two negroes slowly crossed the
cotton field, carrying their tools upon
their shoulders, and cheerily singing
a camp-meeting hymn, to a weird,
monotonous tune.

As she listened the rhythm of the
song seemed to harmonize with the
wild imaginings of her brain, and to
calm them. Of thoughts—thoughts
that resolved themselves into definite
forms—she had none, and the past
and present became a void to her; her
mind lost its weight of agony, and
for hours after the hymn had ceased,
and when the belt of pines were but
as the farthest ether, she sat there,
like one entranced. At last she was
aroused—but only to bodily pain—by
a sensation of cold, which pervaded
her entire frame. She went into the
cabin then, and without closing the
door, or even remarking that it was
open, threw herself upon the bed beside her child, and fell into a deep,
untroubled sleep.

" O heart, sore tried, thou hadst the best
  That Heaven itself could give thee—rest—
  Rest from all bitter thoughts and things!"

CHAPTER XVII.

" Undue suspicion is more abject baseness
  Even than the guilt suspected."
                          Aaron Hill.

MISS HOLMES makes a discovery.
The partial stupor that fell upon the
mind of La Guerita DeCuba upon
that calm summer night happily did
not pass with the stupor it induced;
she awoke on the following morning
with a passive brain and a deadened
memory. The remembrance of the
past was with her still, but its terrible
anguish was gone, and in its stead
remained a dull, subtle pain—a
wound so deep and tender that a
word or look would often cause the
most exquisite torture—torture that
would blind and stifle, but never
rouse her.

The young mulatto girl, who had
brought the supper on the previous
evening, appeared at about eight
in the morning, with a well-filled
tray, which she placed on the rickety
table.

"Miss Addie wanted to send your
breakfast an hour ago," she said,
"fur eberybody gets breakfus' mighty early heah, but Mass Norton he
jiss would n't let her do it. Fust ob
all, she said you could cook your
own victuals, like de res' of de nig-
gas, and I neber see Mass Norton
look so mad in my bressed days,
and he jess spoke right up, and ses
he: 'You will send her from dis
table de bes' of ebery ting ebery day,
Adela.' Well, Miss Addie neber
said a word more, but, Lor', she did
look blacker nor ole Aunt Fanny
does dis bressed minit."

"What is your name?" asked La
Guerita.

"Roxanna Deliny; they call me Roxy, for short. I tends upon Miss 'Tildy, and does all kind o' odd chores. I'se to bring you your meals ebery day; but, Lor', I don't mind if you is n't white. De rest of 'em don't like you, though."

"Why not?" said La Guerita, indifferently.

"'Cos Massa Norton's been an' sot you up 'bove the res', jes' 'cos you's white, and the real blackies can't abide de white ones no way; and now dey tinks dat Massa's jiss brought you here to sit and watch 'em."

La Guerita smiled faintly. "They need not fear that," she said; "I am one of them; I am in bonds as well as they."

Roxy looked as if she scarcely knew what was meant, and discreetly changed the subject by saying: "Miss Addie told me I was to take you ober to de school-house soon as you'd finished breakfus' and wus fixed up. How quar you've made dat bed; looks like you'd neber teched one afore. Miss 'Tildy she goes inter de cabins ebery day, to see ef dey's fixed up; she'd be arter you ef she seed dat lookin' heap."

Roxy re-arranged the bed to her satisfaction, and then conducted La Guerita to a small building that stood about a hundred yards back of the principal dwelling.

"Dis is de school-house," she said, and left La Guerita standing upon the low, broad step, looking listlessly at the white walls and the long windows, with their bright-green shutters. For a moment she forgot where she was and what was expected of her; then Harold pulled her dress, and whispered: "Look, mamma, look, there's the pretty lady."

She entered the school-house then, and bent her head meekly to Miss Holmes, who was speaking to the children. She stopped when she saw La Guerita, but Alfred said, quickly: "You need n't tell me how to behave myself, Addie; I like her first-rate."

"Besides," said Rufus, proudly, "Cousin Claude said, when he was here, that if I wished to be a gentleman like him, I must begin by treating my inferiors well."

His sister's lips curled slightly, but she answered: "That is an excellent precept; I hope you will remember it;" then turning to La Guerita, added: "You are late this morning. I shall expect you always to begin school at eight o'clock, and continue until three. You may give a few minutes' recess at ten, and an hour's at twelve. From four until five you will give Minna a music lesson, or hear her practice."

"I'm not going to stay in school from eight 'till three," exclaimed Rufus.

"Yes you will!" cried Alfred; "you used to do it when Miss Fitzgerald was here. It's an awful long time, but we did it easy enough after she made us a few times."

At that moment Mr. Holmes appeared. "I am glad to see you here, Rita," he said, kindly. "How do you like the school-room? Pleasant, is it not? Now, I am ready to see you begin school; you'll read a chapter in the Bible first, eh?"

La Guerita mechanically turned to the bible that lay upon her desk, and opened it at the thirty-fifth Psalm, be-

ginning : "Plead my cause, O Lord,
with them that strive with me ; fight
against them that fight against me.
Take hold of shield and buckler,
and stand up for mine help."

Miss Holmes looked upon her
steadily as she read this Psalm from
beginning to end. Even the children
listened with delight to the calm, so-
norous tones. La Guerita alone remained unaffected by that solemn
prayer, which eloquently appeared to
plead for her from the depths into
which she had fallen. She was unconscious of their significance ; but
not so at least two of her hearers, for
as she closed the book and looked to
Mr. Holmes for further orders, he
merely said : "Read from the New
Testament in future," and followed
his daughter from the house, turning
at the door to say : "Remember,
Rita, you are mistress here. Boys—
Minna, let me hear of no miscon-
duct."

The children looked at each other
and then at La Guerita, who, with
Harold at her side, stood calmly before them.

"Alfred," she said at last, "bring
me your books and let me see how
far you are advanced."

He obeyed, treating her respectfully, and listening intently to all she
said, thereby making it easier to
force words from her unwilling lips.
Rufus, in his turn, went to her desk
frowning malevolently, and muttering, as he returned to his seat : "I
shan't mind *her ;* I'll just do as I
please, for all that I care for her."

La Guerita's eyes flashed, but she
said nothing, choosing to bide the
time when she might effectually
prove her authority.

Oh, how drearily that long, long
day passed by. Harold ran out to
play in the shade, while she, who had
never known toil before, learned, in
part, what slavery meant, as she listened to Minna's monotonous tones,
as she read her dog's-eared primer,
or enduring patiently Alfred's stupid-
ity, or Rufus' outbursts of sullen
temper.

It was very warm. La Guerita
felt faint and weary, and would gladly have dismissed the children to
their play, but she remembered that
she was a slave ; and when at last
the weary toil was over, and the children had burst with wild shouts from
the room, she sank down in the apa-
thetic way that now seemed almost
natural to her, and vaguely wondered
what next would come for her to do.

The school-room was littered with
books and papers, but it did not occur to her to make it tidy. No
thought entered her mind without
some prompting from another ; and
so she sat, only conscious of extreme
bodily weakness, gazing dreamily
upon the scene without until Roxy
entered uttering an exclamation of
surprise at seeing her sitting idle
with the litter around her, and then
energetically placing the scattered
articles in their places as she said :

"Law sus, Rita, this'll never do ;
'spose Miss 'Tildy should come in ;
she'll be awful mad ef you don't clar
up sooner den this every arternoon ;
and Miss Addie, she'll soon tell you
that yer can't fold yer hands in dis
cabin ; she sent me to tell ye to go
inter the house, Miss Myra wants
you."

La Guerita arose and slowly crossed the grass-plot that lay between the

school-room and the back porch of the house. As she passed the parlor windows she heard a strange voice, saying :

"I am quite anxious to behold this prodigy of yours, Mrs. Holmes."

La Guerita shrank back, with a momentary impulse to retreat. "No, this is a part of my sacrifice," she muttered, "and must be performed," and approaching the parlor door, knocked resolutely.

"Come in !" said a voice; and obeying the summons, La Guerita found herself in the presence of Mrs. and Miss Holmes, and a strange gentleman.

He looked at her curiously as she entered, and bowed, coloring thereafter as if he had been surprised into the condescension. La Guerita stood in the door-way, with eyes bent down, painfully conscious that the eyes of the stranger never left her.

Suddenly he muttered an excuse and left the room. Mrs. Holmes laughed, while Adela looked surprised, and not the less so when, entering the room as suddenly as he had left it, Mr. Russell declared he had been unable to withstand the temptation to rush into the garden and pluck a magnificent moss-rose, which he offered her, with a gay excuse for his impetuosity.

Miss Holmes took it and placed it in a vase on the table, and which she directed La Guerita to fill with water.

She obeyed, glad to escape the searching eyes of the stranger, but, although she did not look at him, she knew he was still regarding her when she returned with the flowers, and as a chance for evading his scrutiny turned to the piano, as Mrs.

Holmes said : "Mr. Russell wishes to hear you play, Rita. Play the piece we all admired so much yesterday."

That was impossible, but the nocturne she selected was equally beautiful.

At the conclusion, Mrs. Holmes looked at Mr. Russell triumphantly.

"She does, indeed, play very finely," he said ; "her mistress must have spent a small fortune upon that one accomplishment. Has Mr. Holmes found a gold mine, or obtained the freedom of a mint lately?"

Mrs. Holmes laughed. "Neither the one nor the other, I can assure you," she returned. "I asked Norton something of the sort yesterday when Rita came, but he said she cost a mere nothing. Play something else, Rita."

She turned to the instrument most sorely puzzled. Where had she seen this Mr. Russell before? Was it fancy, or was there really something familiar in his voice and appearance? He was tall, fair, decidedly good-looking, but with a good-natured and in no way remarkable countenance ; yet it haunted her, leading her back step by step over her life, yet taking no fixed place in it, seeming rather as a shadow than a reality. She was aroused by an exclamation from Mrs. Holmes.

" Play something less monotonous," she cried. "How dreadfully stupid that is ; one might imagine Minna was playing. You don't mean to tell me you can only play one or two pieces well ? "

Mr. Russell arose and walked carelessly to the end of the piano, looking at her curiously as he said :

"Give us something lighter—a polka, for instance; I remember there was a very pretty one called 'La Guerita,' that they used to play when I was at school at Fairview."

She turned deadly pale at the sound of the well-loved name, struck to the heart more by that simple word than the knowledge that she was recognized.

She remembered him well then. Years ago he had been at Fairview for a term—for only a single term; yet, after all the changes that had passed over both, he had known her at a glance.

Obeying the impulse of flight, she arose and hurried from the room, casting behind a frightened look, like that of a hunted fawn. Mrs. Holmes in vain called her back, and then followed her, in high displeasure, which, fortunately for La Guerita, was changed to loud lamentations as she beheld Alfred entering the house, holding in one hand a nest of young mockingbirds, while he wiped upon the bosom of his shirt the blood that was freely trickling from the other.

"Oh, my dear, dear child," cried his mother, "what *have* you been doing? *Are* you killed? You are scratches *all* over!"

"I can get lots more near the same place that I got these!" he cried, gleefully, referring to the birds, not the scratches. "I am going to take these to Miss Rita and get her to raise them for me; you know Dilsey let all those die that I got last spring."

"*Miss* Rita!" echoed Mr. Russell, in a tone of amusement and slight disdain, and then he rose to say farewell.

"Will you not wait until my mother comes in?" said Miss Holmes, hesitatingly, for it was an unusual thing for her to urge Mr. William Russell to remain at Holmsford on any pretext, and she colored to see that he availed himself of her invitation, as if it were an inestimable boon; and scorning to engage in even the most harmless deception, she quickly added: "You have seen our new servant before?"

The young man sighed, but answered courteously: "I have, indeed, Miss Adela."

"And under far different circumstances, I presume," she continued, cautiously.

Mr. Russell placed himself on his guard, and scarcely knowing what to say, muttered: "Certainly; but, doubtless, you know all the past history of—of—"

Miss Holmes waited anxiously for the name, but Mr. Russell bit his lips and remained silent.

"I will buy his speech," thought Miss Holmes, the color rushing over her face as she said: "At least, if you will tell me nothing, you will let me know whether the tale I have already heard is true? Of course, my father did not attempt to deceive me with the tale that has satisfied my mother. He repeated to me the tale he heard from her lips. She was born a slave —I know not where or who was her master—she was given her freedom, and sent North, and there educated; after deceiving one lover she married a second, and a few months ago the husband learned through the rejected lover the secret of his wife's birth, and went mad over it, I believe, and died. After all this trouble she became disgusted with her freedom, and, in order, she says, to make atonement for the sorrow she has wrought, has returned to her original state of slavery, choosing, for some unexplained cause, my father as her master."

"Poor soul!" said Mr. Russell, thoughtfully.

"Well, what do you think of her conduct?" asked Miss Holmes, triumphantly.

"I think it worthy of a mad woman!"

Miss Holmes shrugged her shoulders. "And what of her story—is any of it true?"

"Yes, yes—in part, at least; I know it to be true in part, for I was acquainted with her before she married."

"At what place?"

I cannot tell you without her permission, Miss Adela. Whatever may be her motive for coming here, I, as a gentleman, must respect her secret."

Miss Holmes colored at the implied reproof, but said, with a smile: "I have given you my confidence, Mr. Russell"—adding, in an aggrieved tone—"after that, I think it but just you should honor me with yours."

The young man colored with pleasure, and a multitude of thoughts—some of them not of the purest—flashed through his mind; but he said, quietly:

"I tell you, Miss Adela, her tale is true; though I scarcely think she has betrayed her true motives for coming here; unless, indeed, she is mad."

"She is not mad," returned Miss Holmes, impatiently; "but, Mr. Russell, did you know anything of her first lover?"

"Yes," he returned, hastily, as if he could not allow himself time for after thought; "perhaps you will be able to judge more correctly of her motives for coming here when I tell you that his name was Claude Leveredge."

"Claude Leveredge? Impossible!"

"He met her before he went to Europe," continued Mr. Russell, as if his astonished hearer had not spoken. "They were engaged during the time of his absence, and upon his return she jilted him, and married another."

"Heartless creature!" cried Miss Holmes, her eyes flashing with indignation; "and Claude, too! But, Mr. Russell, you must be mistaken; he would never have engaged himself to a girl in such an equivocal position."

"He did so, nevertheless," returned Mr. Russell, "and now she is a widow."

Miss Holmes sprang to her feet and paced the room rapidly. Mr. Russell saw how greatly she was excited and discreetly took leave, smiling to himself as he mounted his horse and rode slowly away.

Passing the window in her rapid walk, Miss Holmes looked out and cast a contemptuous glance after him. "I know why you told me that, Will Russell!" she said, flushing angrily, "but it will do you no good; nothing that you can tell me about Claude Leveredge can affect me now."

But she was provingly conscious that his words had affected her. She remembered what affectionate letters, in virtue of their cousinship, had passed between Claude Leveredge and herself during his European tour, and how generally it was understood that a closer relationship would some day be established. The thought had flattered her greatly, in her early girlhood, and it was not without shame that she remembered how long she had waited for the words that never came, and how long she had fretted under the mysterious silence he had kept—a silence which all his actions had rendered eloquent of love.

"He has deceived us shamefully," she muttered angrily. "Oh, to think that he should have been engaged to that creature all the time he was in Europe. Well, well, that passed long ago, thank Heaven! I am glad she married another; it served him right. Yet since, ever since, he has doubtless loved her, and yet he dared make every one believe he had set his heart upon me, by parting me from the only man I ever loved; yes, and whom I will ever love in spite of him."

She paced the room with increased excitement, and after a lapse of a few moments commenced a series of fresh ejaculations expressive of her thoughts.

"Adela Holmes has never been called uncharitable," she cried, "Yet I cannot, I *cannot*, see anything right or pure in this mystery from beginning to end. That girl married, doubtless, from spite; my cousin, perhaps, irritated her beyond endurance. She was beautiful, young, weak, and yes—wicked—would she have married so if she had not been? Claude has haunted her, has produced a fatal influence over her—we quarreled when we last met; he swore he would humble my proud spirit, and he has sent *her* here as his tool. I see it all; she has come here to be my slave, and as my slave, to mock my youthful confidence, to bring low my womanly pride, to show me how, for all these years, she and Claude Leveredge have flouted and scorned me. Oh, the double-dyed treachery!"

She had worked herself into so furious a passion that even Miss Matilda would have started back in alarm from the usually quiet Adela.

Her wrath, with true womanish instinct, turned from her cousin to the offender of her own sex. "Oh, the fiendish creature!" she exclaimed, "how she rejoices in the thought of taking him from me. A great triumph surely when I have wished him won and out of the way a thousand, thousand times. But she shall have her triumph at some cost, I promise her. Yes, she shall suffer all that one woman can devise to torture another; she shall writhe, until she writhes free of her bonds. Not a day, not an hour, not a moment shall pass but that she shall know that she *is* a slave."

Miss Holmes caught the reflection of her face in one of the long mirrors. It was so distorted, that she started at the sight, and hastened to her room that no unexpected intruder might see it. When she reached the shelter of her apartment, she locked the door, and with her hand still upon it, burst into a flood of tears, moaning out: "Oh, my love, my love, you would have taught me how to bear this. But oh, fool—fool that I was to give the promise that prevents me from even writing to you of it."

Could La Guerita DeCuba have known how fierce a battle was waged by love and duty in the heart of Adela Holmes, and how she longed to reveal her outraged feelings, and the cause of them, to one doubly separated by distance and a parent's will, she would have trembled even more despairingly for the bonds she held so precious.

For a few moments after she fled from the house, she remained almost stunned by her emotions at the door of her hut. At last she remembered that William Russell had been held by his acquaintance to be the soul of honor, and a wild hope sprang up in her heart that he would not, at least on that day, betray her to Miss Holmes, and that she might throw herself upon his mercy, and induce him to keep silence forever.

Without pausing for further thought she ran across the fields that lay between her cottage and the road, and standing near the fence, eagerly looked for the appearance of Mr. Russell.

Meanwhile, having left Holmsford in an unusually hopeful frame of mind, and quite unconscious of the thoughts of Adela Holmes concerning him, he slowly rode along the quiet road, lost in reverie, until a voice calling softly, yet eagerly : "Mr. Russell, Mr. Russell," suddenly aroused him.

He recognized the voice even before he saw La Guerita, and drawing rein, looked round and said : "Mrs. DeGrey what do you wish with me?"

"Hush, hush," she cried entreatingly ; "not that name ; do not call me by that name here."

"'Tis no wonder that you shrink from hearing it," he said sternly.

"Oh do not use those cruel tones to me," she entreated. "Ah, if you knew all, you would pity rather than scorn me."

"I cannot scorn you," he replied ; "I cannot look upon your face and do that, and yet—" He paused, as if uncertain what else to say, and then suddenly added : "Good God, are you mad?"

"No, no, no," she cried. "Would to God that I were ; but I am not mad."

Her passionate voice and gestures turned aside all his contempt and distrust, and bending from his saddle, he looked at her more gently, and said :

"Then, Rita, why are you here? Why do I find you in this position?"

She told her story wildly, incoherently, but in such a manner as to leave no doubt in the mind of her hearer that, as she said, she had entered into slavery because freedom—life itself—had become hateful to her.

His heart thrilled with pity as he listened, and when she entreated him not to betray her, that she would die rather than return to her home, and involve her brother in her shame, he begged her to be calm, but she still moaned out :

"For God's sake do not tell them I am here."

The thought of doing so had not for a moment entered his mind, and so he impulsively told her.

"Thank God! Thank God for that!" she cried. "And you will never tell them, Mr. Russell? Oh, you will never tell them."

"Well," said Mr. Russell slowly, as if more to convince himself than his hearer. "I don't see that the matter is any business of mine. I am not your keeper, though I think you would be the better for one."

"Then you will promise to be silent?"

"Oh, yes, I promise," speaking more slowly than before. "You're safe in your bonds for me."

He bowed, and rode slowly away, muttering to himself: "She will do me good service here. There was a devil in Adela's eyes when I spoke of her and Claude to-day."

Mr. Russell rode home very gaily that day, after his meeting with La Guerita, saying often to himself: "The battle is not always to the strong, Claude Leveredge. A word to the wise is enough, and Adela Holmes is wise. God bless me what a world this is we live in! That woman is mad, by Jove; but I wonder what Adela thinks?"

He would not have ridden home so blithely had he known how small was his share in Adela's thoughts, and even that was more indicative of contempt than any other emotion. "How abominably Claude must have acted," she said. "I hate him for it," adding a moment after, with woman's inconsistency: "Well, if he has, Will Russell had no business to insinuate it to me, and make a parade of his own strict morality, by pointing out the delinquencies of my cousin."

CHAPTER XVIII.

"There needs no other charm, no conjurer,
To raise infernal spirits up, but fear.
Butler.

DREARILY the first months of slave life passed to La Guerita DeCuba; her mind was dulled, and her delicate hands were hardened by toil, for her task-mistress was pitiless. Deeper and deeper the iron sank into the tortured soul, yet no awakening came. No, when insult upon insult was heaped upon the once proud head, it meekly bent to receive them all, and the bruised heart never once complained or questioned the justice of its fate, finding comfort in the thought that Harold was spared from misery, for from the first Miss Holmes had loved the boy, and proved it in a hundred ways; and the mother was content, and trod her thorny path, and shrank not from the sharpest woes that came.

Through all that time there was but one to comfort her—the child Alfred. Oh, what a thousand darts sprang from the lips of the careless Minna, and sullen Rufus; how they stung her very soul; but Alfred seemed to recognize in her something higher than his father's slave, and to preserve some remnant of her old life to her.

She was even in a certain way happy when alone with him, and in his company drew the first breath of freedom when one Saturday afternoon she was sent by Aunt Matilda on some trifling message to Asenith Bray's.

Her heart leapt at the name. At last she was to see the woman who had determined her future, who could tell her if her father had been a villain or no, and whether her mother had been weak or wicked.

It was late when they left Holmsford, for Miss Matilda had been about the negro cabin all day, and did not notice until long after noon that Celia's baby would surely die if it didn't have some fresh catnip from Asenith's that very day.

"Isn't aunt an old fidget," said Alfred laughing; "I don't believe there's a thing the matter with that baby, but she drenches them all around once a week with catnip, or some other bitter stuff, on principle. But we must hurry, Miss Rita, or else—though it isn't two miles—we shan't get home till dark, and then you'd be afraid of the ghosts in the pines."

"What ghosts?" she asked, listlessly.

"All sorts of ones. The negroes see them every night; nobody else does though. There's uncle 'Riah's ghost that sits in the fork of a great tree; we call him the angel Gabriel, though 'Riah himself says it's his old master who died years ago, and was never in these woods in his life. Then there's Aunt Elsie's pet ghost, a young lady who walks by the river with her hair all down, and a looking-glass in her hand, like a stranded mermaid."

"And who is that ghost?" asked La Guerita.

"Nobody can decide. I guess, as you say to Rufus about his dreaming sometimes, it is a fancy sketch. But the ghost that Aunt Dilsey sees is the best of all. I'd just like to see and hear that fellow myself."

"What, does Aunt Dilsey's ghost speak?"

"No, he's awfully provoking; won't say a word, though it must be able to, for it cries and moans for hours together."

La Guerita felt a strange terror creeping over her as she listened to the boy's laughingly-spoken words; but not noticing her, he continued: "Yes, he cries and moans for hours together. We children were awfully frightened when first we heard of it, for Uncle Acton hadn't been dead but a few weeks, and it was enough to scare a fellow to have him come back so soon. Rufe says now that when he is alone in the dark, he feels as if he was being lifted up by the hair, and rushed off into space by some invisible hand. La, Miss Rita, I've scared you, why 'tain't nothing to be afraid of."

"But Acton Holmes," she gasped, "who dares say that he walks the earth? Who dares say it?" wildly asking herself if he knew the sorrows that had befallen his child, and if they had made him restless in his grave.

"Why, I told you Aunt Dilsey," cried Alfred in astonishment, laughing as he added, "she's always seeing something. But what do you think Aunt Matilda said when she heard of Uncle Acton's ghost? 'It's just what I expected, said she, 'I told him when he was a dying that it was just like his perverseness, and that he'd regret it before a month. But sakes alive he might have remained put; when any body once gets into a box, I believe in their staying there, but Acton never did have any respect for anybody's feelings.'"

"These are gloomy woods," said La Guerita, striving to say something. "No wonder the negroes see ghosts in them, or fancy that they do."

"But 'tisn't here that Aunt Dilsey sees the ghost," said Alfred, still laughing; "that is to say, not just here, though you can see the old cottage through an opening in the woods a little further on."

"A little cottage!" said La Guerita eagerly. O Alfred, can you show it to me?"

"Of course I can, Miss Rita. But how funny that you should care about it. It is nothing but a ruin now."

"So I supposed," she returned eagerly, "but I love ruins, Alfred. Ah, is that the place?"

"Yes," returned Alfred, "I can just see the chimnies now. Why, how quick your eyes must be?"

"I wonder if we could make time to go there," she said eagerly, glancing at her watch, the only relic of the past that she wore; "O Alfred, I wish you would go over there with me, it is not so very far out of the way."

"But we are almost at Aunt Sene's," said he doubtfully; "I don't think we had better go there now. Let us do our errand first, and then we shall see what time we have left," thinking to himself that it would be hard to miss a luncheon at Asenith's because of the whim of Rita's.

La Guerita followed the boy as he strode quickly on, with the slavish impulse of obedience that had for months rendered her a mere machine, yet still with her eyes fixed on the old ruin.

"It's strange that you should care;" Alfred said again, as he noticed her fixed gaze, "but I tell you what, Miss Rita, we'll go there as we come back. 'T would be fun to brave the ghosts in the twilight, you know."

"Ah, perhaps after all that will be best. Let us walk faster, Alfred."

"All right; I am willing to run if you ain't tired. But I say, Rita, don't you think Aunt Matilda's a funny old woman. Oh, I know you do, and you'll see another directly."

"Indeed!"

"Yes, that you will; not that Aunt Asenith is a bit like Aunt Matilda. She's just as good as she can be, but you'll see her pretty soon. There's her house, and—yes—there is Aunt Sene at the door."

They had reached a bend in the road, and turning it came suddenly upon a little red house with a low gabled roof, and half-a-dozen wings and porticoes, which was set in the middle of a few fields that had been cleared in the midst of the dark pines.

House and fields seemed alike to belong to a by-gone age. The first because of its tiny windows, its dull red hue, and the giant trees that shaded it; the latter from the stunted corn, and the tangled weeds that filled the corners of the low, straggling fences.

"Did you ever see such a queer place?" said Alfred, as La Guerita gazed wondering around. She indeed never had, and it seemed to her scarcely possible that such a quaint, weird place should be upon the earth. The garden was filled with a thousand varieties of flowers, fruits, vegetables, and herbs. Here a copse of roses so thick as to be impenetrable, there a patch of corn or cotton. On one side a hill of potatoes, and on the other a bank of creamy lilies, with a bed of onions, and another of turnips, as neighbors.

La Guerita glanced at these and the thick-stemmed grape-vines that covered the broken trellises and clambered over the old trees, in surprise, but her attention was presently riveted by a figure which stood in one of the porticoes, and beckoned them in. It was that of a woman far advanced in years, yet slender and straight as an arrow. She was clothed in a gray homespun dress, with a kerchief of snowy net folded across her bosom, and a cap of the same material drawn closely around her face—a face that had evidently once been beautiful, that bore the traces of many tears, and that in spite of the furrows upon it was beautiful still with that serenity which in old age rewards a well-spent life.

"There's Aunt Asenith!" cried Alfred, and rushed forward to greet her, kissing her with boyish enthusiasm.

La Guerita slowly drew near, and looking at her sharply with her glittering black eyes, Asenith said: "And who is this with thee, Alfred?"

The boy glanced at his companion in some confusion, and stammered out: "Why, this—this is Rita, Aunt Sene"—adding, in a whisper, which was, however, distinctly heard by La Guerita: "She is a new one, that pa bought the other day, and she teaches us."

Asenith did not seem at all surprised, though her face wore a grieved expression as she greeted La Guerita, and invited her to enter the house, leading the way from the portico, hung with strings of red peppers, onions, and herbs, into a low, dark room, filled with articles of every description and of every form and size. The room was, in reality, quite large, but it was so surrounded with shelves and filled with tables—all of which were laden with heaps of barks, roots, and parcels of herbs—that it looked less than half its real size.

"I keep everything in sight," remarked Asenith, in explanation of the disorder, as she dislodged a huge pumpkin from a chair and swept an armful of herbs from another, that her guests might be seated. "I dare say, Alfred, thee couldn't find a given thing upon any of these tables."

"Not unless it was by accident," he returned, laughing; "though, goodness knows, it looks as if there was a little of everything here. I suppose you know where to lay your hand on everything, Aunt Sene?"

"Oh, yes," she answered, smiling, "these tables and shelves are like open books to me. Here, under these pine cones, is a basket of the red apples thee loves so well, and there are a good many bunches of grapes ripe at the south end of the garden; thee'd better run and get some before thee goes."

Alfred waited no second bidding, but rushed into the garden, and La Guerita was left alone with the Quakeress, who had not even cast a glance upon her since her entrance into the house. When, however, they were alone, she turned toward her with a grieved look in her keen eyes, and said, slowly:

13

"Thee'rt very like thy mother! Ah, I knew it could be none other than thee when I heard of the white slave at Holmsford."

La Guerita made no reply, half resenting in her heart the pity expressed in Asenith's gentle voice.

"Tell me why thou art here," she continued, persuasively, after a moment's pause. "Ah, child, child, I thought I had secured thee from this."

"What could you expect but that I should return?" cried La Guerita, excitedly. "What right had you to place me in a sphere so foreign to my own? Did you think you could thwart the purposes of your God?"

Asenith looked up in amazement and alarm. "My God!" she ejaculated, "and why not thine? Hast thou no belief in God?"

"Yes, I believe!" she retorted, fiercely; "I believe in God, because none but a supernatural power could have poured into my life this overwhelming flood of bitterness."

The Quakeress shrank from her visitor's outstretched hands and fiery gaze. "Tell me!" she cried, imploringly, "what has come upon thee?"

And once more the passionate words burst forth by which her tale of agony was made known, and from Asenith Bray not one word was withheld.

Asenith Bray knew not, could never tell, how she was pledged to secrecy; but although she would have given worlds to have used the power that lay in her hands, and to have freed the maddened woman, she dared not hope to do it, for still she breathed forth that awful vow: "I will not return alive to the home and family I have disgraced!"

Ah, how bitterly she felt her helplessness; but there came a ray of comfort in the thought that this dreadful madness would not last, and she said, brokenly: "My poor child, I pity thee! God pities thee!"

"Don't speak to me of God!" cried La Guerita, impatiently; "it maddens me. I have felt His wrath, but never, never His pity! Speak to me of something else; tell me of my parents! Tell me how you dared take me from my mother's arms and cast me forth to meet my horrible fate?"

The old Quakeress bowed her head and wept; and then, in faltering accents, told all that had passed, dwelling long upon the magnanimity of Acton Holmes, and the repentance of Dolores. Her tears, her words, softened the obdurate heart of La Guerita; for the first time her heart yearned for the mother she had despised, and it was in a gentle voice she said at last: "I must see the house where she lived and suffered, Asenith. Come, let us go to the house where I was born."

Asenith consented, though apparently struck with some surprise at the unexpected proposal. "Perhaps it is best," she said, musingly; "wait for a moment and I will go with thee, although the sun is already low."

She went into the garden, and after a few minutes returned, saying to La Guerita: "Alfred will follow us; let us hasten. But first give me thy little basket; thee must not forget the catnip."

All this was said as quietly as if nothing had occurred to disturb the tranquility of her mind. Throwing on a sun-bonnet of drab cotton, she left her house, with all its windows and doors open, saying, with a smile: "No one will trouble aught of Asenith Bray's."

In a few moments they were in the woods, the Quakeress traversing them like one who knew well each winding path. Presently she selected one that seemed less trodden than any other, and which, indeed, the drifts of pine straw rendered almost undistinguishable. La Guerita followed her silently, catching at intervals glimpses of the yellow river through the dark pines, and at length coming suddenly upon the ruins they sought.

The narrow path terminated suddenly in a gap of a straggling, broken fence, that surrounded what was once a garden, but which was now a wilderness of rank herbage. The rear of the little dwelling was toward them, and over it trailed a poisonous vine, with its scarlet and yellow trumpets floating gaudily in the evening breeze. Great patches of moss clung to the roof of the ruinous porch and down the tottering pillars, while loose shingles and staves of the railing flapped uneasily together, awakening the only sound that disturbed the scene.

Passing through this porch, Asenith Bray led the way into the house, gazing sorrowfully around the one large room, and the two smaller that were revealed by great rents in the partitions, from which the plastering fell in great pieces as they softly moved over the tumbling floors.

"In that room thee were born," said Asenith, softly, pointing to the right, "and in this thy mother gave thee to Acton's arms when she could only turn with cries and moans from me. Ah, how well I remember the day she bade all these scenes farewell forever."

Asenith looked at La Guerita as if she expected—almost wished—to be questioned, but she was in no mood for speech. She wandered from room to room silently, passing through them each a dozen times or more—returning to them again and again, as if seeking some relic of the past. She found none. The house had been deserted twenty years; not a trace—not a vestige of human life remained.

"The hand of Time has fallen heavily here," said Asenith, musingly. "It seems but yesterday that these rooms were radiant with their gilded cornices and crimson hangings, and echoed the merry laughter of children; now the spiders and bats alone inhabit it, and the owl's shrill cry is all that breaks the stillness."

La Guerita DeCuba stood silently in the open door-way, gazing fixedly before her. Asenith looked upon her keenly, seeing that she gradually became pale and trembling in every limb; and at last sprang back, shrieking wildly: "Look! look! look! I knew he would come. There—there, in the roses at the gate?"

"My God, then she *is* mad?" exclaimed the affrighted Quakeress, tearing herself from the rigid clasp and ejaculating faintly: "Be calm—be calm, there is nothing there; there are no roses at the gate."

"Hush! you have driven him away!" she returned, in a fierce whisper; "he was there at the gate;

he stood among the roses, and looked at me as he did one day in the bower at Greymont."

"Thee'rt dreaming, child," said the quakeress soothingly, but firmly. "I did wrong to bring thee here. But here comes Alfred, thee must say nothing to him of thy excited fancies."

"I knew he would come," she said, in the same fierce whisper; "he wanted to speak to me, and now you and that boy have frightened him away."

Asenith clasped her wrist tightly, and looked into her flashing eyes. Thee knows thee's dreaming," she said; "Come with me to the gateway, thee'll see thy senses have deceived thee."

La Guerita drew her hand across her brow, and sighed deeply, saying at last: "Yes, yes, you are right; but—but dreams more than realities have to do with me now."

"Thee must cast them away from thee child."

She shook her head, saying hurriedly as Alfred entered the inclosure, whistling gaily: "They will come—these terrible dreams. Oh, they rush over my poor brain thick and fast—thick and fast."

"But they are quite gone now?" queried Asenith anxiously: "Quite gone! Farewell; 'tis growing late."

La Guerita turned toward Alfred and hurriedly left the house. The Quakeress looked after her, muttering: "Poor child; poor child; thy reason has a mighty task before it ere it shall regain its throne, and I dare not act till then. I know too well the blood within thee! Ah, those dreams! thy mother had them be-

fore thee, when these crumbling ruins were fair and beautiful."

She left the old house, slowly and sadly returning to her dwelling, while Alfred and La Guerita walked hastily through the gloomy woods, the former talking gaily of the old Quakeress, and her isolated mode of living.

"Through the summer," he said, "she scours the woods for miles around for roots and herbs, and puts them in readiness for use, giving freely to all that ask for them. I don't think she would even let a dog want while she had a morsel in the world. Aunt Matilda said one day that 'Senith would give the heart out of her body if the Lord hadn't made it so good that it was no use to anybody but an angel."

So he chatted on, and La Guerita hearing yet not heeding his words, with a mighty effort put away the light—demon peopled—that strove to enter her darkened mind. Exorcising the demon of memory by all the cruel logic of madness, and muttering to herself once more: "I am making atonement!"

"I thought you were waiting for that catnip to grow," said Aunt Matilda as the twain entered the gate at Holmsford.

"No, we were waiting for ghosts in the pines!" returned Alfred laughing.

"And found them, too, I reckon," muttered the old lady, looking keenly after the retreating form of La Guerita. "Now, you Alf. go right into the house, and don't be talking any nonsense to Rufe. Such catnip as you've brought me! Nothing but old stalks, I declare, that haven't got strength enough in them to affect a fly!"

CHAPTER XIX.

" When I take the humor of a thing once, I am
like your tailor's needle—I go through."
Ben Jonson.

A WEEK from the day that La Guerita DeCuba made that, to her, ever
memorable visit to Asenith Bray,
Aunt Matilda thought as the day was
fine that she would take a walk, and
accordingly after putting on an extra
cape, and filling her snuff-box, she
set out, complacently enjoying the
snuff as she went.

She walked on briskly for some
time, neither looking to the right
nor to the left, but straight before
her, as if she half expected to meet
a friend.

That expectation was not disappointed, for soon she descried Asenith Bray, in her neat Quaker array,
approaching.

Miss Matilda paused, and observed her keenly, entirely ignoring the
fact that she was some months older
than Asenith, and looked at least a
score of years her senior, and the accent of pity in her voice was quite
genuine, as she muttered :

" Yes, yes, they tell upon her, the
years tell upon her ; she's beginning
to stoop ; and her hair—bless me
how white her hair is ;" fancying to
herself, no doubt, that her own *fri-
sette* was above suspicion.

" I thought you would come to-
day," she said, as she shook hands
with her friend. " 'Twas a week ago
to-day you saw her, so I didn't expect you before ; you are always so
deliberate about everything."

" Ah, yes," returned the Quakeress with a genial smile, " thee re-
members that ever was the difference
'twixt thee and me. How is thy
health ? Thee looks a little worn, I
fancy."

" It's not to be expected that I
look as young as when I was a girl,"
retorted Miss Matilda ; " neither do
you for that matter. Am I mistaken,
'Senith, or did I see a pair of spec's
in your hand as I came up ? "

" It's very probable that thee saw
them, Matilda," replied Asenith,
smiling. " Thee will wonder at their
richness. I question whether it is
right for me to wear these golden
rims, but Claude Leveredge gave them
to me, and 'twould have seemed ungracious to refuse."

Miss Matilda shrugged her shoulders, saying, contemptuously : " So
he went to see you when he was
home, eh ? I didn't have a chance
to see him, but from all I heard, I
should think he was as mad as a
March hare."

" Verily it seemed so," returned
Asenith.

" If he didn't belong to the family,"
said Miss Matilda, frowning myste-
riously, " I'd give you my opinion
of him. I'd tell you that there was
murder or something worse in that
man's mind."

Asenith was used to such confi-
dences from Miss Matilda, and smiled; saying :

" I didn't come to thee to talk of
Claude Leveredge, Matilda, but of
his cousin, thee knows which one I
mean ? "

" Yes. But you needn't call *her*
his cousin," she returned peevishly :
" You'll be making her out some
relation to me next."

" No. Acton Holmes was no relation of thine. Thee said just now

thee thought Claude Leveredge crazy last spring ; what does thee think of her ? "

" Rita ? "

Asenith nodded.

Miss Matilda shook her head sagely. " Well, well, 'tis hard to say ; if she was white, I should say she was mad—mad as anybody in Bedlam ; but, as Uncle Ben says : ' Niggers is mighty apt to 'possum.' But if she aint 'possuming, she's mad. What do you think ? "

" Hast thee heard her story ? " asked Asenith.

" No. No one ever tells me anything any more than they'd whistle to a snake that they did not want to stop and bite them."

Asenith laughed, and laying her hand upon Miss Matilda's arms, said : " I am not afraid to tell thee of this, and I know thee too well to think thee will breathe a word of it to another."

She repeated La Guerita's tale, word for word, thinking to herself, " Poor child, I will at least win one friend for thee."

" I'd like to find out that fellow who told her husband," exclaimed Miss Matilda. " I'd like to seal up his eyes and mouth with melted lead. I'd teach him to peer and pry into other people's concerns, and then to blazon them all over the country. Shallow fellow that husband of hers must have been, too ; dying because his wife had a drop of negro blood in her. Not worth going mad about, I'll wager."

" But she loved him ! " said Asenith gently.

" 'Sposin' she did ? " retorted Miss Matilda, " she needn't have gone crazy about him. I wonder what folks would have said if you'd have cut up so the day that Nathan Ireton was found dead ; the very day you were to have been married to him, too."

Asenith turned pale, but she replied in a low, steady voice : " The Lord helped me ; I had been taught to trust in Him, but this poor child had no faith, and the mighty burden crushed her."

" And another burden is crushing her now," said Miss Matilda.

Asenith looked at her inquiringly.

" If you'd stay at Holmsford a week, you'd know what I mean," continued Miss Matilda, " I suppose you've heard that it's the last straw that breaks the camel's back, and although I don't mean to say that Rita's a camel, Adela treats her as one in a moral sense, and never had a poor animal a more pitiless driver than she makes herself to that mazed creature we're talking of."

The Quakeress looked disconcerted.

" So you can't fancy Adela a loader of camels, eh ! " asked Miss Matilda.

" It is hard to, verily."

" Well I can tell you she isn't a new hand at the business ; she's been packing her straws on to me ever since she was knee high. If ever there was a tyrant born in this world, it's Adela Holmes."

" No, no, she is not a tyrant," returned Asenith quickly, " but only too quick and suspicious—only too fond of power for a woman."

" That's all very well to talk of," said Miss Matilda, " but I don't understand her."

"Neither does she understand herself, but a day will come when she will, and when she will deeply repent her folly—if indeed she has been guilty of it—of persecuting that poor, mad girl, that has made herself a slave from motives too pure and high to be known to common minds."

"I wish I could tell you how Adela manages to torment her," said Miss Matilda, "but I can't for the life of me. When I see them together it makes me think of a picture in Minna's primer, of an eagle beating its wings and screeching in agony, while a tiny humming-bird bores its sharp beak into its brain, quite undisturbed by the fury it awakens."

"That is horrible—exquisite torture!" murmured Asenith.

"'Taint in nature not to feel bad when a body sees it," said Miss Matilda; "makes me think of all kinds of scratchin', bitin' things. You've knocked your hand sometimes against a nettle, I guess?"

"Yes."

"Well, then, you remember how it stung you—viciously and sharply —without breaking a single point. And so Adela stings that girl, making her wince and groan, but never losing an atom of virus—never blunting the points of her animosity."

Asenith listened in horror, knowing that in these few sentences she was gaining more than anyone else either could or would tell her.

"I am grieved, I am astonished," she said. "Thy niece must be as changeable as the weather."

"More so," returned Miss Matilda; "she used to be a regular abolitionist, always botherin' Norton to free his slaves, and now her whole life and soul is bent on persecutin' Rita. I only wish the stupid creature would grasp the nettle that's always stingin' her; I expect to see her do it yet—slave or no slave—it is not because she's powerless that she bears Adela's thrusts so gently."

They had reached the gate of the garden at Holmsford, and looking around her keenly, Asenith made ready to accost anyone that might be in sight. There were only two or three negroes on whom to bestow her smiles and nods of recognition, so she followed Miss Matilda into the house, where they found Adela sitting alone in the parlor.

She greeted the Quakeress warmly, saying, with joyful surprise: "I am so glad to see you here, Aunt Asenith, and so sorry that mamma is not at home, she would have been delighted to see you."

She removed the bonnet and shawl of her aged visitor, chatting gaily, until Aunt Asenith said: "Thee looks pale, Adela."

"Ah," she said, "it would be no wonder if we all looked pale, Aunt Sene. I learn by to-day's paper that Lincoln is really elected, and there can be no doubt that South Carolina will secede."

"Well, let South Carolina secede! Who cares if she does?" cried Aunt Matilda defiantly. "I'm sure she's welcome to go. Always was like a rattlesnake in a prairie dog's burrow, always hissing and coiling, and making things uncomfortable. I never could abide South Carolina."

Adela smiled, saying: "And she, too, I think does not waste much love on us. But you know, as Mr.

Gordon says, the Southern sisters will cling to each other, and if South Carolina secedes, the Old North State will follow."

"I'd just like to know what Ernest Gordon knows about it?" returned Miss Matilda contemptuously. "Ernest Gordon thinks everybody is like him, and would do anything in the world for a parcel of slaves. I never shall forget the first one he owned. There was a speculator drivin' a gang through M——, and among them he had a little sickly girl about a year and a half old, and it was so weak and puny he 'lowed 'twarn't no use to take it any further, so he took it out of its mother's arms, and she a cryin', poor thing, like rain —and gave it to Ernest Gordon. I never saw anybody so pleased in all my life. You see his folks had been nothing but white trash before, and that little creetur' seemed to set 'em right up. He showed her to everybody, and declared 'twas the finest child he'd ever seen in his life. Well, Mrs. Gordon had twin babies then, and took boarders besides, with only a little slip of a white girl to help her, but she just worked over that little darkey, as if her own life depended upon it. But 'twas all no use, the creetur died, and Ernest Gordon didn't hold up his head for six months afterward."

Adela's mind was evidently oppressed, for she did not laugh, and when Miss Matilda left the room threw herself down by Asenith's side, and said in a tone of anguish:

"Oh, Aunt Sene, if South Carolina secedes there will be war. We shall be separated from the North, from all that I love in the world!"

"Not from all," murmured the Quakeress, stroking her hair fondly; "Ah, thee has a true woman's heart, for all thy waywardness. Does Norton still persist in grieving thee so?"

"It is not papa," she sobbed, "'tis Claude. Yes, Claude!" she added passionately; "what have I done that he should persecute me so?"

"He's like the dog in the manger," said Miss Matilda," entering the room suddenly, and overhearing her niece's last words; "He's like a particularly surly dog, too—wont take you himself nor let any one else have you!"

Miss Holmes looked up frowningly, vexed and ashamed that Miss Matilda should have seen her tears. "What is the matter with Claude now?" she asked, as if she had never entertained a thought of anger against him.

"The matter with Claude!" echoed Miss Matilda excitedly, "why, good gracious, haven't I told you a dozen times before that his blood is the essence of iron, his heart is a flintstone. As for soul, he has none, and not as much sense as the horse he rides, or a hundredth part as much as the one Balaam rode."

"That was an ass," corrected Miss Holmes, smiling in spite of herself.

Miss Matilda looked somewhat abashed, but swiftly rallied, saying: "Well, if 'twas an ass, it's all the more fit to be spoken of in connection with Claude!"

"Thee knows I came here to speak with Adela," said Asenith, quietly, "And if thee would leave us alone for ten minutes, I should be greatly obliged to thee."

"You're learning to be polite in

your old age !" retorted Miss Matilda, leaving the room, however, and closing the door carefully.

"I am very sorry that thee is in trouble," said Asenith, turning toward Miss Holmes with a comforting smile ; "I am very sorry for thee, dear child ; but I came to talk to thee of one that has more trouble than thee has ever dreamed of."

Miss Holmes looked at her inquiringly.

"Thee has never refused help to the needy when I came to thee for it," said the Quakeress, "and thee has always known how to give without offering offense at the same time."

"I have plenty of money just now, Aunt Sene," returned Miss Holmes, readily, and rising to leave the room, "How much do you want?"

"None just at present, Adela ; don't leave the room, for I want what thee has been always equally ready to give."

"And what is that, Aunt Sene?"

"True sympathy and tender counsel for one in affliction ; I want thy pity for thy slave Rita."

Miss Holmes' face darkened, but she answered readily : "Why do you ask that?"

"Adela, if thee knew her story."

"I do know it," she said, excitedly ; "Will. Russell told me, too, that every word was true, and he told me more than you perhaps know—he told me who the lover was that betrayed her."

"And we know him?" cried Asenith, in surprise.

"Ah, yes, we know him well. It was Claude Leveredge that taught that woman to feign madness, to

come here and bring disgrace upon our family. Claude, you know, has alienated himself ; nothing can affect him, and he scruples not to use any means to fulfill his threats and humble my pride."

The Quakeress listened in amazement as Miss Holmes poured forth her convictions, thinking to herself : "If the poor girl had only told me it was Claude I might have saved her, but that reticence is only another proof to Adela of the baseness of her motives."

In her gentle voice she urged every excuse and justification of her silence which she could, in the excitement or her feelings, bring to bear upon the the case. But nothing that she could say was noticed in the slightest degree, and Asenith Bray knew that her mission was fruitless, and that she had only increased the anger and suspicions of Miss Holmes against the woman she had hoped to defend.

"I don't know how thee would ever imagine such things," she said at last, looking at the young girl in blank amazement. "I believe thee is all wrong, Adela ; Claude is no fool to wish to mortify and disgust thee by such conduct, nor malicious enough to revenge himself upon thee for withholding a love which, by thy own showing, he never truly desired."

"I didn't say that he never wished me to love him," replied Miss Holmes, as sullenly as her piquant nature would permit her to speak.

"But he never wanted to marry thee," persisted Asenith, "and thy refusal to gratify his vanity by giving him unsought love would never have led him to insult thee so."

"'His blood is the essence of

14

iron, his heart is a flint stone,'" returned Miss Holmes, musingly repeating her Aunt Matilda's words.

"And thee has been said to resemble him," said Asenith reprovingly.

Miss Holmes colored to the temples, crying vehemently : "*She* shall have cause to think so; she shall *know* it, for I hate that woman ; I hate and despise her a thousand times worse than I do Claude himself, for he *is* a master mind, while she is but a base tool ! "

Asenith felt it would be useless to say more, and so arose and went grieving away, passing a child at the gate whom she stopped and kissed, leaving a benediction upon him, and taking from his lips one word of comfort, for he said in answer to her question :

"Yes, Miss Adela loves me."

CHAPTER XX.

"Despair it was come, and she thought it content;
She thought it content, but her cheek it grew pale,
And she droop'd like a lily broke down by the hail."
Sir W. Scott.

La Guerita DeCuba knew not that Asenith Bray had appealed to Miss Holmes in her behalf, or even that she had visited Holmsford at all, and through the long winter she had no opportunity of meeting the Quakeress again, for she quickly noticed that Miss Holmes utterly prevented her from leaving the plantation, or having any intercourse with any one beyond its limits.

Not that she desired any, for still her mind remained incapable of any new emotions—deadened it seemed by all that had swept over it before. She was fully engrossed in her dull routine of duties, and even when some word or deed of her hard taskmistress forced her heart to bleed, it did not rebel ; all strength of resistance seemed gone forever.

There were two things that reached her sensibilities, dead though they seemed. One was the strange, protecting love Miss Holmes devoted to Harold—a pure love, not exhibited to give the mother pain, but for the boy's sweet sake ; the other was the tender sympathy of her fellow slaves —they did not understand, but they pitied her.

The enmity of Miss Holmes toward her was often the subject of conversation in the cabins, and often Aunt Dilsey would gravely shake her head and say :

"A queer critter is Rita ; I'll jist tell yer what she makes me think on."

"Law, now, what kin it be ? " Aunt 'Mandy would ask as eagerly as if she had not heard the sage opinion twenty times before.

"Why, she's jist like my young Missie Nina used to wus ; looks jis as she would when she 'd git up in de middle ob de night and walk about, fas' asleep all de time, and wid her eyes wide open like a owl's. Rita's jist got dat los' look 'pon her face, and 'pears jis as if she wus a walkin' about among us fas' asleep, awaitin' to be woked up."

"O Lor' ! " Aunt 'Mandy would exclaim, her eyes wildly staring, as if she were listening to the latest ghost story.

"Turrible things them walkin's is, too," would Aunt Dilsey continue, shaking her head wisely. "I've seen my missus go right inter convulu-

tions when she's been suddenly woked up, and that's de way we'll see dat
Rita sometime if Miss Addie keeps
on wid her so. 'Taint in natur fur
her to sleep forebber."

But the spring time brought no
signs of awakening. Still Mrs.
Holmes' querulous complaints; the
petty tyranny of Rufus; Miss Matilda's sharp speeches, and the constant
persecutions of the niece—all failed to
arouse more than a momentary thrill
of anger. Nay, the portentous tidings of disruption and war that filled
every other heart with ambition, anger, or dismay, had no effect upon
her. But she could not fail to remark
that Miss Holmes each day grew more
irritable and more sad; but it was
not for some weeks that she learned
the cause of this extreme depression.

Miss Holmes had been in the garden all day, giving orders to the servants who were employed in trim-
ming vines, tying up rose bushes,
and preparing the garden for the
wealth of bloom that was already
bursting over it. She called to La
Guerita as she left the school-room,
to give her some orders concerning a
difficult piece of needle-work upon
which she was engaged, but had
spoken only a few words when Mr.
Holmes and Mr. Gordon rode up to
the gate.

"How d'ye do, Miss Addie,"
cried the lawyer; "you're looking
as fresh and blooming as one of your
own roses, and I've brought you
some news that will make your eyes
dance so that you'll look better still."

La Guerita noticed that Miss
Holmes suddenly grew as white as
the robe she wore, and that her
hands trembled so that her garden-

ing tools fell to her feet. "Oh, Mr.
Gordon," she cried, in accents almost imploring, "the State has not
seceded? Oh, tell me, papa, the
State has not seceded!"

"I am sorry to be obliged to state
anything that is not agreeable to you,
Miss Adela," said Mr. Gordon, gal-
lantly, "but the long-expected—not
to say joyful—news has come at last.
North Carolina has joined the Southern Confederacy."

Miss Holmes wrung her hands as
if in almost unendurable anguish.

"You know we have been expecting this ever since the special meeting of the Legislature was called,"
said her father, almost timidly.

"Governor Ellis is a traitor," she
replied, passionately, "or he never
would have called it."

"For your father's sake, if not for
your own, I should think it would be
best for you to restrain, if not to mod-
ify, your opinions," said Mr. Gordon,
coolly.

"Nothing will ever make me mod-
ify my opinions," she cried, in the
same passionate voice, and stamping
her foot upon the ground to empha-
size her words. "I may never again
be able to say so publicly, but I now
say, that our State has now devoted
herself to infamy that all the blood of
her sons will be insufficient to wash
away!"

Mr. Holmes looked at his daughter, quite appalled by her words and
manner, while Mr. Gordon laughed
slightly, saying: "I am not surprised at your sentiments, Miss Adela;
you have so many friends in the
North, you know."

She colored, turning away, yet saying, defiantly: "It would be the same

if I had not one. I love my *country*, not my *friends!*"

"I've promised myself a long argument with you after dinner," uttered the lawyer, with imperturbable coolness. "But, bless me, whom have we here? What—Um—Um—what's the, name? Rita! Strange I should have forgotten it. And how well you look; how much you have improved. Holmsford agrees with you, eh?"

Without knowing wherefore, La Guerita felt her very soul sicken as this man cast his keen eyes upon her. She stammered out a few words and turned away; and without seeming to notice her manner, Mr. Gordon rode on to the house with Mr. Holmes, and Miss Adela looked after them, and, forgetting the presence of her slave, moaned out: "We need hope no more; our separation *will* be forever!"

"Miss Addie's right smart cut up 'bout de news, shuh," said one of the men when his mistress had passed out of hearing. "'Pears to me de poor ting is nigh distracted at de tort of war; she's as tender-hearted as a lamb, bress her."

"All I know is," said his companion, "if dere's gwine to be a war, I hope 'twon't stop 'till Massa Linkum gits what he's tryin' fur; tho' I reckon he's like all de oder quality, an' don't think much ob de nigs any way. But, Lor' bress us, de squire says de Yankees won't fight, an' it'll all be ober in a month or two anyway."

"I'd sooner b'lieve Miss Addie," said the first speaker, "an' I know by her grievin' face dat dare's heaps ob trouble ahead."

A new light at that moment seemed to fall upon La Guerita's mind when she heard those words: "Our separation *will* be forever." This war, then, the rumors of which had not excited her in the remotest degree, was to raise a bulwark between the North and the South—the very nation was to arise to make her bondage more secure. Some dim sense of loneliness came over her. She experienced that feeling of desolation to which the veriest misanthrope —hating all his kind—might awaken were he thrown upon some desolate shore. Suddenly she felt utterly forsaken. Although she had never dreamed of availing herself of it, there had been one way of escape open to her, but now it was closed— closed forever.

And she learnt from those few passionate words the secret of Miss Adela's deep sadness too, and, strange to say, she felt no triumph, no gladness, in knowing that her enemy loved in vain. Her womanly sympathy was even faintly aroused, and she pitied her, watching every change thereafter with a solicitude that would have driven Miss Holmes to the verge of desperation had she known of it.

Mr. Gordon passed the night at Holmsford, and in the morning strolled carelessly into the schoolroom. But La Guerita was perfectly conscious with what eager scrutiny he regarded her, and something like pride awoke in her breast as she noticed how purposely he addressed her as a pampered servant, and strove to discover whether she remembered that she had been aught beside.

But he could not rouse her, or produce any impression upon the slowly awakening mind; and all that he found to wonder at was the air in which La Guerita owned herself a slave, and yet proclaimed herself a mistress, and how completely the children — even Rufus — recognized both characters.

"Well, well," he muttered, as he left the school-room, "she is really a most wonderful creature; not but that all women play, in turn, the characters of slave and mistress. Heaven knows they're all slaves as soon as they're mothers, and often as soon as they become wives; but that doesn't establish a precedent for this case. There's something more in that woman than any of us can understand."

This remark he repeated to Mr. Holmes during the afternoon, as they sat on the piazza smoking. "Women all make themselves slaves, sir—all," he affirmed, knocking the feathery ashes from the end of his cigar; "but all do not succumb so readily to their fate as this one has done, and she absolutely seems contented with her lot."

Mr. Holmes had heard Aunt Dilsey's opinion, and quoted it, to the great amusement of the lawyer.

"Well, well," continued the planter, impatiently, "I may as well own that there's a look upon Rita's face that I don't like. Aunt Matilda said one day she was like a dead woman set on springs; and, indeed, she does seem incapable of motion; her very quiet and content renders me uneasy, though I dread the wearing away of that horrible indifference, lest, with animation, a desire for freedom should come."

The lawyer looked at the speaker keenly. "You know you were a little doubtful of the justice and legality of enslaving her," he said; "so, if she should fret in her bonds, you have only to go back to your original feelings, and set her adrift."

"It's all very well to talk of going back to one's original feelings," exclaimed Mr. Holmes, impatiently, "but how am I to do it? You know the Holmes' have been slaveholders for generations past, and just at this crisis, as you remarked yesterday, one cannot afford to cast a slur upon the old faith. Now, as I've taken my stand with the South, I am bound to do nothing to weaken its cause, even to my own mind which I should do if I freed Rita—but, pshaw, what need is there for me to think of such a thing? She is perfectly contented now, and may always remain so, but still I always feel as that fellow did who had the sword suspended by a hair over his head."

Mr. Gordon smiled. "She came to you a free agent," he said.

"You're right," exclaimed Mr. Holmes, eagerly. "I am sure I tried to dissuade her from taking such a decisive step, but she would'nt listen, and now that she's here I find her uncommonly useful. And if awakening from this sleep is going to make her restive and unhappy, I hope her nap will be prolonged for many a year. I am sure I don't know what we should do without her, she is the only one that could ever manage Rufe; Myra would go wild if she were to leave."

"I don't understand why you are apprehensive of losing her," said Mr. Gordon. "She seems quiet enough now. There is no lurking devil in her eyes that I can see ; I should tremble for your Adela if there was. I've only seen them together once or twice, but I can see that the little lady hates her most thoroughly."

"That vexes me more than anything else," cried Mr. Holmes, testily. "I believe it's true, Gordon, that Adela positively hates the poor woman, and, strangely enough, as positively adores her child. She has taken it into her head that he is a poor little martyr, sacrificed to the evil desires of a wicked and unnatural mother."

"What can be the reason of her hatred ?" asked Mr. Gordon ; "Adela is not one to act without a motive."

"Oh, doubtless, because she has made herself a living proof of the fallacy of the opinions she has so long held regarding slavery. You know how at one time she shook even my faith with her arguments. You know Addie is not likely to forgive any one for forcing her to yield her opinions, and she positively has not been her real self since that girl came."

"But there may be other reasons for the change in Adela," suggested Mr. Gordon ; "reasons entirely unconnected with Rita."

"I know what you mean," returned Mr. Holmes, gloomily ; "and I declare I sometimes am half inclined to reproach myself for having listened to Claude, for Addie might have been happily married long before this if I had'nt."

"And in the North," added Mr. Gordon.

"Damn the North !" ejaculated Mr. Holmes.

"With all my heart ! In fact we mean to do it !" returned the lawyer,

smiling. "It is a pity your daughter does not see the advisability of such a course as clearly as you do."

"She will have to see it !" muttered Mr. Holmes. "We have gone with the South, and it is utterly useless for her to cry out against it. I used to be proud of her because she was unlike other girls, but now I wish to heaven she'd be a little more like them. Any other girl would have forgotten that Yankee fellow months ago."

"We must try to replace him," said Mr. Gordon coolly. "There are plenty of fine young fellows here she might choose from."

"Plenty !" said Mr. Holmes, despondently.

"But she won't look at them. Now, there's Burton Elwood ; what rational girl would object to him, and Will. Russell too, who is absolutely mad about her."

"That's the man for us !" exclaimed Mr. Gordon, decidedly. "One of the wealthiest families in the State. Secessionist from the start. It would help you wonderfully if you could gain a connection with that family. You know you laid yourself open to suspicion by opposing the Convention, and Adela's avowed Unionism won't allow it to die out. But bless you, if she was married to Will. she might talk Abolitionism to the end of her days, and nobody would think it anything but a good joke."

"Well, well," said Mr. Holmes, uneasily : "we must talk of that some other time. One scarcely knows what to do or say. I should like to know what Leveredge is doing in Europe all this time."

Mr. Gordon shrugged his shoulders and looked wise. "I sent him some heavy drafts last week," he remarked, "and I don't altogether like what I hear about him. Putting aside that other story,—which I consider ridiculous—they say he is playing like a madman, and is keeping up the finest establishment in the Quartier."

Mr. Holmes frowned, and said : "He can do as he likes with his money of course ; but if that other tale should be true, I'd never forgive him."

Mr. Gordon laughed. "Claude is wild, but not a fool ! Bah, he has an eye to charms more solid than a pretty face."

"Well, well, I wish he'd come home !" said Mr. Holmes with a sigh. "He surely will come when the country is in such peril."

Mr. Gordon shrugged his shoulders doubtfully.

Mr. Holmes, though secretly indignant, affected not to notice the action, but said quietly : "Claude's not a man to shrink from danger, and I'll wager if there's any fighting to be done he'll be foremost in the fray."

" There seems to be some fighting on hand now," exclaimed Mr. Gordon, starting to his feet, and hastening to the steps of the piazza ; " what the deuce is the matter."

Something unusual certainly, for La Guerita was standing near the school-room door with Harold in her arms, confronting Miss Matilda, like an enraged tigress.

"How dared you touch my child?" they heard her explain in shrill, passionate tones. " No one shall touch my child. Hush, hush, don't cry,

my darling, mamma is here ; no one shall whip you again. There, there, there, don't cry."

"A pretty way that for you to allow your niggers to speak," cried Miss Matilda, turning to Mr. Holmes. " Pretty discipline you've got on this plantation when one's life is in danger for touching a brat like that. Just wait till I get hold of you"— turning to Harold—"and I'll shake you well."

" No you wont," returned La Guerita, her eyes flashing with passion ; "you shall never touch my child again. No one shall touch him. I will protect my boy as long as I live."

" What is the reason of this ? " demanded Miss Holmes, appearing upon the scene ; "Aunt Matilda, what occasioned this ? "

"Why, I was going from the house to the kitchen," she answered, when I caught sight of this young vagabond a spading up the sod under the white rose bush.

"What are you doing there ? " I asked, as gently as you please.

"I'm going to bury my bird," said he, as bold as possible, holding up a little no-account thing.

"'Twasn't a little no-account thing," sobbed Harold, "'twas a pretty little pet bird."

" That's just what he would keep on a sayin' before," remarked Miss Matilda, in an aggrieved tone ; "that's just what he said before, and just because I threw it over the fence he burst out cryin' as if his heart would break. 'Twas passion—passion every bit of it, and I just gave him a poke with my stick to make him be still, when out flies his mother as if she would kill me. I'd like to know what you expect is to become of you and yours, Norton Holmes, if you let things go on at this rate. Everything's going to wreck and ruin anyhow! All I can say is, I wont stand it, and if you don't correct that child, and all the rest of them, I will."

La Guerita, who had seemingly become conscious that she had exhibited uncalled-for passion, here excused herself to the spectators, and hurled defiance at Miss Matilda in the words : "I will protect my child ; I must protect my child."

"You have no power to do anything of the sort," said Miss Holmes, firmly ; "You are a slave, and have nothing to do with the government of even your own child."

La Guerita turned toward her fiercely, but met a scornful, commanding glance that made her quail.

"Go to the school-room," continued her mistress, in measured tones, "and leave the child to me."

La Guerita knew that he would be safe, yet for a moment she hesitated. Was it true that she, his mother, had no right to protect or correct him ?

Another word from Miss Holmes recalled her to herself, and she did as commanded, passively, unconsciously casting upon Mr. Gordon a look that haunted him for days.

"That slumbering devil awoke and looked out of her eyes then," he muttered an hour afterward, as he sat alone with Miss Matilda on the shaded piazza, while the old lady thought exultantly : "She grasped her nettle then !" "But if I was Norton," she added aloud, "I'd sell that boy as sure as fate."

"What, Rita's?" asked Mr. Gordon, with a laugh, "What's the matter with him ?"

"The Lord only knows what isn't the matter with him," retorted Miss Matilda, in a tone of virtuous indignation ; "He is the triflin'est, most aggravatin' child that ever was born. 'Twould be a mercy if he'd die, for if he lives he'll surely be shot or hung, whichever is most convenient. I declare he makes me tremble for the family's good name. If you'll believe me 'twas only the other day I sent Roxy to Foustville on an errand, and she of course must needs take Master Harry with her. Well, as she was walkin' down the street, along came a gentleman that could not keep his eyes off the boy. 'Who's child is that?' said he. 'Massa Norton Holmes',' said she. 'Indeed,' said he, 'I thought his face was familiar ; I used to know your master years ago.' And then he went into ecstasies about the boy's beauty, and took him into a candy store and loaded him with sweets and toys. I never felt so ashamed in my life as when Norton came home and told the story, and laughed as a good joke, too. I just told Myra my mind then. It's a disgrace to have him about the place ; besides that, he's such a little imp that he's always getting into mischief. I'd sell him just as sure as fate."

Mr. Gordon laughed at the story, and could not help reverting to it with much inward amusement as he rode homeward in the dusk of the evening. "But I'm puzzled, puzzled. What did that act of self-enslavement mean ? Was she mad, or as Adela thinks, only carrying out some deep-laid plot ? By Jove ! that look on her face to-day was enough to make one tremble. I can't see through it. I'll go back next week and watch that woman; her face is worth studying. Heavens! what a beautiful face it is in repose—what a peerless, magnificent face in anger! Holmes may well fear her awakening. She is the most queenly captive that ever was chained to Slavery's triumphant car. Heigh ho! A few month's later we shall see. But I'm puzzled now! I'm puzzled!"

CHAPTER XXI.

" There is a power in the strength of love ;
'Twill make a thing endurable, which else
Would overset the brain, or break the heart."
Wordsworth.

THERE was in the house at Holmsford a small room opening in from the common parlor, and looking out upon the lawn, the school-house, and the negro cabin. Before the window stood a sewing machine, and in the center of the apartment was a large table, usually bestrewn with sewing. At this table sat La Guerita DeCuba one afternoon, early in the fall, busily engaged upon some fine work, which Miss Holmes, in accordance with the plan of keeping the white slave ever toiling, had intrusted to her hands.

Of late La Guerita had grown weary of her endless tasks, and often longed to cast them down. Toil was not sufficient to keep her mind from wandering to forbidden topics, and often she felt a strange pleasure in living over again her by-gone days; and, strangest of all, it seemed to her the sight of her child often filled her heart with a burning pain; she could not tell of what, for still she was not

15

conscious of one thought of wrong toward him. The frequent visits of Mr. Gordon had served to disturb her thus. He was ever coming at unexpected times, and she knew it was to gaze on her. Yet, though he watched her narrowly, he found but a thoughtful face, somewhat less placid at every visit, perhaps, but with none of the fierce passion upon it which he almost expected, yet dreaded to find.

The visits of the lawyer had a strange effect upon her. They aroused in her a dim sense of the unprecedented deed she had accomplished, and almost to her horror she found herself sometimes questioning herself why she should have done it, and failing to find in the words, "It is my atonement," that complete satisfaction that had often silenced her.

She was thinking of these things, in a wandering way, as she sat in the sewing-room that afternoon, when she heard two persons enter the outer room.

One was Miss Holmes; but she had assuredly forgotten her seamstress, for she made no sign of approaching her, but, on the contrary, took a seat near the parlor table, tapped the marble nervously with her finger nails, as she said: "I am so glad we are in the house alone, papa, for I have something important to tell you."

La Guerita arose, and would have left the room, but the only mode of egress was by the parlor, and she knew by experience that Miss Holmes would probably order her back to her unfinished work; so she resumed her seat and her sewing, as Mr. Holmes said, kindly: "Well, Addie, what is it!"

Miss Holmes for once seemed perplexed, for she did not immediately answer, and when she did, it was in a faltering tone, altogether unnatural to her.

"Dear papa," she said, "I scarcely know what to say, but you wont be angry with me?"

"I am not often angry with you, daughter," returned her father, "but I really think, Addie, unless you feel sure of what you wish to say, you had better put it off until some other time."

"No," said Miss Holmes, resolutely, "I cannot do that. I see you half anticipate what I wish to say; but whatever it is, papa, I beg you to hear me patiently."

"Certainly."

"And, oh, papa, if you would only hear me with sympathy, too!"

"I should be glad to be able to do so, my dear."

"First of all, then, papa, I want to know if you really think it wrong for me to deplore the secession of the Southern States, when I can't help thinking their course wrong. You have seemed so angry with me about that lately."

"Because, child, you have openly shown your sympathy with the abolitionists, and have actually rejoiced in their triumphs, and wept over their reverses."

"Never before you, papa."

"Adela, you cannot easily disguise your feelings; every one in the county knows what they are. But all that would be nothing, if you would only listen to William Russell."

"Oh, papa, don't, don't!" exclaimed Miss Holmes, pleadingly.

"I cannot see why I should not speak of it, Adela; for you must by this time know that no past feelings can be regarded now, and that you should wish them to be so is preposterous—unnatural!"

"Oh, papa, you never said that before!"

"Didn't I? Well, I have thought so, and I wish to hear nothing more of them. I tell you, Adela, once for all, if you wish to retain my affections you must put away this childish nonsense."

Miss Holmes made no response, and La Guerita, hoping to attract attention before more private matters were discussed, dropped her scissors upon the table; but at the same moment Miss Holmes spoke.

"Papa," she said, "I must speak, though you have endeavored to show me that it will be of no avail. But I must speak to you, because I have received this note."

She took from her pocket a sealed letter, and passing it gently through her fingers, handed it to her father, saying: "Will you allow me to open it?"

He took the proffered missive, frowning darkly as he looked at it carefully.

"I see you have kept your promise," he said at length; "not that I ever doubted that you would do so."

Mr. Holmes paced the room in deep thought for a few moments. At length he paused before Adela, and said: "Adela, I tell you now, that all I said two years ago I shall maintain to-day. I should still do so if all Claude Leveredge's words were disproved. You shall never, with my consent, demean yourself so low as to become the wife of even the best of that accursed race."

"Papa, may I read that letter?"

Mr. Holmes hesitated, but he had an uncontrollable curiosity, such as often characterizes weak men as well as women, and half relenting before his daughter's beseeching eyes, said: "We will think of it, Adela—we will think of it."

Her suspicious nature took alarm; she thought he meant to tamper with her, and starting to her feet, exclaimed, passionately: "Papa, if you destroy that letter I will never forgive you as long as I live!"

"I can scarcely believe that you are my daughter," returned Mr. Holmes, sullenly; "you are no more like the Adela of old than Rufus is like Alf. Confound this fellow; it is he that has changed you so! There, read the letter."

She took it joyfully, and opened it with trembling fingers.

"Oh, papa?" she exclaimed, a minute later, "It is all as I feared! He has joined the Northern army!"

"Ah! and what else?"

"He only begs me to be constant."

"Constant! By heaven, that is too much. Now, then, Adela, I hope you are satisfied of his love when he has taken up arms against all your kindred. Now, then, I hope we shall have no more nonsense of your loving him still."

"Oh, papa, I cannot help it; I do love him still! I should love him still even if he were the villain Claude Leveredge painted him. Ah, if he were hanging on a gallows for mur-der or treason I should love him still."

"A pretty confession that for a lady to make, upon my word! I wonder what you will say next? Perhaps you will want permission to write those words to him?"

"No, papa, not those, but only a single line to tell him I have received his."

"Adela, you shall not do it! Why, good God, child, putting aside all personal feelings in the matter, do you know what jeopardy you would place your whole family in by such an action? You are already suspected and watched. Do you want us all to be utterly ruined? Oh, Adela, Adela, it would break my heart should it become known that my daughter, whom I have loved so dearly—ot whom I have been so proud, was a traitor to her home and friends. No, Adela, you must not tempt me. Ask me anything else, but not to seal your death warrant."

"Papa, you startle me!"

"I want to, child, for you blindly shut your eyes to your danger. It horrifies me to think of it. Oh, Adela, if you would only do as I beg you—"

"Papa, don't say any more. But since you have allowed me to read that letter, I will not ask you again to be allowed to reply. He will not doubt me. Whatever happens, he will believe me true."

"Adela, child, don't cry. You know I can't bear to make you cry. If you asked anything else which it is in my power to grant I would do so."

"Papa, I was thinking of something else," she said, brokenly; "I want you to give me something. You have often offered me a little slave ; will you give me one now ? "

"Why, Adela ! " exclaimed Mr. Holmes, thoroughly surprised, "what an extraordinary idea ! How whimsical you are, Addie. Well, which one do you want ? "

La Guerita listened breathlessly. The answer she expected, yet dreaded, came. "I want little Harry—Rita's child, papa."

"What in the world do you want of him ?"

"Poor little fellow, I want to put him out of the way of Aunt Matilda. She positively hates the child, and makes his life miserable ; and, besides, I want to remove him from the influence of that wicked mother of his."

"There is an adjective in that sentence that I object to, Adela. The woman has done nothing to *prove* herself wicked, has she ?"

"Not that I know of," admitted Miss Holmes, reluctantly.

"Very well, then, you should not condemn her."

"I think I have reasons enough for doing so, papa. But never mind them ; I only want to know whether I can have Harry ? "

"What would you do with him ?"

"I would put him where his mother would not be likely to see him again. I'd try to make him forget that such a woman ever existed."

La Guerita bent her head and groaned, crying in the depth of her soul : "What have I done to merit such a fate?" She listened eagerly for what Mr. Holmes should say, and drew a deep sigh of relief as he remarked :

"Really, Adela, I think it would scarcely be right under the peculiar circumstances in which Rita came to us, you know."

"Is Harry a slave ? " asked Miss Holmes quickly. "He was born while his mother was free."

"I think you would find it pretty hard to prove that he is not," he answered, laughing uneasily.

"Here, yes, and perhaps everywhere ; but at any rate, while this war lasts, his bonds are strong enough, But, papa, whether he is a slave or not, you surely do not intend to have that bright little fellow brought up like the negro children, his intellect neglected, his very body forced into brute strength, and both rendered unfit for aught but toil ; you surely cannot intend that Harry shall be brought up like that ? "

"Well, I'm sure I don't know, Addie ; I suppose not, though the truth is, these white fellows among the blacks are like fire among straw, and education only makes them worse."

"Papa if you will give that boy to me he shall not be as fire among straw. I will sacredly promise you that he shall never give you any trouble."

"I don't half like it, Adela. I can't help thinking of his mother."

"Papa you needn't ; she must hate the child, else would she have disgraced him by bringing him here ? By what possible course of reasoning could she have persuaded herself that she was benefiting him by taking him from affluence and love, and plunging him into the very depths of degradation and mental darkness."

"Good Heavens, Adela ! how do

I know? But still I don't like to separate him from her. I dare say she would be glad enough herself to teach him to read and all that."

"Indeed, papa, she has more than once utterly refused to do so. Ah, poor little fellow, she would ruin him both body and soul. She is an infidel!"

"Ah, that is bad, very bad," said Mr. Holmes, gravely. "Bad for her, I mean ; the boy can go to camp meeting and learn everything needful when he is old enough."

"Papa, *will* you let me have the boy?"

La Guerita arose when that question was asked and glided softly to the door, and bent her head, as if fearful of losing one word of the master's answer. Her face looked ghastly in the twilight, her lips were ashen, and her eyes wildly staring. Had calm Adela Holmes beheld the white slave thus gazing upon her she would have shrieked in terror and dismay, but, unconscious of her vicinity, she calmly repeated her question.

Mr. Holmes paced the room uneasily, saying, at last, "I think not, Adela."

"Oh, papa! why not?" she exclaimed, in a voice of genuine sorrow and disappointment.

"Because I think the mother is right, and that it is best for the child to remain uneducated. Rita has been free and is now a slave ; she ought to know best about the matter. No doubt she would herself have led a happier life if she had been suffered to remain in ignorance."

"But, papa, you must know there is a higher destiny for that child.

Oh, that woman's curse cannot always rest upon his innocent head."

"You are talking wildly, Adela."

"No, no, I am not. Just think of all the evil she has brought upon him. Has she not torn from him his birthright of freedom? Has he not been taken from the midst of plenty to be that vilest thing on earth—a slave? Has she not divested him of his very name, this mother whom you reprove me for calling wicked? Oh, papa, I loathe her! She fills me with horror when I think that she has done all these things—when, worse than all, she has denied him a knowledge of God, and his mercy and love. Oh, papa, I am pleading for that child's very soul. Let me save him from his wicked, wicked mother. Let me put him away from her forever."

"What was that?" Both started, and Miss Holmes, crying "Oh, I forgot! I forgot! She has heard all!" rushed into the inner room, and to her amazement found La Guerita lying across the threshold, as if in death.

Miss Holmes screamed in affright, and hastening in, Mr. Holmes exclaimed, "Good God, Adela, you have killed her!" and lifting her in his arms carried her to a sofa.

"It is nothing," returned Miss Holmes, regaining her self-possession ; "She has only fainted."

She stepped to the door and locked it, continuing, "There is no use in alarming the whole house about it. Here is a vinigrette and some water ; she'll come round very well, I dare say. It's all passion, no doubt."

She bent over the motionless figure, applying such remedies as were at hand, and as she looked upon the faultless countenance, with all its lines of suffering displayed by its utter lifelessness, some unpleasant doubts of the truth of her suspicions darted through her mind, and caused her to shudder like a guilty creature.

But when La Guerita unclosed her eyes and gazed around, she dissembled her feelings, and as she cried piteously : "Oh, no ! I was not wicked ! I am not wicked ! I was mad !" she turned from her with a trembling heart, and hurried from the room.

"Be calm, be calm," said Mr. Holmes, gently, knowing that the awakening he had feared had come ; "Be calm, and forget what has passed."

"Oh, I cannot be calm !" she cried, springing to her feet ; "Stay and hear me, Mr. Holmes, I entreat !"

But she spoke to bare walls. He would not stay to listen to the truth, and blinded by the sudden light that had rushed upon her bewildered mind, La Guerita staggered forth from the house, and groped her way to the lowly cabin.

CHAPTER XXII.

"Sure some ill approaches,
And some kind spirit knocks softly at my soul,
To tell me fate's at hand."
Dryden.

LA GUERITA DECUBA entered her cabin a changed woman. The shock which alone could restore her to her normal condition had thrilled like an electric current through her very being, and on the instant she had been transformed from the mad woman, who had cursed her Creator, to a rational creature, beholding at once her duty, and the mercy of her God.

She realized at once that she had been mad, and that her mind was once more restored to her, and throwing herself upon the bare floor, she poured forth her soul before the Lord, and wept long and passionately—the first tears that had fallen from her eyes since Harold died.

The precious drops soothed and refreshed her. They trickled over her fingers like rain ; and as she looked upon them she exclaimed : "Thank God I am sane ! Thank God I can weep now."

For a long time she crouched upon the floor, weeping, but not despairingly, thanking God in her heart of hearts that her reason had returned to her, and going over in unbroken order the events of her past life.

The roll of carriage wheels upon the gravel disturbed her. Once she raised her head and thought "Mrs. Holmes must be come. But what a noise they are making, almost as much as if every negro on the place had hurried to meet her. I wonder if this is unusual, or if it is only that I can appreciate joyful sounds tonight, and hear them more readily than ever before ?"

She arose and paced the room thoughtfully. That she was once more sane was to her too joyful a reflection for others of a sadder description to weigh yet upon her thoughts. She lighted her lamp, and as its dim light fell upon her poor surroundings, she started and exclaimed :

"Ah, I had almost forgotten. And this is the atonement I hoped to make. Ah, Harold, Harold, I know now that no atonement was required of me."

She paced the room slowly, muttering at intervals : "I must take the consequences of my madness for a time at least. Mr. Holmes has been kind to me, and I will remain and toil for him patiently until such time as I can find an opportunity to go into the North. Surely Mr. Holmes will let me go. He will not hold a sane woman in slavery, who entered into bonds when mad. He must know that I was mad—and Miss Adela, too, she shall know; I must prove it to her. But how? how? Oh, God, how shall I save my child?"

Some one rattled the latch of the door impatiently; she opened it, and drew in her little son, clasping him in her arms, and again bursting into tears.

Oh, Harold, Harold, darling boy," she cried, as he gazed at her in amazement. " Kiss me, darling, and forgive me. I never meant to harm you, darling. I meant to save you."

Harold kissed her with an expression of great perplexity upon his face. "What is the matter?" he asked; "has any one been scolding you?"

"No, my darling, no," she answered, weeping still; "no my precious one."

She set him on the floor, and bathed her face and hands, remembering the necessity of obtaining composure. "I am enabled to talk to you now, my child," she said at last. " Come sit upon my knee, and tell me that you love me."

"Yes, I do love you," said the child, caressing her fondly, "and I am not a bit afraid of you either now."

She clasped him to her bosom, holding him there long and silently, breathing the first prayer that had parted her lips for him for many weary months.

"I have something to show you, darling," she said, at length, "something I have never looked at since we came here. But first tell me, if you can, what your name is, what it used to be?"

"Why, wasn't it always Harry Holmes?" he exclaimed in surprise.

His mother shook her head, sadly, saying: "Alas, poor child, I was doing my work well. But you can at least tell me where we used to live?"

"Wasn't it at a place like this? No, no, I don't mean just like this—and yet it must have been; there were flowers—yes, always flowers," and the boy looked up with a sad expression of perplexity upon his bright young face.

" Yes, there were flowers, Harry," said his mother, eagerly; "but the place was not like this. Try, dear child, to remember more. Oh, try."

He shook his head, slowly.

"What can you not? Can't you remember anyone that lived there? "Think, now, think.'

" There was a tall man," he said, after a long pause: " But—but he went away."

La Guerita took a miniature case from her bosom. " There," she said, unclasping it eagerly, "this is what I promised to show you. There, look at it carefully, and tell me whether that is the tall man you remember?"

Harold looked at the portrait doubtfully. Then a light seemed to break upon his mind. " Yes," he cried excitedly, " that is his face," and dropping the case into his mother's hands, he continued rapidly, and with a rapt expression of countenance: "Yes, there was another, too, something like him, but darker, and another still; and oh, such a beautiful old lady; and oh, there were more even than that." He slipped from her lap, and leaned upon her knees, continuing dreamily: "Why, I can see faces upon faces, mamma. I can only tell you about them like I do my dreams." He caught up the portrait again, and bursting into tears, cried: "Why, that is my papa, and Uncle Vic.— but papa the most. Oh, I know, I know, I know."

La Guerita clasped the child in her arms in an excess of joy. "Thank God," she said fervently, "you have not forgotten. Your mind, as well as mine, has been awakened to-day."

"Now I remember it all," cried the boy, gleefully. "The pretty flowers, and the water, all flashing, flashing, flashing. Where has it all gone, mamma?"

"It is all in the old place," she answered softly, "and perhaps we may all go back to it, and you will once more be Harold DeGrey."

"There, that's what I was trying to think of," he exclaimed. "Harold DeGrey—yes, that was it. Was'nt it funny I forgot."

"Remember it now, my darling," replied his mother. "Try, darling, to remember it all."

The child looked so excited, that she held him to her bosom for a long time, saying nothing, and only then asking if Mrs. Holmes was at home.

"Oh, yes," he answered, "she came long ago, and there was company with her. I came in to tell you. I——"

At that moment, the door was opened, and Miss Holmes entered, looking unusually pale, and with a perplexed, yet resolute expression upon her countenance as she exclaimed:

"Go to the house, Rita; you are wanted there. Harry, come with me. Rita, hasten."

La Guerita obeyed without pausing to think, and wondered when she reached the house, as she beheld in bewilderment that it was ablaze with light, and that there were sounds of great merriment and rejoicing within. Following the impetus of Miss Adela's hand, she entered the dining-room, but was so dazzled by the glare of the lamps that she could distinguish nothing.

Suddenly a voice fell upon her ear with startling distinctness. "My God, it is La Guerita DeCuba!" she heard, and fell back into the arms of Miss Holmes.

'Twas but an instant's faintness, the glare of the lamps instantly subdued. Though the room seemed to whirl like a ball through space, she sprang to her feet, as she felt her hands clasped in an iron-like grip, and heard again the voice of Claude Leveredge.

"I thought you were dead!" he cried. "They told me you would die. Oh, God, what I have suffered."

His hated touch, perhaps, more than his words, recalled her to herself. She cast off his detaining hands, and glanced at him with an expression of abhorrence, which was not lost upon him, or Adela Holmes, who, white and trembling, regarded the scene. By her side stood Harold, who suddenly threw himself into his mother's arms, crying, in terror: "Oh, mamma, don't let him take me away! Oh, mamma, mamma!"

Claude Leveredge looked at the child fiercely, retreating a step, and exclaiming: "Take him away! take him away!"

"What in the world is the meaning of this?" demanded Mr. Holmes, in a tone of amazement; "Have you all taken leave of your senses?"

"It don't mean anything more than that his satanic majesty is with his friend, as usual," said Miss Matilda, meaningly.

La Guerita never remembered how she effected her escape from the dining room, but a few minutes later she was in her cabin and had bolted the door, feeling that she should die at his feet if Claude Leveredge entered there.

One fervent prayer burst again and again from her lips as she stood in the center of her room, pressing her hands upon her burning temples, exclaiming: "Oh, God, preserve my senses; my reason totters. Oh, Christ, strengthen it!"

It was fearful to her to know what great danger this great shock brought nigh her. She knew she had been mad and she feared to be alone, lest terrors should grow out of the darkness, and all the horrors of lunacy once more seize upon her. She feared that, at first, more than the actual presence of Claude Leveredge. She tried to persuade herself that he had spoken more in the accents of remorse than of passion; that he would rather shield than persecute

her, and so, by degrees, she grew calm.

Roxy brought in supper, and although La Guerita could eat nothing herself she selected a few of the choicest morsels for Harold, and forced herself to talk with him upon indifferent subjects. Afterwards she undressed the boy, and putting him in bed, stayed by him until he slept, each moment growing calmer as she watched his quiet and regular breathing. She was herself surprised after that, that she could think so calmly while Claude Leveredge was near. She could not only think, but pray; and for the first time in many months she knelt down and communed with the Lord, feeling when she arose from her knees that her soul was relieved from half its burden.

Then she recalled, step by step, the whole of her past life, dwelling long upon the bliss of her married life, saying, with a shudder, "What horrible darkness it ended in!" With painful distinctness the events that followed her husband's death came before her. She remembered what a dreadful blank her life seemed when she entered the library to read Claude Leveredge's fatal letter, and how a million demons seemed to gather round her as she read, and to demand atonement for Harold's death. She remembered how they had urged her on in her mad career, and then how the voices had grown fainter, as if appeased, but had only ceased altogether when the voice of Conscience was aroused, and Reason regained her throne.

"They thought me half crazed with grief at home," she said, "but here they must have known that I

was *mad* when I gave up not only my
own freedom but my child's. I know
now what it means, though I did not
then. My mother knew that I was
mad, Mr. Gordon knew it, and Mr.
Holmes? No, I cannot tell what he
thought; yet he must have known."

Then she thought wildly that they
had perhaps merely humored her
with a pretense of enslavement. She
even thought that her family must
have traced her, and suffered her to
remain in bonds, merely to avoid
crossing her mad passion. But that
hope quickly fled. The war had
destroyed all sympathy between the
North and the South. Her friends
would have taken her from the block-
aded country at any risk, and she felt
that Mr. Gordon had been fearfully
in earnest in her enslavement, if no
other had. No, no; it was no jest.
She was a *slave*, and Claude Leveredge had discovered her.

There was madness in the thought,
but she cried out that she would be
free: that Norton Holmes would not
hold her in bondage; that she could
buy herself a thousand times, and
that he would surely suffer her to
depart.

And still fighting for this hope,
which a thousand fears strove to tear
from her, La Guerita DeCuba paced
her cabin floor, and longed for morning, that she might go to Norton
Holmes and entreat her freedom.

CHAPTER XXIII.

" They told me, by the sentence of the law
They had commission to seize all my fortune."
                                        Otway.

MR. HOLMES was usually an early
riser, and with feverish impatience,

from the dawning of the day, La
Guerita watched for him to enter the
lawn; but all in vain. And when
Roxy brought the breakfast, some
time later then usual, she said, that
"Massa had been so glad the night
afore to see Mass'r Claude git home
again that he was clear tuckered out,
and wouldn't be able to git up 'till all
hours."

So La Guerita knew that all hope
of speaking to him that morning
was over, and with a sigh turned
to the table and gave Harold his
breakfast, while Roxy stood near,
twirling a napkin in her hand, and
giving a glowing account of the
night's feast.

"And, law, what a time dat wus
when you comed in," said the garrulous maiden. "Did you eber see
Mass Claude afore?"

This was an embarrassing question,
but, fortunately, Roxy thought it too
absurd to require an answer, and
continued: "I s'pose you neber
did; but I'm bressed ef I wa'n't
scared when I seed Mass Claude
jump for'ard dat away, and saw his
eyes look'd jiss like two flames ob
fire burnin' up out ob gray ashes.
But the minute you was done gone
he bust out a laughin', fit to kill his-
self, and ses he: 'What a fool I am.
I actually thought I'd seed dat woman somewhar when she fust come
into de room. Who de mischief is
she?'

"'Papa's slave—Rita,' said Miss
Addie, a lookin' deadful pale and
stern.

"And Mass Claude jiss sat down
then as ef he'd been struck, and said:
'Oh, my God,' like's ef he'd loss his
wits like.

"Then Miss 'Tilda, she goes up to him and bobs and curtsies so, you'd a' thought her cap-borders would a knocked to pieces 'gainst her head, and ses she : ' Yes, that was papa's slave — Rita ; you are s'prised to hear it, I s'pose?'

"'That I am?' ses he, a burstin' out a laughin' again. 'I thought she was a white woman ; and when she fust came into the room I tuk her fur a lady I'd seed in Spain ! But, law, I don't s'pose she's a bit like her.'

"And shuah enuff, Rita, I've often thought you looked like a pictur ob a furrin lady, you'se so differn't from de res' ob us, you know. I was tellin' Aunt Sally 'bout de name he called you, an' she ses she's gwine to gib it to de baby. Lo-wa-ter, wasn't it ? Only soft and purty like."

"She might have said La Guerita, for Harold glanced up suddenly, with flushed face and eager eyes, as if he had heard a well-known sound. His mother caught his eye, and put her finger on his lip, and he colored more than ever with the effort to keep silence, and looked down in his plate, presently dropping back in his chair, with his eyes fixed dreamily upon the view beyond the cabin-door. He did not move until Roxy had gone and his mother touched his shoulder, saying :

"What are you thinking of, my darling ?"

He looked up dreamily. "I can't tell you what I'm thinking of, mamma ; it is all mixed up. But, oh, mamma !" he continued, clasping his arms around her neck, excitedly, "I know I've seen that gentleman before. I know I've seen that black man."

"The gentleman is not black," corrected La Guerita, gravely.

"He is as black as you are, and a great deal blacker than I am," protested Harold ; "and if we are called black, I don't see why he shouldn't be !"

"But no one calls us black," said La Guerita, her heart sinking, as she remembered that she had herself subjected her sensitive child to the possibility of such an insult.

"Oh, don't they, though?" he cried, in an aggrieved tone. "Miss Matilda is always calling me a little nigger ; and Mass Rufe is always calling out : 'Here, little nigger, run and fetch my ball !' 'Say, blackee, go get my bat !' Miss Matilda called me a black imp the other day, and I said I wasn't black ; and she said, yes, I was the worst kind of black. So then I told her, I guess'd she'd lost her specs, and didn't know white when she saw it without them ; and then I ran—I just did !"

"Oh, Harold, how could you be so impertinent?"

"Oh, that ain't anything !" he answered, quite unabashed ; "we don't care for old Miss 'Tilda, except when she pokes us with a stick."

La Guerita could not refrain from smiling at the grimace which accompanied these words : but a few minutes later she left the child with a heavy heart, and went to the schoolroom—the weary treadmill to which she was self-condemned.

She had been there but a short time, and was leaning over Rufus, explaining some difficult passage in French, when, looking up, she saw Claude Leveredge leaning idly upon the sill of the open window. He was looking upon the group smilingly and carelessly, with the air of one quite at home. He nodded gayly, tapping the ashes from his cigar, and holding it out at arms length, that the smoke might not enter the room.

"What a nice school-room you have here," he said, addressing the children rather than La Guerita; "it seems very cool and pleasant."

"'Tisn't a bit pleasant," growled Rufus. "I just wish you had to sit here all day long, as we do."

Claude laughed, and looked at La Guerita, as if he should like to learn her opinion of the plan, but merely said:

"It seems to me you're a pretty big fellow to be here, Rufe; you're nearly fourteen, ain't you? Why doesn't your father send you to school?"

"Oh, because papa thinks Rita can teach us everything!" replied Rufus, in a surly tone.

"Papa knows that she can do very well by us for another year," explained Alfred, "and then we are to go to Chapel Hill, if the College is still open."

"Say, cousin Claude," interrupted Minna, "where have you been this long time?"

"I have been in England and France, Miss Inquisitive Puss, and, by the way, I have brought you the most beautiful dress from Paris you ever saw in your life."

Minna sprang up in a transport of delight, exclaiming: "Oh, cousin Claude, how good you are."

"It seems to me," responded the *good* cousin, "that your discipline is not very strict."

"Oh, yes it is; Miss Rita makes

us behave, and I'm sure she doesn't want you here."

Claude Leveredge looked at La Guerita most earnestly for a moment, a slight flush passing over his brow, which deepened to a crimson as Minna exclaimed: "I say, cousin Claude, I heard Mr. Rathburn tell pa you were married. You weren't, were you?"

He started from his lounging position, and then burst into a loud laugh. "Well, that is a good joke," he exclaimed; "why, Minna, I am waiting for you."

"Are you?" said Minna, innocently; "why, I thought it was Adela; but anyhow, I'm glad you're not married."

Claude Leveredge turned away, but Rufus called him back, saying: "Look here, cousin Claude, are you going to join the army?"

"Can't say, I'm sure," he returned, carelessly; "You know the Yankees might shoot me if I did."

"Coward!" ejaculated Rufus, contemptuously.

His cousin looked at him with an amused smile. "I'll give you a pair of spurs, my young knight, when you go," he said.

"You may be called upon to keep your promise," returned the boy, his cheeks flushing redly; "Mr. Gordon told me the other day that even my young hands might be called into action before the independence of the South is achieved."

"I think it very likely," responded his cousin, drily.

"I don't believe you are going to the war, cousin Claude," exclaimed Minna, "for you don't talk like it; and besides, you havn't got on a gray coat all covered over with gold lace. I say, is my dress red and white? Oh, I'll just *love* it if it is, but I shan't wear it if it's got any blue on it. But I'll be glad if you don't go to the war; I want you to stay home with us. How long are you going to stay, cousin Claude?"

He looked steadily at La Guerita as he replied deliberately: "I shall stay until the work I have found to do here is accomplished; yes, until that business is completed to my satisfaction."

"I didn't know you had any business," replied Minna, naively; "'Twas only this morning I heard Aunt Matilda say you hadn't a bit of business in the world."

"I was of the same opinion once," he answered laughing, yet glancing stealthily at La Guerita, "but last night I found I had still a great deal to do, and I mean to stay until it is completed—yes, until it is completed."

He nodded, smiled, and walked away whistling a lively air, as if in the most hopeful mood, and La Guerita in soul bent down and raised the gauntlet of defiance he had cast at her feet.

She was inexpressibly relieved when he passed out of sight and hearing. For a few moments during which the hum of the children's voices was rising and falling indistinctly around her she stood motionless, thinking that her application to Mr. Holmes would be in vain, and shuddering at the remembrance of the invincible face Claude Leveredge had turned toward her when he said he would stay at Holmsford until his business was completed.

It seemed to her that the morning would never pass. She looked so pale and haggard that the children often asked if she were sick. She was glad for the sake of quiet to say that she was, and indeed she spoke truly, for her veins were filled with fever and her temples throbbed unceasingly with the terrible anxiety that was each moment growing more intense.

She thanked God when twelve o'-clock came, and unable longer to restrain herself, hurried to the house and asked for Mr. Holmes. He was alone in a small study or office, in which he usually transacted the business of the estate.

He was writing as she softly entered the room, closing the door after her, and leaning against it for support.

"Well, Rita," he said, glancing over his shoulder carelessly, and continuing his writing, "children been troublesome to-day?"

She advanced a step into the room, turning very faint and dizzy, as she stammered: "I beg your pardon for disturbing you, Mr. Holmes, but— but I would like to speak to you on— on an important subject."

She would have given worlds to have been able to speak in her usually calm tones, but Mr. Holmes seemed to take no notice of her confusion, but merely looked at her inquiringly.

"I wish to ask one question, sir," she continued, summoning all her courage; "Am I really a slave?"

"Why, good God, yes."

She shuddered. "That is dreadful," she said; "but oh, Mr. Holmes, answer me once more, did you not think me insane when I offered to become a slave?"

Mr. Holmes colored and bit his lips nervously. "Why do you ask?" he said; "what can that matter to you now?"

"Oh, sir," she said, earnestly, "it matters much. I have come to you now to tell you that you were right. I *was mad!* Oh, terribly, terribly mad! But now, by the peace, the discipline, the healthful toil I have found here, my reason has been mercifully restored to me."

"Do you wish me to believe that up to this time you have been a mad woman?" asked Mr. Holmes, coldly.

"Mad on that one subject, yes," replied La Guerita, excitedly.

"On what subject?"

"Oh, sir, you must know. Upon that of making atonement for the evil my birth had wrought. Ah, well I know now that such atonement was impossible, and that it was never required of me, and that all I could hope to make could only make the evil greater."

"What do you wish me to understand by all this?" asked Mr. Holmes, after a pause, in a voice that would have been trivial had the matter of discussion been trivial.

La Guerita was fearfully excited, but she strove to control herself. She clenched her hands and drew her lips against her teeth in order to speak firmly. "It is right that I should speak to you plainly," she said; "it was very easy for me, in my madness, to entreat to become your slave; I scarcely know why it is so hard for me now to beseech you for my freedom."

An expression of displeasure, which

he vainly endeavored to change to surprise, rested upon the face of the planter as he looked upon the suppliant.

"You surprise me, Rita," he said; "I thought you had considered the matter well before you entered into slavery."

He arose and took a parchment from a small tin case. "I suppose," he said, "you recognize this?" Do you not also remember the words in which you promised to become my slave, and that of my heirs, for life?"

"You will not hold that bond against me?" she queried, in faltering tones.

"I wish to hold nothing against you," he answered, quietly; "there is, in fact, no need to do so. Your emancipation papers are in Mr. Gordon's hands. You see I merely wish to remind you that you are lawfully my slave, and that I have as much right to you as to that boy I bought of a speculator, and gave a thousand dollars for, last week."

For a moment she was dumb, then she cried mournfully: "I do not dispute your right to hold me in bonds, Mr. Holmes; but I entreat you to release me."

"I cannot do it, Rita. There, now, let that answer suffice."

La Guerita had half expected this answer, yet it stunned her, and after a few moments she said, calmly: "Will you tell me why you deny me my freedom, Mr. Holmes?"

"What a question!" he returned, angrily. "Had you better not call in all my field-hands, and bid them ask me why I will not give them their freedom. Rita, I with thousands of others, am maintaining a principle;

I have sworn never to free a slave, and I will not free you."

"Sell me, then," she cried ; "sell me to my friends—to those who will buy me at any price. Set some price upon me, and let me buy my freedom."

"I can't do it," answered Mr. Holmes, flushing to the temples, "the principle would be the same as if I freed you at once. Besides," he added, deliberately, "you see, Rita, —you'll excuse the phrase, one never knows exactly how to speak to you— you are a fancy article, not easily found in the market, and the truth is, I wouldn't sell you at any price; to prove that, I'll tell you that I refused four thousand dollars for you, offered by Judge Gaylord only last week."

La Guerita staggered blindly into a chair, thinking this must be the worst degradation that could fall upon her.

"Oh, don't let that trouble you," said Mr. Holmes, reassuringly ; "now you know my thoughts, don't worry any more about freedom. Consider the matter settled, and go back to your work like a good girl. Remember that I tried to dissuade you from entering into slavery, but what has been done is now irrevocable."

"Irrevocable." It seemed to La Guerita the word of doom. It leveled all the little pride that had hitherto sustained her, and throwing herself upon her knees, she entreated him by all things sacred in earth and heaven to set her free. But all was vain.

"I can do nothing for you," he said ; "rise, and calm yourself, you will remain my slave until death, or the fate of war releases you. I have put it out of my power to move in the matter."

She arose, quivering with excitement, and fixing her burning éyes upon him, cried : "It is false ; you could free me if you would. Your word of honor is nothing. You, yourself, offered to restore my freedom, should I ever desire it. Though I was mad, I remember that. But though I am your slave, my boy is not. You have no right to hold him. Send him North to his lawful guardians."

Mr. Holmes seemed startled.

"Prove him free," he cried, panting with anger ; "prove him free if you can."

"I will," she replied ; "his guardians shall be here to rescue him and me, before your cowardly soul has time to grow calm again. Norton Holmes, I warn you that I was mad when I entered into bonds, and consequently not responsible for what I did, and that you are detaining a *free* woman and her child in slavery. Ay, and when the time comes, which will soon be here, when I can prove this before the world, you will rue the day when you denied my prayer for freedom."

Norton Holmes turned toward her, livid with ungovernable rage. "If you have ever been mad," he cried, furiously, "you are mad now. I should be rather justified in giving you a straight-jacket than your freedom. Go."

She obeyed, and a moment later Claude Leveredge entered the study from an inner apartment.

"Bravo, uncle," he cried, "you did that splendidly."

"Gordòn foresaw that this would

come," he replied, wiping his forehead, excitedly. "I did take that oath that I told her of one day, but I should surely have broken it but for what you told me this morning. Good God! what times we have fallen upon, when even one's most private actions may serve to condemn him of treason!" 'Tis all Adela's fault," he added; "she won't listen to reason. 'Tis a pity, though, that that poor soul has to suffer for it."

"Tut, tut, you couldn't have spared her, anyway. Look at her now."

He drew Mr. Holmes to the window, and both looked at La Guerita DeCuba as she passed on to her cabin.

"There is a frightful despair in the droop of her head, the fall of her hands, and in the very motion of her limbs as she walks," he muttered, "that shows her incapable of resistance."

"She looks sad," said Mr. Holmes.

"Oh, yes," said Mr. Leveredge, turning away indifferently, "but like all of her race she is incapable of lasting emotion. But never mind her now, I want to talk to you about business. You have the idea that I am ruined, but I can prove to you very satisfactorily that I am better off now than I have ever been before. Europe, after all, is not a bad place to go to when you have luck on your side, and I can assure you that I had it, though I cared very little for it."

"Having but yourself to care for."

"Of course."

"Well, well; I suppose you know your own business best, Claude, but it would be a comfort to me if you would settle down."

"I mean to, uncle. Look here!" said Claude Leveredge, lighting a cigar and spreading some papers upon the table. "I see you're uneasy about Rita. Well, if you're anxious, we can ask the children when they come in."

But when the children came they had nothing to report of their governess, though they were laughingly interrogated by Claude, who teazed the boys unmercifully for allowing themselves to be taught by a woman at all.

After tea he sat upon the piazza for some time, evidently in deep thought, although he endeavored to take part in the conversation. He sprang up suddenly, saying he would smoke a cigar in the shrubbery, and strolled slowly out of sight. A few moments later Miss Holmes came out of the house and asked for him, and being told where he had gone threw a light shawl around her, and went to seek him.

CHAPTER XXIV.

"Most other passions have their periods of fatigue and rest—their sufferings and their cure; but obstinacy has no resource, and the first wound is mortal."
Johnson.

BUT well as Miss Holmes was acquainted with every nook of the garden, she sought her cousin for some time in vain, and was at last standing, in some perplexity and annoyance, upon one of the most secluded paths, just without a circle of roses, which were so thickly set as to be impenetrable except at one point, when she heard voices, which she immediately recognized as those of Claude Leveredge and La Guerita DeCuba.

Her first impulse was to leave the spot as quietly as she came, and her second to put aside some sprays of foliage and see what attitude those two, who had been all day in her thoughts, held toward each other. She was conscious of a feeling of shame as she bent to the task; but she could not draw back. She beheld them quite plainly even in the dim starlight, and at the first glance saw that she had been wrong—that the white slave was not the tool of her cousin, and that she regarded him, not as a lover, but as her bitterest enemy.

They were standing almost at the center of the circle of rose-bushes. La Guerita was facing her; and Miss Holmes saw without hindrance that her face was deadly pale, and that she was panting for breath, as if she had vainly striven to wrest her hand from that of Claude Leveredge, who was standing beside her, with his hat pushed back from his brow, and his eyes shining defiantly from under his meeting brows. His cigar was smoldering at his feet, and he was muttering between his teeth: "Don't attempt to move, La Guerita! Be silent; how could you explain your appearance here?"

"Let me go! I know not what evil chance brought me here?" cried La Guerita, passionately.

"Don't say an evil chance," said Leveredge, gently; "the chance will lead only to good, if you will listen to me."

"Let go my hand!" she cried, fiercely.

"No, no!" he returned; "I am determined to speak to you."

"Speak, then! For Heaven's sake speak, and let me go!"

Before she could divine his intention he seized her other hand, and, bending down, looked full in her face, as he said: "La Guerita, I thank God that I can hold your hand once more."

"Ah, you thought me dead?"

"How could I think otherwise?" he returned; "how could I dream you were here? Oh, La Guerita, I thought I should have gone mad when I heard that you had killed yourself."

"Did Fabean believe that?" she asked, in a faltering voice.

"I believe so. They traced you as far as New York; then, when no more was to be discovered, was it unnatural for them to suppose that the waters of the bay covered you? I knew nothing of it until I went to Ellisville, two months ago, intending, if you lived, to see you and tell you how terribly Harold's death affected me. Good God, La Guerita, I never meant to kill him; I swear that I did not."

He paused, but La Guerita made no reply; and he presently continued: "I went to Ellisville, and put up at a quiet hotel, where I was not known, and late in the evening, before, however, asking any questions, I strolled over to Enola. Everything was in perfect order. There was no appearance of desolation either about the house or grounds, and yet all seemed strangely still. I noticed that the doors and windows were shut, and as I passed through the garden I asked a man who was watering the flowers if Mrs. DeGrey was at home. By the way he stared at me I knew that the question was a strange one for him to hear. I repeated the question, thinking you might have chang-

17

ed your residence. 'You can't have heard the news, sir!' said the man; 'you can't know that Mrs. DeGrey and her son were lost, a month after the master died?' I must have asked him some questions, though I have no idea what they were. It seemed to me that I was going mad as the man told me of your flight, and of the search made by poor Fabean and Victor for you. 'You seem all struck of a heap,' said the man, in conclusion, 'and surely 'twas a dreadful thing. She seemed crazed like, did missus, after her husband's death, and drowned the boy and herself, I make no doubt. But no body das'nt say that to the family, though they must think it themselves. I am feared that the house that they're always a airin' and dustin' for her will fall about our ears before either the widow or her child come back to claim it.'"

Miss Holmes listened entranced to her cousin's words, and her own eyes filled as she saw the tears coursing down La Guerita's white cheeks.

"I don't know how I moved from that spot, La Guerita, or reached my hotel," continued Leveredge, "but I remember that the first thing I saw on entering my room was a brace of pistols. I took them in my hand; the charges had been withdrawn—if not, upon the impulse of the moment, I should have shot myself. I believe that I was mad that night. I went down to the shore and walked up and down, cursing the hour that I was born, or upon which I first saw you. La Guerita, I had done worse than murder for you, and then—then all seemed lost!

"La Guerita, 'twas love for you

that had taken me back, not remorse, as I had fancied. Ah, you should have been my wife! You know it! you know it!"

"I should have been no man's wife," she said, weeping still.

"Yes, La Guerita, you should have been mine. DeGrey was not worthy of you—I knew that from the first; but I misjudged him even then, for I thought his pride would triumph over his love, and that he would put you away from him when he knew your birth. After that, La Guerita, if indeed he did not at first, I meant by threats of public exposure to make him divorce you, and then, La Guerita, how proudly would I have elevated you to your right standard again, for I would have married you in spite of all."

La Guerita looked at him scornfully. "My husband died before he dreamed of abasing me," she said. "Claim no credit for magnanimity or knowledge of human nature either. Oh, how shallow was your plot! Harold would have protected me, have loved me, in spite of public scorn, if he had been possessed of physical strength to withstand your fatal letter. He would never have repudiated me, and if he had, do you think I should have turned to you for comfort?"

"It matters not now what I thought," returned Claude Leveredge, gloomily. "Enough that all my plans failed. I gave up all hope of them when I heard that DeGrey was dead. I would have given worlds then to have recalled what you call my fatal letter. I determined to save you, if possible, from its perusal. For some reason I had the idea that it had been placed in the library. I crept in at the window and broke open the secretary. You entered the room, and, unable to face you, I fled. You closed and barred the windows, and I walked up and down beneath them in agony, knowing that you were reading the accursed words. I would have given my life to have spared you. In the morning I heard that you were in a raging fever, and later, that you could not live. I came South with the haste and fury of a madman—I was little else then—and finding no peace, I ordered everything to be sold and sailed for Europe, without going to Ellisville, because I thought that you were surely dead, and that it would kill me to hear it. Almost the first person I met in Liverpool was your brother Fabean. He had heard of DeGrey's death, and anxious to hear of you from any source, questioned me. I thought the very sound of your name would kill me! I wonder Fabean did not see my horror and remorse, but he was always an easy fellow and was more overcome by his own emotions than mine. I meant to go to Italy, and live in the strictest seclusion, but something took me to France instead. I threw myself into the vortex of Parisian dissipation, and for a time drowned, though I could not destroy, my agonies of passion and remorse. Then reverses came. I awoke to a sense of what I had done. I was maddened again, and although my luck returned, my stupor of mind did not, but I lost my remorse and hope arose within me. Each day my wealth increased. To leave Paris was to stamp myself a villain, but nothing could hold me back. I was posses-

sed with the idea that you lived, and I was resolved once more to see you. I took passage for New York, and thence hastened to Ellisville, where, as I have told you, I heard the news of your supposed death. I stayed in Ellisville—half mad, I think—for more than a month, haunting the places you had frequented. I kept myself aloof from every one, although there was no one there whom I really feared to meet, for Fabean had already entered the army, and Victor was with his mother in Philadelphia. They say the old lady has never recovered from the shock of your flight. I heard they were fighting here, and in utter desperation I decided to come and help the South. Not that I cared for the cause; that was nothing to me. Excitement was all I craved, and there was something that warned me from Paris, so I hastened here, swearing to lose my life in my first battle. With that resolve I entered these gates last night; that was in my heart when you entered the room and saved me. Great God! I never can describe what I felt when I saw you. I think at that moment, so great was the bliss of knowing you to be alive, that if you had been spirited away I could have been content to resign you forever; but now, La Guerita, that I have had time to think I know that but one thing will satisfy me. You must be my wife!"

Miss Holmes started in amazement. She had not dreamed he would have uttered those words. She could scarcely repress an exclamation as she saw him bend a searching glance on La Guerita, and entreat her to answer him. But she would neither look up nor answer him, and he almost whispered : "I want you to think of it. It is your only chance for freedom, and you must be free."

"Not at that price," she answered, proudly.

"You will remember that DeGrey was weak and my temptation great," he said, imploringly.

"Yes, I will remember that," she answered, bitterly.

"And that I never meant it to fall so hard upon DeGrey."

"Yes, I will remember that also. I will remember that you meant the greatest insult and the greatest agony to fall upon *me*."

"And the greatest triumph," he returned eagerly ; "the greatest triumph, too ! "

"Was it for that you attempted to abduct my boy ? " she demanded, as if struck by a sudden thought ; "did you intend to hold him as a hostage for me ? "

"Never mind now what I thought," he answered, surlily ; "that fellow frustrated me, and gained ample revenge for the slight harm I had done him, as if I would have hesitated to have put a dozen such out of the world if they had threatened, however innocently, interference with my plans."

"How did he do that ? "

"'Tis not worth explaining now, but listen well while I tell you that your freedom and that of your son both depend upon your becoming my wife, and returning to the position you have forfeited."

"I care not for that ! "

"Perhaps not, but you hate these bonds."

"I do hate them ! " she cried, passionately ; "I hate them as the proofs of sin and madness. But for you, I believe they would have fallen from me to-day. It was by your influence that Norton Holmes denied my prayer."

"I don't deny it," he answered, quietly ; "it was through my influence. But believe me my object was as much a desire to save you from the shame that must attend your return to Ellisville as to keep you near me, though what man would willingly lose sight of the woman he loves ? La Guerita, think you that after your wild, almost incomprehensible, conduct, you will be received as a sane person in Ellisville ? Your best friends will have to shut their eyes to avoid beholding either sin or madness, and the thousand tongues of slander will blazon abroad your story, and tell how your retreat in sorrow was the home of your former lover. I know that a mad desire to fly from all persons and places that you had known in your happiness, that could scorn you in your shame, actuated you in your flight, and also a wild thought that you would confront and denounce the authors of your misery. Unfortunately for you, your mother alone remained. Poor uncle Acton would have saved you if he had lived. He would have told you that it was for him to make atonement, and would have sent you back to freedom, possibly to quiet happiness. But it is too late for that now. You cannot, dare not, return to Ellisville. La Guerita, dare you face the court that would decree you worse than mad— vile, depraved ? "

"Say no more," cried La Guerita, warningly. "I will hear no more ; I will not even think of what you have already said." But the trembling of her lips as she spoke betrayed how deeply he had wounded her, and how well she knew she might find his words true.

"I will say no more," he returned, gently, "except that there is a way for you to escape all that. La Guerita, I love you! I will make you my wife. Come with me!"

"Never!" she cried, striving to escape from his grasp. "Let me go; for God's sake let me go!"

"Not until you promise to think of what I have said," he returned; "not until you promise to remember that your freedom, and your child's, depends upon your marriage with me."

"I know it, I know it!" she gasped; I will think of it all! Let me go!"

He released her hands and she staggered back from him in a blind, despairing way. The hedge of roses barred her back; she looked around a moment wildly, then rushed by Claude Leveredge, who with folded arms stood in the center of the plat, triumphantly regarding her. He drew a deep sigh of relief when she was gone, and presently began to move about the inclosure in a restless manner. He lighted a cigar as if from mere force of habit, throwing the burning match over the hedge of roses. It fell so close to his cousin that she started back, and the boughs rustled loudly behind her. So intently had she listened to the conversation between her cousin and La Guerita DeCuba, and had felt so much astonished thereat, that she had totally forgotten her position until aroused by her cousin's abrupt movements.

"He will be coming out directly," she said to herself, "and it will never do for him to find me here. Can I creep upon this thick grass to the further path, I wonder? Yes, he is too much absorbed in thought to notice the slight noise that I may make."

She crept slowly by the circle of roses and gained the path she sought, then rising to her feet cautiously glanced at her cousin, who was still standing within the inclosure, with his face in the direction that had been taken by La Guerita. Following her first impulse Miss Holmes turned into another path, and by a circuitous route reached the cabin.

She stood for a moment upon the steps before knocking at the door, and she heard a cry of passionate despair:

"Oh, if I had but one friend to help me! But one friend, my God!"

Miss Holmes threw open the door and rushed in, crying: "Oh, Rita, you have a friend! You have, indeed!"

La Guerita looked at her in amazement that for a moment destroyed all other emotions, while Miss Holmes threw her arms around her and burst into tears.

She comprehended all then, and her amazement was changed to joy too deep for words. She bowed her head on the shoulder of her mistress—they wept together.

"There, there, don't let us cry," said Miss Holmes, at last, in her usual decisive manner. "Try to compose yourself and tell me your sad story. I have heard it all before, but I could not believe it until to-night. And just think how, in consequence, I have persecuted you. How could you bear it so calmly?"

"I don't know," said La Guerita, "except because all my powers of resistance were gone. But, Miss Adela, don't reproach yourself with unkindness toward me. That first awoke some of my olden spirit, and aroused me from the almost idiotic state in which I entered Holmsford. Indeed, Miss Adela, I thank you for even arousing my resentment."

"Don't thank me," cried Miss Holmes, impulsively, "for I acted only from the most despicable motives. I don't think I ever was ashamed of myself in my life before, but I am so most thoroughly now."

"Oh, don't say that, Miss Adela."

"I must say so. I am thoroughly humbled. I have prided myself upon my judgment all my life, and now I must own myself at fault in every particular. Why, Rita, I have believed you the most designing and the basest of women, simply because I could not understand the agony of grief and shame that seized upon your shrinking soul."

"Miss Adela how could you understand it? I myself can scarcely now understand how I was led to the maddest of deeds—self-enslavement. You have heard my tale, you say, but it has never been but partly told. You shall hear it all. Had you heard it from my own lips at first you would have known me true."

"Don't try to excuse my blindness," exclaimed Miss Holmes. "It was willful, purely willful! Even aunt Matilda believed the tale Asenith Bray told her, but I could not, would not understand. I could not comprehend why you should come here.

I learned that by one word from Claude to-night, and in five minutes I learned the whole plot from beginning to end."

"God is indeed good to me!" exclaimed La Guerita, joyfully. "Ah, Miss Adela, how blessed I was that you were near to hear the conversation, for if ever I needed a friend it is at present."

"And you shall have one," returned Miss Holmes, emphatically; "you shall see, La Guerita, that I can love as firmly as I can hate, and that I will serve you a thousand times more readily than I have persecuted you. It is well for me that you are in trouble, La Guerita, for if I was not sure of being able to compensate, in part, at least, for the pain I have given you, I should be ashamed to look in a mirror, or own the face it reflects."

La Guerita smiled, and Miss Holmes continued: "I am going away now; if I stay longer my absence will be noticed, and Claude must on no account suspect that I am your ally. Do you put Harry to bed, and when he is asleep I will steal an opportunity to come and hear your sad story. You will trust me with it, will you not?"

"I will tell you everything," returned La Guerita, readily, yet in a voice of deep emotion, "and although I have sinned I hope you will find excuse for me, as I hope also will He whom I cursed in my madness."

Miss Holmes listened with a grave and pitying face, and then unbolted the door and passed into the garden, leaving La Guerita to pour forth her gratitude and joy to Him who alone could fathom their depths.

Miss Holmes joined the group

upon the piazza but a few moments after Mr. Leveredge returned from his walk.

"Have you been in the garden?" he asked, in a voice of some apprehension.

"Yes," she returned, carelessly; "I went to look for you. Your old uncle George is bed-ridden, but has not forgotten you, and I intended to ask you to go with me to see him."

"I suppose it is too late now; I'll go to-morrow," he returned; but I fear you did'nt look for me very closely, though that garden of yours is a place to get lost in. By the way, Adela, I have some choice foreign seeds for you."

Thank you, Claude, though I really have but little time for gardening now. Papa, do you know Mr. Gordon says the war is going to last long enough to make it necessary for me to learn to spin and weave?"

"I wonder if he supposes you will ever wear homespun?" asked her cousin, laughingly.

"Some of the wealthiest ladies in the country are already doing so," said Mr. Holmes.

"Yes, from principle," said Miss Matilda; "like the graduates at Foustville last week, looking like perfect 'guys,' in their checks. I asked them how they happened to trim them with Yankee buttons, and have them sewed with Yankee thread."

Claude laughed, and then said, gravely: "Good heavens, what changes a few short months have wrought!"

"Ah, yes, yes!" acquiesced Mr. Holmes, and then began a conversation with his wife upon the changes which had taken place in the neighborhood since the war. His nephew paced the piazza, apparently deeply interested in the conversation, but saying but little, while Miss Holmes listlessly watched him. At last she arose, said "Good-night!" and entered the house. Each accepted this as a signal to retire; and at an unusually early hour all left the piazza.

It was not, however, until nearly two hours later that the light disappeared from Claude Leveredge's window, and that his cousin felt it safe to venture to La Guerita's cabin.

Then, throwing on a dark dressing-gown, she glided softly through the house and across the garden. She found La Guerita sitting at the door, and after exchanging a word of greeting they entered the room together, and sat down in the wide bar of moonlight that lay across the floor. There, half kneeling before Miss Holmes, La Guerita told her tale.

It was soon told; but not so soon were Adela's tears dried. She said but little, save to express her sorrow and remorse. "How you must have loved him!" she exclaimed, when La Guerita showed her the portrait of her husband. "Ah! La Guerita, I can understand your love, though I still cannot the madness that followed it; for, my poor child, it is strange you did not remember that the accident of birth could in no way blacken your fair name."

"Oh, it was terrible! terrible!" murmured La Guerita; "think of the power that it gave your cousin over me; that it gives him now."

"It gave him not an atom!" cried Miss Holmes, excitedly; "but now —now, that you are a slave, it gives him every power. How shall we wrest it from him?" Oh, Heaven, how can we save you?"

"Oh, if my brother were here!" sighed La Guerita.

"I do not not see that his presence would be of the slightest use at present. He is of the proscribed race himself. The moment he set foot upon the soil of North Carolina, Claude would declare him a slave, and the State would claim him as such."

"Impossible!" exclaimed La Guerita, in a tone of such surprise that Miss Holmes hastened to explain.

"My father told me," she said, "when he consented to become your master, that your residence in a free State alone gave you freedom, and that when you returned to North Carolina the State would have claimed you had he not taken you under his protection."

"Then Mr. Holmes forgot to tell you that my father emancipated me by process of law, as a dozen or more of his other slaves were emancipated. Mr. Gordon holds my papers; my brother's are in my mother's hands. No will save our own could make us slaves."

Miss Holmes paced the floor in great anger and excitement. "I have been deceived altogether in this matter," she said, indignantly; "I was led to believe that my father took you from pure charity, and in order that you might be spared the ignominy of a public sale; and now I must bear the shame of knowing that he forged bonds for you."

"No, no; I did that myself," began La Guerita, but Miss Holmes impulsively interrupted her.

"Nonsense! you were a mad woman, and should have been controlled, or humanely delivered. Oh, dear, dear! I believe my whole life has been a failure; for its chief aim has been to persuade my father of the evils of slavery. I thought I had partly succeeded, and I hated you as much for thwarting my abolition plans—for declaring slavery a thing to be desired—as I did for the wicked plot I believed you engaged in. I see now that I was wrong in supposing that I had weakened in any degree my father's pro-slavery opinions; and even if Claude Leveredge had not come, I believe he would still, at your cost, have maintained his principles. It is useless to hope to move him, with Mr. Gordon and Claude both urging him on. You must depend upon God alone to set you free."

"I do!" said La Guerita, fervently; "and, oh, Miss Adela, I know that He who has given me such a friend to-night will do still more."

Miss Holmes was silent for some minutes. "You have many friends," she said, at length; "many you have not mentioned to me by name. The one that rescued Harry from Claude, for instance; besides your brother, and Victor DeGrey, and Prof. Harleigh. 'Tis a pity that your brother must be told all, poor fellow!"

"Ah, poor Fabean!" sighed La Guerita; "rather than he should suffer as I have done, I would die in bondage, were it not for my boy."

"But he must know all," said Miss Holmes, decisively, "and the sooner he does so the better. He might possibly gain entrance to the

State and effect your release now; but if there is delay, even that slight chance may be lost. It is worth trying for, at any rate. You must write to him."

"But I doubt if I could send a letter through the post-office," said La Guerita, doubtfully.

"Of course you could not," said Miss Holmes; "your letter would never pass the public office. But I have a friend at Norfolk, in charge of one of the flag-of-truce boats, who has offered to pass any letters for me. For once I will trouble him. Write your letter to-morrow, and I will forward it, and we will pray God speed it on its way."

"How can I thank you?" cried La Guerita, in a transport of gratitude and delight; "you have smoothed all my difficulties away in one sentence. I feel already free!"

"Do not be too sanguine," said Miss Holmes, smiling gravely; "this is but our first effort; it may require many to accomplish our object."

"Oh, I am full of hope!" cried La Guerita; "you have strengthened me for the contest, Miss Adela. With God's help I shall be able to resist Claude Leveredge until success comes."

She bent down suddenly and kissed her sleeping child. "See how beautiful he is!" she exclaimed, exultantly; "oh, how proud they will be of him. It seems to me now a marvel that his sweet face did not deter me from my act of madness."

"Be calm," said Miss Holmes, warningly. "Go to bed now and try to sleep like a rational creature. You must husband your strength. What would become of you and

your child if you were to allow your excitement to overcome you now. Write your letter to-morrow, and give it to me; but be careful neither to concentrate your mind upon your hazardous position, or to show, by your manner, that aught has occurred to lessen its dangers. Good night!"

She left the cabin in her usual abrupt manner, but stepped back to say: "You must remember that I am a secret ally. It would injure your cause beyond measure if any one should suspect that I have espoused it. Aunt Matilda likes you merely because she knew of my aversion. Unless you wish to bear the sharpness of her tongue, you must endure mine still."

"I can bear anything from you," returned La Guerita, lightly.

"There is a light in Claude's room," said Miss Holmes; "what in the world can he be doing at this time of night? His nerves are, probably, in a disturbed state. I wonder how long it will take him to quiet them?"

It seemed to Miss Holmes and La Guerita an hour or more, as they stood in the cabin door watching for the light to disappear. Once Miss Holmes laughed, softly, and then said:

"I cannot help laughing, although, indeed, poor child, I feel it a sin to draw any amusement from your sad tale—but I cannot help smiling, when I think how ridiculous Claude must have looked when that brave young man forced him to drop your boy upon the road. Aunt Matilda would compare him to the hawk that was glad to escape yesterday from an enraged hen, leaving his prey behind.

18

Do you know, I once used to look upon Claude as a superior being— one of those grand creatures, that one reads of in novels, to whom all manner of eccentricities seem quite proper. I suppose that was because he was dark and somewhat sullen, and much given to quoting choice scraps of poetry on occasions when others would find it difficult to express themselves in the plainest prose. Altogether, he used to bewilder me."

"And me, also," returned La Guerita; "his influence was, indeed, unlimited over me, until he went to Europe. It seemed a species of mesmerism. He caused me to act, without leaving me power to exercise any will of my own."

Miss Holmes mused for some moments, saying, at last: "What a strange story you have told me. Do you know how it would end in a novel? You would rebel against, and strive with, and weep over, this strange spirit, and end in discovering that you had always loved him."

La Guerita turned pale, but said: "That with me is impossible, for I have loved another. I am a widow, not a romantic maiden. I am the widow of the man he murdered— the mother of the child he made an orphan, and my work is to protect him; not to strive for the life or the soul of Claude Leveredge."

Miss Holmes strove to soothe her, grieved, yet re-assured by her words; for through all she had not been able to rid herself of the fear that there might be some spark of love for her cousin smoldering in the depths of the woman's insulted soul; but then she was satisfied.

"I am getting dreadfully sleepy," she said; "I wish Claude was. Ah, there goes the light at last. Now for my run home!"

She glided swiftly across the garden, and La Guerita soon learned that she had safely gained her room, by the light that for a moment illumined its windows. "God bless her!" she whispered, softly; "God bless her noble heart!"

CHAPTER XXV.

"The mechanic who would perfect his work must first sharpen his tools."
Confucius.

THE letters to Fabean and Victor DeGrey were not completed until late the following night, for though her tale could be told in a few words, it was difficult for La Guerita to choose them so as to express clearly why she entered into slavery, and the necessity which existed for her immediate release therefrom. At last the task was completed; the letters were addressed and under cover to the officer at Norfolk dispatched on their way, and then, as Miss Holmes said, nothing more could be done but to await the result patiently.

This proved more easy than La Guerita at first supposed possible, for after the interview in the garden Claude Leveredge refrained from intruding himself upon her, though he usually passed each morning at the school-room window to chat a few minutes with the children. True, the words that he then spoke with apparent carelessness were often full of significance to her, but in her strong hope of speedy succor she bore all his covert prayers and threatenings with an equanimity that equally surprised and baffled him.

Still, with all her faith, the suspense each day grew harder to bear. Fears would enter her mind that the letters might fail to reach their destination, that her brother might delay in coming, or that in indignation at her conduct her friends might suffer her to remain in the position she had chosen, or might even choose to let her and her child die in slavery rather than blazon her history abroad and declare her origin. These last thoughts she dismissed as insulting to the noble heart of her brother, yet they would return, and they haunted her with terrible pertinacity and filled her soul with terror as she saw that Claude Leveredge had no idea of giving up his object, or even of leaving Holmsford.

A few days after his arrival there he spoke of refitting his own house.

" Indeed, Claude, you should do no such thing," said his uncle. " I suppose you will go into the army as soon as you decide upon which branch of the service will best suit you?"

"Oh, of course," he replied, carelessly.

"Then what is the use of fitting up a house that you are not going to live in? It would be a different thing if you had a wife to leave in it. No, no; save your money for the war. It will be sure to be needed, and you will be able to do far more good with it than by buying furniture and servants at the present ruinous prices. You know you are always welcome here."

"Indeed, yes," exclaimed Mrs. Holmes. " It would be quite delightful to have you here on a furlough if you should be wounded or anything, you know ! "

" Delightful ! " echoed Claude, laughing, and after that it was generally understood that his house was to remain in a dismantled state until after the war, and that he was immediately to enter the army.

But though enlistment was in active progress throughout the country, and though Claude Leveredge appeared most deeply interested in the politics of the day, he made no movement to join the army, although it required infinite tact not to do so and still retain his reputation for loyalty and bravery. But although his conduct gave great dissatisfaction, he managed still to retain the faith of his friends and the community at large, taking no notice of any hints or inuendoes, but spending his time very quietly in riding over his uncle's plantation and his own few acres, and in the perusal of the papers.

He was engaged in the latter occupation one afternoon about six weeks after his return to Holmsford, when Miss Matilda approached the piazza upon which he was sitting, carrying in her hand a little chicken, upon which she was looking with great solicitude.

" What is the matter, aunt Matilda?" he asked.

"Matter enough, I should think !" she returned, spitefully ; "that outrageous old gobbler, General McClellan has been beatin' Dixie again. I declare the poor thing can never have a bit of peace ! "

" And what, may I inquire, bears the honorable title of Dixie?" inquired, Claude, with mock gravity.

"Why this chicken does!" replied Miss Matilda. "He broke his leg nearly a month ago; you see now it is all twisted, and turned straight out from his body."

"Why didn't you have it killed, aunt Matilda?"

"Killed? Well that is just what might be expected of you, Claude. You never did have the least idea of economy. Why the poor creature wasn't nigh big enough to eat, and so I told them all the time. I do believe if it wasn't for me Norton Holmes would be a pauper in six months. Law me, there's chickens enough die in this place without having them willfully killed just for a broken leg."

"But I don't see what use the creature will ever be," said Claude; "it will surely never grow any more."

"That is just what all the rest of them said; but I put his leg in splints, though the creetur is always a knocking them off, and I said that if he never grew big enough to be eaten, he would make a first-rate Confederate gauge."

"Confederate gauge!" ejaculated Claude, much to Miss Matilda's indignation, bursting into a hearty laugh. "What in the world do you mean by that?"

"Just what I say," she responded, tartly; "I tied his leg in splints and called him Dixie, and I just watch him close and when I see him kick his splints off and droop down, I say to myself, 'You stand a mighty poor chance, Confederacy;' but when his splints are on all right, and he fights for his corn with the best of them, I say, 'Ah, ah, United States, you had better be lookin' out for your laurels now!'"

"Well, well, if that isn't a funny idea," laughed Claude; "and how is Dixie getting on now, aunt Matilda?"

"Mighty bad," she returned, curtly; "all the splints off his leg and one eye pecked out."

"Illustrative of to-day's news," commented Claude. "The C. A. has met a repulse at Harper's Ferry; rallied again, however—it will be proved to the people a victory next. Dixie has got his splints on again, I see."

"Yes," retorted Miss Matilda, "and his spurs are growing, too. I heard Will. Russell say the other day that some folks would let their's grow rusty from want of use."

"I shouldn't wonder," returned Claude, indifferently; "it is still too warm to ride much."

"You look like a delicate young man, Claude," said Miss Matilda, ironically; "I reckon you're something like George Ware, eh? When they wanted him to enlist, the poor fellow was suddenly seized with rheumatism in his back. He suffered powerfully; none of the doctors could do him a bit of good. I sent him a small, thin sheet of iron, and told him 'twas mighty good for rheumatism, and if he would apply it to the part affected he would be relieved immediately, and be in no danger from bullets either. Now, you'd hardly believe that the young man didn't appreciate my kindness for a moment, but enlisted the next day, like a fool. I wonder now if he thinks that there's a single chance of that poor, weak chicken maintaining an independent existence?"

"Probably he has not the honor of an acquaintance with the illustrious fowl," returned Claude ; "but, by speaking of George Ware, you remind me that his cousin John has taken arms on the other side. He joined a New York regiment just as I left there."

"He did, eh ?" cried the old lady, sharply ; "and a pretty fellow he must be to fight against his own relations. I always did say he was a triflin', no-account creetur."

Claude laughed, saying : "You are the first neutral person I have met yet, aunt ; you condemn both George and John. Now, tell me, which side do you like best ?"

"One's just as bad as the other," she returned, excitedly ; "I can't abide either abolitionists or secessionists. What do they mean by making such a commotion in the country ? But I've seen this trouble comin' in for a long, long time ; I said 'twould come when I saw the first locomotive tearin' and snortin' through the State. I told 'em it looked like the old Harry, and would be doing his work before long."

"Why, I don't see what the railway can have to do with the war !" said Claude, in some surprise.

"It's just had everything to do with it," retorted Miss Matilda. "People weren't careening all over the country before that ; abolitionists weren't a comin' here preachin' their doctrines and makin' the slaves unhappy ; and secessionists weren't a scootin' North with their's. I'll tell you, I'd just like to have a line stretched from Canada to the Gulf of Mexico, and have those fellows strung up, one by one."

"I think it would be an excellent plan of disposing of them," acquiesced Claude ; "but I should think it would hardly do for you to make such remarks publicly."

"I say what I like publicly," she returned, "and I would just like to see anybody try to stop me from doing it. Ain't such things as one constantly sees and hears enough to make a saint talk ? Ah, me ! what a pity it is we can't go back to good old days, when I was a girl. Folks didn't used to talk about cutting each other's throats for a mere difference in opinion then ; and when they went to bed at night they expected to wake up and find themselves in the same place in the morning. But, for my part, I never open my eyes and tell Roxy to light a fire or a candle without waiting a few minutes first to see whether I haven't been spirited off to a place where it wouldn't be allowed."

"Or needed," suggested Claude.

Miss Matilda glanced at him suspiciously, but found no latent meaning in his smile, and she continued : "Speakin' of Roxy, just puts me in mind that I've got her to punish yet, for hiding away that little wretch of Rita's from me yesterday. I just can't abide that child ; and there's Adela makes me wild, a pettin' and fussin' over him all the time."

"Yes," said Claude, carelessly, "he and his mother are great favorites of Addie's."

"No—Rita isn't," said Miss Matilda, decisively.

"Oh, now, Aunt Matilda, I know you are not deceived ; you know well enough that Rita is a favorite of Adela's," returned Claude, flatteringly. Not that he believed one word of what he was saying, but because he wished Miss Matilda to do so. "Of course, you have noticed how often Addie goes to Rita's cabin, and that she has been dressing her in the prettiest calicoes and most delicate lawns of late—and she has looked more beautiful than ever," he added, *sotto voce.*

"So she has!" said Miss Matilda, suspiciously. "Um! um! I guess she learned more than I did six weeks ago. So, so; that's the reason I haven't seen her doing one stitch of sewing for weeks past. Well, its plain enough she has won that stupid, kind-hearted Adela over."

"Well, I don't see why she shouldn't," said Claude; "she was always well enough in her way."

"And a nice way that must have been," said Miss Matilda, in virtuous indignation; "I always did think that Rita the laziest and craftiest creetur in the world. What in the world Norton can see in her I can't imagine."

Claude Leveredge smoked his cigar, complacently, making no remarks, but watching with great satisfaction the effect of his few words.

"There goes Roxy now to sweep out her school-room," continued Miss Matilda, spitefully; "I always said she ought to be made to do it herself, and she shall, too. Here, you Roxy, tell Rita I want her."

Claude Leveredge opened his lips to countermand the order, but paused, anxious to witness the scene that must ensue, and thinking it would certainly turn to his advantage. He sank back in his chair, and quietly smoked his cigar, while Roxy hastened upon her errand.

In a short time La Guerita obeyed Miss Matilda's summons, appearing, with down-cast eyes before the old lady and her dreaded companion.

"I've just sent for you, Rita," said she, slowly, "to tell you that I am not a goin' to have you trifflin' around in this way any longer. If there's anything in this world that I hate it's a lazy white nigger, and hereafter I'm not a going to have my girl a waitin' on you, and you'll have to sweep your school-room yourself."

La Guerita was so thoroughly stunned by this attack, from one who had thitherto stood her friend, and by the fact that she was by it so degraded, ruthlessly degraded, in the presence of her enemy, that she could find no words in which to reply. She flushed to the temples, then turned deadly white, and bursting into tears, hurried from the spot.

Claude Leveredge arose and flung his cigar away, looking after her with a curious mingling of pain and triumph.

"I guess I have let her know that she is to have one mistress here at least," said Miss Matilda, complacently.

"I'd like to break your neck," muttered Claude, regaining his composure with an effort, and lighting another cigar, while he seated himself with an air of attention as she continued:

"I just haven't got a particle of patience with those white niggers. Niggers used to be black in my day; and even then they weren't worth fighting about. I do think, sometimes, when I hear folks talkin' and vowin' they won't give up their precious slaves, that they would be glad enough to do it if they were all like ours—always flouring their tongues and makin' believe sick, or something. My goodness, any one would think that a nation of idiots would know better than to fight about them."

"But, you know, both parties contend that they are not fighting about them," said Claude.

"Oh, they can contend and pretend what they please, I should think I ought to know what they are fightin' for!" returned Miss Matilda, disdainfully; "I've watched them long enough. The Southerners were always as jealous and suspicious as a half-jilted lover; and the Yankees are just like a dog in the manger— an uncommonly surly dog, too— they won't take the niggers themselves, or let any one else have them."

Claude laughed, and said: "I suppose, aunt, as you think the abolitionists such terrible fellows, you will go to the grand meeting at Foustville next week: although I scarcely think it will be safe for you to do so."

"Safe or not, I'm going," she retorted. "There, just look at Dixie! Doesn't he balance himself beautifully on one leg? It's a pity I can't make the other one stay down; it's always getting in the way, from its horizontal position—catches in the bushes and sich and trips him up. The creetur forgets how much room he needs, just as the girls used to when they first began to wear crinoline."

Claude looked at the wretched fowl, as it hopped painfully away, with a glance of mingled pity and amusement. "It is a good thing Gordon is not here," he said, "for I fear he would greatly disparage your gauge of his pet Confederacy."

"I should like to hear him attempt it," she exclaimed, defiantly; "what does Mr. Gordon know of the Confederacy, I wonder? He simply imagines it to be a place that should be peopled with blacks, and ruled over by himself. You'll see if he don't intimate as much in his speech on Monday; though if he could find anything new to say about the 'divine institution,' he'd sell his soul to do it."

"That is so!" exclaimed Leveredge, suddenly starting to his feet and pacing the piazza in great agitation.

"Yes," continued Miss Matilda, "that speech will be slavery! slavery! slavery! from beginning to end. He will give a history of its divine origin, and prove that the first thing that Adam did when he left the Garden of Eden was to take a trip into Africa and capture a negro, that he might eat his bread by the sweat of the slave's brow, in the same gentle, manly manner that is practiced at the present time."

"You seem to know the whole ground that Gordon travels over," said Leveredge, laughing.

"To be sure I do, for he's been walking up and down the same little patch for thirty years or more, and as he has never seen anything on it but cotton and niggers he thinks nothing else can flourish there or anywhere else."

"It is very natural that he should think well of slavery," said Leveredge, "as by it he has in a great measure raised himself to his present position. But, indeed, I think he is crazy on the subject. It was he who persuaded Rita to enter into bonds, was it not?"

"I'm sure I don't know," replied Miss Matilda, in a dissatisfied tone. "Nobody ever tells me anything. They pretended when she first came here that she had been a slave all her life, but I recognized her the moment I saw her, and so did you."

"Of course," replied Leveredge, coolly; "I used to go to school with her. Uncle Acton asked me to look after her a little, and I did so, but it led to unpleasant results."

"I've been watchin' her for some time," began Miss Matilda, in virtuous indignation; "I've been suspecting as much of her for a long time. There's no mistake that still waters do run deep. Well, well, I guess she won't get much chance to deceive anybody here, though I don't know what would become of Norton Holmes if I wasn't here to look after his interests!"

"And I must not forget that I thought of you when I was in Paris," exclaimed Leveredge, entering the house, and presently reappearing with a dress pattern of heavy black silk upon his arm, which he had purchased a few days before. "There, aunt, I hope you will consent to wear that for the sake of the giver."

Miss Matilda was filled with exstacy. Claude had reckoned well upon her great love of dress, and by this timely gift had insured her friendship as long as he could keep up her anger toward La Guerita. "I have got her safely enough now," he said, as she hurried away to exhibit her present, "and if I fail in my next attack it

will be no more aunt Matilda's fault than mine."

He was certainly correct, for no sooner had Miss Matilda shown her new acquisition to Mrs. Holmes, the children and the house servants, than she hastened with it to La Guerita's cabin, where she found her with Harold upon her lap, teaching him to read.

"I'd like to know who told you you might teach that child to read?" she exclaimed. "Don't you know it is against the laws of the State to teach niggers to read. Now you just put down that book and measure the breadths of this skirt, and go to work upon it right away."

La Guerita arose quickly, though her cheeks burned and her eyes flashed fiercely, and taking the silk in her hand bent on one knee to measure the breadths.

"Can't you stoop," cried Miss Matilda, sharply. "What do you suppose your back-bone was given you for, if it wasn't to bend it? I've been makin' up my mind for some time past to give you a good talkin' to!"

After this prelude she poured upon the astonished La Guerita such a torrent of invective and abuse that she quite forgot the source whence it came, and bent before it in dejection as great and real as if Miss Holmes herself had spoken.

CHAPTER XXVI.

"Let come what will, I mean to bear it out,
And either live with glorius victory,
Or die.
                    Shakespeare.

FOOLISH as she endeavored to persuade herself they were, La Guerita could not cast off her feelings of wounded pride and shame, and for sometime after Miss Matilda left her, sat in her cabin in a most dejected mood. Harry at last came in, saying :

"Miss Adela has come home and wants you to go to her immediately."

La Guerita obeyed the summons, but upon opening the parlor door was peremptorily ordered by Miss Holmes, who was talking with her cousin, to go up to her bedroom, "For," said she, "I have bought some new books, and intend that you shall use them instead of the miserable things the children are poring over now."

It was nearly a quarter of an hour before she ascended to her chamber. "I thought I should never be able to get away from that tiresome fellow," she said, as she carefully closed and locked the door, "and I know by your face that something unpleasant has occurred. What is it? Has Claude been talking to you?"

"He has been doing worse than that," returned La Guerita, sadly ; "he has in some way turned Miss Matilda against me," and in a few words she related the events of the afternoon.

"It is very, very annoying," exclaimed Miss Holmes. "I really think aunt Matilda must be crazy, she says and does such strange things. I positively wish we could prove her so, and send her off to the asylum at Raleigh for a time."

"Did you call at the E—— Post-Office, to-day?" asked La Guerita, in a low voice.

"Yes," answered Miss Holmes,

very gravely, "and this is what I got."

She gave La Guerita a package, and turned away. La Guerita was prepared for ill tidings, and with a trembling hand drew forth, first, her own letters to Fabean and Victor, and then a note in a strange handwriting, announcing the death of Miss Holmes' friend, and closing with polite regrets, that from the nature of the inclosed communications, the writer thought it his duty not to forward them.

La Guerita dropped the letters upon her lap, and looked upon them for some time so hopelessly, that Miss Holmes almost feared the shock had been too great for her reason.

She knew not what to do or say, but shortly La Guerita raised her head, and with a faint smile, more expressive of despair than a flood of tears would have been, said : "It is all over now, Miss Adela. There is no more hope. I don't think I shall strive any more. If it is the Lord's will that I should be a slave, it is no use for me to fight against it."

"Oh, we must not be disheartened by the failure of our first enterprise," said Miss Holmes, cheeringly, "I have no doubt we shall think of a dozen better projects before long."

But nothing that Miss Holmes could say cheered her despondent listener.

"I think I will go to my cabin and think of it alone," she said at length, and not knowing how to comfort her, Miss Holmes allowed her to depart. As she passed the parlor door, Claude Leveredge noticed her down-cast appearance, and thought, "My pretty cousin has been helping me. I think I may venture to speak to La Guerita, I may never find her in such a dejected mood again."

But it was not until late in the evening that he found the opportunity he longed for, and even then he was forced to create it. It chanced upon that evening he was engaged to attend a party with Mr. and Mrs. Holmes and his cousin, but so intent was he upon meeting La Guerita, that he determined at the last moment to forego it, and under pretense of writing important letters, which he had unfortunately till then forgotten, excused himself from going with the others, and promised to ride over an hour or two later.

His aunt disclaimed against this, but he easily silenced her, but could not so readily rid himself of the uncomfortable feeling produced by a glance from Adela's eyes, which met his own, and plainly showed she believed his excuses false.

Indeed she would even have remained at home if it had been possible, but Claude had so cleverly managed that there was nothing left but for her to go, and that without even being able to send a word of warning to La Guerita.

Claude Leveredge paced the piazza until the carriage was out of sight and hearing, then entering the house he exchanged his light coat for a black one, and putting on a black hat, strolled into the garden, and avoiding the negro cabins, kept upon shaded paths until he stood before La Guerita DeCuba's humble home.

"Incomprehensible woman," he muttered, "to exchange Enola, with freedom, for this and slavery."

He drew nearer ; so near that the whole interior of the cabin was exposed to view. Harry lay upon the bed, and his mother was sitting by his side, leaning her chin upon her thin delicate hands, and looking upon the child with an expression, that declared to the eager watcher all the horror and desolation of her thraldom.

He could have wept for her then, had he not loved her with such cruel and selfish passion.

"Oh, why will she not let me pity, and love, and shield her ?" he muttered, passionately. "Oh, why am I doomed to see—yes, to rejoice in the suffering of the only thing I love in the world ? Must she die in this horrible servitude? Will she doom herself to that ? No, no, she must save herself; she must; she shall !"

He paused no longer for thought, but entered the cabin. La Guerita started to her feet in terror and amazement, for she had supposed him gone to the party.

Claude Leveredge stood before her, and though he did not even touch her hand, he had almost irresistible power over her—she could neither move nor speak.

"La Guerita," he said, gravely, I passed your door, and saw you sitting here, with such a deep dejection upon your countenance, that I could not forbear entering. Oh, La Guerita, my love, my love, I would give my life to see you happy again—to see your life what it once was."

"That life was a flower thrown into a coffin," she said, almost unconsciously quoting the beautiful words of another.

He clasped his hand over his brow, with a gesture more expressive of sorrowful impatience than remorse.

"One flower may be gone," he said, "but the stalk can bear its life again. La Guerita, it must. Love shall awaken it, and you know that I love you!"

"Yes," she returned, scarcely knowing what she was saying.

He drew nearer, and said in that low, sweet voice which at times was his greatest charm: "And I cannot forget that I once held you in these arms, and you sobbed forth that you loved me—that you would be my wife."

He paused; for to his great surprise she had sunk into a chair, and was weeping bitterly.

"You remember it?" he whispered at length, "you loved me then."

"Oh, Claude, Claude," she exclaimed, wildly, "I thought so then. Oh, leave me, leave me, I am so wretched."

For a moment he stood spellbound as his name burst from her lips, then springing forward he knelt before her, drawing her hands down from her face, and covering them with passionate kisses. "Oh, my love, my love, he cried, "you have then forgiven me? You will let me make your happiness, as I once destroyed it?"

La Guerita seemed for a moment paralyzed. Her brain whirled. "He has mistaken me!" she thought. "But he loves me: he will save my child. Oh, Heaven help me, I believe I am going mad. Oh, Harold, Harold, Harold!"

She sank back in her chair quite powerless, almost senseless, while Claude Leveredge still knelt at her feet. If he had left her then, if he had trusted to the sense of honor which would have controlled her later thoughts, she might never have had power to undeceive him. But he cried:

"Remember, love, that I did not mean to injure Harold DeGrey. I did not think to attain this happiness only by his death."

She sprang to her feet. "This happiness," she cried. "Good God, what have I done? Leave me. I am a miserable slave, but never will I be freed by the hand of my husband's murderer. Never, never!"

He arose and grasped her arm. "What do you mean?" he cried, hoarsely. "Are you mad? Dare you play me false a second time?"

"I cannot be false," she returned; "I have never loved you. I know not what spirit tempted me a moment since, but I tell you now, Claude Leveredge, I would rather die a slave than be your wife."

He made no answer. Great as had been the shock to him, he determined to keep his composure, remembering what high stakes he had often sacrificed by ungovernable excitement. He sat down upon the bed, and toyed with the long, dark locks of the sleeping child. La Guerita shuddered as she saw him. Presently he looked up, and said in a voice of inexpressible sadness:

"You have doomed him! You will not marry me, and by those words have cast bonds as strong as death upon this innocent child. I speak not of you, but of Harold De-Grey's child, the scion of a noble race enslaved forever."

She knew that he was acting a part, yet she found it almost impossible to withstand the emotions he excited, until she thought and said : " Adela Holmes loves him."

"But Adela Holmes is not his mistress," returned Leveredge, impressively, adding in a voice as inexorable as Fate, "but I will be his master. Do you understand me? I shall take your child from you ; he shall be my slave."

La Guerita looked at him hopelessly, appalled by the fresh threat.

"I am in earnest," he continued, remorselessly. "Think of what I offer you and your child—wealth, position, an honorable name. De-Grey himself would have scorned you ; that craven who died because the world could jeer the wife he professed to love. Yes, he would have scorned you, could he have seen you as I do now. But I—I would raise you to the highest pinnacle of honor, slave though you are."

The insult stung her, yet it cowed her too. There was silence between them for full five minutes. Leveredge seemed lost in thought. He paced the room, uttering quick and violent expletives. His passion was culminating. La Guerita saw it with horror, and strove to quiet him.

"Listen to me," she said, "and oh, I pray be merciful. If you love me—if you repent of Harold's death, and crave forgiveness—leave me. I I will not even ask your help, but only that you will leave me and my child to God's own will—whether it

be to live or die. Claude, I cannot marry you ; I feel that my perjured soul would be lost forever if I did. But indeed you have your revenge. I will humble myself even throw myself at your feet, to crave your mercy—to entreat you to spare my child."

"Fool!" he hissed, madly, "do you think to cajole me with soft words? No, no! By Heavens, if you will not be my wife, you shall be a slave ; your child shall be my slave. Have you a care for your good name —for that of your dead husband? They shall be bandied about in men's mouths as the lightest and vilest on earth. Yours will be that of the most unnatural of monsters—the woman whose passions led her to enslave her own child. La Guerita, why do you not bid me save you? Why will you not save yourself even now?"

"I cannot," she said, meekly ; "but God will save me."

"You were wiser once," he said, laughing harshly. "You said there was no God. We shall see if he will work a miracle for his new devotee. I swear to you that if I leave this room in anger, I go to ruin you."

"I cannot appease you."

He muttered an oath and strode from the cabin. She would have given worlds to have been able to call him back—to appeal for mercy once more, but the power was denied her. She sank upon the bed almost senseless from excitement, and remained there hours quite motionless, aroused at last by a bright light falling over her.

She looked up in bewilderment, and beheld Miss Holmes, still in evening dress, standing beside her.

She muttered something confusedly, but Miss Holmes said :

"Try to calm yourself. Try to tell me what has happened. Claude has been here, but what else ? "

"I cannot tell you yet," said La Guerita, in a strange, incoherent way, yet aroused by the sight of her friend's tears ; "but why are you here ? "

"I came from Mrs. Rulofson's five minutes ago. I thought mamma would never leave. Claude promised to follow us there, but did not. Oh, I know why he stayed."

La Guerita was already calmer, and gave a hurried account of what had passed.

"I suspected it, I suspected it," she cried excitedly ; "for I went into aunt Matilda's room and inquired for him as soon as I reached home. 'I believe your cousin is mad,' said she, 'for, an hour or so after you left for Miss Rulofson's, he suddenly came into the sitting room, wild with excitement, and never minded me no more than if I had been a fly buzzin' in his ears. And then he rushed out and ordered Selim, and went off on the M—— road as if pursued by furies.' "

"And did he say nothing ? " asked La Guerita, eagerly.

"Yes ; aunt Matilda said he muttered that he would see him this very night, and that he would have his revenge.' From which she thinks that there is a duel to be fought. Ah, if 'twas nothing worse that is to be done. What can it be ? What can it be ? "

"God only knows," said La Guerita, helplessly. "Oh, Miss Adela, He knows even why it is good for

me to be tortured thus. Oh, my God, my God, I am very weary."

Inexpressibly affected, Miss Holmes for the first time in her life, bent down and kissed her, saying : "Rest, my poor child, rest ; for He giveth his beloved sleep."

Then she went out, and silence brooded over Holmsford, while two hearts, in anguish, awaited the coming evil.

CHAPTER XXVII.

THE CLOUDS DARKEN.

THE next day Miss Holmes was ill, and La Guerita could neither see or hear from her, as both felt the need of circumspection, that neither aunt Matilda or any member of the family might suspect their intimacy. This illness was an additional trial to La Guerita, not only because it prevented her from seeing her friend, but because she knew it had been obtained in her service.

She could scarcely restrain her joy when Roxy entered the school-room and said that Asenith Bray was in Miss Adela's room, and wished to see her there. She went quickly and gladly, and found Miss Holmes sitting in a large easy chair, looking very pale, but not seriously ill, as she had supposed her to be.

"Oh, it has been nothing worse than a bad cold on the lungs," said Miss Holmes, as she embraced her ; "just enough to remind one of the necessity of prudence."

"Thee never had much of that, Adela," said Asenith, after greeting La Guerita, who exclaimed :

"It is I who am to blame for this. It was not the midnight ride, but the visit to my cabin that prostrated you."

" I stayed in the garden too long after it," said Miss Holmes, hoarsely ; " I was so excited that I could not enter the house. I momentarily expected that Claude would come back and do something dreadful. What did happen, Rita ? I scarcely understood you that night."

La Guerita related all that had transpired. Miss Holmes glanced up in momentary amazement when she heard how La Guerita had been tempted to buy her liberty even at Claude Leveredge's own price.

" Do not blame her, Adela," said Asenith, gently, noticing the upbraiding glance. " Thee has never been a slave ; thee can little imagine how great a boon is freedom. But, La Guerita, I came here to-day to give thee some hope. I know thee needs it. It comes from thy mother."

" My mother ! " echoed La Guerita, trembling with emotion ; " Oh, Asenith, what have you heard from her ? "

" Sit down and I will tell thee," said the Quakeress, kindly. " Thee seems weak and excitable, child ; I must stew down some herbs for thee. Last week I was in M——, and went to see thy mother. Poor soul ! she wept bitterly when we spoke of thee."

" Poor mother, she tried to save me," sighed La Guerita ; " she told me I should curse the day I entered into slavery."

" Ay, and she blessed the Lord when she heard that time had come. Thy slavery hath grieved her sorely, and greatly has she striven with the Lord to show her some way of deliverance for thee. At last she heard by

accident Will. Russell speak of thee. Something led her to believe he had known thee when free. She followed and questioned him, and at last gained thy brother's address and that of thy husband's brother. Even after that she could for a time do nothing, but thee knows she can read and write, and is of a deep and crafty nature, and hath made herself a great woman among her race. None fear to intrust their secrets to her, and many go to her for advice, especially those who meditate flight. To one of these she intrusted two letters, and gave him such instructions as enabled him to get into the Union lines in safety."

" Are you sure of that ? " interrupted La Guerita, breathlessly.

" Quite sure," said Asenith, " or I should have told thee naught of this. Thy mother hath in some way gained every assurance of his safety."

" Thank God, then I am saved ! " cried La Guerita, fervently. " Fabean will rescue me ! "

" Asenith always brings glad tidings," exclaimed Miss Holmes. " La Guerita, your faith has not been in vain."

La Guerita took the hand of the Quakeress and kissed it, being for some time too much affected to speak. " I wish I could see my mother," she said, at length ; " I have not deserved this kindness from her."

" You shall see her," said Miss Holmes, " as soon as this annoying illness leaves me. I must be careful not to expose myself so much again. I never fancied myself delicate before, but indeed of late I have been too much excited to remain strong. And not alone because of you," she added, quickly, perceiving La Guerita's eyes bent sorrowfully upon her. "And now, thank Heaven, all anxiety for you may end; we can defy Claude to do his worst."

"Oh, Fabean will surely come!" cried La Guerita, in a voice she vainly strove to render free from doubt. "He surely will not let me languish here."

"There's a gentleman down in the parlor," said Roxy, suddenly entering the room, "and Miss Myra's sent for Rita to go there right away."

La Guerita looked blankly at Asenith and Miss Holmes, both of whom looked blankly in return. "It is Fabean," was the instant and unspoken thought of each; and trembling with the joy, the hope induced, La Guerita left the room and hastened to the parlor. She paused for a moment at the door, fearing to realize her fears or destroy her hopes. Then with a mighty effort she turned the lock and passed in. She was quite blinded by her emotions; she knew she was standing before a gentleman, then suddenly realized that it was one she had never beheld before. The revulsion of feeling was too great for her to bear, and with a faint moan she fell in a swoon upon the floor.

"Most remarkable!" exclaimed the stranger, as he raised her in his arms and gazed in amazement upon her beautiful countenance. "The woman is certainly not robust, though remarkably handsome—too handsome, in fact. I am afraid she would not answer Mrs. LeGrand's purpose at all."

"Oh, my goodness!" cried Mrs. Holmes, "you don't mean to tell me that you came to *buy* her—that Nor-

ton *wants* to *sell* Rita? Do ring that bell for the servants. Oh, dear, what *should* I do with the children if she were to die?"

Miss Holmes and Asenith Bray had heard La Guerita fall, and at first supposed that their first idea was correct, but at the sound of the bell and Mrs. Holmes' incoherent speeches Asenith hurried, in much agitation, to the parlor, where she found La Guerita already regaining consciousness, and Mrs. Holmes and the servants in a state of the greatest excitement.

"To think that Rita is going to be sold," exclaimed the former. "Asenith, only think, Norton is going to sell Rita."

"Hush, hush!" exclaimed Asenith, greatly shocked; "it cannot be true. Hush, she will hear thee."

"Oh, but it is true," persisted Mrs. Holmes, following Asenith to the sofa upon which La Guerita lay. "I never should have thought it of Norton. He sent this Mr. Reeves out here to look at her this very afternoon. He wants her for a waiting maid for Mrs. LeGrand, of New Orleans. Just think of Norton selling Rita to be a waiting maid!"

"Hush, I tell thee," said the Quakeress, sternly. But it was too late; La Guerita had heard it all, and springing to her feet, the color flaming into her cheeks, she cried:

"Who dares to speak of selling me? I will die before I leave this house other than a free woman."

"I just knew she would turn this way sometime," said Mrs. Holmes, helplessly; "she'll put poison in our coffee next, no doubt. These octoroons always do."

"Be calm," said Asenith, in a low

voice, laying her hand upon La Guerita's arm, and striving to draw her
away from the startled servants and
the amazed agent.

"No !" she exclaimed, fiercely,
"I will speak ! I will declare that I
am held here in bondage against my
will—that I will die rather than yield
to another master ! Oh, Fabean !
Fabean ! "

She uttered the name of her brother
in a despairing way, strangely at variance with the defiant tone of her
former sentence. At that moment
Claude Leveredge entered the room,
greatly flushed and bespattered with
mud. He instantly approached the
agent and said :

" My uncle, Mr. Holmes, has
sent me with all speed from M——
to say that he cannot dispose of the
slave in question at the price spoken
of."

"I think I could venture to say
the price would be readily increased—
doubled, if necessary," replied the
agent, glancing admiringly at La
Guerita.

That glance infuriated Claude Leveredge, but he controlled himself
wonderfully well, as he answered,
firmly : " No money will buy her, at
least at present. But, however, that
your journey here may not be in vain,
I recommend you to call at Mr. Stan-
ley's. He has a girl of whom he
wishes to dispose who will exactly
suit your purpose."

The agent looked at La Guerita
and hesitated. Claude Leveredge's
brow darkened, yet he still restrained
his passion, and in a few moments
conducted the agent from the room.
La Guerita was too much astonished and bewildered by all that had

passed, especially by Claude's unexpected interference in her behalf, to
be able for some moments to speak
or move. She was recalled to her
senses by finding herself alone in the
room with Mrs. Holmes and Miss
Matilda, the former of whom was in
tears and the latter more voluble in
her indignation than she had ever
been in her life before.

La Guerita left the room and encountered Claude Leveredge in the
hall. He was leaning against the
door-way in a languid attitude, and
with a haggard, worn expression
which she had never seen upon his
face before. Something prompted
her to stop and look at him. He
turned toward her, saying, almost
sullenly :

"Why do you stop ? Is it to
thank me for saving you to-day ? for,
by Heaven, that was no acting. I
did save you."

" I do not doubt it," she said, sincerely, "but why did your uncle
think of selling me ? "

"Because he was either drunk or
mad," he answered, excitedly, "coward and traitor as he is to us both.
Dolores told him to-day that she had
written to your brother ; he tormented the woman till she even dared do
that ; and in his impotent wrath and
fright he encountered that agent, and
swore that he would sell you. Good
Heavens ! I could have killed him
when I heard of it ; but I thought it
wiser to hurry home, before that fellow left. He would have given any
price for you ; and you and your
child would have been hurried off to
New Orleans this very night."

"Oh, don't speak to me in that
way !" she entreated, quite broken

down by shame that it was possible for him to do so.

"You have only yourself to blame that I can do so," he said; "and you have your mother to blame for your fright this afternoon. Did you know she had written to Fabean?"

"Yes," she replied, hesitatingly.

"Ah, well! let him come! Do you think he could take you from me? No, by Heavens, he shall not!"

She looked at him calmly, but with the calmness of despair.

"I ask you for the last time to trust me," he said. "Good God, is not my love surety enough for your honor?"

"It is not in your power to marry me," she said.

He turned deadly pale, and reeled, as he attempted to stand erect before her. "Ah!" she continued, contemptuously, "that shows me that you would not."

"I would!" he exclaimed, regaining his composure; "I swear that I would. Come with me, to the North, to Europe—anywhere where I can marry you. I ask you for the last time to go with me—to go and be my wife. Remember what I saved you from this afternoon."

"Remember!" she said, "and this let me assure you, that I no longer act from passion, but from reason, and whatever comes I cannot marry you."

She left his presence slowly, and gazing after her in a wild, hopeless way, he muttered: "Then it must be; I will subdue her, even at that cost. I would have spared her; but now it must, it shall be!"

La Guerita left the house more in

wonderment than alarm. "God will send Fabean," she said, in faith, "and wherever they place me he will find me out. Even the hand of my enemy He constrains to protect me; I will not fear."

She related what had passed to Miss Holmes the following morning. "Oh, Rita! Rita!" she exclaimed, "I cannot believe in his good faith, though you, through all, do not doubt it. Remember how your simple question affected him. Indeed, I feel as if, of late, we had all grown utterly bad. My father is different from what he ever was before; Aunt Matilda, even, is more of a vixen, and Claude's worst passions are developed. I feel myself dreadfully wicked at times," she added, the tears gathering in her eyes; "but, oh, Rita, I am so lonely—so wretched!"

La Guerita remembered what she had heard concerning the private matters of Miss Holmes, on the memorable afternoon when she awoke to a full consciousness of her own abject condition; but as the subject had never been alluded to by Miss Holmes, she felt constrained to be silent concerning it, and said, cheerfully:

"Yes, I know the war worries you, but the news from the front is inspiriting to-day, Miss Adela."

"Oh, as to the war," she replied, "nothing that occurs can alter my belief as to what will be the final result; but the end seems so far off. Ah! there is a knock at the door. Unfasten my hair, or do something as an excuse to stay with me longer."

La Guerita obeyed.

"I am going to see what sort of a hair-dresser Rita will make; Annette is so clumsy," said Miss Holmes, querulously, as her mother entered the room."

"I have told you so hundreds of times," said Mrs. Holmes, looking with childish delight at her daughter's long, waving tresses; "but you never would agree with me. How becoming that blue wrapper is. Can't Claude come in to see you; he is dying to do so. Never mind if your hair is down."

"But I do mind," began Miss Holmes, when her mother opened the door and gave the invitation which had evidently been waited for in the hall, for Claude Leveredge immediately entered, and greeted his cousin with unfeigned affection, secretly wondering how La Guerita bore the indignity of being transformed into a dressing maid.

She went on with her work, apparently regardless of his presence. "I have been very uneasy about you, Adela," he said; "I was very sorry, when I heard you were ill, that I did not go to the party and insist upon your keeping yourself well wrapped during the ride home."

"Thank you. By the way, I have never heard the reason of your absence that evening—Rita, be more careful—Mrs. Rulofson was greatly disappointed."

He colored slightly beneath her glance, but answered, readily: "I presume my disappointment was greater than her's; I can't imagine how I was so stupid as to forget some most important business which I had intended to write about to a friend in Richmond, to whom I at last found it imperatively necessary to telegraph that very night."

"Oh, you were always just as careless!" exclaimed Mrs. Holmes; "indeed, you were the torment of all surrounding you when you were a boy; and yet every one liked you."

He sighed, and his aunt laughed, gaily, as she continued: "You need not grieve over your lost popularity, for the ladies were quite in despair at your absence the other evening; you make an impression wherever you go."

"So the committee said when they asked me to make a speech at Foustville, on Monday," he returned, laughing.

"Yes, and only think, Addie, Claude is really going to make a speech, and we are all going to hear him. I'm sure you will be well enough. Alfred and Rufus, and even Minna, are nearly crazy about it."

"You surely are not going to allow the children to go!" exclaimed Miss Holmes; "there will be no peace for any one else if you do."

"Oh, Rita shall go, also. Claude particularly desires them to go; don't you, Claude?"

Miss Holmes flushed. "Leave the room, Rita," she said, suddenly, scarcely able to repress a glance of intelligence, as she obeyed, filled with a vague distrust and fear. Why was she to be present when Claude Leveredge spoke in Foustville? Was it possible that he could find some means to shame or intimidate her there?

"That was quite impossible," so she said to herself a hundred times, yet still her fears remained when, hours later, she obeyed a summons to Adela's room.

"I don't know what is to be done at Foustville," said Miss Holmes, "but I will certainly be there to see. I tried in every way to induce mamma to leave you at home, but, for once, she was quite firm in resisting my whim, as she called it. Of course, Claude rallied me about it, too, or she would have yielded. After all, my first impression, that Claude meditates some step against you is wrong, and may be altogether wrong. At any rate, there is nothing left but for you to go ; and I, too, will be there, if I am even half as strong as I am now. Don't come to my room again unless I send for you ; I have a fancy that Claude is watching us."

CHAPTER XXVIII.

THE CLOUDS BURST.

THE next two days La Guerita spent alone, free from the cares of the school-room and the persecutions of Claúde Leveredge. Therefore she sighed when Monday came, and with a thousand misgivings at her heart, took her place with the children in an open carriage which was to convey them to Foustville.

Miss Holmes had not improved in health as much as she had hoped to do, but according to the determination previously expressed, she took her seat in her mother's carriage, giving as an excuse that she, like the others, must hear Claude speak.

"And so must I," ejaculated Miss Matilda, appearing in her most fantastic apparel, at the last minute. "Help me in Claude. Oh, law, you needn't lift me quite off my feet, I'm as spry as ever I was in my life."

"You'll surely get into trouble," said Claude Leveredge, who seemed at once to get in a restless and teasing mood.

"I don't care if I do," she retorted ; "but law me, I can't do worse than I did that Sunday Parson Simcox preached."

"And what did you do then?" asked Claude, leaning against the door of the carriage, while the servants brought and arranged the numerous articles Mrs. Holmes thought absolutely necessary to her comfort ; "What sort of a sermon did he give that it would excite you?"

"Oh, 'twas condensed thunder and lightnin', of course. What's-his-name never hurled such bolts of wrath against the Yankees as did Uriah on that day. Almost the first thing he said was that every man that died while fighting for the Confederacy went straight to Heaven—got a pass right through—he couldn't help bringin' in some idea of the universal darkey even then, you see. Well, some folks at that got up and left the church, but I went there to hear the whole of the sermon, and I wasn't going to let anything prevent me from doing so. Uriah was a little daunted when he saw the people go out, but immediately went on to prove his words. 'They were doing God's work,' said he, 'and will therefore gain the reward of the righteous. By arraying themselves against Abolitionists, they array themselves against the Devil, for Beelzebub was the first Abolitionist ; he took Job's servants from him.'

"Well, everybody seemed dreadfully excited, and I own I was too, or I should never have spoken right out in meetin' as I did then. 'All that's very true,' said I, 'and it strikes me he was the first Secessionist, too, for we've all read how centuries before Job was born—the Devil was kicked out of Heaven for tryin' to create a division there!'

"Well, Claude, you never saw such a commotion in your life as there was then—leastways in meetin'. All the people sprang to their feet and shouted, and laughed, and hissed; and Norton, he just pulled me out of the crowd, and put me into the carriage, and drove home like one possessed. You never did see such a time, and they say the officers at Foustville didn't get a recruit for a week afterwards."

Claude laughed, but Mrs. Holmes frowned, and shook her head, warningly, as he mounted his horse, and signaled for the carriages to proceed.

The drive to Foustville was most delightful. The road lay through six miles of pine forest, the unchanging verdure of which formed a striking contrast to the scarlet and brown leaves of the vines that clothed their tapering trunks. The greater number of the party were sorry to reach Foustville, a pleasant village, which had been chosen for the place of meeting on account of its central location, and also of the large range of "old fields" which lay at the back of the town, and formed an excellent ground for the exhibition of the county volunteers.

To this ground the carriages were driven, and the gentlemen, who were on horseback, after some difficulty, opened a passage for them, to a point but a short distance from the speaker's stand.

Never had such a crowd met in the county before; persons of all ages, sex, and color were there, striving with each other for precedence, and conversing loudly on the all engrossing subject of war.

Ubiquitous among them seemed Mr. Gordon, who hastened from one part of the field to the other with a smile or a word for every one. At length he espied the Holmsford carriages which, either by accident or design, had been placed in a most conspicuous position. This was particularly annoying to La Guerita, who, sitting in the open carriage, soon discovered herself to be the observed of all observers.

Claude Leveredge remained on horseback at the side of her carriage, talking restlessly, to the children, and noting with many conflicting emotions, the glances of admiration cast upon La Guerita. A party of gentlemen passed by, and one of them speaking more distinctly than the bustle around allowed him to suppose, said:

"Who can that beautiful creature be?"

"Zenobia," answered his companion, Will. Russell, "a queen in chains."

"Ah, a governess, you mean. What a pity," returned the other; "yet there is something queer-looking about her with all her beauty."

The young men passed out of hearing, and turning toward her with flashing eyes, Claude Leveredge said in a low voice:

"Can you bear such irony as that —a queen in chains. Can you bear the laugh that will follow the explanation of that witticism? Say no, no, before it is too late, and I will take you home."

She was sorely tempted then. She was perhaps more sensitive to ridicule than to anything else, and Will. Russell's careless words had stung her cruelly, and she doubted not that worse would come before she left that field.

"Oh," she thought, "if it were possible for me to escape it with honor. But there is not. No honor could follow a marriage with him. Yet anything would be better than these chains. But no, no ; not *anything !*" she added with a shudder ; "to lose my soul would be worse. No, I will not yield. I will bear any torture, but I will not yield myself to infamy."

Claude Leveredge read that determination upon her face, and turned away with a curse.

"I will not be baffled," he muttered, as he dismounted, and walked rapidly to the speakers' stand. "I love her, and my love is deeper and more terrible than my strongest hatred. I cannot have mercy. I will kill her, or yet call her mine."

The exercises of the day were soon commenced. The County Guard and Volunteers performed a variety of of evolutions which were greatly admired and vociferously applauded by the vast assemblage. Then speeches were made by several gentlemen, during which Claude Leveredge and Mr. Gordon stood in earnest conversation near the Holmsford carriage.

"Your name will be called next," said the lawyer at length, as Will. Russell, in his gay captain's uniform, took his place upon the stand. "As

you have as yet done nothing, you must at least assure the people that you will. Prepare yourself, Russell will soon be finished. I prophecy that he will make a much better fighter than orator."

"All the better for the Confederacy then," returned Leveredge. "But you forget that I simply promised the committee to speak a few words after the orator of the day—the Hon. Ernest Gordon."

"I warn you he will leave you no chance," returned the lawyer, laughing ; "he intends to exhaust the subject. So speak before him—the people will expect it of you."

"They, like other sovereigns, must sometimes submit to be disappointed," replied Leveredge ; "I will speak after you to-day, or not at all. Of course, you are prepared. Go, now ; let us have a specimen of your finest oratory."

"That you shall," returned the lawyer, walking with great dignity to the platform, while his late companion took a position at the side of his aunt's carriage, and with folded arms, and gloomy brow, waited the announcement of Ernest Gordon's name.

Soon it was made, and a general movement of increased attention was visible among the vast audience as the popular lawyer stepped forward to address them. As his pro-slavery opinions were well known, it was generally supposed he would again declare and strenuously uphold them. But this, at first, seemed far from his thoughts, for he spoke of the war as a grand necessity, solely that the chivalrous South might free itself at once and forever from the encroachments

of a race of mountebanks and ped-
dlers. Then he spoke of the glorious
age that would follow the accomplishment of that feat, picturing in the
choicest terms the wealth and distinc-
tion each scion of the white race
would acquire by means of the cotton
and tobacco of the South, the triumphant result of the labor of their
slaves. From that point slavery was
his theme. He spoke of it first from
a political point of view, and successfully proved to himself and his audi-
tors that no government could be
sustained which had not the "divine
institution" as its basis.

La Guerita and Miss Holmes, in
common with the entire audience,
listened to the orator with delight.
His command of words, his extraordinary ingenuity in their application,
all tended to charm even where they
could not convince, and impressed
the excitable mind of La Guerita as
if they had held the very spirit of
truth, instead of the base and hollow
ring of falsehood.

"How will he prove the benefit of
slavery from a social and Christian
view!" she asked herself, as his intention to do so was declared. "Ah,
if he can only from those points exhibit it in a light as favorable as he
has from the political, I shall myself
be induced to bear it unmurmuringly."

Unseen by her, Claude Leveredge
was watching her with undeviating
gaze. He smiled grimly as he saw
her head bend forward in an attitude
of increased attention, and fix her
eyes intently upon the orator. He
had been speaking for more than an
hour, but not for a moment had the
attention of the audience, or his own

energy, wavered. He continued steadily and enthusiastically pointing out
the vast difference of the state of the
negro in his native country and that
enjoyed by him in the South. "There
he is naked, ignorant, barbarous," he
exclaimed ; "here he is clothed and
fed, subjected only to wholesome restrictions, and made happy by the
truths and consolations of the Christian faith. Under the protection of
a master he is free from all cares that
oppress others. Guided in his natural imbecility, he by this means be-
comes a rational creature, a blessing
to himself and the land that supports
him. Left to himself his small mind
refuses to control the mass of bone
and sinew in which it dwells, and the
semblance of man is degraded to the
useless position of a beast. A negro
left to his own resources has scarcely
even the instinct of an animal to provide food and escape from danger.
The negro was born to be a slave ; it
is a necessity of his nature to rely upon the stronger intellect of the white,
and woe to him of the superior race
who neglects and disavows this man-
ifest duty to a fellow mortal and to his
God !"

Long did he speak after this manner, adding argument upon argument, proof upon proof. Again and
again he reiterated the words : "The
instinct of the negro teaches him to
find relief from the cares and responsibilities of life in the sympathy and
protection of a master."

"And yet," at length cried a voice
from the crowd, "our slaves run away
from us."

"Ay, and return to prove my
words," said Mr. Gordon, firmly.

There was a laugh, and a shout

from some one of : "We have never seen one."

"There is one here," cried Mr. Gordon, glancing at La Guerita, who sank back in her seat in speechless terror and shame. "There is one here! She came to me more than a year ago—the most beautiful woman my eyes ever rested upon. 'I was born a slave,' she said, 'and my master freed me when I was an infant. He sent me North, and there, in ignorance of my birth I was most excellently educated, and married a wealthy and high-born gentleman. Some years after the marriage my husband discovered the secret of my birth, and died of shame and grief. I am rich, I have friends, but I can find no peace. I must cast the burden of my existence upon another. I have come here with my child to enter into slavery!'

"Friends, I reasoned, I plead with her, but in vain. A slave she would become, a slave she is here to-day—contented and happy. Yes, there she sits in the carriage of her master, Norton Holmes. She who was once the belle of Ellisville, the wife of Harold DeGrey, whom some of you knew in your school-days—there she sits, the happy slave Rita."

He attempted to say more, but his voice was drowned in shouts and applause, and he left the stand amid cries of: "Where is the woman? Where is the self-made slave?"

La Guerita heard the roar of their voices like that of the great sea-waves. She struggled and strove to rise, as if it were possible for her to flee. Her strength and senses alike deserted her, and she fell back into the arms of Miss Holmes and Claude Leveredge, who had both entered the carriage."

"You shall not touch her!" cried Miss Holmes, fiercely, as her cousin attempted to raise La Guerita in his arms. "Traitor, villain, that you are, leave this poor girl before God strikes you to the earth for your wickedness. See, she is returning to consciousness. Leave her, unless you wish to complete the work you have begun—to kill her outright!"

Claude Leveredge drew back from his cousin in consternation. He glanced at La Guerita, muttering: "I have made you feel your master to-day! I did not know I had Adela Holmes to conquer, too."

He sprang from the carriage, but turned quickly as a scream of horror from Adela, and a cry of: "She has killed herself!" reached him. He sprang again into the carriage. He caught La Guerita in his arms; a purple stream was flowing from her mouth and dying her neck and dress.

"A doctor, a doctor!" he cried; "she has broken a blood-vessel—she is dying! Oh, God, help! help!"

He wrung his hands in the helplessness of despair. Three doctors were near and hastened to the carriage. In an incredibly short time the hemorrhage was arrested, and La Guerita DeCuba slowly came back to life.

Oh, the cruel people, the soulless crowd that pressed around. Their eyes seemed piercing her like arrows of scorn, their tongues lashing her with contempt! She realized it all, and buried her face in Miss Holmes' bosom, and madly prayed to die.

But she lived—lived to give the lie to the lawyer's false words, for the people turned away pitying a slave, trying in vain to silence doubts which had never troubled their minds before.

CHAPTER XXIX.

"I falter where I firmly trod,
And falling with my weight of cares
Upon the great world's altar-stairs,
That slope thro' darkness up to God;
I stretch lame hands of faith, and grope,
And gather dust and chaff, and call
To what I feel is Lord of all,
And faintly trust the larger hope."

Tennyson.

THENCEFORWARD for many months there was almost a blank in the life of La Guerita DeCuba—a time when she hovered between life and death—sanity and madness.

For weeks she lay in her darkened room, utterly exhausted, both in body and mind, incapable of movement or thought; and during all that time Miss Holmes never left her cabin. Another, too, was there, of whom, for a long time, La Guerita took no heed, but who watched and tended her with the untiring zeal and tenderness a mother only could know.

At first they feared she would drop into a state of hopeless imbecility and speedily decline; but as time passed the strength of her corporeal and mental natures exhibited themselves, and they gained hope that her recovery was but a question of time.

Claude Leveredge was the first to seize that hope. Almost maddened as he had at first been by the effect of his cruel plot, he soon grew to look upon it as a necessary consequence, and as essential to his success. To his cousin he did not attempt to disguise his thoughts, and, meeting her in the garden one day, told her calmly he was only biding his time, but

waiting for health and sanity to be re-established ere making La Guerita his bride.

"You will not so disgrace us," she said, proudly.

"What! by marrying one of the inferior race?"

"Yes!" she answered, firmly; "that would disgrace us, while it remains impossible for you to make her your legitimate wife in any part of the world—while you must live with her in solitude—while you dare not mention your affection to any Southron but me, whom you cannot deceive."

"I would declare it before the whole world!"

"That is false!" she said, contemptuously; "I know how you have stooped to deceive my father and Mr. Gordon. Oh, Claude, Claude, may I die before I see another of my family so utterly depraved as you!"

"You give me a good character," he said; "is it, then, a sign of utter depravity to love as I love La Guerita—to live only in the hope of making her my wife?"

"Claude, I would give a fortune to know if what I heard of you last year is true."

He laughed: "I am not a fool, Adela."

"I should consider any other man in your position one. Can a man be called rational who sets his whole mind and heart—yes, risks his very soul—upon the poor aim of marrying a woman that hates him?"

"La Guerita does not hate me!" he cried, excitedly; "I will stake my life on that. Love, such as mine, must beget love again."

"Claude, don't force me to add to your other qualities that of a romantic dreamer."

Her quiet tone of contempt was most galling to him. "You shall see," he said ; "I know Le Guerita DeCuba better than you. I only wait for her to regain strength of mind and body to take her from your power. It is you, Adela Holmes, that I have been fighting against all this time. The battle would have been shorter had I known that sooner."

His cousin was terrified ; she felt that she had a desperate game to play, almost single-handed ; she felt almost powerless while her cousin remained upon the plantation ; but at last, happily for her, there came upon him so great a pressure from without that he was compelled to choose one of two alternatives—to leave the country, or to take the sword in its defense ; and, to Adela's delight, she was at last free of his dreaded presence.

The news of his departure was the first that aroused or excited La Guerita in the slightest degree. After hearing it, she seemed to rally slowly. "I was like a deer hunted down," she said, one day, "and now I feel that the dogs are held back, and breathing time is given me."

After that she took some slight notice of passing events, and lay for long hours with her eyes fixed sadly upon her mother, or upon the blessed words of her bible, which seemed then to contain the germs of divine consolation and strength.

At last there came a time when her mother bade her farewell, and returned to her own lonely home, and La Guerita once more took her place in the school-room, changed both in body and mind — in both a mere wreck of her former self. There was no trace of madness about her, but her mind seemed like that of some aged person slowly becoming blank.

Miss Holmes, with all her acuteness, did not understand this, and fortunate it was that she did not, or she would, in pity, have avoided the discussion of those subjects which alone could command her thoughts, which, as months passed, served to rally her failing senses. Two things alone sustained her through that time—fear of Claude Leveredge, and trust in God. Worldly hopes she had none, but while she was left in peace, she almost hoped to die in slavery, that her presence might not embitter the freedom of her boy.

She said something of that sometimes to Miss Holmes, entreating her that she would not compromise herself further in any attempt for her rescue, saying no more of shame would befall her in slavery, and feeling, as months passed on, and Claude Leveredge still remained away, that she could wait with patience until the gates of her prison were unbarred.

"They will be," she said, "in the Lord's good time, if not for me, at least for my child."

" 'Tis strange to see you so tranquil," said Miss Holmes, one day as she was sitting with La Guerita in her cabin. "One thing only seems to arouse you now—to fill you with your former zeal for freedom—that is, the fear of my cousin Claude."

"Yes, that cannot be overcome," replied La Guerita quickly ; I cannot forget how he has tortured me. But yet my reason tells me, I have no cause for fear. He has yielded, and war is now his only love."

Miss Holmes remembered the conversation in the garden.

"I would not be too sure of that," she said, "his duties bind him closely, no doubt, but still I am convinced he is keeping strict watch over you. His regularly conducted correspondence with Rufus is not kept up from mere love of the boy, but because of the information he unwittingly gives of you. For a time, you know, you seemed lost and childish, yet at times exhibiting passions which would utterly prevent his influencing you. Now that is passing away, you have returned to that condition in which he may hope to strive with you, as most rationally-minded men strive with rationally-minded women, and to conquer, as they usually do, laying heart and reason beneath their unbending will. You know I am a true woman, and believe in the supremacy of man. If I had been in your place, I should have yielded to my cousin long ago. As a looker-on I can scheme and advise where I should utterly fail if I was personally concerned."

La Guerita smiled, remembering what she had heard in the sitting-room months before, and how Miss Holmes had been sorely tried since by the entreaties of a later lover, to forsake that one her friends condemned as a villain and a traitor. La Guerita saw that she thought of it, too, for she began to speak of a recent battle, which had resulted in great slaughter on both sides, and ended her sentence with a flood of tears.

Miss Matilda entered the cabin at that moment, exclaiming :

"I thought I would find you here. One would think you could see enough of negro cabins without living in one half your time. You'll leave it now for awhile, I dare say, for Asenith Bray is in the house askin' for you. You'll have to speak pretty loud to make yourself heard," she added, as her niece rose and left the cabin, "for the poor old soul seems to be gettin' deafer and deafer every day." It is astonishing to see how some folks break down. Why, I'm just as spry now as ever I was in my life."

She stayed a few moments to rate La Guerita, in a sharp tone, for some imaginary offense, and then went to see after the welfare of "Dixey," who still lived with his broken leg in a horizontal position, and his entire frame drawn into the most grotesque shape ever assumed by beast or fowl.

In a short time afterwards, La Guerita saw Asenith returning to her home, and almost at the same moment Miss Holmes entered the cabin, exclaiming :

"Prepare yourself instantly for a ride to M——. Your mother is ill, and has sent for you."

"But will Mr. Holmes allow me to go ?" cried La Guerita, anxiously ; "You know he has not permitted me to leave the plantation for nearly a year."

"That is all settled," returned Miss Holmes, "I have ordered the carriage, and shall go with you."

In a short time they were on their way to M——. Many and varied were the emotions of La Guerita as she entered the town, in which three years before she had signed away her freedom.

"Oh, not there, not there," she exclaimed, when Miss Holmes directed the driver to the hotel.

"I am sorry," said Miss Holmes, after she had for a moment considered the matter, "but we really have no other place to go to. Mrs. Gordon is the only person upon whose kindness I would presume, and I suppose you would rather go to the hotel than there."

"Oh, yes, yes," said La Guerita, eagerly, adding mentally, as she strove to lay aside the fearful shame and terror of strangers that had haunted her since that dreadful scene at Foustville, "after all, I may not be recognized in this dress, and in the evening light. God support me if I am."

She needed that support, for the hall was ablaze with light, and a score of eager eyes were bent upon her as the landlord involuntarily exclaimed :

"What, have you come back? Well, well ; if you're being one of them octoroons didn't beat all. And there's the boy, too. Well I never."

"Show us to our rooms," said Miss Holmes, sternly, and startled by the unusual tone of command, the host preceded them up stairs to the very rooms occupied by La Guerita three years before.

"Oh, my God !" she thought, "if I could but recall them. Ah, if I could but place myself now where I was then ; and yet not altogether, Oh, Lord, for then I knew not thee. Then I hated the mother I have now come, in love and forgiveness, to see die !"

She would not stay at the hotel even for some slight refreshment, but taking Harold with her, hastened to her mother's cottage. The child recognized it at once, and though it seemed no different to her from a score of others, it was rendered sacred to her at once by the scene within that met her view.

The room was comfortably furnished and scrupulously clean. Upon the walls hung a few highly-colored prints, and a bright homespun carpet covered the floor, showing at once the station and taste of the occupant of the little cabin. She lay upon the bed, heedless of all that had once delighted her, her olive face contrasting painfully with the snow-white pillows which an old negress was carefully smoothing. Silently and softly La Guerita entered the cabin and approached her dying mother.

"Oh, Death, where is thy sting?" Oft thou bringest to us love sought for in vain through life. Thou broughtest it then to Dolores from the heart of her daughter. As La Guerita looked upon that death-like face, with the holy shadow of another world falling over it, she forgot the woman that had sinned, and wept for her mother.

"Thank God you are here," said the dying woman, faintly ; "thank God you are in time to see me die."

"No, rather to nurse you back to life," sobbed La Guerita. "Oh, mother, mother, you must not die when I have just begun to love you."

"'Tis better that it should be so," she whispered. "I am ignorant and have sinned. You could not love me if I lived, perhaps you will when I am dead ; and my boy, too, when he knows—my pretty, pretty boy !"

Fabean was always a child to her. For some time La Guerita wept in silence. Those tears—that natural and quiet grief—seemed to strengthen her. She felt again the bonds that hold other women to life and its duties, and that a holy one was that of smoothing a mother's pathway to the grave.

Dolores was an ardent Methodist, and at intervals poured forth her soul in snatches of hymns and prayer. All were of Heaven, of home, and rest. Rude as they were, they were to La Guerita sweet as the words of angels. Bending over her mother she said, at last :

"You are happy, then, dear mother, perfectly happy ? "

"Oh, yes, so happy and peaceful. Angels have been around me all the day. They have waited for me many, many hours, but I couldn't go without one look on you. Oh, my daughter, tell me I am forgiven."

"Dear mother, I have nothing to forgive. To God, God alone, you should appeal."

A peaceful smile overspread the face of the dying woman. She spoke no more for some moments, and then her mind seemed wandering.

"Kiss the boy," she murmured ; "kiss my little son, and tell him how I have mourned for him. When he grows to be a man he will understand and forgive me. He is like Acton ; he will have the same heart, you know."

"Oh, mother, mother," cried La Guerita, unable to restrain her emotion, "do you not remember that Fabean is now a man. Give me some message that I may give him from his mother when I am free."

"Free, free ! Oh, God, yes, I forgot. You are a slave ! " The dying woman raised herself upon the pillows with almost superhuman energy, and gazed upon her wildly. "Oh, my child, those bonds ! those bonds ! They are worse than death. And Claude—Claude Leveredge ! Oh, fly from him, fly ! for I know he ——. Oh, my God, this is—death—this—is—death ! "

She strove in vain to speak further. She clasped her daughter's hands in an agony of despair ; she struggled to utter but one word, which La Guerita knew must be of the greatest importance, but all in vain.

Rapidly the last changes came upon her. The death-rattle sounded in her throat, her eyes became fixed upon her daughter, who even in her grief was comforted when some one entered the cabin softly, and she felt instinctively that Miss Holmes was at her side.

Shortly after the dying woman became composed, and at last for some time was so still that the watchers were uncertain whether she lived or not. Then they saw the glazed eyes turned Heavenward, and, sinking upon her knees, La Guerita poured forth an impassioned prayer for the passing soul.

Colder and colder grew the hand she held, and ere long it stiffened within her grasp, and a faint, strugling sigh gave her the tidings that her mother's spirit had passed beyond the reach or necessity of prayer or psalm.

She arose then and looked with tears upon the dark and still beautiful face of the dead, and pressing a kiss upon the faintly smiling lips, repeated those words of comfort which have filled with peace many a doubting soul : "Her sins, which were many, are forgiven, for she loved much."

CHAPTER XXX.

"True friends visit us in prosperity only when invited; but in adversity they come without invitation."

Theophrastus.

THE little cabin was closed and tenantless. Dolores Holmes had found another home, and at last slept peacefully beneath the waving pines on the hill-side. Upon the day of her burial her sins had been forgotten, and the lowly friends, and the daughter who had scorned her for years, wept over her as one without guile. As she turned away from the lowly cottage, La Guerita rejoiced that there had been lamentation and mourning, for she said: "I can tell Fabean of it; it will comfort him in his shame to know that our mother was beloved."

She walked thoughtfully through the little lane, and entered the hotel. She was painfully conscious of the curious glances of all she met, and for that reason, as well as the indulgence of her sad thoughts, was glad to find herself for once truly alone. When she entered the sitting-room she found Mrs. Holmes and Harold both absent, and sitting down, meditated upon the life that had begun in that very apartment, and which, henceforth, was to be borne with one friend less on earth, but with one more, she trusted, in that heavenly throng that loved and guarded her.

The shrill scream of the railway whistle startled her at last. "Ah!" she thought, "how I used to shrink from that sound when I sat in this room waiting—imploring—my fate! How I feared it might herald the coming of Fabean or Victor to tear me from my cherished purpose.

Oh, if I could but imagine it such now, how even the vain fancy would comfort me; but, alas! my friends can gain no entrance here! I must wait—wait for the Lord's own time. But it will come; it needs *must* come. He will not leave His people in this terrible bondage! Are not their shackles already loosened? Oh, Lord, hasten the day when every yoke shall be broken, and the oppressed go free!"

In her enthusiasm she had spoken the last words aloud. "Amen!" said a voice behind her, and, turning, she beheld Miss Holmes, with face so pallid and expression so wild, that she cried, involuntarily:

"What has happened? Are you frightened? Are you ill?"

"Oh, La Guerita, help me!" she cried, excitedly; "those words you uttered assure me that you will help me to save him!"

"What do you mean?" demanded La Guerita, alarmed at Adela's incoherent words. "Who are we to save?"

"Ah! I had forgotten you know nothing of it; and yet you must have heard that I am engaged to a Northerner. Oh, La Guerita, he is here sick—wounded—a prisoner; I saw him in the cars not ten minutes since!"

She wrung her hands and wept like a child, totally forgetting the dignity she, in all circumstances, strove to maintain. "Oh, he must not go on!" she continued, wildly; "he will die in either of those dreadful prisons! We must save him. La Guerita, have you nothing to suggest?"

She seemed suddenly to remember

the necessity of caution, and spoke the last words in a whisper. La Guerita could answer nothing, but remained for some moments deeply perplexed by the unexpected appeal.

"Oh, do speak!" sobbed Miss Holmes; "Oh, I know he is dying even now!"

"I can suggest but one thing," said La Guerita at last, slowly and reluctantly, "and that is, that your father and Mr. Gordon have influence, and might use it to save the gentleman."

Miss Holmes stopped her by an impatient gesture. "You know not what you are saying," she exclaimed; "Neither possess the influence you suggest; and if they did, neither would use it for this Northerner; but *we* must do something, La Guerita—you and I. Oh, I have helped you in your hours of trouble, will you not think for me now? Oh, he must be rescued; he will die in that dreadful prison!"

"I would do anything for you, Miss Adela," said La Guerita, earnestly, "but, indeed, I can divine no plan for saving him. Where is he, and when does he leave town!"

"I suppose he is at the depot now," returned Miss Holmes; "I heard that they would be detained there until the train from Richmond came in to-night."

"When is that due?"

"About half-past ten, I believe."

"Are the prisoners closely guarded?"

"I don't know, but I suppose so. I wish you would go and see. Try to get into the baggage rooms in some way; the wounded will be sure to be there; you will know Thorn-

ton immediately by his major's uniform, and by his lazy brown eyes and dark curling hair; besides, poor fellow, his right arm is in a sling."

La Guerita sank into a chair, turning deadly pale and trembling violently, as she said: "Thornton! Is it Thornton Leslie?"

"That is his name," cried Miss Holmes, in surprise; "where have you heard it?"

"I knew him well," exclaimed La Guerita, excitedly; "he was one of my earliest and best friends; he stood beside my husband when he died, and he was appointed one of the guardians of my children."

"How strange," ejaculated Miss Holmes, "that you never mentioned his name to me! Did you," she added, suddenly, "remain silent all this time to avenge yourself for my first distrust of you?"

"No! no!" cried La Guerita, greatly shocked at the unjust suspicion; "I never knew that he held any place in your affections, or that he was even known to you. You asked me to save him! If mortal can, I will. I would shrink from no danger to aid Thornton Leslie!"

"Go! go and see him quickly!" exclaimed Miss Holmes; "he will know that friends are near when he sees you."

"But he must not recognize me!" returned La Guerita; "the shock would be too great for him to bear calmly, and the least excitement on his part might be fatal to our plans."

"That is true," acquiesced Miss Holmes; "in my terrible anxiety for his rescue I forgot even the most ordinary precautions. But how can you disguise yourself so that he will not know you?"

"The simplest means will do it," returned La Guerita; "the possibility of my being here at all will not enter his mind; and if it should, the sight of this dress will dispel all idea of my being before him."

As she spoke she left the room, but returned, after a short time, with a basket on her arm. "I have been to mother's cabin," she said, and taking from the basket a homespun dress and a large bandanna handkerchief, arrayed herself in the one, and wrapped the other around her brows, completely hiding her luxuriant hair, and suddenly assuming, with the dress, more of the look of a negress than was agreeable to her own feelings, or than Miss Holmes could have considered possible.

"He will not know me," said La Guerita, smiling bitterly; "I do not think that even my own child would. By the way, where is he?"

"I sent him on an errand to Mr. Gordon's a short time ago."

"Ah, then he is safe. On no account, Miss Adela, allow him to go to the depot. I am sure he would recognize Thornton immediately, and that would never do."

"But what are you about to attempt?" asked Miss Holmes, anxiously.

"To sell this fruit to the prisoners," returned La Guerita, filling her basket with some fruit that lay on the table; "I have no other plan as yet."

"Come back to me as quickly as possible," whispered Miss Holmes, as La Guerita tied on a large Shaker bonnet and left the room. "I shall be dying with anxiety until I see you again."

La Guerita hastily left the hotel, and proceeded toward the depot. She had proceeded but a few steps, when she met Mr. Gordon. Her heart sank within her, but he passed her with a cursory glance, that assured her more than a thousand words could have done, of the completeness of her simple disguise."

She noticed as she approached the depot that it was well guarded, rendering impossible any project that might be made for any escape thence. She was stopped at the entrance by a sentinel, who demanded who she was, at the same time gazing curiously upon her face.

"I b'long to Massa Norton Holmes, and Miss said I might come here and sell some fruit, 'cos gen'ally the prisoners hab got lots ob greenbacks to trow away," she replied, readily.

So well she imitated the negro dialect that, supposing her to be some favorite house-slave, he suffered her to pass, saying:

"You'd better not talk too much 'bout greenbacks. It's against the law to traffic with them, but I s'pose you ain't accountable."

Falling into a leisurely pace, which but illy accorded with her excited feelings, La Guerita walked into the baggage-rooms, where most of the prisoners had been lodged. She looked around her anxiously, not only for Thornton, for she remembered that Victor DeGrey, or even her brother, might also be there. She was called hither and thither, and had disposed of most of her fruit, and was about to enter another room, when she saw an officer extended upon some bales of cotton. A Union private and a Confederate sentinel were near him, but she approached with steady head, and with a thrill of delight recognized Thornton Leslie.

" Don't go thar," said the sentinel. " He don't want yer fruit, and won't want anything long, I reckon. You havn't got any business here, nohow. I don't b'leive in lettin' niggers in with the prisoners."

Thornton Leslie wearily turned his head and looked at her as he heard these words. A puzzled expression passed over his face, which was quickly followed by one of pain.

" Why don't you pass on ? " said the sentinel, roughly, as she still stood gazing upon the wounded man.

She saw that Thornton was too ill to take more than a passing notice of her, and instantly resolved, even at some risk, again to claim his attention.

"I was just standin' here," she said, indifferently, but in a voice totally unlike her natural one, "because I s'posed the sick men will buy fruit quicker'n most others, and not care what they give for't. Leastways that's what Miss Adela said."

"And who's Miss Adela? Some Yankee sympathizer, I s'pose?"

"No she hain't ; she's my missis," returned La Guerita, with difficulty retaining her false tones as she saw Thornton Leslie look eagerly upon her. "She's Massa Norton Holmes' daughter. Guess you have heard o' Massa Norton Holmes."

"Lor' yes ; I know all them Holmes' like a book. There's no foolin' 'bout them, an' they all hate the Yankees worse nor they do p'isen any day."

The private who had been standing near Thornton then approached La Guerita, and said the major would like some of her fruit.

Thornton raised himself and greeted her eagerly as she drew near, feeling ready to weep as she noticed his prostrated condition. The sentinel looked at them a moment, and then passed on.

"Who are you ? " whispered Thornton, eagerly.

"Only Miss Adela's waiting maid," she returned, in the same tone ; "she sent me here to tell you not to despair. We will liberate you."

"God bless her ! " he said, fervently.

"Handle my fruit as if choosing some, and listen to me."

He obeyed, and two citizens approached, speaking of the prisoners.

"There are three hundred of them," said one, "and they're to be sent on the eleven o'clock train, which goes through without making any stoppages, you know."

"Yes ; but it seems cruel to send men wounded, like that one, for instance, in box cars, as they say they will."

"Oh, it is safest," returned the other, carelessly, "and all we can provide them with until our ports are open. Those baggage cars are not uncomfortable, after all, and even the most agile cannot escape from them. One fellow actually jumped from the window of a passenger car and got free not a month ago. He deserved his liberty, but evidently the guards were at fault. I have seen hundreds of prisoners go through on the tops of cars, and couldn't see that there was any chance for escape. Do you stop in town to-night?"

"No; I shall go on this train to the E—— station. It will stop there for wood. I'm lucky in having my plantation so near it. Hello, major," suddenly turning to Thornton, "how did you get that bullet in your shoulder?"

"By defending my country from traitors!" he retorted, proudly, eliciting a hearty laugh from his comrades and causing the hasty retreat of the inquirer and his friends.

During the few moments occupied by this apparently unimportant conversation a thousand thoughts had chased each other through the mind of La Guerita, and her plan of action was matured before the laugh occasioned by Thornton's remark had subsided.

She glanced hastily around. The sentinel was near, and also several citizens. "I will come back presently," she whispered, and hastened to a soldier who had for some moments been calling her.

None but prisoners were near when she returned.

"Listen to me," she whispered, deliberately filling Thornton's cap with fruit, which she polished with her coarse apron. "To-night the train will stop at a station for wood; it lies about ten miles from here. Wrench up the floor of the car and lie on the track till the cars pass over you and all is quiet. Creep then into the copse on the left and I will come to you."

He looked at her in astonishment, but she continued calmly to fill his cap with fruit, asked for her payment, and counted out the change, saying:

"You'll find it all right, sir; you needn't be afraid," adding, in a whisper, "have you a large knife?"

"My dagger."

She smiled, said "Good-day," and passed on to another officer. To him she sold all her fruit, and then hastened from the building. She was about to enter the hotel when, to her surprise, she met Mr. Russell, whom she had supposed to be in Virginia. He looked at her closely as she passed, then turned and followed her a few steps, but presently, to her infinite relief, paused, and with a short laugh, as if at the utter absurdity of his suspicions, turned again toward the depot. Waiting until he had disappeared from view, La Guerita hurried into the hotel, and to Miss Adela's room.

"What news?" she cried, eagerly. "Have you seen him?"

"Yes," she answered, and in a few words related her meeting with Thornton Leslie, and the plan she had formed for his release. "You know the box cars are but very slightly made," she explained, in conclusion. "The flooring, I am sure, may be easily wrested up by a strong blade and a willing hand."

"Oh, the escape from the guards is not so difficult," said Miss Holmes. "I have seen Union soldiers actually waiting at the stations at which they had been accidentally left for chances to be taken on to prison, but how we are to conduct him to a place of safety is my great trouble. Now that you have suggested a plan of escape from the train, I have no doubt he will try to follow it out."

"Yes," said La Guerita, "we may trust to his ready wit to help him out of any danger connected with that which we cannot foresee. My only care now is to be near the station in time to conduct him to a place of safety before his flight is discovered, for however careless they may be as to common soldiers, the authorities would not relish the idea of an officer running through the country at will."

"That is quite true. My poor Thornton has everything against him. But with his wounded arm he can never wrench up the floor."

" He will find others to help him, and as there will be several in the car we may safely reckon that all will not trust themselves to these unfriendly woods, therefore several hours may elapse before the flight of any is discovered. I ask but one; that will take us some distance toward Asenith Bray's."

" Asenith Bray's ? "

"Yes ; we can find no safer place for him. There is not one retired nook at Holmsford. If we can cover up our tracks, no one would suspect Asenith of harboring any one. She must be prepared for our coming."

" It can never be done," said Miss Holmes, despairingly. " They expect me home to-day ; I must go. How am I, then, in the first place to account for your absence ? My father is so jealously careful of you. But, even if I could arrange that satisfactorily, how are you to conduct Thornton over roads you have yourself never trod ? "

" The first difficulty is the greatest," said La Guerita, after a moment's thought, "and I own it did not at first occur to me, although it now appears to me insurmountable. As to the rest, I know the general direction of the roads leading to and from the station. But has not Harold yet returned ? Can it be possible that he has wandered to the depot ? Oh, I hope not ; if he is seen by Will. Russell our plans may be utterly ruined."

"What? Is Will. Russell in town ?"

" Yes, and even Thornton did not eye me so closely ; yet I think I escaped unrecognized."

"Thank God for that. Oh, La Guerita, we must not fail. We are running a frightful risk. I am even placing my father's life in danger. Oh, God, the thought is agony ! "

"We will not think of danger," said La Guerita. "God will not suffer so just an undertaking to fail. But now we cannot draw back. I would not at any cost."

"But the danger is frightful," said Miss Holmes, turning pale and shuddering, as she pictured the hundred chances of failure and detection they must have. "Much as I long to rescue Thornton, I cannot bear to risk my father's honor, and to place you in such terrible jeopardy. Oh, Rita, be careful ! be careful ! My father would never forgive you if you were discovered. He would part us forever."

" I know it," returned La Guerita. "But let us think of how we shall account for our absence from Holmsford to-night. Can you trust Henry ?"

" Not an iota. Fate seems truly perverse in awarding him as our driver."

"That is unfortunate ; but we have Harry. There he is now, at the door."

" Have you considered," said Miss Holmes, "that it is more than ten miles from Holmsford to the station, how can you ever walk such a distance?—or, at any rate, in time to rescue Thornton."

"There must be no delay," replied La Guerita; "Let us call in Harold, and you can send him to order the carriage. It must be nearly five o'clock now."

"It is quite that. Come in, Harry."

He entered, and delivered a note to Miss Holmes, and then turned to his mother, in great glee, exclaiming:

"Oh, ma, they're having such a time down at the depot; there are thousands of Yankee prisoners there. I went down myself and saw them."

"Oh, Harold, Harold, what have you done?" she cried, in a tone of such grief that the child shrank back as though he had been struck.

"I didn't mean any harm," he faltered.

"I know you did not," she returned in a gentler tone. "Who did you see at the depot? Any of the prisoners?"

"No," he answered, half crying, "I was going into the big room, when Captain Russell came along and wouldn't let me."

"Captain Russell!" ejaculated Miss Holmes, in affright, "and what did he say to you?"

"He only put his hand under my chin, and made me raise my face so's he could look at it, and then he ask me who I came to town with; and I told him Miss Adela and ma, and he told me to run home, and I did just as quick as I could."

La Guerita, for the first time in her life, was thoroughly angered at her child, and for a few moments was almost filled with despair. She went with Miss Holmes into the bedroom, leaving Harold in tears.

"This has totally discomposed my plans," she exclaimed; "had we better not forego them, and apply at once to Will. Russell for aid, he knows Thornton well, and can have no personal enmity against him.

"You forget; they are rivals," answered Miss Holmes, blushing; "Captain Russell has many reasons for preferring to see Thornton in prison than free, and, at any rate, he is not the man to recognize a personal friend in a political enemy."

"You cannot, then, trust to his generosity?"

"No, no; and additional caution is necessary now, for undoubtedly he knows that Thornton is here, and his seeing you in that disguise has aroused his suspicions."

"Perhaps they will say that I am planning my own escape instead of Thornton's," said La Guerita, cheeringly; "at any rate it is now too late for us to draw back. When shall you be ready to leave town?"

"Immediately; if you think it best. Here, Harry, see if you can be a man and order the carriage; and then go into the office and pay my bill for me."

She gave him her purse, and he left the room proud, and once more happy.

"Do you remember," said La Guerita, "that the E—— road crosses the Holmsford, about seven miles from here? Now, I am well assured that a walk of three miles on that road, and of five miles more through the woods, directly east, will bring me to the station.   Eight miles south-west from that point is Asenith Bray's.   By some good fortune, I remember hearing that some time ago."

"Sixteen miles to walk," said Miss Holmes, aghast.

"I am not sure that I ever walked so far before in my life ; but I can do so now, or as much further as need be.   There is the carriage now. Henry is in a hurry to leave town I suppose ; no doubt he is thinking of that long, stony hill which will prevent one reaching the junction until nearly eight o'clock at least."

Hastily arranging themselves, they left the room.

"I had forgotten we must have some brandy," whispered La Guerita.

"I have some," answered Miss Holmes ; "I brought it from home for your mother.   But we will have some sandwiches."

She dispatched Harold for them, and the landlord conducted her to the carriage, leaving La Guerita to follow as she best could.

"Drive quickly, Henry," said Miss Holmes, when Harold had joined them with a small basket well filled.

He obeyed, and for some time they proceeded in silence ; and when they were fully free from the town, they in whispers matured their plans.

"Yes," said Miss Holmes, at last, "Harold must help us ; I cannot trust Henry.   Harry, listen to me, I have a reason why your mother shall leave the carriage without being seen by Henry.   Will you help her to do it ?"

"Why, of course, Miss Adela,"

he answered in astonishment, "I'll do anything you want me to."

"That is right.   Now, presently, we shall get to the top of this hill, and I shall send Henry to a spring in one of the fields to get me some water ; you must get out and hold the horses.   Your mother will leave the carriage, and when Henry brings the water, you must take it from him."

"I'll do it," he said, "but I'm sure ma will get lost, it's pretty near dark already."

"Never mind that.   I have, besides, something else for you to do.   I am not going to Holmsford to-night, but to Asenith Bray's ; I shall send you home with a note to mamma, and if they ask you about us, tell them that you left us at Asenith's."

"What, if ma a'int there ; that will be a lie," said Harold bluntly.

Miss Holmes colored.   "A lie is nothing where a life is concerned," she said, more to herself than to the child ; "I will explain to him when you are gone," she added to La Guerita.   "Now, then, for the disguise as before."

La Guerita hastily assumed it, and when they reached the top of the hill, Miss Holmes said to Harold :

"Now, then, let me see how well you can perform your first task ; tell Henry to go for the water."

He did so, and took his place at the horses' heads, while the driver departed on his errand.   As soon as his face was turned steadfastly toward the spring, La Guerita arose, and taking the basket of food and the brandy, and the "pass" which, as an additional safeguard, Miss Holmes had prepared for her, hastily left the carriage. Uttering a word of farewell, she looked around her cautiously for a moment, and then entering the thick woods that bordered the road, crouched down, and awaited impatiently a chance for action.

From her hiding-place, she presently saw Henry return from the spring, and Harold run to him, exclaiming that he could not hold the horses, and snatching the water from his hands, conveying it himself to Miss Holmes.

To her great relief Henry mounted the box without looking into the carriage, and drove slowly away.

CHAPTER XXXI.

"I dare do all that may become a man."
Shakespeare.

LA GUERITA then felt herself fully launched upon her perilous adventure ; and yet, strangely enough, she felt far more anxiety for Miss Holmes than for herself. Would it be possible for one so well known to drive so many miles without encountering one that knew her ? Might not her father even, rendered anxious by the lateness of the hour, ride forth to meet her, and ask the cause of her own absence ? In such a case, what answer would she give ? These questions long tormented her, even after she had arisen and begun to walk boldly on the open roadway.

"It must be nearly eight o'clock ! " she thought, glancing at the sun, which was fast setting ; "it will soon be dark among these gloomy pines ; but, after all, that will be all the better for me."

Within the first three miles she met many persons, but, as it was almost dark, she passed almost unnoticed. "Now for the labyrinth ! " she muttered, as she made a sudden detour into the woods. "This path is scarcely distinguishable. I might have found my difficulties greatly lessened if Miss Adela had taken Henry into our confidence. Those old negroes know every turn. Let me see—where am I ? "

She paused for some time at the junction of two roads, which were, in fact, little more than mere footpaths. "This," she thought, doubtfully, at last proceeding in one, "must be right, I know I must go east. But, oh, if I could but see a few paces before me, how thankful I should be ! "

She went on, however, quite blindly for more than a half hour longer. The faint starlight failed to pierce the gloom of the forest ; and at length, utterly wearied, she sat down at the roadside to rest.

She had sat there but a short time, when a man on horseback went by. She drew back from the road, hoping he would pass without speaking ; but he drew rein, evidently surprised to see a woman in the woods alone at that late hour.

"Who are you ? " he asked, suspiciously, "and where are you going ? "

Evading his first question, she answered, carelessly : "I am going to E——."

"Then you have a good walk before you." He evidently took her for a white woman. "There are lots of runaway negroes and conscripts in these woods ; I wonder you are not afraid of them."

"I am too poor for them to trouble me, sir," she returned ; "but I am not quite sure I am on the road to E——."

"Oh, yes ; you're all right."

Her heart sank. Then she had diverged far from the road leading to the wood-station ; but dissembling her emotion, said : "I was afraid it might be the other road—the one that crosses this more than two miles back."

"Oh, no ; that would take you to R——," mentioning a village which she knew to be but a short distance from the wood-station.

The man rode on, with a cheery "Good-night" to her, and the advice to hurry on, as there were conscripts and conscript-hunters within a mile, and they might annoy her were they to meet her.

After he was gone she stood for a few moments quite motionless. All those weary miles, then, must be retraced. With difficulty she restrained her tears ; but, with a silent prayer for help, she walked back to the junction, and, almost hopelessly, took the other road. She thought the five miles she had decided she must proceed interminable, and several times felt inclined to turn into one of the numerous small paths that intersected the greater on every hand. She knew that to reach the station it was necessary for her to do so.

Her perplexity increased with every passing moment, and at last she mentally exclaimed : "It must be nearly eleven o'clock ; and here is another road. Oh, Heaven direct me, or all may be lost ! "

She stood for some minutes at the junction, afraid to move ; when, to her great terror, she heard the sound of wheels. She sprang into the woods, and in a few moments a buggy, driven by a negro, rolled rapidly by and turned upon the very road she had been pondering over.

"That is the buggy for the gentleman who was to leave the train at the wood-station," she thought, joyfully ; "I am, indeed, all right now."

She hastened hopefully upon her new path, and almost at the same moment the shrill scream of the engine awoke the forest echoes, and she knew that the train was approaching the wood-station, and thought that at that very instant Thornton Leslie might be striving for freedom. Which would he gain, Freedom or death ? "

The thought quite chilled and sickened her for a moment ; then again the whistle sounded, and, quite regardless of her fatigue, she ran eagerly in the direction of the station.

At last she saw the red lights of the engine before her. She paused, drawing into the covert of the wood, as the buggy, containing her unconscious benefactor, drove by on its homeward way. The whistle again sounded—the heavy train moved on —the flickering lights at the wood-pile vanished one by one, and all was dark and still as death.

She stood for a moment quite awed by the thought of the joy or sorrow she would shortly know. "I shall never reach Asenith Bray's if I must go there alone," she thought, and then moved a step forward and scanned the track with eager gaze.

She fancied she saw two or three dark objects move slowly across it, and, with a beating heart, she descended the hill, crossed a rustic bridge which spanned a ravine at its foot, and entered the copse that lay between it and the railway track.

No sound was to be heard but the croaking of the frogs in the stream and the howl of a distant dog. By the faint lights but few objects could be distinguished, and putting aside the boughs of the shrub pines and wild-rose bushes, she stepped into the copse, holding herself ready to be accosted in any way; yet she could not repress a shiver of terror when her dress was firmly, yet gently, seized, and a low voice whispered: "Adela!"

At that word she looked down, and saw a stranger lying at her feet; but he was clothed in the Union blue, and kneeling beside him, she whispered: "How many of you are here?"

"God bless you, five—the major and four privates. Tell me the nearest point we can hope to gain the Union lines."

"At Kenston—about eighty miles north-east. I can give you only the general direction. Where is the major?"

"God save you for a brave girl!" replied the man; "my comrades and I will never forget you for your work to-night. Tell me who you are, and to whom you belong."

"Detain me no longer," she whispered, "but tell me where the major is."

"Close under the covert of the wood yonder, unless he has gained courage to rise and walk away; he was not able to creep, because of his broken arm. Let me shake hands with you."

She gave him her hand, and answering "Good-by" to his fervent blessing, hastened away, returning, on a second thought, to say: "Have you money or food?"

"The first, yes; the last we need most."

"Have you a brandy-flask?"

"Yes."

He produced it, and by the uncertain light she filled it, shared with him her slender stock of food, and said: "That must serve you until you reach the house of a Quakeress, ten miles south. Tell her nothing but that you are hungry, and you will be fed. You will know the house by its large, brown, wooden blinds; there are none beside them hereabout."

She left the copse before he could utter a word of thanks, and after a careful survey of the ground stepped lightly across the open space, and at the spot designated by the soldier found Thornton Leslie.

"I saw you go into the copse," he whispered, "but was too faint to move or speak. For God's sake, let us leave this place; there is a man in the hut yonder; he might discover us at any moment."

Without uttering a word, she led the way across the bridge. At the top of the hill they paused and listened. In the distance—at M——, they conjectured—the whistle of the cars sounded shrilly, and, as if it heralded pursuit, they hurried desperately on.

"How far have we to go?" whispered Leslie, at last.

"Eight miles."

"Good God, I am fainting already!"

She stopped and gave him some

brandy. It revived him, and after resting a moment he continued his walk, leaning heavily upon a stick which La Guerita placed in his hands.

"Why do you walk behind me?" he asked.

"My dress sweeps over your footprints and obliterates them," she replied.

"None but a negro used to flights would have thought of that," he mused.

Oh, how wearily the next hour passed. On they pressed through the gloomy woods, often startled by some distant sound, or obliged to yield for a moment to the fatigue that threatened to overcome both.

They at last sat down, at a few rods from the roadside, and partook of the food La Guerita had reserved. "'Tis the first food I have eaten with an appetite since I was made prisoner," whispered Thornton.

"Was your escape easily managed?" she queried.

"Yes; though there was a double guard placed at our car; and after the boards were loosened they came in, and actually trod upon them. Heaven knows what would have become of us if one had slipped. One of them stood at the door all the time we stopped at the station; but part of our brave fellows blocked his view while the four others and myself raised the boards and dropped upon the track below. There was a terrible glare from the engine shining upon it; but, thank God, in a moment the train thundered over us— the station-master slowly passed by, putting out, one by one, the dull lights, and at last went into the cab-in, leaving us in the blessed darkness."

"Lie down," muttered La Guerita, warningly, throwing herself back. Thornton instantly obeyed, and a few minutes later four men on horseback passed. One was a conscript, and the others were so much engaged in taunting him that they fortunately looked only at him.

"I guess the next time you run, it will be from the Yankees," remarked one, jeeringly.

"I'll run to them," retorted the conscript, sullenly.

"You will, eh?" replied the captain, with an oath. "Well, at any rate we caught you nicely to-night. We should have had your brother, too, but that my horse stumbled on that cursed tree that lay across the road by Deacon Wright's."

They passed on, and were soon out of sight. La Guerita arose and beckoned to Thornton to follow. They made but slow progress, for Thornton faltered at every step, until they came to a path leading across some fields that surrounded a large white house.

"I did not know before that Deacon Wright lived there," she thought, "but I know his house is but a few miles from Asenith's. Yes, we are right; there is the fallen tree."

They entered the fields, then, creeping along under such covert as presented itself, yet often obliged to take to the open field, and run the risk of encountering their worst enemies— the seemingly ubiquitous conscript-hunters. When they again entered the woods Thornton sank down, faintly declaring himself unable to go farther.

La Guerita gently forced him to take some brandy, but it seemed to have no effect.

"It is no use," he muttered, "I can go no farther. Oh, the agony of this wounded arm is intolerable."

La Guerita silently took his dagger from his belt and slit up the loose sleeve of his coat, and loosened the bandages slightly, not daring to remove them, as he begged her to do, lest the blood of an artery should burst forth.

"Come now," she said, cheerfully, "it is only a mile farther, and I know the road well. I am sure all danger is past."

"It is no use," he muttered, sinking back after a vain attempt to rise.

"Oh, Thornton!" she exclaimed, bursting into tears, and for the first time speaking in her natural voice, "rouse yourself! for God's sake, rouse yourself! The morning will soon break, and unless we reach Asenith's before that, all will be lost."

"Who are you?" he cried, suddenly, rising to his feet as if electrified; "are you yourself Adela, or whose voice is that I hear?"

"Her waiting maid's," she replied, gaining, by a moment's thought, time to answer him calmly, "and she will kill me by the sight of her grief if I do not take you to her to-night."

"No, it cannot be possible. You cannot be——. And yet——. But lead on."

"To Adela!" whispered La Guerita.

The name seemed to give him fresh strength. He pressed onward, though slowly, often scarcely able to repress a moan of pain. La Guerita spoke no

more until they had passed through the woods and the wild, uncultivated garden, and they stood before the little porch of Asenith Bray's house. She took Thornton Leslie's hand; it was cold as ice, and he trembled like an aspen. His former danger, and his escape from it, she knew were for a moment forgotten.

"Where is she?" he murmured. "My love, my Adela!"

That moment he was answered. The door opened and he fell forward into her outstretched arms.

CHAPTER XXXII.

" To his eye
There was but one beloved face on earth,
And that was shining on him."
Byron.

THERE was no time for words of welcome, or tears of joy. Thornton Leslie had fainted, and at the sight of the strong man so utterly prostrated, the three women instantly became calm, and even La Guerita was unconscious of fatigue as she assisted to raise and carry him into an inner chamber. Scarcely had they laid him upon the bed, when to their utter consternation a heavy knock sounded upon the door.

"Oh, my God, you have been followed," ejaculated Miss Holmes, throwing herself despairingly on her knees beside her lover. "Oh, Thornton, Thornton, we are lost!"

La Guerita would not move for very terror, but leaving the room and closing the door, Asenith demanded firmly:

"Who is there?"

"It's only me," replied a voice which, to the infinite relief of all, they recognized to be that of the coachman, Henry. "I'se come for Miss Addie."

"And why?" said Miss Holmes, hastening to the door, "what has happened?"

"Oh, Miss Addie, you'se to go right off. Massa Rufe is wid me to see you safe! Dey's jest havin' de most orfulest times—Miss Myra's done gone inter de hystricks, and Massa Norton's nigh 'bout crazy; let 'lone Miss Tildy, who says she jest know'd 'twould happen so!"

"That what would happen?" cried Miss Holmes, breathlessly, her heart palpitating with a thousand fears.

"Why that Massa Claude would be killed! He was just shot all to pieces!"

"Claude shot!"

"Yes," cried Rufus, who had just entered, "shot by those cussed Yankees, but if I live a year longer I will avenge him. But how does it happen that you're all dressed?" he said, suspiciously.

"Asenith has been so dreadfully sick," she replied, hurriedly; "Rita, I must go home—you shall stay."

"No she musn't," interrupted Rufus, "she is to go home with us. Father particularly told me that."

They went up stairs ostensibly to put on their bonnets and cloaks, but in reality to consult together. Asenith presently came to them.

"I see by Rufus' manner that there are some suspicions afloat," she said. "Go home, both of you, and leave him to me."

There was nothing else to be done, and not even a glance of farewell could be given. Adela was almost glad of a pretext for her tears, as she entered the carriage and asked Rufus how the news had come.

"Mr. Gordon received the telegraph late in the night, and sent it right out," he answered.

"But it may not be true!" said his sister.

"Nonsense," returned Rufus; but she repeated the words to her father as he came out in the early dawn to meet her and assisted her from the carriage.

"Alas! it must be true!" he replied. "Only look at that, my dear."

He placed a telegram in her hand which she read aloud. There were but a few words, but they were definite enough to convince the most unbelieving.

"Col. Claude Leveredge was killed at ——, on the 20th instant, while leading a charge on the enemy's works. Body not recovered."

Miss Holmes burst into tears, and hurried into the house, while La Guerita turned slowly toward her own cabin, saying to herself: "Dead! dead! Gone into the presence of God and Harold without one word of forgiveness from my lips. Oh, Claude! Claude! how gladly would I have spoken them; for, base as all your other feelings seemed, your love for me at least was pure!"

She found a strange pleasure in that thought; she felt that the pure love she pictured had honored her, perhaps, more than him; no other woman would have commanded it from such a heart. She could not grieve for him; 'twas hard for her, so far as to triumph over her weak human nature, as to refrain from some slight joy when she thought how great a boon his death was to her; yet withal, her heart softened toward him, and she gave a sigh to Claude Leveredge dead, that no art could have gained from her during his life.

Mrs. Holmes, as Henry had represented, was indeed in hysterics, and remained in them during most of the following day; and not only Mr. Holmes, but the children and servants seemed crazed. And worst of all to Miss Holmes and La Guerita Mr. Gordon came out to advise and condole with the family in their affliction.

For nearly a week the only news gained of Thornton was through Harold, who was sent to Asenith's on some pretext each day. He was never told the name of the stranger whom he knew to be concealed, and whose cause he espoused for Miss Adela's sake with exemplary zeal and discretion.

Never had Miss Holmes passed a week of such terrible anxiety. The sadness of her home was aggravated by her fears for Thornton. Day after day she heard that he was growing stronger, but that in no degree lessened his chances of discovery, for the news of the escape of the prisoners ran like wild-fire through the country, and means for their recovery were eagerly adopted.

One alone was captured, and he would reveal nothing of the locality in which their dangerous experiment had been made.

Later in the week Asenith Bray sent word that she was herself extremely ill, and notwithstanding the protests of her father and mother, Miss Holmes hastened to her, de-

claring she would not leave so good a woman to die alone.

"I shall probably stay there three or four days," she said, when alone with La Guerita. "I know it is Thornton that is so extremely ill. Oh what joy it will be to see him and to tell him who was his deliverer!"

"But that you must not do!" returned La Guerita, hastily. "I cannot bear that he should see me here. He cannot help me, and I have nothing now to fear in slavery. Promise me, then, that you will not betray me."

"Betray you!"

"Yes. If he reaches the Union lines he would relate all to my brother, and give him years of misery that he may as well be spared, for, indeed, he cannot help me. Promise me, then, that you will not tell Thornton who saved him."

"I promise until I again see you," said Miss Holmes, sadly; "yet I think you are wrong. But I can refuse you nothing."

"There is Minna calling you," said La Guerita.

"So she is, dear child, with Rufus by her side, looking as black as a thunderbolt. He characteristically remarked this morning that if Claude had sent him his spurs which he promised should be his if he was killed, he would put them on and never take them off until they were dyed red with the blood of his cowardly Yankee murderers. The child actually makes me shudder."

She left the cabin, and shortly after proceeded to Asenith Bray's. She found the old Quakeress sitting, as usual, in her outer room sorting herbs.

"I am glad thee has come at last," she said, as Adela kissed her cheeks, which she noticed with a pang were unusually pale.

"And I am glad," she answered, "not only for his sake, but yours. You must go now and lie down, your pale face reproaches me."

"It need not, child, it need not, for he was quieter last night, and I had some rest. But the neighbors have troubled me sorely each day; so many have come in, and I have been in constant fear the poor lad would betray his presence by a word or moan. Go in now, I will move about these dishes of herbs if any one comes in, that the rattling may warn thee to keep silence."

"I will remember," said Adela, and stealing softly away to the chamber where Thornton was lying, looked fully, for the first time in years, upon the face of her lover. It was sadly altered. He seemed, indeed, altogether but a wreck of his former self; yet never had Adela loved him so well as now, in his helplessness, when she was called upon to endure trials and danger for his sake.

She bent over him and kissed him, and awaking, with a cry of delight he rapturously bade her welcome.

"I know why you have stayed away!" he exclaimed; "but I thought that you would never come, my precious Adela!"

"Dear Thornton, you know it was hard for me to stay away," she said; "but I could not leave my home without seeming unkind or arousing suspicions."

"I know it—I know it, my love; but no reasoning could quiet my im-patience to see you. I am quite content now that you are here."

He seemed so, indeed, for he lay for a long time with his hand clasped in her's—too weak to talk, but listening with delight to what she related of her life since they parted.

"But you have told me nothing of that brave girl—Rita," he said, at last.

"She is well," she replied, coloring; "she has been unable to leave home; they would miss her even more than they do me."

"I had such strange thoughts about her while I was delirious," said Thornton; "I remember them all now. I kept on fancying that she stood beside me vailed, and that I sometimes fancied her one person, and then, again, another. I am sure I must have seen her somewhere. Has she ever been North with you?"

"No, Thornton, never," answered Miss Holmes, almost unable to restrain her secret, yet doing so more for his sake, perhaps, than that of La Guerita. "You must be silent now. You have talked already too much. Asenith will think me a careless nurse."

On the contrary, Asenith declared herself perfectly satisfied, and at an early hour retired to seek the rest she so greatly needed; and for hours Adela sat in the darkened room, bending anxiously over her sleeping lover. He awoke at last with a start; but a word from her lips calmed him.

"Then I was not dreaming," he muttered; "you are my love, in truth, beside me?"

"Yes, dear Thornton; yes!"

"But you will go again?" he said, uneasily. "All those weary years

Claude Leveredge kept you from me will be repeated?"

"You forget, dear Thornton, that Claude is dead."

"Ah, yes! so he is! I must bear malice no longer; but, indeed, it is hard for me to forgive him when I think what our home would have been all these weary years!"

Miss Holmes sighed.

"Yet, perhaps, after all," she said, at length, "this separation may have been for our good. Remember you would still have been a soldier and a prisoner, and God, knows, I might soon have been your widow."

"That is true, my love. God bless you. You are, then, true to the Union as well as to me. Oh, I have longed for one single assurance of that."

"I must not let you talk, Thornton," said Miss Holmes, gently, "though it is hard indeed for me to bid you be silent. It is so long since I have heard your voice, save in my dreams."

"Oh, blessed dreams," murmured Thornton; "they have brought you to me a thousand, thousand times. Through them I have felt your hand in mine, your kisses on my lips. But I would not exchange one moment of this reality for a world of dreams."

She bent and kissed him, and he held her head a moment to his bosom, calling her his wife, his very own.

That was indeed a season of delight. But as the night passed on, Thornton's feverish vagaries returned. He lay fearfully awake, listening anxiously to every sound, and filling Adela with his own vague fears. The window was closely curtained, yet he declared, nervously, that some

rays of light from the table lamp were surely falling upon the garden. At last Miss Holmes arose and, almost fainting with terror, entered the garden. All was dark. She even pressed her face to the window, but Asenith had covered it so well that not a glimmer could be discovered behind the black screen. She re-entered the house to assure Thornton of this, and found him filled with the most agonizing fears for her safety.

"Don't leave me again," he entreated. "Something might happen to you. Give me your hand and sit beside me. I can be sure of you then."

"The second night was a repetition of the first; and as Adela had refused to leave Thornton even during the day, she could not conquer the drowsiness that came upon her in the early morning, when Thornton slumbered under the influence of some herb, for the virtues of which Asenith vouched, and sinking back into her chair she fell into a deep sleep.

So Asenith found her an hour later, and awakening her cautiously sent her to her chamber, where she sank upon the bed, and, with a muttered prayer for Thornton, again slept. At about ten o'clock she was again aroused by Asenith, who came to her bedside to tell her that her father was below.

"And verily," she added, "I had no call to feign sickness, for his coming startled me so that he said I was as white as a sheet, and chid me for getting up, but I told him I could not bear to keep thee longer from thy bed, for thee hadst been up much of the two nights thou hadst passed here."

"Then he will be prepared for my haggard looks," returned Adela, hastily bathing her face, and smoothing her hair. "I wonder what he has come for? Perhaps only to see me, or with fresh news of Claude."

The last conjecture was correct, although Mr. Holmes said truly he had been longing to see his daughter. He gave her half a dozen telegrams relating to her cousin, all verifying the intelligence of his death.

"I think I should have been better satisfied if we could have got the poor fellow's body," said Mr. Holmes, sorrowfully. "I cannot endure the thought that his body should lie upon the field undistinguishable from those of the cursed Yankees."

"Oh, papa, hush!"

"Don't look so shocked, Addie; I didn't mean to hurt your feelings. After all, as Claude was an officer, they may have buried him. Poor boy, poor boy!"

"His fate was very sad," said Miss Holmes, sorrowfully, "and yet it has been the same with thousands during the last two years."

"That is so, but very few young men were like Claude," answered Mr. Holmes, "and my greatest trouble is to think that none of us ever understood him. You know, Adela, contrary to all expectations, he never declared love for you. I know now the reason."

"What was it?" Miss Holmes asked, anxiously.

"He feared that it was not reciprocated. I have not the slightest doubt now that he did love you most devotedly."

"Indeed!"

"Yes; for yesterday, in a way that women all have, your mother went to soothe her grief by looking at everything that could remind her of Claude, in that way hoping to accustom herself to his loss, I suppose. Well, in a little pocket in one of his trunks she found a miniature case, containing the likeness of a beautiful, fair-haired girl, and under it, in tiny seed pearls, was placed the word 'Adelé.' It was evidently a fancy picture he had picked up in France and fancied like you, and convinces me that the poor fellow really loved you."

She perceived that the thought gave him far more pleasure than pain, and although she had a thousand reasons for freeing his mind of the false idea, she knew she could only do so by betraying La Guerita's secret, and blackening the memory of her cousin to the only man on earth that loved him.

He continued to talk on his favorite topic for an hour or more. Never was his daughter so thankful as when he took his departure. She hurried into Thornton's room, and found him in a perfect fever. He had recognized the voice, and heard most of the conversation.

"It was true, then, after all. Claude did love you, and that was why he separated us."

"You are mistaken," she answered, gently. "It was that young girl at Fairview that he loved; that he told me the last time I saw him he should love forever."

"True, true; I had forgotten. Can it be possible that he had anything to do with her disappearance?"

"Her disappearance?"

"Yes; did he not tell you? Her husband died, and she, I think, must have become insane, though we did not notice it at the time. At any rate, she left her home, and nothing, literally nothing, has been heard of her since. She dropped out of our world as completely as if the earth had opened and swallowed her."

"Was she sought for?"

"Certainly. Her brother arrived from Europe a few days after her loss, and devoted months to her pursuit, beside which, instantly upon her departure, her brother-in-law and myself sought her in every direction, besides employing the most active of the secret police throughout the country."

"And what does her brother think?" asked Adela, scarcely able to retain her secret as she gazed upon her lover's sorrowful face.

"He will not say that he has given up hope," he returned, "and her house is still kept in readiness for her return, but in reality he must think, with the rest of us, that she in some manner destroyed herself and her child."

That cruel, cruel thought Adela would have destroyed in a moment, but that she was hurriedly called from the room by Asenith, and she remembered before returning the promise she had given. She determined, if possible, however, to learn something of La Guerita's friends, and to that end said:

"And what is her brother doing now?"

"Oh, he is in the army, and was badly wounded, poor fellow, the day before I was taken prisoner. He was shot through the shoulder, and it will be some time before he will be fit for service again, and Victor DeGrey, poor fellow, I heard was taken prisoner."

"Oh, dreadful!"

Thornton supposed she alluded to the fate of the young men, while she in reality was thinking how entirely useless it would be for her to disclose the position of La Guerita.

"I wish," he said, "I could know how poor Fabean is getting on. No doubt he is at this moment lying at the hospital thinking of me. We have fought together through all the war, and love each other like brothers."

"It is so sad that he should be in ignorance of his sister's fate," said Adela; "the constant suspense must be dreadful."

"It is. I think his mind would be comparatively relieved if he could know she and her child were really dead. But if, as I sometimes think, she is pursuing some wretched life, from which he would find it impossible to wean her, it is better for him ever to remain in doubt. It would kill him to see her unhappy."

These few words decided her. Miss Holmes needed no second entreaty to keep silence.

"Doubt is in this case better than certainty," she mused, "until we can give that blessed certainty that she lives, and can be free."

CHAPTER XXXIII.

UNDER the skillful treatment of Asenith Bray, and the tender care of his betrothed, Thornton Leslie rapidly grew better, and at the end of a week declared his intention of striving to gain the Union lines; but the entreaties of Adela, and his own disinclination to part from her, detained him somewhat longer; and anxious as he was to reach the army, fearing that she would still, in his weakness, have found some cause for delay, he would have still stayed, had not a most unexpected event accelerated his departure.

He was sitting one day talking to Adela, when he was silenced by voices in the outer room, and presently Asenith came to the door and softly called: "Adela!"

She obeyed the summons, but presently returned to the room, with a face as white as snow, crying, in a voice of affright: "Thornton, you must go; you must leave us instantly!"

"What has happened?" he demanded, in great agitation; "is my presence here discovered? Oh, God! I shall never forgive myself if I have brought you into danger!"

She made no reply, but gave him a paper—weeping on his shoulder as he read it. There were but a few words; "Asenith's house will be thoroughly searched to-night."

"Who brought you this?" he asked, in amazement; "and who wrote it?"

"The last we do not know; I cannot even guess," replied Adela; "it proves, however, that it is known to at least one person that you are here."

"I have not a moment to spare," said Thornton, rising; "give me a wallet of food, my love, and let me go."

She left the room, but instantly returned to say, that Asenith was making everything ready for his flight. "Oh, Thornton!" she exclaimed,

"if I had only let you go before! Rita begged me to do so; but I could not send you away."

"Who came with this note?" asked Thornton, suddenly; "was it Rita?"

"Yes!" answered Miss Holmes, reluctantly.

"And you did not bring her in to see me. Ah, Adela, that was really unkind."

"She would not come, Thornton, although I begged her to do so; but Rita is so strange; one can seldom comprehend her."

"So I should think; but where did she get the note?"

"She was walking in the field, at the back of her cabin, when a negro boy ran out of the woods, sprang over the fence, placed that note in her hands, and disappeared without a word. She thought it must be of importance, and brought it directly to me."

"God bless her!" cried Thornton, fervently; "she has, perhaps, saved my life for a second time; I wish I could have seen her, if but for a moment, to tell her how I appreciate her efforts. She must love you dearly, Adela, to be willing to risk so much for your lover."

It was decided that it would be best for Thornton not to begin his journey until after sunset, as fewer people would then be abroad to be attracted by his strange and haggard appearance. At an early hour they sat down and partook of the evening meal together; and afterwards Adela took from her pocket a small map, drawn on tracing-paper.

"This," she said, "was brought to me with the note. You must un-

derstand that Rita has a good knowledge of the geography of her State,
and that she also draws quite fairly.
By putting the two accomplishments
together she has produced this map.
I am sure I cannot tell where she
gained all the information ; you will,
however, find it correct."

Thornton looked at the map in
the greatest astonishment. "This is
a treasure beyond price," he exclaimed, and Rita must be some benefi-
cent fairy. Tell her, dear Adela,
how I hope one day to thank her for
all she has done. Stay ; take to her
this little locket ; it contains the hair
of my mother and sister. Try to
make her understand how they will
bless her name."

"I will," said Adela, as Thornton
disengaged the locket from his chain
and placed it in her hand. "I know
she will prize this little gift more than
untold gold. By the way, you have
some gold ?"

"Plenty ; and greenbacks, too."

"Either of which would lay you
open to suspicion if you should be
stopped and searched ; so you must
consent to exchange a part of them,
at least, for Confederate notes."

He readily consented, looking rue-
fully at the crisp pieces of paper and
the "butternut" suit with which Asenith had provided him, saying :

"I wish I dared resume my uniform. If the Lord permits, I will
resurrect some day the suit you have
buried, and wear it at our wedding,
Adela."

She sank into his arms, crying out,
with a moan, that it was so hard to
part from him ; her heart would
break. He soothed her gently, holding her to his throbbing heart, pray-

ing God to bless and preserve his
promised bride.

He bade her farewell at last, and
vainly striving to be calm, that she
might not unman him by the sight
of her grief. Adela witnessed his
farewell to Asenith, and saw, with
surprise, that she gave him a pair of
handsomely mounted pistols, saying,
as she placed them in his belt :

"I pray thee not to use them
wantonly, and aim high, if thee
needs must fire at all."

"The mark often is high," returned Thornton ; "and now good-
by ; take care of my Adela, as you
have cared for me, and Heaven will
reward you."

Asenith returned his parting kiss,
and then, as he turned and caught
Adela to his bosom, begged him to
hasten, pointing to a path, which
could be dimly seen through the
darkening woods. He pressed a kiss
upon the lips of his betrothed, and
rushed from the house ; and when
she raised her head he had disappeared from view.

He was gone—gone—and into
what dangers—what privations—her
loving heart alone could picture.
Asenith went away to arrange and
close the chamber, that Thornton's
coming had opened for the first time
since her mother died there ; and
Adela wandered out into the garden,
to breathe in with the air of evening
that tranquility of spirit which dead-
ens sorrow, arouses hope, and fills
the mind with peace.

She went into the house at last,
calmed and strengthened. Asenith
met her at the door and they stood
together for sometime regarding the
heavens and exchanging remarks up-

24

on the weather, but breathing not a word of him upon whom their hearts were centered. They spent the evening in cheerful conversation, and at an early hour parted for the night. Adela went to an upper chamber, and partly disrobing sat down at the window and looked steadfastly in the direction Thornton had taken, as if she could hope to pierce the recesses of the forest, and assure herself of his weal or woe.

She sat there a long time, mournfully looking out upon the bright stars, and the pines that swayed beneath them, filled with such visions of terror that she dared not retire, and listening intently to the sough of the wind through the trees, fancying at times the rustling of their boughs to be the echo of countless footsteps, and the shrieks of the night-birds' cries of despair.

At last it was possible for her to doubt no longer. She heard footsteps both of horses and men. She listened intently for a few moments, her face growing white as their steady tramp drew nearer.

"They are coming," she muttered, at last. "Well, well, they are welcome; they will find no trace of him, I know."

She hastily dropped the curtain of her window, and knelt below it in order to hear all that might occur. Soon the garden gate was opened and a number of men walked up the path, dropping their guns heavily upon the porch, while the captain demanded admittance. It was readily granted, and a few minutes later she heard them passing from room to room, opening the doors of closets and the lids of chests. She hastily threw a wrapper around her, and stole on tip-toe to the landing at the head of the stairs. She heard the men leave the kitchen and Asenith's chamber, and enter the sitting-room.

"Nothing discovered yet," said the captain. "Let us see what is kept up stairs."

"Thee must wait until I call down the young woman who is tarrying with me," interposed Asenith, as he stepped toward the stairs.

"Oh, certainly, but be quick about it," he replied, adding in a whisper to one of the men, "make sure that it is a woman. Ah, here she comes."

He touched his hat and apologized for disturbing her as Miss Holmes entered the room.

"Do not mention it," she returned, courteously; "but I beg you will complete your task as quickly as possible."

With admirable self-possession, although she felt most painfully abashed by the gaze of the soldiers, she waved her hand toward the staircase, and said :

"Continue your search, if you please."

The captain looked as if he would willingly have restrained his men, but without waiting for orders several at once rushed up the stairs, presently returning with the tidings that no one was to be found.

Adela's face burned. It seemed to her that by this search she had been personally insulted, and with proud disdain she stood beside Asenith and looked at the baffled soldiers.

"We havn't looked into that room, captain," said one, pointing to the door of the chamber lately occupied by Thornton.

"Give me the key, if you please," said the officer to Asenith, as he placed his hand on the lock.

"I pray thee not to enter that room," said Asenith, with so much emotion that Miss Holmes for the first time guessed how great a trial it had been for her even to place Thornton there. "That was my mother's room—she died there. I pray thee to take my word that no person is there concealed."

"I must look into the room, my good woman," returned the captain, smiling at the delicacy of feeling he could not understand. "I have my orders to search every nook and corner of this building, and I must and will obey them."

"The very heart's blood of thy people, O, Lord, is drained by the hands of their persecutors," exclaimed Asenith, bitterly ; "yea, verily the tombs and consecrated places do they enter and lay waste !"

"Give me the key," said the captain, looking at her, darkly.

"Cant !" ejaculated one of the soldiers.

"Peace preacher !" cried another.

"Open the door !" cried a third. "Let's see whether the old Quaker traitress tells the truth !"

"Stand back !" exclaimed Asenith, her face becoming suddenly pale and determined ; "not one of ye revilers shall enter in."

She beckoned to the captain and a few others, who had maintained a respectful silence, and opening the door bade them enter. They did so, peering cautiously about the quaint apartment.

"We have been deceived," said one, "there is no one here."

"Nor has there been for years," added the captain. "Our business is now ended."

The soldiers shouldered their arms, and after uttering courteous adieus, the captain led his troop from the house.

"They are watching us still," said Asenith, a few minutes later, smiling grimly as they caught the sounds of stealthy footsteps without. "I did wrong to-night in hesitating to admit them to that room. By doing so I aroused their suspicions, and trouble may yet come from it—but I could not bear that these rude men should enter my sanctuary."

And then she whispered to Adela the tale she had often heard from other lips—how that her lover had died in that chamber, stricken suddenly, upon the night before that appointed for his bridal.

"Hark ! What is that ?" said Adela, suddenly.

It was a great outcry, followed by the sound of men running to and fro. Suddenly a bright light filled the room and, with a cry of fear, Adela sprang to the door and unbolted it. Flames were shooting forth from a building at the right of the house, and were being blown by the fresh wind directly toward it.

"Oh, my barn, my wheat, my hay !" cried Asenith, standing as if riveted to the spot, while Adela rushed into the gardens, where she heard various ejaculations from the soldiers.

"That drunken Jackson did it," said one, "by holding the candle too close to the hay."

Adela ran past the group and approached the fire. The men were stupidly looking on ; the captain alone seemed excited by what had happened.

"This is most unfortunate," he exclaimed, "and perfectly accidental, I assure you."

"Then for Heaven's sake," cried Adela, "why do you not take some means to stop the conflagration? There is water in the well."

"And a gourd to dip it up with," laughed a soldier, while the captain explained that the house was so old, and all within it so combustible, that it was useless to attempt to save it.

"But the house, the house is burning!" cried Adela, rushing toward it, as she perceived that the left wing was ablaze. "Help, help; try to save the furniture, at least."

Several men, roused by her cry, rushed to the building and carried out the first articles they could lay hands upon. Adela alone had sufficient presence of mind to think of the small amount of plate and other valuables, while Asenith herself, still possessed with the ruling passion of her life, rushed frantically about with bundles of roots and herbs, which she carried to the door and threw out, only to meet destruction from the insatiable flames.

In a few minutes the whole building was on fire, and perceiving the utter uselessness and extreme danger of any further attempts to save anything, Asenith drew back as she was about to re-enter to save some bottles of eye-water which had been made from the snow of March.

"Never mind," said Adela, "it is too late to save it now," and turned aside to ask the captain to send one of the men to her father's with news of the disaster.

"Certainly I will do so," returned he, "but where is the old woman?"

Adela screamed and darted forward—she was entering the burning room. Remembering only the danger to Asenith, she rushed after her into the fire and smoke. She felt the flames lick her dress and pour their hot breath upon her face, while clouds of smoke enveloped her. It was an awful moment! She could not see although she touched Asenith, and exerting all her strength clasped her in her arms and rushed through the fire again into the open air. Some one dashed a pail of water upon her burning dress and hurried them back, while the roof fell in with a terrible crash, sending columns of smoke and sparks into the air, into the very room whence she had escaped but a moment before.

They were safe—that was all she could think of; while poor Asenith, stunned by the calamity that had befallen her, looked at the single bottle of eye-water she held in her hand and muttered: "And there may never be snow in March again as long as I live, and all the summer yerbs gone besides!"

That was all she mourned over, even when the neighbors came and condoled with her, and bound up her burnt hands and arms.

"The Lord does all for the best," she murmured. "He has not bereft me in my old age without some good purpose; yet I had hoped to die in the place where I was born, where *he* died, and my father and mother. But the Lord's will, not mine, be done."

Thus spoke the poor old woman who, without one relation in the world to offer her a refuge, had suddenly been bereft of her home and all her substance, save a few worthless acres.

Adela wept more for that than for the pain of her scorched hands and arms, and for the beautiful hair, scorched even from her very temples. When her father came she distracted his attention from herself to the poor old Quakeress, who was lifted into the carriage and taken to Holmsford, which was thenceforward her home.

CHAPTER XXXIV.

" We thought her dying when she slept,
And sleeping when she died."

Hood.

WITHOUT sadness or repining Asenith Bray made her home at Holmsford. Seldom even speaking of her old home, yielding it up unmurmuringly to the cause she loved. Yet Miss Holmes and La Guerita were not deceived ; they saw that her life was gradually failing beneath the stroke, and both with a feeling very nearly akin to remorse, mourned over the disaster they had indirectly brought upon her.

But she—meek saint—did not live to feel it long. Her soul became more and more lost to earth, and one day, about six months after the fire, she fell asleep in her chair at the fireside — and her awakening was in Heaven.

She died with but one wish unfulfilled. She had not heard of the safety of Thornton Leslie, for during all that time not one word had reached Adela from her lover, and daily she grew more anxious and despairing.

At times the suspense she endured became almost unsupportable. Again and again she pictured Thornton in the hands of the Confederates, wearing his life away in some foul dungeon. Often would she start from feverish dreams, in which she had looked upon his dead face through the slimy waters of some shallow pool, lying ghastly amid the clinging sods of the pestilential swamp. But for La Guerita, she would at such times have given herself up to despair. But she whom Adela had once comforted and protected, became in turn the giver of hope and peace. For hope and peace were hers.

The autumn of 1862, and the spring of 1863, were periods of great distress throughout the South—not only of physical, but of mental distress—that which is of all the most difficult to alleviate. A class of people were then created which had had no existence before—conscripts, and their wretched wives and children. Among these, La Guerita found her true work, and in ceaseless toil and care for them, had no time for vain repinings at her own sad lot, and at last learnt to say in faith and humbleness of heart : " It is good for me to be here."

It was strange how tranquilly the long winter months passed to her. She thought it so, when some cessation from her daily toil gave her time to overlook the past. She had never hoped for peace, yet she had found it —even in bonds, even far from the friends and the home of her youth. She shuddered sometimes when she thought that the death of Claude Leveredge had brought this peace ; yet in the depth of her soul she knew that his persecution, and all her long experience of woe had bowed down her rebellious soul to the very feet of Christ, and in the peace she there had found, she could exclaim : "Thy chastening has been my salvation, O, Lord."

She was sitting in the little sewing-room one morning in March, engaged upon some trifle for Minna, when Miss Holmes entered, and throwing herself into a rocking chair, looked at La Guerita for a moment, and exclaimed impatiently :

"How can you bear your life so patiently, Rita, when mine, which is so much brighter, seems almost insupportable to me? Do you care for your friends ; do you think of your brother who was so cruelly wounded but a few months since? If so, how can you do your duty day by day so cheerfully, while I am so torn by the agonies of suspense, that I can neither clearly think, nor act like a reasonable being?"

"I have seen nothing very unreasonable about you," replied La Guerita, smiling. "This is your first trial, Miss Adela ; suffering has not given you patience, and hourly I pray it never may. Miss Adela, can you not have faith to believe that He who preserved Thornton from one great danger, will also deliver him from others? Can you not even contemplate the worst that may befall, and say : 'Thy will be done.'"

"No," cried Miss Holmes, desperately, "and now for the first time I can comprehend the spirit with which you regarded your husband's death. Not that in any event I could deny, or curse my God, but

that I *could* not bow calmly to all His decrees. Have you even now faith to do so?"

"Yes," returned La Guerita, in a low voice. "So great has been the goodness of the Lord toward me that I can endure, though doubtless with pain yet still with fortitude, all sorrows that it may please Him to send, feeling assured that I shall some time be free from them and from these bonds. Free in spirit, if not in body. Sometimes I feel that my probation will be short, Miss Adela."

"What do you mean?" cried Miss Holmes, in alarm. "Are you ill, La Guerita? Have you been suffering in silence, while I have been accusing you of insensibility?"

"Oh, no," she answered quickly, "but still I feel that this long season of tranquility has been given me in which to prepare for some great change. God knows, it may be for the joys of heaven, or the bitterest trials of earth."

"You have strange thoughts, sometimes," said Miss Holmes, thoughtfully ; "it seems often as if you obtained dim glimpses into futurity. You speak as an oracle ; how can you?"

"Aunt Dilsey says because it is of the old 'Eboe' blood in me," she returned, smiling : "I have even myself been led to believe that negroes have some peculiar power of divination."

Miss Holmes looked up in amazement ; it was the first time she had ever heard La Guerita own her connection with the slaves, not only of condition but of blood, and it seemed to her that by that simple avowal, she had raised them nearer the level of other men.

She sat for some time musing in silence.

"I wish I could imitate your courage and resignation," she said, at last; "I think I could have both faith and patience if I could only hear that Thornton lives."

She bent her head upon her hand to hide the tears that gathered in her eyes. La Guerita saw them trickle slowly through her fingers, and was about to speak some word of sympathy, when Roxy came in to announce Captain Russell.

It was long since Adela had seen any of her old friends, and she hastened to the parlor, and welcomed Captain Russell with unfeigned pleasure. She cordially offered him her hand, and drew back in surprise when it was touched lightly, almost coldly, by her former playmate and lover.

The conversation that ensued was constrained on both sides. Captain Russell inquired for Mr. and Mrs. Holmes, and Adela replied that they had driven into Foustville. He expressed regret at their absence, saying that as his furlough was but for a week he would be forced to return to Richmond on the morrow.

"I am very sorry," said Miss Holmes, earnestly, "papa would so much like to see you, and have your opinion of war matters. Do you really think that there is any truth in the report that General Lee contemplates an invasion of the North?"

"I think time will prove that there is more faith to be placed in that than in most other newspaper reports, Miss Adela," he replied; "I pray heaven that there may be. I for one am anxious for the Yankees to feel, as we have done, the stern realities of this war, and to know what it is to have an enemy upon their very hearthstones. But I beg your pardon, Miss Adela, I forgot for a moment that you had no sympathy with such feelings."

There was an awkward silence then, which was broken at last by an exclamation from Miss Holmes who for the first time had noticed a deep scar upon Captain Russell's left temple.

"How did you get it?" she involuntarily exclaimed.

He smiled quietly, saying: "I have been waiting for you to ask, Miss Adela, for I thought that you would be interested in knowing that that was dealt by the hand of Thornton Leslie."

Surprise for a moment held her speechless. She sank back in her chair, pale and breathless. Captain Russell noticed her agitation with a smile, and sought to relieve it by adding:

"I saw Leslie about three weeks ago, for the first time since his escape from the cars. That really was cleverly managed. We met in a skirmish, and I received this wound."

"And Thornton?" gasped Adela.

"Recognized me, and rode away unhurt."

"Thank God!"

"Good-by," said Captain Russell, rising and extending his hand; "Good-by, Adela, and though from my very heart I condemn the opinions you hold, I honor the devotion you have exhibited for your lover, and am happy to be able to give you the assurance of his safe escape from the Confederacy."

The blood rushed into Adela's cheeks at his words. This Captain Russell, then, whom she had shrank from intrusting with her secret, knew it all, and believed her a traitress. For a moment her heart quailed with fear, then calming herself, she said :

"I shall never forget your kindness, Captain Russell, but I was not aware that you"—

"Knew how Major Leslie made his escape," he interrupted. "Shall I tell you how I learned it? I met a woman in the streets of M——, well disguised, but whom I thought I knew ; I passed her by, uncertain as to her identity. I saw her son an hour later, and could doubt no longer. That woman—La Guerita DeCuba—had been to the depot where the prisoners were confined, and was hastening to you to give you news of your lover and her friend. I felt convinced of that in my own mind, and that Major Leslie would strive to escape that night. I felt it to be my duty if possible to prevent it, and going to the officer in charge —I was myself but a passenger in the train—told him that there were a desperate set of men in Leslie's car, and advised him to put a double guard upon them."

"Ah, then, it was by your advice they were so closely watched," cried Miss Holmes, energetically ; pausing as she recollected that by those words she had implicated herself openly in the matter.

"I did what I considered right," said Russell, firmly ; "I did all that I could to prevent the escape of even a single person, while the government thought fit to retain them. I am not the man, from a sentimental feeling of friendship or party, to place a sword in an enemy's hand that he may strike at me or my friends."

Adela cast down her eyes, blushing violently at those words for she knew that they were uttered to rebuke her.

"Then it was by your advice that so strict a search was made throughout this country ? " she faltered.

"It was," he returned. "I tell you plainly that I desired the capture of Leslie and his friends. But," he added, in a low voice, "I could not bear that *your* name should be mentioned in so disgraceful an affair."

"It was not disgraceful," retorted Miss Holmes, with a flash of the temper for which she had once been noted. "Remember, Captain Russell, that we have both honestly adopted different opinions of this sad affair ; but even if I thought as you do, I should still have considered it my duty to have saved one whom I had once loved from such a loathsome den as a Confederate prison. They are a disgrace to humanity, and when this war is ended, their record will be too horrible for even friends to read without a shudder. How, then, can you call it disgraceful for me to have risked my honor—yes, almost my life, to have saved from them my betrothed husband ? "

He winced at the word. "I beg your pardon," he said, "I was looking at the case only from my own point of view. Believe me, much as I regret the stand you have taken, and the part you have acted, I admire—nay, reverence—the courage which has enabled you to do both."

Adela mused for some minutes.

"Captain Russell," she said at last, "you have given *me* much to thank you for, in so faithfully keeping my secret, though you must have had many temptations to betray it. Let me ask you if I—if Thornton—has not also more to thank you for. Did you not send me word that Asenith's house would be searched?"

"It was only done to save you and Asenith," he returned, bluntly : "I did not choose that the name of Adela Holmes should become a by-word through the country round. I made sure they would catch Leslie on the Foustville road, and gave them a hint that conscripts and deserters generally took that route. Of course you know how he escaped them there? I had no idea that he could do so."

"You say *them ;* did you not yourself join in the search?"

"My dear Miss Holmes," he cried, indignantly, "I am an officer of the regular army. I have nothing to do with conscripts and escaped soldiers. I happened to be able to send you that item of information because Captain Owen of the detailed force, told me that day, as I was passing through E—— on my way to Charlotte, that there was a great hunt in perspective that night, and among other places they should make a clean sweep of Asenith Bray's house, so I immediately dispatched my servant to give you warning."

"And you cannot refuse my thanks for the valuable information," cried Adela, warmly ; "but for that Thornton would never have escaped."

"I thought he would certainly have been captured on the Foustville road," observed Russell, regretfully.

Miss Holmes laughed merrily.

"Pray don't allow such a good act to weigh upon your conscience," she said, gaily ; "let my thanks for your tender consideration of me soften your self-reproach for the escape of Thornton," adding, gravely, as she remembered their late encounter : "Believe me, Captain Russell, had he but known your kindness, he would not have ignored it so cruelly."

"Oh, this scar !" exclaimed Russell, touching it lightly with his forefinger. "Do not imagine, Miss Adela, that I regret his escape on that account. He could not have acted more magnanimously than he did the moment he recognized me. He turned to another point of the field, and permitted me to regain my sword, allowing me at once to retain my liberty and honor."

"Then, surely, you can feel no further reproach concerning his escape," said Adela ; "for, after all, a life for a life has been given. I think 'prisoner for prisoner' synonymous with that, you know."

"I know you had always a horror of bonds of any kind," replied Captain Russell, smiling ; "I believe the only arguments I ever had with you were upon the subject of slavery. Let me tell you now, that I do see some evil in it ; it is wrong in the case of La Guerita DeCuba, for instance. I have felt that ever since the meeting at Foustville ; that was a terrible scene, and thousands of times have I reproached myself for not informing her friends of her whereabouts when it was in my power to do so."

Why did you not?" asked Miss Holmes, abruptly.

The young man flushed to the temples, and looked at her nervously. She felt her cheeks burn, and could have bitten her tongue for its hasty speech.

"I will tell you," he said, in a low yet steady voice; "you know, Adela, that I loved you. Knowing what I do, it would be an insult to say with what feelings I regard you now. I had heard that a gentleman at the North had proposed to you, and that Claude Leveredge had broken off the match—that you had suffered him to do so. I was unconscious then of the great influence held by Claude over your father; or that you had yielded only from a sense of duty. Can you wonder, then, that I imagined your cousin Claude to be my rival? I saw when La Guerita came that you were jealous, and fearful of her—I beg your pardon, I will say no more."

"Yes, yes; go on," said Miss Holmes, ashamed of the flush of anger his words had called to her cheek.

"I am ashamed to say," continued Russell, after a slight pause, "that I kept La Guerita's secret because I knew how Claude had loved her, and reckoned upon the effect the sight of her would have upon him. I even wrote some letters, addressing him, in a friendly spirit, to return home and defend his interests during the coming war, not daring, however, to compromise myself by naming La Guerita DeCuba. Well, well, I was justly punished at last by finding all my plotting vain. Claude Leveredge himself told me who my rival really was. Forgive me, Adela, for though I loved you above all treasure, I could have resigned you almost contentedly to so good a man as Thornton Leslie."

"Who would have supposed that you could have concocted a plot, even so slender as that?" exclaimed Miss Holmes, extending her hand. "Indeed, my friend, I forgive you, and thank you from my heart for the reparation you have made."

He was deeply touched.

"Thank you—thank you!" he murmured; "I can think of the matter with a lighter heart now; especially as I suppose La Guerita's secret is one no longer. Yes; I can even think with some satisfaction of the part I took in Leslie's escape, in the consideration of the good news he has undoubtedly taken to her friends."

Miss Holmes found it painful, and difficult to explain, that the secret was a secret still, and yet more painful to hear his exclamations of surprise and sorrow.

"I assure you you have done wrong—very wrong—" he began, when the door was thrown open, and Mrs. Holmes entered. She shooks hands with him, and commented volubly upon his improved appearance.

"And that scar makes you look quite warlike," she said; "I called at your mother's on my way home, and she told me your furlough was so short that your calls upon your friends would necessarily be so also. Therefore I had no idea I should have the pleasure of seeing you here; but I am delighted, and so is Addie, I am sure," and Mrs. Holmes looked from one to the other, enjoying the slight confusion into which her abrupt entrance had thrown them; for, like most idle women, Mrs. Holmes was a match-maker, and had not yet given up her favorite project of seeing her daughter Adela Mrs. William Russell.

The young man stayed but a short time after her arrival, much to her chagrin. After bidding farewell to the other members of the family, he walked through the garden with Mr. Holmes, saying, as he mounted his horse at the gate :

"I had some conversation with your son Rufe, while waiting in the parlor for Miss Adela. What a young fire-eater he is, and a strapping fellow, too. If you are not careful he will be in the army before another month."

"Pooh! nonsense!" laughed Mr. Holmes; "he is not out of the school-room yet; though he ought to have been, and at Chapel Hill long ago. The idea of his going into the army; why he is a mere child still."

"But well able to carry a musket," rejoined Russell; "and I can see he has been brooding over his cousin's death, and all sorts of romantic stories, until they have driven him wild. He is puffed up with the idea of becoming a hero, and, of course, will rush to the army. Still, my prophecy may prove false; I hope it will. Good-by!"

But to the amazement and distress of the whole family, in less than two weeks Captain Russell's words were verified. Rufus Holmes left his home and enlisted.

Upon first hearing of it, his father was overwhelmed with anger and grief, and hastened to take the necessary measures for withdrawing him from the army; but at last, yielding to the popular feeling and the entreaties of the boy, he withdrew his objections, and, in spite of all the argu-

ments and prayers of his sister, he was allowed to proceed to the camp of instruction; whence, in a few weeks, he passed into the ranks. Even Mrs. Holmes, who had at first appeared half wild with grief at the departure of her child, soon felt positive relief in his absence, saying it was the only peaceful time she had known since his birth; and flattered by the representations made by admiring friends, of the valor and patriotism of the boy, meekly replied to all Adela's remonstrances :

"Well, well, my child, I suppose it is our duty to allow him to go."

"Duty! duty!" thought Adela, sadly; "If he should be killed, or come home ruined in health or principles, I wonder if that thought will comfort her, when she shudders over his wasted life!"

CHAPTER XXXV.

"Why the sepulchre
Wherein we saw thee quietly inurn'd,
Hath ope'd its ponderous and marble jaws
To cast thee up again."
Shakespeare.

EARLY in April Miss Holmes left home on a visit to some relations in Charleston. La Guerita gladly saw her depart, though she felt most deeply their separation. Though Miss Holmes had regained part of her elasticity of spirit after Captain Russell's announcement of Thornton Leslie's safety, much of it had been almost instantly destroyed by the wayward conduct of her brother. The great anxiety she felt concerning him, added to her constant sympathy in the miseries of those around her, preyed seriously upon her health, which during the winter had not been robust. Although she prepared for her journey languidly she could not but feel that it was her duty to go, and seek, in change of scene and air, her wonted strength.

She had been gone two weeks, and La Guerita being unable to find sufficient employment for her active mind in the light duties of the schoolroom, which now seemed mere child's play when Rufus had gone, or in the woes of the few conscripts that yet remained in the woods, and besought her advice and aid, felt most deeply the absence of her friend. She seemed quite lost and bewildered without her, so used had they been to consult together in any occasions of perplexity.

"I suppose it must be my 'Eboe' spirit longing for its superior," she said to herself at times, smiling bitterly. "Well, whatever may be the cause, I cannot do away with it. Oh, that she would come back; I feel so utterly alone—so miserable."

Such had been her thoughts one afternoon, when she entered the house and found Mrs. Holmes crying over two letters she had received. That did not alarm her, as the excitement of war-time had increased the natural nervousness of Mrs. Holmes to such an extent that she wept at everything, and often much to the annoyance of stronger-minded people.

"Just listen," she cried, "what Rufus says. Did *ever* any one hear of such a boy? 'Every one prophesies a brilliant career for me, and I feel in my heart that the South will one day tremble with pride, and the North with terror of my name.'"

"A noble boy," said Mr. Holmes, proudly. "I must show that to Gor-don; how he will glory in the lad's spirit. But you have a letter from Addie, I see. What does she say?"

Mrs. Holmes opened the missive and read a few lines, and with a slight scream of surprise, exclaimed:

"I never heard of such a child, Norton. She is actually coming home in a few days—will leave early in the week, she says. Who ever heard of such a thing as a two weeks' visit to Charleston!"

"Well, she never did like Charleston much," said Mr. Holmes, secretly pleased at the prospect of his daughter's quick return; "neither are the Charleston Leveredges favorites of hers. Addie has some good reason for returning so soon, you may be sure. What does she say about it?"

"What does Addie ever say to satisfy people?" returned Mrs. Holmes, impatiently. "She merely states that she is coming home, and with her usual kindness leaves us to guess the reason."

"And it will prove a sufficient one, I'll wager," said Mr. Holmes, decidedly.

"And whatever it may be," thought La Guerita, "thank God she is coming. Thank God I shall not be much longer alone."

Just at that moment a great noise arose in the garden beneath; a dozen negroes were crying out in various tones of horror, amazement, and delight. La Guerita started to the window to discover, if possible, the cause of the hubbub, and presently above it all heard a voice that stayed her heart from beating—the voice she had believed silent forever—the voice of Claude Leveredge.

In a moment he was in the room, and his aunt was sobbing out her welcome in his arms. Mrs. Holmes embraced him delightedly, and the children half smothered him with kisses. Miss Matilda, meanwhile, stood aloof, with a most dissatisfied expression of countenance, for although she had deplored his death most sincerely, she could not reconcile herself to this unusual proceeding of a dead man coming to life, and at last gave vent to her injured feelings by exclaiming :

"Well, Claude, this is just like you. Who would ever have dreamed of your coming back to give us all such a shock. For my part, I feel as if every nerve of my body had been taken out, a pin stuck through each, and then put back in the wrong place.

Claude laughed, kissing her warmly, "to settle her nerves," he said, and to assure her that he was really flesh and blood ; a fact which she, like the negroes, seemed to doubt.

"Ah, and so you also thought me dead," he continued, intercepting La Guerita as she was leaving the room. "How exceedingly pale you are. Have you been ill ?"

He spoke kindly, yet looked penetratingly into her face.

"I have been very well," she answered, not knowing what she was saying.

"Oh, yes," Mrs. Holmes interposed, much to La Guerita's relief, "we have all been very well. But how dreadfully pale you are yourself, Claude."

"What else could be expected of a resurrected man ?" asked aunt Matilda, grimly.

"And no wonder," he replied, "for I have been sick and in prison since you saw me last. But where are Addie and Rufe ?" he added, glancing around the circle. "I was in hopes that all the family would help to welcome me."

"Rufe has volunteered !" cried a chorus of voices.

"What ?" cried Claude, looking at the group with an expression of blank amazement.

"He has volunteered," explained Mrs. Holmes, "and gone like a brave, high-spirited lad, as he is, to fight the base invaders of our soil."

"And you sanctioned his going?" asked Leveredge, reproachfully, fixing his eyes keenly upon his uncle.

"Not at first. But I could not withstand the boy's eloquence. How could I, when his sole desire seemed to be to revenge your death ?"

"Then recall him at once, I beg of you," said Claude, much agitated. "You see I am not dead, but am abundantly able to revenge for myself all the wrongs I have suffered. But we can speak of this later ; where is Addie ? I suppose she has not also volunteered."

"No," answered Mrs. Holmes, smiling, "she is visiting the Charleston Leveredges. We expected her home next week, but I will telegraph her to come immediately."

"Oh, let her have her visit out," said Claude. "I shall not be ready for service for a month, or three weeks, at least. I want her to come home and find a surprise awaiting her."

"Addie isn't fond of surprises," said Miss Matilda, dryly, "and Rita is not either. Where did you get that scar on your face? It looks as if a horse had kicked you. That's part of Claude's honor, I suppose."

Mr. and Mrs. Holmes laughed, and Claude looked at them interrogatively, wondering to what the words "Claude's honor" had reference.

"She is thinking of old Mrs. Clayton and her son William," explained Mrs. Holmes, laughingly. "You know they never owned a negro in their lives, and when some one remarked so to the old lady, asking at the same time what her son was going to fight for, 'Why, for honor, to be sure,' answered the poor old soul innocently, as if her booby Will. would ever get honor as a soldier, or anything else. Well, after a time Will. was wounded, and Mrs. Clayton exultantly told every one that Will. had got honor on his arm ; a battle after, it was in his leg, and about a month ago, to use the old lady's own phrase, 'He got so much honor all over him that it killed him.'"

"I am afraid aunt Matilda has made some additions to the original story," said Claude, laughing.

"I can assure you not," replied Mrs. Holmes, earnestly, "but now, dear Claude, tell us really where you got your honor."

"In the fourth day's battle near Richmond," responded Claude, "and faith quite an overpowering honor it proved to be. I was left on the field for dead ; a dozen officers have sworn to me that they saw me draw my last breath, and when I came to myself I found that I was in an ambulance, and on my way to an hospital, where I remained for some time an involuntary guest of Uncle Sam. After that I was sent to Fort ——, from

whence I was exchanged about a week ago. There is my history in a nutshell."

"But you have been very ill, Claude," said his aunt, anxiously.

"I have indeed," he answered, gravely. "Had I not received the best of care your mourning garments would not have been worn without cause."

Mrs. Holmes burst into tears and left the room, returning an hour later in colored apparel.

La Guerita caught a glimpse of her figure during the afternoon, and straightway began to reproach herself most bitterly that while every one else upon the plantation, from the eldest to the youngest, was putting on the robes and feelings of joy, she alone remained unable even to feign the semblance of pleasure. Never had she felt more utterly miserable or more forsaken. Her enemy had come, as from the grave, to torment her, and there was not one to whom she could go for comfort or protection. For the first time in months the realization that she was *a slave* came home to her, and it was with the deepest shame and the most bitter self-reproaches that she reflected that the resurrection of Claude Leveredge had brought it to her.

"It is just," she said, at length. "The Lord is punishing me as I deserve, for I found *peace* at the thought of my enemy's death, and in my heart of hearts I found pleasure in it."

Fain would she have written to Miss Holmes, had she but dared, urging her immediate return. Five days seemed to be an interminable time to be alone. Never dragged hours so drearily by, yet often she could but smile at her disquietude. Her faith in God was too strong for fear of mortal to shake it. No, she knew well through all these days that it was not *fear* that agitated her, and caused her to tremble like an aspen leaf at the sight of Claude Leveredge. It was that old feeling of shame that had maddened her twice, and which had slumbered so peacefully for the few months of repose that had follow-ed her adventures in Thornton Les-lie's behalf. She realized that fully on the third day after Claude Lever-edge's return, when he walked into her school-room, and glancing keenly at her, asked abruptly :

"What did you think when you heard I was dead ?"

Alfred and Minna were present, and, in great confusion, La Guerita stammered :

"We were all greatly shocked, of course, Mr. Leveredge."

"I am dreadfully tired," he said ; "Alfred, I wish you would go in the house and get me a cigar. You will find one on the study mantel-piece."

Alfred was off in an instant.

"Oh, I forgot," said Leveredge, looking at Minna, "'twas the parlor mantel I meant. Run and tell him so."

She quickly obeyed. Claude Lev-eredge looked up at La Guerita, as she stood calmly at some distance from him. He advanced a step, the blood rushing over his pale, olive face as he whispered :

"I could not die, La Guerita ; the thought of you won me back to life. What welcome have you for me ?"

He held out his hand, and looked at her as if he would read her very soul. He saw she was afflicted, but it was only for a moment. She waved aside his proffered hand, and turned away. He looked at her with the longing and ferocity of a baffled tiger, muttering a few words between his clenched teeth, which gave La Guerita to know that the vows made years before were not forgotten.

She knew then that any slight hope she had entertained of a change in his feelings toward her, was futile. His long illness had not made him a better man, and his incarceration had given him time to think over the dif-ficulties of the chase he had in the excitement of war apparently aban-doned. She saw that his long ab-sence had but given her vantage ground, but had served also to height-en and intensify the ardor of her pur-suer.

These thoughts flashed upon her mind in an instant, leaving their im-press on her face. Determination to resist to the death, Claude Leveredge read in her flashing eyes and com-pressed mouth. Determination to *strive* till death, she read in his. They understood each other fully then. He knew it, and turning from the house, entered the garden, mutter-ing :

"Fool that I am. Why could I not have feigned indifference for a time ? That might have accomplish-ed what all my love and cruelty have striven to do in vain. How is it that before *her*, I cannot hide that I love her ? I love her ! She would ques-tion that if she knew all ; but 'tis true. What am I thinking of ? Hers is the love I want. Good God, what love she could give me if she would. How I would glory in it ; how I would laugh all other love to scorn. My wife! By ,Heavens, she was promised to me years ago, and mine she shall be. What do I care if she hates me with a power strong as death? I would rather have her hate than the undying love of any other wife. Any other wife! What am I thinking of; I believe my fever has not left me. Ah, here are the children."

"Swift messengers, you are," he cried, gaily, as they approached him. "You see I had got tired of waiting for you."

"We could not help it, cousin Claude," they explained eagerly; "We had to go to your room for cigars, there were none in the parlor or study."

"All right," said Leveredge; "go on to the school room, and, Minna, if you have perfect lessons to-day, you may come to me for a real gold dollar in the evening."

Minna opened her eyes very wide, and then with an exclamation of delight and astonishment, ran off to the school-room, followed by her brother.

Mr. Leveredge lighted one of the cigars they had brought him, and strolled on, endeavoring to confine his thoughts to the same channel in which they had flown before, but the unpleasant flavor of his cigar, entirely diverted them, he threw it from him with an exclamation of impatience, and hearing the sound of high voices in a distant part of the garden, he strolled, indolently, in the direction from which they came.

It was not long before he discovered the cause of the unusual hubbub. Miss Matilda was soon seen advancing toward him, holding Harry by the ear, and followed at a respectable distance by half-a-dozen little slaves, whose wildly-rolling eyes and significant howls, declared that they had been engaged in some mischief for which they expected condign punishment. Harry was the ringleader; Claude Leveredge could easily have seen that, even if Miss Matilda's voluble expressions of indignation had not assured him of it.

"You must come right along with me," exclaimed the irate old lady, "he'll teach you how to make forts, and turn his cigars into guns. Oh, you dreadful creature; what do you expect will become of you? Where do you think you'll go to when you die? Don't you speak!"

The poor child had not attempted to utter a word.

"Just come right into your master, and if he don't order you whipped I'll tie you up by the heels and make you pick cotton till Christmas; what do you think of that?"

Mr. Leveredge laughed heartily, asking: "What is the matter, aunt Matilda? What has the boy done?"

"Ask me what he has not done," she returned, "and I might be able to tell you—'no good,' for I am sure he has done everything else. I verily believe he's getting up a revolution among the niggers now. Here, you sir, come back and give me your ear," she added suddenly as Harold escaped from her grasp and retreated a few paces.

Involuntarily he covered his ears with his hands, withdrawing them, and flushing hotly as he caught Claude's eye fixed laughingly upon him.

"I am going to put out my guns," he muttered, turning away.

"Let him go," said Claude, as he saw Miss Matilda was about to follow him ; "you take care of the others, I will take care of him."

Miss Matilda did as she was wished ; not, however, to please Claude, but because she saw that most of the offenders were looking around for chances of escape, and she was determined to allow them none.

Claude Leveredge followed Harold out of the garden, and a short distance into the meadow, where, much to his surprise and amusement, he discovered the fate of his choice cigars. They were actively engaged in bombarding and defending the miniature city of Vicksburg. The city, which was made of a vast number of wooden buildings, gaily painted churches, and tin savings' banks, the combined wealth of the plantation children, was situated upon a high bluff of the meadow brook. It was surrounded by walls of brick, on which were planted continually active cannon in the form of lighted cigars. There were four hide boats lying in the stream below, also mounted with cannon, which presented fire toward the city or the spectators on the opposite shore with perfect impartiality. Thin spirals of smoke constantly arose from both the city and the boats, almost enveloping their respective flags.

Claude Leveredge laughed for a few moments heartily.

"You are a pretty fellow," he said at last ; "who gave you permission to use my cigars in this way?"

"No one, sir," said Harry, flushing and trembling ; "I beg your pardon, sir, the fire crackers all gave out, and I didn't know what else to do."

"You have been using crackers for cannon before, then?"

"Yes, sir, and they did beautiful for Norfolk and Newbern, and all the battles around Richmond ; only sometimes they would fizzle, and they don't make such a big smoke as cigars."

"But how do you manage the report?" asked Claude, laughing.

"Why, for the distant ones, sir, we beat a little drum, and for the others we have still a few fire crackers left. I am very sorry, sir, we didn't use them, but I was afraid they would give out before the fight was over."

"But what in the world could make you think of taking my cigars? Do you know that I ought to whip you for it?"

"I didn't take the cigars, sir."

"Who did?"

"I shouldn't like to tell, sir. Besides, it was I that was to blame ; I ought to have sent them back, but he brought one to me lighted, and it just seemed as if I couldn't help using the others."

"So you won't tell me who did it? Suppose that I whip you then."

Harold looked at him defiantly, then dropped his eyes. Claude Leveredge saw him working his hands together nervously, and biting his lips, to force back his rising tears ; yet though again asked, he would not reveal the name of him who had brought him the cigars.

Something arose in Claude Leveredge's throat and choked him, as he looked upon the boy, and suddenly, with a strange passionate gesture, he caught him to his heart and kissed him again and again.

Harold released himself roughly from this unwelcome embrace, muttering angrily :

"I'm not a baby !"

Claude colored to the temples, annoyed at and ashamed of his sudden emotions.

"I know you are not," he said, but I knew you when you were a baby. I even knew your mother when she was."

Harold looked at him in astonishment.

"Put out these smoldering cigars," said Mr. Leveredge, pointing to the miniature city and fleet, and throwing himself indolently upon the grass. "I am not angry at you, Harry."

The child gathered up the cigars silently, and tied a wisp of long straw around them, often glancing furtively at the lounger by his side.

"Where did my mother live when she was a baby, sir ?" he ventured at last to inquire.

Mr. Leveredge informed him ; and emboldened by his kindness, Harold asked a series of questions, receiving satisfactory, if not always truthful answers to all. So they talked together a long time ; and it in some way happened, that in that single afternoon, Claude Leveredge gained a power over the child that perfectly obliterated all his former dread and dislike.

La Guerita was detained in the school-room until late in the afternoon ; when she went to her cabin, she found Harold sitting on the steps with his face resting between his hands. She sat down beside him, and playfully asked why he was so thoughtful ?

"I was thinking of Enola. You know, mamma, you took me away from there and put me in this little cabin. What did you do it for ; when I am so rich, and have such a beautiful home of my own ? "

She was so totally unprepared for the child's questions, that each seemed a dagger in her heart. He repeated them, looking at her anxiously with his wistful eyes, and unable to bear their reproachful glances, she covered her face with her hands, and burst into tears.

"Oh, mamma, don't cry ; please don't cry," cried Harold, in great distress ; "don't you want to go back, mamma ? I thought you did ; and Mr. Leveredge says he will take us if you will go. Do go, mamma."

"Then Mr. Leveredge has been talking to you ?" La Guerita raised her head and looked at the child steadily.

"Yes, mamma, he has told me all about Enola, and he wants to take us there. Let us go. Mr. Leveredge told me just what it was to be a slave, and I can't bear to be what he says I am."

"What did he say you are ? But never mind ; don't think of it, Harold."

"Yes, I shall think of it," he persisted ; I can't help thinking of it. Mr Leveredge says I ought to go to Enola—that I should be a master there, and I am a *slave* here."

"My child ! my child !"

"Will you let Mr. Leveredge take us back, mamma ?"

"No, Harold."

"Not to Enola, mamma ? "

It was hard to encounter his looks of utter incredulity, but still she answered, firmly :

"No, Harold."

"Then I don't believe you love me," he cried, passionately ; "I am not a black nigger, and I won't be a slave. Oh, take me back to Enola ; let me go back ! "

So it had come at last. The child she had despoiled of his birthright had arisen and demanded it of her, and though her very heart bled for it, she could but answer sternly, and bid him be silent. Yet hours afterwards, she paced the floor of her room, praying for power to give her child his freedom, and for strength to resist the temptation his lips held out to her.

"Am I ever crying to God for help, and yet ever putting aside the hand he stretches forth to me," she cried more than once. "Claude Leveredge loves me ; other women have married a second time and been happy. Happy, I could never be ; but should I be right ? O, God, should I be right? No, no, no ; a thousand times *No !* My very soul revolts from such a union—angels seem to warn me from it."

She bent over her sleeping child, in anguish, crying :

"Not even for thee can I do that. I will sacrifice my very life for thee, but I cannot lose my soul."

A hundred times during the three succeeding days did she find it necessary to strengthen her resolution by such words as these. It was hard to utter them in the face of her child's rapidly-increasing intimacy with Leveredge, and his growing discontent

with his lot. It seemed to her that her direct punishment, or rather trial, had come. She could not look upon her sorrows as punishment, for she remembered she had not sinned. From the hour she had sternly silenced Harold in his entreaties and demand to be taken home, she felt that she had lost the child's confidence, and with an agony that cannot be described, saw that he was rapidly transferring it to the man whose power over him she dreaded, not only as affecting his physical, but his moral weal.

She had, herself, neither spoken or encountered Leveredge since his visit to the school-room, and was greatly in hopes that she would not do so until Miss Holmes' return, which was expected to take place on Wednesday or Thursday. She was thinking of this as she sat in her cabin, on the evening of Monday, patching a hole in Harold's coat, and often glancing at him anxiously, as he lay sleeping calmly upon the bed, when Roxy entered with a message from Mr. Holmes.

" Dere ain't nobody thar but Massa, and Missus, and Massa Claude," she said, in answer to La Guerita's inquiries, "an' you must go in right away. Massa Claude said he was mighty dull, and I 'spect he wants you to play de panny."

"Oh, I hope not," involuntarily exclaimed La Guerita, for she had not touched the piano for many months, except when instructing Minna, or alone with Mrs. Holmes ; she, however, hastened to the house, and with a fast-beating heart entered the parlor she would as gladly have avoided.

"Oh, no, Aunt Myra," she heard Leveredge say as she entered, "I don't want her to play for me. Minna gave me music enough this afternoon to last any reasonable man a month; and very well she plays, too," he added, looking at La Guerita, and acknowledging her presence with a smile; "far better than her sister does. Who would ever have dreamed that you would have made such a successful teacher? Now, uncle, we are ready for a game at whist; Rita and I against aunt and yourself. You will have to do your best; for I remember that Rita played a splendid game years ago."

Mr. and Mrs. Holmes looked at each other, and at La Guerita, as if greatly astonished, and somewhat displeased. As for La Guerita, she could not for a moment comprehend the audacity of the speaker; the next she turned and was proudly leaving the room, when Mr. Holmes called her back.

"Rita," he said, "did you not hear what Mr. Leveredge said? What do you mean by leaving the room? Sit down instantly, and take your part of the game."

She stood for an instant, uncertain whether to rebel or obey; her eyes flashed and her bosom heaved, but she did not entirely lose full control over either her temper or person. Claude looked at her narrowly; she saw it, and thought: "He expects me to refuse submission; I shall give him some pretext for insulting me more deeply if I do." She approached the table slowly, and with the air of a queen—a haughty queen —took the chair that Claude Leveredge placed for her. For a few min-

utes she seemed quite blind; her surroundings faded from her sight; she was again at Enola, with Harold, Victor, and Mrs. DeGrey. The tears rose to her eyes, but she forced them back, knowing if she suffered them to come she should lose all composure; and she presently found herself following Mrs. Holmes' lead, and taking an active part in the game, in which she had been forced to participate. By good fortune she held good cards, and played them well, though without taking the slightest interest in the game, or any part of the conversation, which Claude Leveredge strove to make most constant and agreeable. She played as if in a dream—a dream that was endless—taking no note of anything. She heard Mrs. Leveredge make a remark about a carriage, without at all comprehending what it was. A few minutes later she heard footsteps in the hall, the door was thrown open, and Adela Holmes entered the room, followed by a tall, elderly gentlemen and a troop of servants. The group at the table arose to meet them, uttering exclamations of pleasure and surprise. Miss Holmes recognized her cousin, and, turning deadly pale, gasped out: "Oh, Claude, they did not tell me you were here."

He greeted her warmly, quickly dispelling her wonder and alarm; then she noticed for the first time that La Guerita was in the room, and the game in which she had been engaged. Instantly her countenance clouded with indignation. She sprang forward and snatched the cards from La Guerita's hand, and without a word motioned her to the door. She left the room gladly, but saw Miss

Holmes turn upon her cousin a glance of ineffable scorn. "So, you could not let me know you were here," she said, in a tone of cutting irony; "and this is the way you keep your vows? This is your sense of honor?"

CHAPTER XXXVI.

"O, Lord, my boy, my Arthur, my fair son—
My life, my joy, my food, my all the world—
My widow-comfort, and my sorrow's cure."
Shakespeare.

WELL as La Guerita was assured that she had no share in Miss Adela's anger and scorn, the hours passed wearily until she could hear the fact from the young lady's own lips.

"How could you for a moment suppose that I accused you falsely?" she said, in reply to such a remark of La Guerita, when they met in the school-house, after lesson-hours, the following day.

"No; all my anger and scorn was for Claude—my sympathy for you; but last night was not the time to show it. I remembered that, even in the height of my indignation. But, say, were you not for a moment more startled than delighted at my appearance?"

"I must own that I was," returned La Guerita; "for much as I longed for your coming, I had no expectation of seeing you until to-morrow, at the earliest."

"I often laugh at you for your shrewd prophecies and strange presentiments," said Miss Holmes; "but I don't think I shall ever do so again; for my mind has been full of them since I left home. My cousin told me I was nervous, and rallied me about it; but it was of no use; I could not shake my dismal forebodings from me; perhaps they grew all the more rapidly because I would not mention them. At last I became convinced that some danger was threatening you, and I wrote to father that I should leave Charleston this week—that being the earliest time I could possibly name. Strangely enough, just after that letter was sent my forebodings increased a hundred fold; so that I most earnestly begged my cousin Charles to take charge of me to Raleigh, instead of causing me to wait for his brother Will., who had first proposed to escort me, and who could not have been home for three days later. The whole family protested against my leaving them so hastily. I think, indeed, they were half offended, and would have been wholly so had any other visitor acted so obstinately; but their displeasure troubled me little. Indeed, I scarcely think anything on earth would have kept me from Holmsford a day longer; and the sequel shows I am right. You are in danger, my poor Rita; you do need my sympathy and protection. I thank God I am here to give it. But, La Guerita, tell me, did Claude look so wild and haggard when he first reached home? It is almost impossible for me to believe even now that he has not come from the grave, and you can well imagine his appearance at first startled me."

"I need not imagine it," returned La Guerita; "I felt, perhaps, even more deeply than you, certainly more remorsefully."

Miss Holmes looked at her and sighed. "Ah, did you feel remorsefully?" she said; "and yet you should not have done so, for you have never rejoiced in his fancied death, though it brought you peace. What has his return to life done toward destroying that peace? What has he said or done to you?"

La Guerita could not, even in the midst of her own anxiety, repress a smile at the tone of defiant solicitude in which these last words were spoken; still she gladly proceeded to place her newly awakened fears and perplexities before the clear mind of her questioner, feeling assured that they would be understood, and that she would receive the sympathy, and perhaps, also, the counsel she needed.

"Was ever man so bewitched before?" said Miss Holmes, musingly, when she had heard what La Guerita had to tell. "It seems almost incomprehensible that he persists in continuing this persecution; he must, by this time, be satisfied that it is useless; he shall know it, at any rate, to-day. I have opposed him silently too long. I will find what my tongue can do. That is called woman's best weapon, you know."

"Oh, I beg you not to speak to him!" cried La Guerita, in alarm.

"I certainly shall; I intend to know why he persecuted you so; I intend to know, La Guerita, whether he really proposes to marry you. You know I have doubted it. I think such a question from me will cause him to reflect upon what he is doing."

"I think he debated that question years ago," returned La Guerita, coloring, a little proudly; "and I most positively believe his intentions in that respect are strictly honorable."

Miss Holmes said nothing, feeling sorry she had said anything to arouse La Guerita's sensitive pride. "He is a Southerner," she thought, "and, thank Heaven, Southerners do not marry slaves."

"There he is," she added, aloud; "I am going to speak to him."

He was standing in the garden, intently watching a pair of ants, that were pushing a tiny grain toward their hole. He did not see his cousin until she approached and laid her hand upon his arm. He started, and laughed, as he called her attention to the tiny laborers.

"Work is a good thing," he said, lightly; "it keeps even these ants out of mischief. I haven't a doubt, if they were idle they would be looking around for some person or thing to sting."

"You are quite a philosopher, Claude."

"Any man gets to be that who has been on the sick-list three or four months."

"That is very true, or he ought to. I came to tell you so, Claude. I have been talking to La Guerita DeCuba, and I came to tell you so."

He colored, quickly and angrily, at her unexpected words. "What has La Guerita to do with me?" he at last said, sullenly.

"Nothing," returned Miss Holmes, promptly; "you know, Claude, that she is never so happy as when separated from you; but you have much to do with her; you take from her all the happiness of her life."

"I take from her the happiness of her life?" he exclaimed, excitedly; "it is not so; I would restore it to her. It is your father, and our accursed laws and law-givers, that take it from her; it is those that keep her in slavery."

"And are you not one?"

"Have I not offered her freedom a hundred times, and I offer it to her again. Go, Adela, and tell her so; tell her I will take her and her child out of this accursed bondage."

"Would you marry her, Claude?"

The question was asked very quietly. She saw him grow pale and tremble for an instant.

"What right have you to ask me such a question?" he said, at length.

"I was thinking of her happiness, Claude."

"Her happiness? and you keep her in bondage here, on a level with the lowest of the low. Do you expect her to find happiness here? You were thinking of her happiness. You would do better to believe that I think of it, and of my own honor."

"And you would marry her?"

"Good Heavens! Adela, why should I not?"

"Have you ever considered that your family—that the whole world would suggest many reasons why you should not. You must have done so, or you would have told my father years ago that you wished to marry Rita, and would not have so grossly deceived him as to your real motive in keeping her in durance here."

"Your father is her master," he said, sternly.

"*You* are her master," retorted Miss Holmes, angrily, striving in vain to keep her temper; "my father would have freed her years ago had you not bound him by an oath to hold her; and if you had not forced that oath from him by hold-ing over his head menaces of the vengeance of her family should her hiding-place be discovered. You practiced well upon my father's fears, Claude Leveredge, and upon his love for you. You told him that your life would not be worth the asking if she returned home. You confessed to him the base part you had acted in making her parentage known to her husband, and cajoled him into the promise to keep her in slavery until all danger of your life, by the hands of her brother, was overpast. You are not a coward, Claude, but you feigned to be, with good effect, then."

He actually cowered beneath the gaze of scorn she threw upon him; but rallied immediately, saying, with a careless laugh:

"Are you ubiquitous, Adela?"

"No," she said.

"Then you were eaves-dropping instead. I think you have belied the promises of your childhood as much as I, Adela."

"No," she answered, flushing; "I was not eaves-dropping, my cousin; but your plot was easily read by one who studied your character as I have; and as to belying the promises of my childhood, I have never broken vows, as you have done. But I did not come here to exchange reproaches. I came to tell you that you are persecuting La Guerita in vain; she will never yield to you; she will never marry you."

"Then it is you that will prevent her," he burst forth, angrily; "but, by heaven, you shall find it a hard task. Do you think I am like you, so narrow-minded that I weigh the drop of Ethiopian blood in her veins against her beauty, her accomplishments, and her thousand natural charms? I tell you, Adela Holmes, that though La Guerita DeCuba was born a slave, you might be proud to see her the wife of the worthiest of your family."

"Not against her will; not when she has only contempt, and fear, and hate, to give with her hand."

"I care for none of that," he ejaculated, with an impatient gesture; "I swore years ago that she should be my wife, and my wife she shall be. I love her! Is not that enough?"

"It would have been better, Claude, that you had killed her at Fairview. It would have been better that you had proved your love for her so. You are killing her by slow torture now; it could have been done by a blow then."

"You talk like a mad woman, Adela."

"You know I was the companion of one for many weeks, and I may be again."

He winced under her look, crying out, desperately: "I cannot help it; I will not give her up. I will make no vows to do so; for I have given up my very soul to the attainment of the one object. You can go and tell La Guerita so. Tell her that I am a man, and cannot tire, while she, sooner or later, must. And, Adela, I warn you that you had better caution her to yield before she aggravates me farther; for I have my hand upon the tenderest part of her heart, and I am not a man to spare it. Stay, I will tell her so myself."

He strode rapidly toward the school-house; she saw him enter and close the door, and watched long for his reappearance, but turned away at last unsatisfied. La Guerita came to her room two hours later, with face and lips of ashen paleness, and told her how he had striven with her—how sorely she had been tempted to yield, and how, at the moment, some angel seemed to whisper her that more sorrow and shame than ever she could dream of awaited her if she did. "I know not how it was," she concluded, "but some visible presence seemed to bar him back from me, and she seemed to take the form of that pale, lovely girl whose picture you found among Claude's effects, after his supposed death. I did not take much notice of it when you showed it to me, and it seemed almost a miracle that it appeared to warn me back when I was so sorely tempted to yield to his entreaties and threats, and win my freedom even at his fearful price."

It was the last time that Claude Leveredge ever tempted her by word or look. That very evening he announced to his uncle his intention to go to Richmond, and remain there until able to rejoin the army.

Rejoiced as La Guerita and Adela were to hear of this determination, they did not repress the feeling of uneasiness at the suddenness of his resolve, although they could not conjecture how it could be made to operate to La Guerita's disadvantage.

"And I shouldn't wonder if Harold is hidden away somewhere, crying his bright eyes out for him," added Miss Holmes. I never saw such an extraordinary thing in my life; the child seemed perfectly bewitched by him the last few days of his stay."

"La Guerita went to the door and called: "Harry!" but instead, Miss

Matilda came, frowning like a sphynx, and looking as wise.

"I know what will come of it ; he will make him a hundred times more of an imp than he is already ; but what upon earth Claude could want to take him to Richmond for I can't imagine. Reckon it must be because it is a good place to finish off associates of his Satanic Majesty."

"La Guerita had listened to her as if in a dream ; but she sprang forward then, her eyes flashing like fire.

"What are you talking about?" she cried. "Where is my boy? Has he taken my boy?"

The old lady was startled into a direct answer. "Yes ; didn't you know it? They went three hours ago."

"Oh, my boy—my pretty, pretty boy !" screamed La Guerita, in agony ; "he will ruin him ! he will kill him—body and soul. Oh, Miss Adela, save my boy !"

Miss Holmes drew La Guerita into the cabin, shutting the door, and leaving Miss Matilda upon the steps, in a state of bewilderment, from which she did not recover for many minutes.

"Listen to me !" she said, very quietly, though her face was pale as snow, and her heart throbbed longingly for the lost boy ; "Claude can do the child no harm ; he has only done this to frighten you. It is cruel —very cruel, but think of it calmly."

"I cannot !" cried La Guerita, starting to her feet. "Oh, my God ! think what he has taken from me ; but you cannot think ; you have no child."

"Claude is not a brute," said Miss Holmes, persuasively ; "he will do the boy no harm, and he shall restore him to you. I will go to my father

and tell him all. Don't cry so wildly, Rita—be still ; for heaven's sake, be still ! "

"Oh, I shall never, never see my boy again ! My Harold's child is lost to me forever ! Oh, that I were dead ! Oh, that I were dead ! "

So she moaned, traversing the floor with rapid steps, and pressing her hands wildly to her burning temples. In vain Miss Holmes strove to comfort her by caresses, hopeful words, and tears. Suddenly she threw the door open and darted across the garden, into the house, and to Mr. Holmes' study.

She found the master there and demanded her child, breaking out into such a storm of entreaties and reproaches as overwhelmed him.

"Leveredge wanted him ; Leveredge will take care of him," was all he could say until his daughter came and added her voice to La Guerita's.

"Papa, why did you give Claude Rita's child?"

"He wanted him—he had a fancy to take him to Richmond ; he is going to send him back in a week or so."

"He will never send him back," moaned La Guerita.

"What do you think he will want him for when he gets well enough to join the army," said Mr. Holmes, angrily. "Go away, Rita, and don't make a fool of yourself. Is it going to hurt the child to stay with Mr. Leveredge a week or a month?"

"Promise her, papa, that he shall return immediately," said Adela, earnestly ; "you must, indeed, you must."

"Yes, promise me, promise me that," cried La Guerita, entreatingly. "I shall go mad if you do not.

Promise me, and I will pray the Almighty God unceasingly to make you faithful to your word."

"But I tell you Claude only wants him for a little while. The boy was glad to go—he was delighted, though he cried a little because his mother was not here to bid him good-by. There, Rita, don't cry," for her tears burst forth at the mention of the child's grief; "I never thought you would mind his going. Addie shall write to Claude to send him right back, if you like."

With this promise she was somewhat comforted, and left the study to find relief for her surcharged heart. A little reflection convinced her that no immediate danger need be apprehended for the child, but she could not, in all her reasoning, silence her grief and anxiety at this forced separation from the nearest and dearest of all things upon earth.

Adela's letter to her cousin was quickly written and sent. She not only demanded the return of the child, but in the most moving terms entreated him to pity the desolate mother, and give her the only blessing that had for years been left her.

Miss Holmes thought La Guerita must have anticipated the reply that was made to this, for she received it very calmly, even the scrap of paper to her, on which was written :

"I shall keep the child as a hostage for you. When you get tired of waiting come for him."

"O, God, I am sick of waiting already," she muttered ; "sick, sick unto death, but I cannot go. O, God, help me to say that, even for the sake of my child, I cannot perjure my soul. I cannot, I cannot ; would

not the child be overwhelmed in his mother's shame ? "

Miss Holmes took the letter she had received from her cousin, and, burning with indignation, laid it before her father. He was much disturbed at its contents.

"It seems strange," he said ; "I thought he would have sent the child immediately. Write to him how woe-begone the mother looks."

"It would be useless," said Adela, vehemently, "and worse than useless. He has taken him from her to torment her. He attempted to do so once before." And in a few words she told how Thornton Leslie had rescued Harold from him on the cliffs of Ellisville.

"Ah, then that is the secret of your friendship for her," exclaimed Mr. Holmes, angrily. "You weep and wail over her because she knew that Yankee lover that you should blush to name."

"Papa," returned Adela, pleadingly, "put Thornton out of your thoughts, and let me tell you of La Guerita DeCuba, and of the wrong you have blindly abetted so long. Claude Leveredge is persecuting her now, and has persecuted her for years, with his unwelcome attentions."

"Adela," said her father, severely, "such thoughts should never have entered your mind. Claude is a gentleman, and Rita a slave."

"A lady, papa. Claude acknowledges that, if as well not you."

"What do you mean ?"

"Should you think it possible for Claude to marry Rita, papa ?"

"Certainly not ; it would not be even possible for him to do such a thing."

"In other countries it would, and his sole aim for more than ten years has been to make La Guerita DeCuba his wife."

Mr. Holmes looked at his daughter in blank amazement.

"To make her his wife? Impossible!"

"Do you think I would tell you a falsehood, papa?"

"No, daughter, no."

"Then I assure you most positively that he has assured me he will never cease his endeavors to make her his wife until one or both die. He has taken that child as a hostage; this note, written by his own hand, will tell you so."

Mr. Holmes read and reread the few lines as if he could gather no clue to their meaning. Firmly and clearly his daughter pointed it out to him. It was pitiful to see the utterly hopeless and sorrowful expression of his features as he said, brokenly:

"So even Claude has deceived me, even Claude has made a tool of me, to bring disgrace upon our family. But I can't believe it," he added, impulsively, forgetting for a moment the presence of his daughter; "he might have taken her away, but he cannot have disgraced us by marrying her."

"Papa, would you have him disgrace us more?" asked Miss Holmes, quietly.

"I forgot you. I forget things often now," exclaimed her father, irritably. "Oh, dear, how I wish I had never seen the woman's face. It was beautiful enough to bring me a fortune, and it has half ruined me instead. Nothing goes right with me now. I have not a friend in the world. Claude Leveredge, that I had

done so much for, almost insulted me because I allowed Rufus to enter the army to avenge his supposed death, and Rufus himself has written me four pages of the most terrible abuse because I wrote him advising him to return home. I don't believe I have a friend in the world, or that there is one to care for me."

It was touching to see the abject way in which the old man bent his white brow upon his wrinkled hands. His daughter found it deeply so, and throwing her arms around him begged him to believe that she loved him with all her heart, and when he was somewhat comforted, entreated him to comfort the slave he had oppressed so long by giving her her freedom and restoring to her her child.

"I will see about it to-morrow," he said to this, first, "and I will write to Claude to-day. Tell her to be easy, Adela; tell her I'll bring the child back if I have to go to Richmond for him to-morrow. But Adela, indeed, indeed, it is hard for me to think that Claude has deceived me so. He begged me for my own sake to keep the woman in slavery, quite true; and now to think that he did so only for his own purposes, and that he may bring disgrace upon us by marrying her."

"By breaking her heart," thought Adela.

CHAPTER XXXVII.

"Leaves have their time to fall,
  And flowers to wither at the north winds' breath,
And stars to set; but all—
  Thou hast all seasons for thine own, O, Death!"
                              Mrs. Hemans.

WITH a joyful heart, Miss Holmes hastened to La Guerita with the promises her father had made ; and upon the hopes they raised, the weeping mother strove to live, but her faith in man perished, when day after day wore by, and brought no tidings of her child. But for that other faith—her faith in God—born amid tribulations, she could not have patiently endured them—those weeks of waiting would have been unsupportable.

As it was, there were times when her brain seemed reeling, and her heart bursting, and Miss Holmes feared to leave her, lest the old madness should come upon her. No one knew what prayers she breathed to be kept from that. No one knew how she strove with the Lord to turn aside the frenzy that oftimes threatened her—not that she feared with Miss Holmes, that she should be tempted to take her life. Calm and inviting as the waters looked, she knew she would never seek their embrace while Harold lived. Often as she looked longingly at the grassy mounds on the hill side, she prayed that one might not rise upon her breast while Harold was in bondage. The weary days of her life were uncounted then—her miseries, save the parting from her boy, were all forgotten ; all merged in that. The child, the child ! Oh, for how many weary months her constant cry was : "My lost child ! My ruined child !"

Alone though she was—a slave in bonds most irksome—a widowed mother with nought beside to love—she could have spared him had it been for his good. So she said a thousand times a day ; but what of good could he learn of Claude Leveredge. Rather, what prayers could

ward off—what tears wash out—the evil he would gain.

Truly it appeared, as Mr. Holmes had said, that none cared for him, or paid the least respect to his wishes. The days of his power, the wavering powers he once held, were gone. He had, through all his life, been a man of doubtful mind ; seldom advancing an opinion, and never clinging to it. For a year or two preceding the war, his daughter Adela had, by the firmness and decision of her character, done much to give the same qualities to his ; but her efforts were indeed useless, when the approach of war drew around him. The most prominent men of his State, on account of his wealth and influence, used every argument in their power to induce him to enroll himself with the active secession party. They flattered his vanity by presenting to him a grand estimate of his own importance, and that of the cause in which he was engaged. It may be, too, that Ernest Gordon, his chief adviser, laughed jeeringly, yet pleasantly withal, over the power his daughter had over him. Be that as it may, it is certain that when he cast aside that power, he cast aside his own ; and in the third year of the war, he found himself neglected by the political party that had formerly courted him. Spoken of lightly as a man without wit or influence by his personal friends, and even by his children regarded with more pitying than admiring affection.

Very drearily passed his days, during the fall of '63, when all others, if sad, were active. A strange lethargy seemed coming upon him ; people called him "an old man," and said he was growing gray and stupid very fast.

They would not have wondered that he did so, could they have read the thoughts that filled his mind, at the sight of La Guerita DeCuba, the woman he had enslaved in her madness—the woman he had, in his folly, bereaved of her only child. For so it seemed he had done forever, by giving Harold DeGray to the care of Claude Leveredge. For the winter wore away, and still the child was not returned to his home.

From time to time Mr. Holmes received from his nephew a vague assurance that the child should be sent shortly, and with that he would rest content until aroused by remonstrances from his daughter, or passionate appeals from La Guerita.

"I will go to Richmond, myself," she said at last, "I shall die if I stay here in this dreadful suspense. You cannot be so cruel as to forbid my going; if you do it will make no difference, for my heart is breaking for my child. I will, I must see him."

"Go to Adela about it," was Mr. Holmes' reply; "Heaven knows, I want you to have your child. I told Claude so in my last letter. I don't want you to go to Richmond; it would not be safe for you to do so; it is a dreadfully wicked place, I hear. But go to Adela, and she will tell you what to do."

"Stay at home," said Miss Holmes, decidedly, when her father's words were repeated to her. "Stay at home, unless you wish to put yourself wholly in Claude's power."

"But my child; I think of my child," she returned, almost fiercely. "Can I think of my own danger when I know the peril he is in. O, God, can it be that I am wrong. Have I mistaken contemptible and unwomanly obstinacy for virtuous and most righteous determination?"

"Certainly you have not," replied Miss Holmes, warmly; "It is not necessary for me to assure you of that. Your conscience must do so every moment of your life."

"It does, it does," cried La Guerita, earnestly, "and yet I am almost persuaded to make any sacrifice to save my child from the hand that holds him now. My very hope of eternal happiness I would give."

"La Guerita!"

"Oh, you cannot know the depth of a mother's love, Miss Adela. What is even my eternal welfare when staked against that of my child? I tell you there is but one thing that keeps me from yielding to Claude Leveredge now, and that is that I cannot perjure myself before God, and dishonor further my child's dead father. No, no, it is better for him to live and die the slave of his bitterest enemy, than in freedom to groan in shame and misery over a mother so lost and vile as I should seem to him. I have felt the curses of the son of my parents, and never, never, shall he bear the misery that has been mine—the misery a thousand times more keen than any that servitude can bring."

At times she would speak of the matter more calmly, saying, that she felt that the Lord would suffer her to free the child she had enslaved. Death could have no power over her while such a mighty tie as the duty she owed her child, held her to the earth.

When her agony seemed unsupportable, when those around were anxiously striving to derive some mode of allaying the agony under which her mind and health were visibly declining, help came from an unexpected quarter. Help—yet in the form of a mighty temptation. It was a letter from Harold. A thousand times was the little missive read by his mother, and fondly was every word pondered over, though she could not but believe that each had been dictated by Claude Leveredge, or allowed to reach her fresh from the heart of her child only to tempt and agonize her soul.

"My dear mamma," ran the missive, "Mr Leveredge has told me that I can write to you, and I am so glad, for it is so long since I have seen you, that I feel as if you must be dead, else you would have written to me or come to see me. I did not know I was to stay so long when Mr. Leveredge took me away, and though I wanted to see you, yet there were so many fine things to see in Richmond that I was contented for a while to stay. But I could not help thinking of you, and that made me feel dull all day, and cry all night; and then I was sick, but I thought you were with me then, mamma; and it was so dreadful to find that I had been dreaming all the time; and when I cried about it again, the gentlemen all laughed at me (there are a great many gentlemen here all the time, and they give me champagne, and teach me to play cards with them, and the other day I won ten dollars); but Mr. Leveredge does not laugh when I cry about you, and he told me to-day to write you, and tell you

he is willing to take us all to some beautiful country, where we shall never be lonely or sick any more. Dear mamma, won't you go? Doctor Pillow said to-day I should die if I did not see my mother, and indeed, indeed I shall, for though I love Mr. Leveredge dearly, and he is very good to me, he is not like my dear mamma. Ask Miss Adela to come with you, and tell her I want to see her next to you. I shall look for you next week, and I know you will come to your affectionate son,

"Harold DeGrey."

A fresh temptation did I say this letter was? Ah, not so much a temptation as an agony. She had known ever since the child's departure that his safety lay not in her hands, but in God's. Scarce did the thought occur to her as with breaking heart she read the childish words, to her so expressive of the child's loneliness and pain, that she, by yielding—as many women would have been glad to yield—regardless of the sin, could save the child. Was he to die if she did not? Had she not said that "Death was better for him than the misery he would some time know, were he saved at such a cost?" Her heart was rent at the thought of her child sick and alone, but her resolution was not shaken.

"My child, my child," she said, firmly, "Heaven is better than this breath we draw. We will choose it, even though moments of incalculable agony lie before, rather than gain a little lease of life, perhaps of pleasure, at the cost of our souls."

She could not write this to him, but she wrote what Claude Leveredge would understand to mean the same, and which would comfort and cheer the heart of the suffering child. Hope whispered that his illness might be exaggerated by his fears, or by Claude Leveredge, in order that the sensibilities of her heart might be excited, as they often before had been, to act with a power her mind could not balance or sustain—but that time had passed. Reason, that had tottered on its throne, was seated there forever by the hand of that God who guards all those that put their trust in him.

Strangely enough, this letter quieted her late distracted mind.

"I can contemplate his death and mine," she said, "far more calmly than slavery for him or dishonor for myself."

"I don't believe the child is ill," said Miss Holmes; "he would not dare to keep him if he were, he would not dare to let him die in his hands. There will come a day when he will have to give an account to the child's guardians of all this; he knows that as well as I. I wonder that he did not threaten to sell the child. It would have been but a fitting climax to what has gone before."

"Ah, if the child were out of Richmond—any where out of Richmond," replied La Guerita. "It is no place for him. He has a pure soul, but I fear greatly it will be made black enough by the atmosphere he breathes. Nor is it even safe for his body, for I hear the Northerners are advancing upon the city now, and ere long it will be beleaguered."

"We believed that once before," remarked Miss Holmes.

"And I have faith to believe it again," said La Guerita. "The Lord worketh in his own good time, yet it seems to me the hour of freedom is at hand."

"God grant it!" ejaculated Adela, earnestly. "I have been thinking much of late of our dear, wayward Rufus. You know if they are fighting now he is with them."

"Poor boy," said La Guerita, sighing, "poor boy! So young and yet so eager to rush into danger."

Adela's eyes filled with tears.

"The fact is never absent from my mind," she said, "and though he has been thus far mercifully preserved, and has been a wonder of valor and daring, I cannot but fear that Claude's words will come true, and that papa will rue the day he consented to allow Rufus to join the army. He was so young, and is still so young, to view the bloody scenes which have passed before him from Gettysburg until now. Poor boy, poor darling! I would give the world to see him safely home."

She saw him soon, but alas, not safe. The gallant boy, the proud, handsome young soldier, returned to the home he had left so gaily, a shattered cripple, shot through both hips in the defense of Petersburg, and conducted home by his cousin Claude, during a lull in the mighty tempest of battle that was raging. Ah, it was a pitiful sight to see him carried upon a litter into the house, followed by his stricken father, his weeping mother, and younger sister and brother, and preceded by his cousin and his sister Adela, who, struck to the very heart, could give no expression to her grief, and who knew at that crisis she must not allow it to prostrate her.

"I have come home to die;" so

whispered the poor lad again and again, manfully striving to keep back the groans of anguish that *would* come.

None dared to hope that he was mistaken, Death was written on his face so plainly. Amid all their grief they wondered how he had survived the frightful wound so long. Claude told them how it had been received, when he rushed to the top of a breast-work to replace a flag that had been swept down by the enemy's fire. It was strange and touching to see how tenderly he bent over the dying boy, interpreting instantly every glance and faintly uttered word, and with his own hands administering to his wants more gently than the most tender woman that stood beside his bed.

From the sick chamber Aunt Matilda and Mrs. Holmes were excluded—the one because of her violent indignation against the authors of the mischief, and even against the poor lad himself, for so recklessly hastening into danger, and the other because of her uncontrollable outbursts of grief. Even Minna was quieter, and sat for hours weeping silently beside her brother, and watching every look and movement of Adela in attending the dying boy. It was a strange sight to see those three, kindred by blood, yet aliens at heart, the woman and the man, bending together in present sympathy, over that couch of pain, consulting together in whispers, standing side by side, their hand often hurriedly meeting as they reached for some wanted article, and yet to know that outside of that room all such intercourse would be abhorred, at least by two, and that the third would give the world to even touch the hand he now was suffered to hold in a firm grasp to raise the dying boy.

The presence of death makes many changes. It seemed so then, when for a long night and day those three toiled and grieved together, and when, at last, in the still eventide stood at one side of the couch whence the spirit of Rufus Holmes was striving to depart. They knew that the hour was at hand when rest for the tortured body would come, and had bidden his father and mother to bid him farewell.

He knew that he was dying, and tried to tell them so calmly, but broke into a shuddering wail : "So young, so young."

His father groaned in the bitterness of his spirit : "Oh, Rufus, my son, can you forgive me for allowing you to sacrifice yourself?"

The boy's eyes flashed, and a momentary gleam of passion and strength passed over his face as he answered : "Don't say that it is a sacrifice, father. I should be glad to die if I thought by so doing I could help the cause, but I wanted to live to fight for it, and now I am dying, so young and with so little done."

His mother burst into such a paroxysm of weeping that Claude was obliged to lead her from the room. Rufus detained her face a moment to kiss her grieving lips, and beg her not to grieve for him ; she had still a son left, who had always been much better than he."

He talked but little after that, but simply asked them to kiss him. They did so, bursting into irrepressible tears as their lips met those so lately full of youthful life, now fast growing cold in the awful chill of death.

La Guerita was the last to approach him. He had never been a favorite with her; he had been an unmanageable and careless pupil, and had caused her to feel much of the pain of her early servitude. But she forgot all that—forgot all but his heroism, his devotion to his cause, his patient suffering and his near departure, as she bent over him to give her first and last caress. But all that he had been to her seemed then to flash upon his mind.

"Dear Rita," he whispered, "I want you to forgive me. I was very hard on you when you first came here; I want to do something to atone for that."

"Dear Rufus, it is all forgotten, all forgiven," she answered, with tears. "Don't let it distress you; it is all past, you know."

"Rita," he whispered, in so faint a voice that she had to bend very low to hear it, "don't you want to be free? You ought to be free."

"Rufus, don't trouble yourself about that. I shall be freed in the Lord's good time.

"Pa," he said, with sudden energy, "I want you to free Rita and Harold. Cousin Claude, remind him of it when I am gone, and take care of her. Light a candle—it is very dark."

Alas, the candles were lighted, and it was the darkness of death that fell upon Rufus Holmes. Adela's courage gave way at that moment, and it was La Guerita who bent forward and whispered:

"Though I walk through the valley of the shadow of death, I will fear no evil, for Thou art with me; Thy rod and Thy staff they comfort me."

The dying boy smiled and whispered, brokenly, "It is getting light."

Then there was a short struggle, and in the arms of Claude Leveredge and La Guerita DeCuba, those two so strangely brought together, that the young hero heaved his last sigh, and took up the palms of everlasting peace.

They laid him gently back upon the pillow, and thought of each other for the first time then. Death had passed, and with him the magic of his presence. Claude Leveredge became, in an instant, to La Guerita the man she dreaded more than all the powers of earth; and she, the woman he would barter heaven to win.

He told her that, in a few impassioned words, when he left the side of the dead boy and followed her into the garden; but she bade him be silent in such a tone of horror that he could not but obey her. Yet still he followed her to the door of her cabin, detaining her in his iron grasp when she would have entered, and crying, passionately, that there never was love so strong as his, and entreating her to grant the last wish of the dead boy, and let him shelter her from all pain.

"I cannot! I cannot!" she exclaimed—not desperately, but with a voice, of such high determination that all the hope he had for years, through all her coldness cherished, died out of his soul. Yet he strove with her—wildly painting his love and despair—describing, in words that made her heart stand still with anguish, the loneliness of her child, and his future doom.

All was useless; she could not

yield, a higher power than her own sustaining her. It appeared to herself, and to her desperate lover, that she was but passively enacting the will of an all-powerful being, who would not suffer her to be moved.

"La Guerita DeCuba," he cried, at length, "you were a woman once, as weak and fickle as any of the sex; now you are an enthusiast, pursuing the chimera of duty—cold, passionless, and immovable, as if no mortal fire had ever lived within you. I know now that you are dead to me —dead to all love; even that holy flame that burns within a mother's heart. I have told you that your child is in the power of one that will crush him forever beneath the heaviest chains of slavery ever worn by man, yet you will not stretch forth a hand to save him."

"I cannot!" she cried, with an expression of resignation almost sublime; "I cannot! but he is in God's hands."

He laughed, in a hollow, mocking way, that was terrible to hear. La Guerita turned from him in horror; but he held her back, looking into her face with a grim smile and saying: "You are pale; you are haggard; you are dying. Ah, yes! there is still enough of woman's nature left in you to die, and I tell you, you are dying."

The words seemed more like a curse than a prophesy. She staggered back from him, and faintly said:

"You are keeping my child from me!"

"You are asking me for your life," he said, "and are asking your child's; but in vain. Let your hopes die, as mine have died to-night; you will never see your child again; you will never be free. Let your hopes die, I say, as mine have done, and your misery endure, as my vengeance will."

It was little wonder that she tottered into her cabin when he left her, and for hours lay prostrate on her bed, entirely overcome by his awful words, and the tone in which they were spoken. His words, his look, his gestures, haunted her through all the night, filling her mind with images of terror, which she almost feared would drive the light of reason thence.

When the morning came she was in a high state of fever, and much too ill to rise. It was then that the grief and anxiety of the last year revealed the havoc they had made upon her. When the fever passed, she could not rise from her bed. Her energy was gone, and it became apparent to all that her hold on life was each day growing weaker.

Her form was but a shadow of its former self. Never in her great misery had she been so haggard and wan. Never had her eyes shone with such painful brilliancy.

Miss Holmes marked with amazement the deep and holy resignation with which she spoke of her approaching fate.

"The hand of God seems to work so slowly," she sometimes said, "that I cannot even hope that Death will find me before Freedom; but it will not be so with my child. I know it will not be so. God will give him his birthright, even though he suffered me to take it from him."

With faltering lips they often tried to cheer her. Even Mrs. Holmes awoke to a vague sense of what the self-enslaved woman had suffered, and promised her that even if Mr. Holmes heeded not the request of his dying son, that she would do so, and that she and her child should again be free.

Miss Matilda, too, noticed, with a strange mixture of vexation and sympathy, how frail she was growing, and in some sort of awe of the death she believed so near, treated La Guerita with a consideration most unusual to her, and quite wonderful to those who for years had looked for such an exhibition of tenderness in vain.

Of all upon the plantation, there was, perhaps, but one that throughout the summer and autumn of 1864 failed to perceive the terrible effect the loss of her child had had upon La Guerita.

That one was her master, Norton Holmes, who, since the death of his son Rufus had noticed nothing; his faculties seemed paralyzed. He sat all day long in his library in a sort of stupor, from which nought but news from the war could arouse him, and that excited him to such frenzy that his friends were careful never to mention the subject in his presence.

It was sorrowful to view this stricken man ; not old, yet bearing all the infirmities, both bodily and mentally, of extreme age—indifferent to all passing things—dead to all passions and emotions, save those aroused by the mention of that cause for which he had risked and lost so much.

When Christmas came the family invited many of his old friends to visit Holmsford, hoping thereby to arouse and enliven his mind. They

had been carefully entreated not to mention the ever-recurring, all-absorbing subject of war before him ; and all, without exception, abstained from doing so. On the last day of their stay, however, Mr. Holmes, having fallen asleep upon the sofa in the parlor, the guests repaired to the study to smoke, and soon fell into an animated discussion of the proscribed topic. All were unanimous in their detestation of the Northerners, but divided in their estimation of their power—many believing that Sherman's march through the South would be successfully accomplished, and even Richmond be forced to yield to the thousands surrounding it. Mr. Gordon loudly scouted the idea ; and in the midst of their excitement all failed to perceive that Mr. Holmes had entered, and was listening eagerly to all that was said.

"I, for my part, should not be surprised to behold this very country in possession of the enemy before another sunrise," said Mr. Russell, at last; "I tell you that the power of the Confederacy is melting away, and I greatly fear that our peaceful fields will be trodden by the invader, and our homes ruthlessly despoiled, as those of our brethren have been."

"Then God grant that I may not live to see it !" cried Mr. Holmes, with sudden energy, his eyes flashing and with uplifted hands, grieving with emotion ; "I have suffered enough from the vandal hordes. If there is mercy in heaven, I pray that it will be shown me at least as far as to keep me from sight or hearing of the murderers of my son—the cursed destroyers of my peace."

The mercy he so passionately

craved was granted him.   Early in the new year, Norton Holmes found a hiding place from the coming foe beside his son, in the great church-yard.

A few days after his decease his will was opened and read.   To the sur-prise of his family, it was discovered that his estate was heavily mortgaged, and that the greater portion of his property had been disposed of in the cause of secession, and the remain-der left to his wife and children. Claude Leveredge was appointed sole executor.   By a codicil, he re-stored freedom to La Guerita and her child, directing that they should be committed to the care of his daugh-ter Adela, until they could return to their lawful guardians.

This codicil surprised them all, for it was dated on the evening of Ru-fus' death, when and after which they had believed him incapable of per-forming even the most trivial act. The news of her freedom seemed for a short time to arouse and strengthen La Guerita, who, in the fullness of her heart, thanked the Lord that her child was free, and thus openly declared throughout the land, and that even she was thus graciously permitted to cast away her bonds, if but for an hour or a moment.

Mr. Gordon was greatly disgusted at what he termed the deplorable weakness of his deceased friend, and was in his heart delighted to know that La Guerita could not receive the symbols of her freedom until the es-tate was settled, and that, he knew, would not be for many months, for the executor remained throughout in Richmond, both unable and un-willing to leave.   But though in the eyes of the lawyer, to La Guerita the papers of emancipation were nothing ; it was enough for her to know if she died, or lived to meet those she so dearly loved, it would not be with the shameful bonds of self-enslavement upon her.

CHAPTER XXXVIII.

"Lives there a sound more grateful to the ear
  Of Him who made all Harmony,
Than the blessed sound of fetters breaking,
  And the first hymn that man, awaking—
From Slavery's slumber, breathes to Liberty ?"
                                   T. Moore.

" That sound bespeaks salvation on her way."

IT was March ; and as La Guerita lay upon her humble couch, and gazed through the window of her cabin across the bleak fields to the dark pine woods which waved beyond, it appeared to her sad eyes the most desolate scene upon which they had ever rested.   A drizzling rain was falling, through which the uprisings of the sodden earth appeared more like darksome shadows than tangible ob-jects, and the sky, a frightful cloud that no sunshine would ever have power to dispel.   It was a day for tears, and La Guerita felt it to be so, and wondered whether a day for smiles would ever dawn for her on earth.

She felt that she was dying, that the separation from her child was wearing away her life by slowest tor-ture.

"They think I am dying—as my mother did—of consumption," she thought ; "but no ; it is no bodily disease that is hurrying me to my grave, but my heart is breaking ; I cannot live apart from my boy.   My heart is breaking ! "

Sometimes she bethought herself, and tried to rise above her grief, but she could not ; it crushed her to the very earth. Claude Leveredge had indeed placed his hand on the vital point, and slowly she was yielding beneath the agony of his relentless grasp.

Strange it was, that through all her anxiety for her boy, she was content to leave him. "When I am gone, she thought, "Claude Leveredge will give him up to Adela, and she will see that all his rights are restored to him."

At that moment, she saw Miss Holmes hurrying through the rain. In a few moments she entered the cabin, and in surprise, La Guerita exclaimed :

"How could you venture out in this weather, Miss Adela ? What has happened ? "

Oh, the most glorious thing," ejaculated Miss Holmes, throwing off her waterproof cloak, and, to La Guerita's amazement, casting her arms around her and bursting into tears. Happy tears she saw they were, and Miss Holmes next explained why they were shed.

"The news has just arrived that the Union troops crossed the Pedee the night before last ! La Guerita, the hour of our deliverence is at hand. The Northerners will be here within a week ! "

Who can describe the deep, almost sacred joy, that filled those two faithful hearts.

Confusion reigned through all the country ; terror filled every mind but theirs, and though they dared not yet even openly express their happiness, unto God it was poured forth in a ceaseless tide of thanksgiving.

Miss Holmes had in her zeal accelerated the movements of the advancing host by nearly two weeks. It was on the first of April that they beheld the pioneers of the army, whose coming they had hoped and prayed for so long. Was ever an April day so glorious as that when they first heard the soul-inspiring airs of victory and freedom, and beheld the colors of the Union floating proudly on the balmy air ?

At Holmsford, the soldiers involuntarily felt themselves welcome, at least to the fairest and most potent member of the family, and neither their persons or their goods and chattels were in any way molested. On the day of their arrival, Adela had in a few words revealed her sentiments to the leader of the party, and all gave three hearty cheers for the fair loyalist.

At that moment, Miss Matilda, who had upon the Union victories declared herself an unyielding secessionist, appeared upon the · scene, and much to the alarm of Mrs. Holmes, and the amazement of Adela, cast looks of direst hatred upon the soldiers.

"I just knew this was a goin' to happen," she exclaimed, loudly ; "I just knew this Yankee horde were a comin' to trample down all the rose bushes, when I've been thinkin' all winter they would yield sich heaps of leaves to send to our poor, sick defenders. I told them they must be sick when they went to defend us. I just knew that they was a comin'. Dixie's been prognosticatin' it all day, and just now I found him a whirlin' and a whirlin' round and round as if he was crazy, which, the

Lord knows, it's a mercy we all ain't."

The soldiers burst into a hearty laugh, evidently considering that she at least, was not very sane ; upon which she proceeded, as she said, to give them a piece of her mind, which she continued at intervals throughout the day.

Another fortnight passed, full of welcome excitement to La Guerita, which reached her even upon her weary couch, and also of sickening pain, for from the time she had heard of the entrance of the Union troops into North Carolina, she had encouraged the hope that her brother, or Victor DeGrey would be with them, and would, by a kind Providence, be led to the spot in which she was. Miss Holmes confessed to a lesser degree of disappointment in regard to Thornton Leslie, though she would not allow one thought of his safety to cloud her joy, and remarked philosophically, that he could not be expected to leave his regiment at such a time, simply to hasten to her. But she knew in her heart that he would do so at his earliest possible opportunity.

Soon came the tidings of the fall of Richmond, putting a climax upon the triumph of the Union forces.

The news filled the heart of La Guerita with many conflicting emotions. Joy for a moment prevailed, and then the thought of her child rushed over her. Where was he? Doubtless Claude Leveredge had sought safety in flight, as many of his comrades had done. Would he not strive to leave the country, to hasten to Europe, and take Harold with him ? The doubt became to her almost a certainty. It was agonizing —almost maddening.

"O, God," she moaned, "have I borne so much only to die on the very threshold of my happiness."

One day she sat up in bed, and strove to write a letter to her brother. The sight of his name opened the floods of her heart ; she could not proceed, and burying her face on the pillow, she wept bitterly.

Suddenly the door opened ; she looked up. An officer stood on the step. She sprang from the bed, and with a scream of joy, fell fainting into the arms of her brother.

His kisses, his words of endearment, and his fast-falling tears, brought her back to a sense of the great joy that was hers.

"Oh, Fabean, my brother, you have saved me," she cried ; "Thank God, I have seen you once more."

The scene that ensued can perhaps be more easily imagined than described. For a moment, all else was forgotten in the bliss of again beholding her brother, who exclaimed :

"Thank God, indeed, that I have found you once more, my sister. Ah, La Guerita, He alone can know what I have suffered because of you —and what agonies you, too, have endured to save me from the shame of our parents ! "

"Then you know all," she ejaculated, ineffably relieved to discover that she was spared the task of making the disclosure.

"Yes, Claude Leveredge told me all upon his death-bed."

She started up trembling, yet strong with hope :

"And did he tell you where to find my child," she cried ; "Oh,

Fabean, brother, have you brought me back my boy ? "

She was answered at the moment. The door flew open, and Harold —taller, paler, yet all her own, rushed into the cabin, and threw himself upon her bosom.

" Oh, gracious Father, this is too much joy, she murmured. " My brother, my child, both given back to me. Oh, how great is Thy mercy."

"We praise Thee, we worship, we glorify Thee ! " added Fabean, reverently, and sinking upon his knees offered unto God such thanksgiving as never before had been echoed from those cabin walls.

After Harold had gone to tell the story of his joy to his beloved Miss Adela, the reunited brother and sister sat together ; they spoke not much of the past, that was too full of pain to be contemplated then, but of the peaceful future which they had hoped to share together.

"I was dying ; yes, dying ! " exclaimed La Guerita, "but now I shall live. For this joy, thank God, is tempered so that it will not kill. But, my poor Fabean, you are maimed—your right arm is gone ! "

"Yes," he said, quietly ; " that I lost at that famous battle at which Thornton Leslie was taken prisoner. Ah, now I see that *you* were the wonderful slave that rescued him from a fate worse than death itself. I wonder that we never thought of that in the thousand times we have talked of it and you."

"Where is Thornton ; is he quite safe and well ? " she inquired, anxiously.

" He was both, as far as a soldier can be, when I saw him last ; it was on the glorious day we entered Richmond. We are on different branches of the service. I, strangely enough, am the colonel of a colored regiment. Something led me to solicit the post. My friends will think it was blind instinct when they hear all."

He spoke with some bitterness, and La Guerita bent her head low, as she whispered :

"Oh, Fabean, can you bear that shame, or must my fears be realized ? Will it madden you as it did me ?"

"No, no," he answered, gravely ; "the name of Fabean DeCuba is honored wherever I am known, and I will so live as to compel respect for you and myself, in spite of all adverse circumstances. Yet think not that I count the shame lightly. I know what it will do for us ; I know what it did for me years ago, for *she* must have known."

La Guerita shuddered.

"Oh, Fabean, Fabean," she murmured, "did you then love her ? "

"No, 'twas but a boyish passion that I had for her—unworthy of the sacred name of love. Yet if I had loved her with unconquerable devotion she would have cast me off ; because I had in my veins that cursed thing—a drop of negro blood ! Well, I cannot blame her ; we, in her place, should have done the same thing ; and, at any rate, I should have married her with a breaking heart, and perhaps have broken hers, while she is now happy with another."

La Guerita sighed ; she saw that some barb rankled in his heart, even if it had not been cast there by Carrie Leslie. But she saw that it was not yet to be revealed to her, and striving to put the thought aside, she gave herself up to the joy of being once more with her brother and her child.

It was soon to be perceived that her illness had been indeed that of the mind. Joy gave her strength, and in a few days she even sat up for an hour or two, and feebly interested herself in the womanly pursuits she had for months entirely neglected.

CHAPTER XXXIX.

"Men must die—one dies by day, and near him
　　moans his mother;
They dig his grave, head it down, and go from
　　it full loath!
And one dies about the midnight, and the wind
　　moans—and no other."

Jean Ingelow.

MISS HOLMES was scarcely less thankful and rejoiced at the coming of Fabean and Harold than was La Guerita herself; yet, as days passed on, she could not repress a sigh that her own loved one tarried so long. Could it be that at the very last he had been stricken down? The thought haunted her, chilling her very heart, and throwing a deep shade of sadness upon her countenance, which even her participation in the contentment of La Guerita could not banish.

But, like magic, it flew when, at the close of the last day in April, a horseman galloped up the road, and Fabean sprang to his feet, exclaiming: "Thornton at last!"

She could not restrain herself; she ran down the garden path and met him at the gate. He sprang from his horse and clasped her in his arms. That moment was one of sacred joy. When it had passed, and he had leisure to think of another than Adela, he recognized Fabean.

"How in the world came you here?" he cried, in amazement; "what business have you away from your regiment? No one could tell me where you had vanished to; and now to think of you being here."

"I will show you just cause for it presently," returned Fabean, gaily, as Thornton asked for the slave Rita.

To his intense astonishment he was led into the presence of the long-lost Mrs. DeGrey. His ecstacy knew no bounds. He could find no words in which to express his joy and gratitude; and after vainly attempting to declare both, he turned to Miss Holmes and exclaimed, reproachfully:

"Why did you not tell me, Adela? Why did you allow me to remain in ignorance of so important a matter?"

"I will tell you when you have leisure to hear," interposed Fabean, gently pushing him from the room, whence he was followed by Adela, looking somewhat downcast at his hasty speech—seeing which, Thornton applied himself to the pleasant task of bringing smiles to the face he had clouded.

It was no difficult task. "She is an angel!" he enthusiastically exclaimed to Fabean, as they paced the garden path together late in the evening, smoking their cigars and inhaling the perfumes of the fresh May flowers. "She is an angel worth waiting for another five years. Thank God, it need not be so many months! But, Fabean, how came you to meet Claude Leveredge? And is it true that he gave you the information which led you to seek your sister here?"

"It is, indeed, true," replied Fabean; "I had not been in Richmond four hours, when a colored man came up to me and handed me a note, saying his master had ordered him to find the — Colored Regiment, and deliver the note to the colonel. It was addressed to me, and, to my surprise, contained a most urgent request that I would visit Claude Leveredge, who was lying at the point of death.

"I lost no time in obeying the summons, and early in the evening repaired to the house designated in the note. It was a small, but handsome villa, situated on the outskirts of the city, and, by its neglected appearance, gave evidences of the riotous days that had been passed within it. I found Leveredge there, attended by a single servant—the one who had accosted me. The rest, upon the entrance of our troops, had left him, to live or die, as the Lord willed.

"Leslie, I never saw a man so much altered as was Claude Leveredge. You know he was, when we knew him so well, a man of most commanding appearance—one to command the admiration of women, and the envy of men. How can I describe to you to what he was abased? He lay upon his bed, bloated and stupified with brandy, the fumes of which filled the close apartment—suffering agonies from a wound in his right shoulder—insufficient in itself to cause death, but the pain of which was constantly aggravated by his frequent bursts of passion and use of stimulants.

"He raised himself upon his left arm when I was announced, and looked at me with a fixed stare. I approached and offered my hand. He took no notice of it, but sank back upon the pillow, still regarding me with that awful stare. Supposing that his mind was wandering, and that he did not know me, I called him by name, and said: 'Do you not know me? I am Fabean De-Cuba—for whom you sent to-day.'

"'I know it,' he said; 'though you have changed much. You are bronzed by exposure, and look grave; from grief, perhaps?'

"I made no reply, and he presently continued: 'I sent for you, Fabean, to make a confession. Only to think that of Claude Leveredge! But he's dying now, you know. All men do strange things then.'

"I shuddered to hear the laugh with which he ended. I thought him delirious, and was relieved when he said:

"'First tell me how the city looks, and how your men are enjoying their long-sought triumph.'

"I complied, giving him the information he desired in as few words as possible. He grew excited towards the close, and exclaimed, through his set teeth:

"'Woe to the conqueror!
Our limbs shall be as cold as theirs,
Of whom his sword bereft us,
E'er we forget the deep arrears
Of vengeance they have left us.
Woe to the conqueror!'"

"'Tom Moore, in these lines, breathed the very spirit of the South, Fabean!'

"It was terrible to me, Thornton, to hear that dying man quote the fanciful words of another, when he had scarcely breath enough left to breathe a last farewell. I think he must have seen something of that feeling in my face, for he said, abruptly :

" 'Why do you let me waste my time on such nonsense? Why don't you ask me why I sent for you?'

" 'I do so now,' I said, wondering greatly what reason he could have had, for, strangely enough, no suspicion of the truth entered my mind. It seems incomprehensible now that we never guessed that he knew of her whereabouts. I did, indeed, suppose that his words would relate to his early love for La Guerita; but that she lived — that he knew her hiding place — I never for a moment conjectured. I had believed her dead, and could not harbor for one instant such a thought.

" It was some moments before I could believe it true, even after the dying man had told me all. He thought me overwhelmed with shame; but I was not — I was not. All the dreams I had cherished that instant took flight forever; though I felt myself an alien to all the world, yet, with all, it was not shame that caused me to drop into a chair and cry; 'O, God! O, God!'

" I saw it all — all my sister had suffered — all she was suffering still. My darling, my beautiful sister. Oh, it was terrible — terrible!

" He gave me a little time to grow calmer, and then told me where she could be found, if she still lived.

" If she still lived! Oh, how terrible was the thought that she should die alone, in her shackles — even before I could behold her, and through that man, too, as her husband had before her; for he said boldly, that when he found her she was sane, and eager to return to her home and friends, and that he had kept her four years in slavery because he loved her.

" Because he loved her! I almost forgot he was dying, and might have cursed him, but I suddenly remembered that my sister's child was in his possession, and demanded whether he was in the house.

" 'No, no,' he answered; 'anticipating the evacuation of Richmond, I sent him to Raleigh for safety. You will find him there, at the house of Mr. R——.'

" He then gave me the necessary directions for finding him, and said, in conclusion :

" 'The poor child loves me; he begged me not to send him away. Ah, if I could have foreseen this I could not have parted with him. Yet, perhaps, it is better as it is. I should not like the only creature that loves me to see me die like this.'

" It was wonderful to see how his countenance softened when he spoke of that child. Tears gathered in his eyes and rolled slowly over his cheeks. He was too weak to raise his hand to wipe them away, or perhaps even to be conscious of them.

" 'Ah, yes,' he murmured, 'that poor child will mourn for me. He, at least, believes me good and noble, and loves me. Ah, I have deserved but little love through my life, and, alas, have had but little!'

" There was something in these few words, spoken in a tone of deepest melancholy, that subdued all my anger. I knew by the gaze the dying man cast upon me that he craved my forgiveness, and yet, even in that solemn hour, he was too proud to ask it. I could not speak, though I would gladly have done so, as I saw the expression of despair that settled upon his face. He hoarsely called for brandy, and though I found voice to beg him not to take it, it was in vain. The servant handed him some, and he quaffed it eagerly, as if he sought oblivion in the draught—and I quickly saw that death, if not oblivion, was drawing near. He sank into a stupor, in which he remained for an hour or more. I feared he would die in it, and the idea so horrified me that I forced between his lips a restorative the doctor had left on his last visit.

"After a time he opened his eyes and looked at me, but the glaze of death was over them. Scarcely knowing what I did, I muttered a prayer, such as we have often breathed over a dying comrade. I think even in his extremity it was a comfort for him to know that a fellow-creature stood near, who took interest enough in him to utter a prayer for his passing soul. I took his hand in mine; I think, I hope he took it as a sign of forgiveness, for he pressed it gently.

"A few moments afterward his lips moved, and he looked at me eagerly, oh, so eagerly, as if beseeching me to hear what he had to say. Alas, I could not. It may have been nothing of moment, yet I cannot think he would have striven with such mighty ardor to utter trivialities.

He lay in comparative quietness, yet in terrible agony, until about three in the morning. All that time I knew he was dying, and could not leave him, though I was imperatively needed elsewhere. Then he began to toss wildly from side to side, uttering, in constant succession, the most unearthly groans. Never, never heard I such before. The memory of them haunts me even now.

"In the midst of his terrible agony the power of speech suddenly returned to him. 'Oh, find her,' he cried. 'Adela!'

"Then he fixed his eyes upon me wildly, and moaned: 'Oh, my ruined life! My—lost—soul!'

"These were his last words, spoken with his last breath. When they ended, I stood beside a corpse.

"Why, Thornton, you are shivering! Is it with cold, or with horror of my tale? I need not tell you much more. I saw him buried next evening, and an hour afterward started in quest of my sister. I found Harold at Raleigh, sad and lonly enough, poor fellow. He fell into a perfect paroxysm of grief when I told him of the death of Mr. Leveredge, and was only comforted when Holmsford was reached, and he gained the arms of his mother."

"God bless her!" ejaculated Thornton, fervently. She deserves the love of her child if a mother ever did. Yet it is a wonder to me that in the company and under the influence of Claude Leveredge, Harold cherished his affection."

"Leveredge encouraged him to do so," replied Fabean, "for by means of it he hoped to gain that power over La Guerita, which his own love could never give. But enough of that. Thank God, her trials are past—she is free, and though now so frail and wan, I earnestly pray that in her own peaceful home she will find strength and contentment."

"She must be removed thither as

quickly as possible," said Thornton ; "she will never regain her strength amid these scenes, where her life of slavery must be ever before her."

"And you, I hope," said Fabean, shaking his friend's hand warmly, "will bear hence the bride you have waited for so long, and I shall be spared from hearing longer your lovelorn woes."

"For shame," said Thornton, good-humoredly, "I had no idea you were laughing in your sleeve all this time you have pretended to condole with me. I wish you would give me a chance to pay you in your own coin, Fabean. Do you never mean to fall in love? It is a duty that you owe society."

"I · have other duties," said Fabean, gravely. "Henceforth I shall devote my life to my mother's race. Poor, blind people, they need guides, and I will be one to them."

Thornton pressed his hand, and they walked together for some moments silently.

"I was going to tell you of our marriage," said Thornton, at length. "I entreated the dear girl to marry me this very day, but she said she could not wed and part from me so soon, and you know it is impossible for me to leave my regiment at present, and I declare it seems equally impossible for me to leave her. But I see clearly that I must do so, and Adela Holmes will be safer under the protection of Curtis and his men than Mrs. Leslie, the wife of an Union soldier. So I must e'en yield to my fate with the best grace possible, and pray that I may soon be 'a disbanded volunteer.' Then, ah then, we will take our loved ones home."

CHAPTER XL.

" After long storms and tempests overbloune,
 The sun at length his joyous face doth cleare ;
 So when as fortune all her spight hath showne,
 Some blissful homes at last must needs appeare."
 Spenser.

THE next day Thornton Leslie left for Richmond, accompanied by Fabean DeCuba, but within a month both returned. Was there ever such a June ? Thornton declared there never had been to him, and Adela, too, blushingly confessed that it seemed sweeter than all that had passed since the cloudless days of her childhood. They were to be married on the morrow, and to leave immediately for the North, and they could not go without visiting the scenes of their former peril, and together they walked to the spot where once had stood the home of Asenith Bray.

The air was full of fragrance and summer sounds. They listened with new pleasure to the carols of the birds among the trees, and to the distant murmuring of

" The busy beck, that still would run
 And fall, and falter its refrain ;
 Aud pause, and shimmer in the sun,
 And fall again."

Often they left the beaten road to enter the woods, crushing beneath their feet the odorous pine straw, or stopping to gather clusters of wild roses or yellow jasmine, that hung in rich festoons from many a tree.

"We shall not reach our destination to-day, if we loiter so long upon the road," said Adela, at last. "I am surprised, Thornton, after all the marching you have done that you prove yourself such a laggard."

."This air is balmy enough to make any man lazy," he answered. "Did you ever breathe any so clear and pure before? And it is so laden with sunbeams, too. Ah, stand where you are. It is beautiful to see the glory of Heaven thus shimmering down upon you. You should always stand in sunbeams, my darling—your golden hair forms a halo around your sweet face, and your eyes shine like the blue depths of some wood-fringed lake."

Adela laughed and blushed at his impassioned words, and the radiant light of pleasure they cast over her made her appear, to her lover's eyes, a thousand times more charming than before. She looked so youthful as she stood there, although dressed in mourning, that Thornton Leslie could scarce believe that five years had passed since he had won the first blushing confession of her love, and that, instead of nineteen, her life marked twenty-four years.

He told her so, remembering, too, how wan, and indeed how old she looked when he parted from her at Asenith's door, and with a thrill of gratified love, he knew that his coming had worked the change.

"My precious love," he thought, "if I can prevent it—and what cannot a husband's love prevent?—your eyes shall never more be dimmed with tears, or your dear lips grow white with fear or pain. Heaven knows it was my deepest agony, even in that time of suffering, to witness how she suffered, too."

They spoke together of that time when they stood by Asenith's house, and looked around upon the quaint garden, now more than ever overgrown with herbs and flowers, which the rank weeds were vainly striving to o'ertop. Thornton thought of the time he had tottered up the narrow path, now almost overgrown with grass, leaning upon the arm of his unknown deliverer, and remembered what a tide of joy had rushed over him as he was received in the arms of his beloved under the humble roof now fallen forever.

His heart swelled with pain when he thought that he had been, perhaps, the cause of the affliction that had come upon Asenith.

"Ah, I would rather have died in prison," he thought, "than to have bereft that good woman of her home, and to have sent her forth to die of grief among strangers."

But Adela comforted him by relating again how peacefully she had passed away, and they gathered some of the choicest flowers from the garden, and carried them to Holmsford to scatter upon her grave.

"If there are saints in Heaven she is one," said Thornton, as he knelt upon the turf and planted tufts of violets above the mound. "Well, well, perhaps it is well she passed from earth before this time, for it would have broken her heart to see the changes that have already been wrought, and those which still must come."

"Yes," answered Adela, "for she took a mother's interest in all these ruined and scattered families. But over one thing she would have rejoiced."

"Our marriage?"

"Yes, and La Guerita's freedom."

"Ah, yes; the very angels must rejoice over that. Adela it makes me feel keenly the frailty of poor human nature when I think of her madness. She was such a lovely girl, so queenly and devoted a wife, such a tender mother. And even after her deep degradation of self-enslavement, there are few women so sweet and noble upon this earth ; yet I fear she is gradually fading from it."

"No, no," answered Miss Holmes, "that cannot be. She is growing strong again—she even leaves her room sometimes. She will live. Her soul is calm, and if not happy, she is, at least, content, and contentment is the surest medicine for such sickness as hers."

"Perhaps you are right," said Thörnton. "We men shudder if a woman we love grows pale, and I cannot but regard La Guerita with love and admiration akin to that I hold for you."

"I am not jealous," said Adela, with a smile, "and again I say that she will live. She is naturally a strong woman, Thornton. Her life for the past four years has proved that. She was dying of a breaking heart when her child was restored to her, and now that her sorrows are overpast, I believe as well as pray that she will live to know the hallowed bliss that follows pain."

They left the burial place and hastened to the house, to think of other things almost as solemn—those relating to the bridal.

Never rose a brighter sun than that which gilded the tops of the pine trees on the following morn. La Guerita arose early, for the first time in months, and with the aid of the willing servants, decked the house with flowers. It was a gala day on the plantation. The negroes, who had wandered off in their first days of freedom, had all returned to wit-

ness the marriage of their beloved Miss Adela. Roxy was especially joyous and triumphant, for of late she, too, had had her little dream of love, which promised now an unclouded future. Aunt Matilda alone seemed discontented. She wandered from room to room, surveying the different arrangements for the wedding, declaring "everything was going to wreck and ruin," and facetiously offering to sacrifice even Dixie to grace the marriage feast.

Thornton Leslie had in some way gained possession of the suit of regimentals which Asenith Bray had buried years before, but with her usual foresight had so carefully incased that they were as fresh as ever. Adela smiled as she recognized them, while he gazed delightedly upon her, as in her simple muslin dress and wreath of white jasmine, she entered the room, leaning upon the arm of Fabean DeCuba.

The ceremony was performed at eleven o'clock by the chaplain of Thornton's regiment, and was witnessed only by the members of the family and the servants.

Mrs. Holmes was, as usual, exceedingly tearful upon the occasion, and Minna, for some cause unknown, but seemingly incidental to young ladies at such a time, quite shocked her brother by sobbing aloud, and induced Miss Matilda to ask sharply if she was already crying because she was not married too.

Meanwhile the wedded pair were receiving the congratulations of all present, and were almost overwhelmed by those of the rejoicing negroes, when the notes of a magnificent band were heard upon the lawn.

"It is the band of my own regiment," cried Thornton, in delight. "Ah, Mr. Reeves, I owe this to you."

The doors of the house were quickly thrown open, and Thornton led his bride out, followed by the whole party. A deafening cheer rent the air as they appeared, which was followed by congratulations from the members of the band, and Captain Curtis and his men. Thornton thanked them in a few expressive words, for with delight he beheld in the unexpected appearance of the band the good will and affection with which he was regarded by those he had so often led into battle, by whose beds of sickness he had stood, and over whose dead comrades he had so often prayed.

After a luncheon the wedded pair, accompanied by Fabean DeCuba, his sister and her son, left Holmsford, and turned their faces to the North.

Adela felt some natural sorrow at leaving the home of her childhood, her mother, and her brother and sister, but the tears were soon driven away by the smiles of her husband.

Though it was not grief that oppressed her, it was long before La Guerita could cast off the painful thoughts that clouded her mind, as the carriage in which she was seated followed that of the bride and groom from the home where she had known so much sorrow and so little joy. She thought of the time when she had first entered it. The house was whiter then, the gardens more luxuriant, yet a glamour seemed to rest over them, which was all gone as, with lingering gaze, she marked each favorite spot, hallowed to her—some by pain, a few—a very few—by joy.

When they reached the cross roads at which she had alighted on the ever memorable day of Thornton's escape, she would gladly have hastened from the renewed expressions of gratitude he poured upon her, as his wife pointed out the path she had taken. It was indeed joy to her to meet her brother's approving glance, and to hear his softly spoken words :

"That deed blessed your servitude, and should make the memory of your darkest days endurable."

Upon entering the town of M—— they drove immediately to the depot. The whole party from, however, widely different motives, wished to avoid meeting acquaintances, but scarcely had they left the carriages when Mr. Gordon approached, greeting warmly, yet with a subdued air, his "dear Miss Adela."

She received and returned his greetings, and then introduced "Colonel Leslie," adding, in a lower tone, "my husband."

"Is it possible?" exclaimed the lawyer, in tones of genuine surprise. "Why, I supposed ——. But never mind ; times have changed. I wish you much joy, I'm sure."

The last sentence was uttered in a lugubrious voice, strikingly adverse to the sentiment expressed.

"How is Mrs. Gordon?" asked Adela, "and Lillie and Katie. All well, I hope."

"Yes ; but ladies can't be ladies now-a-day's—they have to be well and strong. I left them cooking the dinner. Just to think after all that I have said and done in their behalf, not one of my former slaves will remain with me. But I forgot it makes no difference if the wretched creatures do betray all the latent laziness and ingratitude of their race. You are on your way North, I presume."

"Yes, Mr. Gordon, with our dear friends, Mrs. DeGrey, and her brother and son. Colonel DeCuba, allow me to introduce Mr. Gordon."

Adela afterwards laughed heartily over the expression of rage and dismay that passed over the lawyer's face when called upon to respond to this introduction. He did so, however, gracefully enough, turning to La Guerita with the remark :

"This must be a sad time for you, Rita."

"Mrs. DeGrey," interrupted Fabean, frowning.

"Oh, indeed ; I beg pardon, but I have been accustomed to the name of Rita. Ah, as I said before, this must be a sad time for you ; but you must remember that you have still a refuge in Cuba. How many of you poor creatures, so suddenly bereft of protection, will be happy to seek it there ?"

Fabean's eyes flashed, and the muscles of his arm contracted with a sudden impulse to knock the audacious speaker to the earth. He restrained himself, however, and merely said : "He who dares insult Mrs. DeGrey will find, to his cost, that she has both a home and a protector in a free land."

"La Guerita, the cars are waiting," said Mrs. Leslie, turning from Mr. Gordon with a distant bow. She was almost sorry afterward that she had thus punished his insult, when she saw how deeply humiliated he was by her coldness and scorn.

In a few seconds the last whistle sounded, and the train moved slowly onward. La Guerita looked back upon the town, and remembered how she had first gazed upon it through the gloom of a summer night, long years before. Its lights wore to her then an unearthly, spectral glare. It was, she knew, but the result of her distempered fancy ; yet she wondered if the awful terror that fell then upon her heart was not sent to warn her back from the fate toward which she was hastening. She shuddered when she thought of it, and involuntarily turned toward her brother, whose arm instantly encircled her. She lowered her head and thanked God for His merciful kindness toward her.

She had entered that town mad, cursing God, and almost denying His existence ; she felt it meekly, blessing Him who had chastened her, and filled with the "peace that passeth all understanding."

These reflections, painful though they were, melted her to tears, and feeling a strange and sweet reliance on Him who so fondly supported her, she wept long and silently such tears as follow pain and hallow its memory.

A blessed calm possessed her soul as she shed those lightly flowing tears. The voices of the bride and groom floated toward her, filling her with content, sweet and perfect, though they brought to her the remembrance of the time when she, too, was a bride, and listened to such words of love.

"Though my husband can never be forgot," she mused, "there are voices that have the tone of his. Ah, my boy—my beautiful boy ! I will live for thee, and for the helpless and down-trodden of my race !"

CHAPTER XLI.

"So word by word, and line by line,
   The dead man touched me from the past,
And all at once it seem'd at last
   His loving soul was flash'd on mine."
          Tennyson's " In Memoriam."

ALTHOUGH La Guerita was most anxious to reach her home, traveling fatigued her so greatly that the party were, on her account, obliged to remain a short time in Norfolk. Upon the second day, as Mrs. Leslie was sitting alone in her private parlor, her husband entered and said :

"Where is Mrs. DeGrey ? "

"In her room," she replied ; "I have just persuaded her to lie down for a few hours. But what do you wish with her ? "

"Nothing in particular, my love. Perhaps, after all, it is just as well she should not know. Fabean found her hopeful son a few minutes ago in one of the rooms down stairs, watching, with entranced interest and offering to bet on a game of faro."

"Is it possible ? "

"Yes ; and exceedingly angry he was when Fabean first asked, and then commanded him to leave the room. He declared at first that he would not, and that his uncle had no right to speak to him in such a manner, and that he was doing no wrong ; that his 'dear Mr. Leveredge' had taught him to play faro, and that he should do so when he pleased.

"That is really shocking ! " exclaimed Mrs. Leslie ; "I had perceived that the boy was changed, but I had no idea of such things as that."

"Of course, you had not, my love ; but Fabean and I have both been troubled about him. You must remember the child was for months among a set of roystering men, who would have no scruples in teaching him every vice. If there is any good left in the boy, it is all owing to his deep love for his mother."

"Poor soul, she has a hard task to perform to eradicate from the child's heart the evil planted there by my misguided cousin," sighed Adela. "Where is Harold now, Thornton?"

"With Fabean, who is endeavoring to reason the matter with him."

"His uncle is almost a stranger to him," said Adela, with hesitation ; "perhaps if I were to speak to him it would have more effect. Ask Fabean if he may come to me, Thornton."

"Certainly ! " he answered, leaving the room, into which, a few minutes later, Harold entered, looking so sullen and defiant that Adela's heart sank within her. But she knew his nature, and talking to him kindly, yet firmly, showed him the evil into which he was straying.

"Mr. Leveredge used to do it," he said.

"That may be," she replied ; "but what may be proper for a man, is not for a boy like you. It is not right, Harold, even if Mr. Leveredge allowed you to do it."

"I don't want you to say anything against Mr. Leveredge," he exclaimed, passionately, bursting into tears.

Not for worlds would she have darkened the memory of her cousin in that young mind ; she knew it would grow hateful far too soon, and so she turned from the discussion of him to bid him remember that his uncle was then his guardian, and must be obeyed.

"If you don't want me to play cards again, I won't," he said; "but I don't see what right uncle Fabean has to order me around; I am not a slave now!"

But the memory that he had been accounted one rankled already in his heart. Mrs. Leslie knew not what more to say to him, and was gazing upon him sadly, when the door, which had been thoughtlessly left ajar, was pushed slowly open, and a boy, apparently four or five years of age, peeped slyly in. Mrs. Leslie looked at the child, and gently bade him enter. She was irresistibly attracted by the beauty of his face; there was, also, she thought, something very familiar in its appearance. Yet she could not remember where she had seen it before. She spoke to him again, and he slowly drew nearer her—timidly, yet with an air that showed he was used to receiving and well pleased with the attention of strangers.

She was still gazing upon the dark-eyed boy, with momentarily increasing interest, when her husband entered the room, and glancing at the child, exclaimed, hurriedly: "Who is that? What is his name?"

"I do not know," replied Adela, and, turning to the child, asked his name.

At that instant a female voice called: "Claude! Claude!" and the child bounded away, exclaiming: "Mamma!"

"Claude!" The name both had had in their thoughts. Thornton stood for a moment in deep thought, and then hurried from the room.

It was an hour or more before he returned. Harold had gone to his uncle's room, and his place was supplied by his mother, who was conversing cheerfully with Mrs. Leslie.

Colonel Leslie looked flushed and excited, and paused, irresolutely, when he saw La Guerita; then muttering: "It will be as well," said:

"I have just heard a strange tale, Adela, from the mother of that child."

"Indeed! what was it?"

"It relates to your cousin, Claude Leveredge."

"I suspected that," she answered; "Do tell me, Thornton, what it is."

"She claims to be his wife."

La Guerita turned deadly pale, while Mrs. Leslie exclaimed, excitedly:

"Oh, that cannot be true! My cousin was never married. Yet there were rumors of it years ago; yet it cannot be true."

Thornton shrugged his shoulders, and, turning to La Guerita, said:

"Will it be too great a trial to you to hear the simple tale the lady has just told me. If Adela approves, I propose to invite her into this room, and give her an opportunity of offering proofs that her claims are just."

"I should be glad to hear all she can say," replied La Guerita, striving to conquer her emotion, and to regain the self-possession she had for a moment lost, and speaking in a tone that intimated her utter disbelief that the claimant could substantiate her words.

"Yes; let her come, by all means!" exclaimed Mrs. Leslie; "one must listen to her, though I positively believe she will speak falsely. Why didn't she claim her rights when Claude was alive?"

"She shall explain all that to you," returned her husband, hastening from the room. He met Fabean in the hall, and asked him to join the ladies. He did so, and found them sitting silently together—each wearing an expression of extreme perplexity. He had not time to ask of his sister the cause before Thornton entered, ushering in a lady, whom all involuntarily rose to meet, and whom both Mrs. Leslie and La Guerita, with surprise and emotion, recognized as the original of the portrait found by Mrs. Holmes among Claude Leveredge's effects, at the time of his supposed death.

They were both so greatly embarrassed that it was with difficulty they could command themselves sufficiently to acknowledge with composure the introduction of Mrs. Claude Leveredge.

She was quite young; certainly not more than twenty-two or three. She would, indeed, have readily passed for less even than that, though her fair face was shadowed by an expression of melancholy, which deepened around her small, rosy mouth and in her large, blue eyes. She was small and slender, of most graceful form, and distinguished by an air of dignity that commanded, at once, admiration and respect.

A deep flush dyed her cheeks for an instant, as she replied, in a slightly foreign accent, to the salutation of Mrs. Leslie, "Mr. Leveredge's cousin." Then she sank gracefully into a low chair, and passing one hand lightly over her brow and across the bandeaux of luxuriant blonde hair that graced her head, turned toward Colonel Leslie, as if awaiting his pleasure.

With a pang, La Guerita noticed upon her hand a ring Claude Leveredge had been wont to wear long years before. Mrs. Leslie saw it too, and with heightened color listened to her husband, as he said:

"Madam, these ladies and the gentlemen present, are relatives of the late Colonel Leveredge, and will be greatly interested in any communication you may make concerning him,"

"Ah, sir, I will but tell them the truth," she responded, earnestly; "I scarcely think I could have revealed even that if you had told me at the first that my husband was dead."

She spoke in tremulous tones, faltering a little at the long words, and pronouncing them all, though with correctness and delicacy, in such a manner as to show they were strange to her tongue.

"Pray do not hesitate to repeat your sad tale," said Colonel Leslie, reassuringly; "it will be received with due consideration both to yourself and to the memory of Colonel Leveredge."

"I wish it to be," she answered; "Ah, gladly would I praise rather than blame my husband, if I could do so."

"Mrs. DeGrey," said Colonel Leslie, turning toward La Guerita, you are looking excessively fatigued. Pray lie down on the sofa. Thornton, there is a fan on that table."

La Guerita gladly obeyed Colonel Leslie's request, for she felt quite overpowered by the presence of that fair young creature who called herself Claude Leveredge's wife. Fabean seated himself beside her, and all, with the deepest interest, listened to the tale of the young stranger.

She began it very simply, without hesitation, or preface either of word or sigh :

"My maiden name was Adele Roquencourt ; my parents died when I was an infant, and left me penniless, to the care of an aunt—Madame Dujunois. She was a childless widow, and bestowed all the wealth of her affection upon me. But deeply as she loved me, I knew it was more for my beauty and cleverness than from any other motive ; for she was exceedingly proud, and although quite wealthy, occupied but a medium station in society, which she hoped to raise by my marriage with a noble. She often said I was beautiful enough to win any heart, and liberally bestowed upon me an education that would adorn a countess. I was exceedingly vain of my beauty, which I imagined of the most dazzling type, because, at an early age, I was named the belle of St. Croix—the village in which I lived. I aspired most eagerly to reach the honors my aunt prophesied for me, and as an important step toward them applied myself to study with a devotion which other girls, as frivolous as myself, would naturally have given to flirtations with rustic swains. For that reason, I speak so readily to you in your native tonge, for at the age of fifteen I was well versed in English, as well as French literature ; I also played on the piano and guitar, and accompanied them with a voice of considerable power and sweetness ; beside which I was an adept at all species of embroidery and fancy work.

"I tell you this that you may understand why I had many lovers, not only in my own station but above it. Among the latter, the most devoted, and the one which I favored most, was Monsieur DeLisle. He was an elegant young man—a gentleman in the highest sense of the word—the owner of the finest estate within many miles. My aunt was well pleased at his attentions, and I encouraged them, feeling justly flattered by the preference he openly avowed.

"I was walking near the village with him one evening, when I saw a gentleman loitering along the road, as if wandering there without any object unless perhaps it was to drive from his brow the cloud of care which rested upon it. I called the attention of my companion to him, and instantly, with an exclamation of pleasure he sprang forward and greeted him.

"A few moments later, I was introduced to Monsieur Leveredge, whose gloomy face, unlighted then by a single smile, was expressive of a melancholy—it seemed to me a despair—that filled me with admiring pity, while I saw with a thrill of gratified pride, that though in appearance the veriest misanthrope, he was not insensible to my charms, and from that moment the attractions of Monsieur DeLisle faded from my sight.

"Monsieur Leveredge remained in the village, at the house of Monsieur DeLisle whose intentions I still endured that I might see his friend. I believe now that I dissimilated so well, that even Monsieur Leveredge, for some time, believed me totally indifferent to him, and piqued at my coldness, he pertinaciously sought my society, and paid me attentions, of which at last both my aunt and Monsieur DeLisle demanded explanations.

"Until then I am quite sure he had never thought of marriage ; even then he did not ask me of my aunt, who had indeed declared, that she would never consent to my marriage with a heretic, but privately induced me to elope with him.

"We were married in Paris, by Le Abbe Marchand, and though I know now that I was not of age, my aunt could have claimed me, she, on the contrary, disowned me, and declared her intention of leaving her wealth to the church.

"Monsieur Leveredge installed me in fashionable apartments, and, for a time I was perfectly happy. My love of dress was gratified by the rich presents my husband lavished upon me, and my admiration satiated by the admiration of his numberless male acquaintances who visited us. I sometimes wished that I had one friend of my own sex, but it seemed that women were rigidly excluded from our circle, and I was exceedingly offended and mortified when I discovered that my husband often attended the assemblies of high-born dames, while I was by them altogether ignored. But he laughed at my anger and quickly dispelled it, and my suspicions, and on his continued attentions, and those of his gay companions, I rested content.

"So matters continued for nearly a year, when suddenly we were compelled to leave our elegant apartments for others far more retired.

My husband had lately lost vast sums at the gaming-table, and my jewels were sold to pay these debts of honor, while, in actual penury, we awaited remittances from America. Never shall I forget those gloomy days. My husband seemed plunged into the depths of melancholy. For a time I attributed it wholly to the lack of that excitement in which we had constantly lived, but at length I discovered that though that was doubtless the immediate cause, the more powerful one lay farther in the past, for then I discovered that my husband cared nothing for me, that he madly loved one whom he had wronged even unto death.

"Once in his sleep I heard him mutter a doubt whether she was really dead, and from that time my peace of mind fled.

"The remittances from America came ; we returned once more to our life of excitement, but I abhorred it. My husband won immense sums at the gaming table ; everything that he touched appeared to turn into gold. We lived in the greatest magnificence, but I was deeply unhappy, for my husband seemed like one demented, and I knew him to be the victim of passion and remorse.

"At last he suddenly declared his intention of leaving me at Paris, and visiting for a few months his native land. I was filled with despair, for at that time my fondest hopes were to be realized—I was about to become a mother, and I believed our child would bind him to me."

"Let me tell you the rest, quickly." She panted for breath, and grew pale, as if it were almost impossible for her to speak at all.

"My entreaties were in vain. He placed me in more retired apartments, gave me a sum of money, assuring me that his friend, Monsieur Dacre, would look after my welfare, and that he would shortly return. With that I was obliged to feign contentment, though my heart was bursting with anguish and distrust when he left me.

"A month afterward my boy was born. Monsieur Dacre was very kind to me. He visited me every day, and brought me fresh flowers and fruits when I could enjoy them, but he never mentioned my husband, though I asked for him repeatedly.

"At last I was quite well, and then one day — *mon Dieu*, I shall never forget it—he told me Monsieur Leveredge had left me forever.

"Oh, they were cruel, cruel words. I could not believe them. I demanded proof, and it was given me. Oh, I cannot tell you what he said, *Santé Vierge*, it was too vile! But he made me understand that Claude had never owned me as his wife—that I had never been imagined to be such by any who had visited us.

"I understood all then; why I had been made mistress of that gambling haunt. Alas, before I had been too young and innocent to know he would never have taken his *wife* there; why ·I had been excluded from all female society, and why I had been deserted.

"First came anguish, and then shame. I was daily insulted by Monsieur Dacre and such as he. All laughed to scorn my protestations that I was Claude Leveredge's wife— that our boy was our legitimate child.

"I escaped from them; I can scarcely tell how. But though my husband had branded me as the vilest thing on earth, he had not left me quite destitute, or Heaven knows, only death could have saved me from becoming so.

"I swore that I would prove the truth of my assertions, and although the priest who married us was dead, the record still existed and I found two living witnesses. They tell me my marriage is worth nothing in law —that I was under age, and Claude Leveredge a foreigner and heretic. But that is nothing to me ; it vindicated my honor—it saved my child from shame. I was triumphant in France ; I dared aspire to be so in America also. With the little money I had, I came to this country ; it was involved in war ; my object was delayed, I could not reach Claude Leveredge to force him to acknowledge me as his wife."

At that time Fabean DeCuba rose, and approaching the speaker, held out his hand to her, saying earnestly :

"I believe now that Claude Leveredge's last wish is fulfilled, that I have found ' Adela '—not his cousin —but his wife."

The young lady burst into tears.

Mrs. Leslie looked at her in painful indecision, and at Fabean, as if somewhat vexed at his officious recognition of the stranger's claims.

The young Frenchwoman perceived it, and striving to regain her self-possession, took from her pocket a packet of papers, saying :

"I toiled for my bread in New York, three long weary years, that I might force him to acknowledge the genuineness of these documents. He is dead! He has gone too far for either my hate or my love to reach him; but I have still my son to strive for."

She opened the package and spread upon the table the records of her marriage and the birth of her son—both attested by well-known names. There were also two letters from Claude Leveredge, beginning "my dear wife," the genuineness of which—those who knew his peculiar calligraphy, could not for a moment question.

Mrs. Leslie looked over the papers one by one in silence. She believed in her heart that what she had heard was true, yet she was unwilling, by acknowledging it, to cast upon the memory of her ·cousin the infamy he merited.

"Well, my love, what shall I tell her," asked Thornton, in a low voice.

"She must wait a little," she whispered; "I must talk over the matter with you. It is very, very, distressing."

She glanced at the stranger, and saw that she was overcome by her emotions, and was weeping bitterly.

The sight conquered her; her suspicious nature was vanquished, and clasping the delicate hands of the young widow in her own, she caught her to her heart, and wept with her, exclaiming:

"My poor girl, I do believe you; I do believe that you were the wife of my cousin Claude before Heaven, that is enough for us, whatever the law may be."

Thornton smiled, saying, "How like you, Adela, to rush from the ex-treme of doubt to that of certainty in an instant," while Madame Leveredge burst into hysterical tears, and rushed from the room.

She soon returned, bearing her child in her arms.

"Ah, Madame, she exclaimed, "my son is an outcast no longer. God bless you. God bless you."

Colonel Leslie interposed, and led the excited lady from the room, motioning his wife toward La Guerita, for whom the scene had evidently been too much.

"Oh, my brother, Oh, Adela," she cried, "I know she has spoken the truth. Her face has more than once risen between me and Claude Leveredge, and warned me back from him. Oh, had I yielded! O, God, what an abject creature I should this day have been."

They soothed her as well as they were able, and at last succeeded in restoring some degree of composure to her excited mind. But from that day, all the faith she had ever felt in the purity of Claude Leveredge's love—the last dream of her life—passed from her, and she saw it as it had ever appeared to others, as vile, as damning, as it had been insatiate.

CHAPTER XLIII.

"Were my whole life to come one heap of troubles,
The pleasure of this moment would suffice
And sweeten all my griefs with its remembrances."
Lee.

FABEAN DeCUBA and Colonel Leslie manifested the greatest interest in the case of the young Frenchwoman, and Adela, rushing to the opposite of the dislike and suspicions she had entertained of her at first, evinced for her the kindliest sympathy, feeling as she had before done for La Guerita that it was her duty, by every means in her power, to make compensation for the distrust with which she had at first regarded her. To this end she wrote to her mother and to Mr. Gordon, expressing her entire belief in the tale the stranger would tell them, for she was in no wise debarred by the news of the death of Claude Leveredge from declaring herself his wife, and proving the legitimacy of his child. In this she was most heartily supported by the Leslies, and also, though more gently, by La Guerita and her brother, who felt but too keenly how necessary to the happiness of the boy was the recognition of his mother's claims.

Mrs. Leveredge proceeded south on the following day, provided with full instructions how to act from Colonel Leslie, and from his wife with letters to all whom it was necessary she should meet, and on the same day the travelers north took the boat for New York.

Two days later, just at sunset, they stood on the pier at Ellisville. It was almost impossible for La Guerita to believe that so many years had passed since she left it. There were, she fancied, the same buildings, the same steamers discharging their freight or loading for the downward trip, the same little boats gliding down the stream propelled by youthful rowers. There was the same row of carriages, the very vehicles seemed familiar, and the same motley crowd of hurrying men of business, loungers, vendors of small wares and beggars, that had appeared to watch her so curiously when she left them five years before.

She stood in a maze of bewildering thoughts, the Past and Present each striving for the mastery. She was confusedly conscious that the Leslies bade her farewell, that Fabean placed her in a carriage, and that she was driven rapidly away. But it was not until they had left the streets of the busy little town that she recovered her self-command sufficiently to realize that her brother and son were seated before her, and that they were passing over the road to Enola.

Enola — Alone! Alas, she had prophesied her fate in naming her home. Home! Ah, that word. What a tide of emotions swept over her heart. She remembered the day she first entered it, and wondered if it was half as beautiful as then. Oh, no, it could not be. Her husband was then at her side—he who had ordered every beauty and perfected every charm. Now, the place so lovely then, knew no master. For years it had been deserted and neglected. Who would care to decorate for her coming; who would welcome her to it?

Then, for the first time, she wondered that Victor DeGrey had not been at the depot to meet her. The remembrance stung her to the quick. Were, then, her fears yet to be realized? Was she to be a stranger and an outcast among those who had once loved and honored her so greatly?

Happily their progress was rapid, and her arrival at the gates of Enola was too soon to allow a long continuance of these gloomy thoughts. A thrill of genuine delight, for an instant unclouded by any thought of the past, filled her heart. It was unchanged, beautiful, glorious!

Harold uttered exclamations of delight as the carriage rolled over the smooth roads, and paused before the steps. In a moment La Guerita found herself standing upon them, bewildered by a thousand thoughts of pleasure and of pain, but above all rose that, that here was no one to welcome her.

She felt a deadly chill at her heart. She staggered and would have fallen, but at that moment the door was thrown open and, with a cry of delight, Victor DeGrey bounded down the steps, and catching her in his arms, rushed tumultuously into the parlor, exclaiming :

"Thank God, mother, the wanderers are home again!"

La Guerita in an instant saw why she had been so disappointed at the depot, and on her arrival at the door of Enola, the mother and son had intended to give her a great heartfelt welcome that would neither excite nor sadden her. It was well that their plan had failed, owing to the uncontrollable emotion of Victor on beholding the agitation and weakness of La Guerita. The excitement attending her greeting was exactly what she needed to draw her thoughts from the past, and fix them upon the present.

And supported by it, she returned with delight the caresses of Victor and his mother. The latter after a single embrace and a fervent "Welcome, my child," turned to Harold.

She drew him toward her, and looked at times as if she could never turn her gaze elsewhere, then catching him to her heart, lost all the haughty calmness that had sustained her in her greeting of La Guerita, and burst into a paroxysm of joyous tears, exclaiming that she could bear to die now that the Lord had permitted her to look once more upon the face of the boy—the child of her dead son.

La Guerita could with difficulty afterward remember how that evening passed, she had pictured to herself her arrival home a thousand times.

She had believed that it would be joyful—yet, oh, how sad. How every room by its discolored walls, its moldy furniture, would cry out to her of her absence and neglect, and awaken bitter memories of the last lone hours she had passed among them. How different the reality. The walls were as spotless as the day she first beheld them, the furniture was the same, and arranged as she best loved to see it. She could almost believe that the stand of flowers near the window, was the same that Victor had placed there as a bridal gift.

The memory of the dark days appeared as a lively-remembered dream, while the first happy hours of her married life seemed actually present. She even in a nervous, excited way, turned every time the door opened, expecting to see her husband enter. She missed him all the evening; but not as one gone forever. He was absent but would return. So it seemed during the happy hours she spent that night with Mrs. DeGrey and Victor; later came the realization that his stay would be forever— that she was a widow not a wife.

But she was then better able to bear it, and though a deep tinge of sadness rested upon her heart, and clouded the beauty of her home, faith in a merciful God, and peaceful reliance in the love of her friends, stood sentinels at the door of her heart, and barred the entrance of anguish and despair.

Within her bosom, hope, crowned by love divine, sat enthroned, and every tear she shed sprang from that blessed source, even when she stood above her husband's grave, and mourned his early fate ; she wept as those whom the Lord comforteth, and left him to his long repose, not as once, in the fury of despair, but in the hope of a blessed immortality in which she, in life's fitful fever, might share.

She was happy. Aye, happier—more deeply, truly so—than her most joyous days.

Then she was joyous, as the birds are, because sunshine warmly shown upon her, and she did not dream it would ever fail. Now she was happy in that higher sense that only souls can know that have battled with life's sorest sorrows and temptations, and through them have found God's truth and peace.

It was a wonder to her friends how she took up the thread of her higher life so readily, when she had lost the clue so long. A stranger going into her home would never have guessed that the mind of the calm, graceful woman that so quietly presided there had ever been distracted so cruelly, or that she had for years been a lowly slave—not even mistress in the lowly cabin in which she had been a stranger to the luxuries and refinements that she now looked upon so indifferently, as if she regarded them as the common necessaries of life, that she could not even conceive the possibility of existing without. To Adela, who had never beheld her in that home before, the sight was not simply strange, but a mystery—a perfect mystery—as she emphatically told her husband, one evening when they were returning home from a visit to Enola.

"One would think that she had never known any other life," she said ; "She sat in a low chair engaged upon some trifle of knitting work, which she said was to be developed into a present for me, and entertained her guests, calmly and gravely it is true, but as pleasantly, as if to hear and answer their light talk, and to pass a needle slowly through such trivial work, had ever been her sole employment. Your sister was there, Thornton ; she came and went while you were absent with Fabean, endeavoring to decide upon a site for the charity-school."

"Yes," said Thornton, "La Guerita has learned by sad experience that toil soothes pain, when no reasonings can. She has set apart her life to the benefit of the women of her mother's race, while Fabean tells me he intends to go South to purchase a plantation, and make it a practical school for the young freedmen."

"Indeed," exclaimed Adela, "you astonish me. Fabean is so fond of society—so fitted to shine in it. How will he ever endure such a life?"

"His sense of *duty* will uphold him," answered Thornton ; "he, as well as his sister, possesses a noble soul. They will, together, in their generation, do more toward raising the negroes of America, than all the arguments and schemes of politicians could accomplish in ages."

"I believe you," said Adela, warmly, "La Guerita is a noble woman, and from those poor simple creatures she is gathering around her, she will produce noble women—noble in their sphere."

"And Fabean will do the same for the men," replied her husband, "already his heart and soul are centered in his work."

"Yes, but it makes me sad to see them so," returned Adela, musingly. "He is young, and it seems to me, formed for the joys of domestic life, yet he voluntarily renounces them all for the benefit of his fellow creatures. I thought of that when I saw Carrie this afternoon. Do you think it is possible that for love of her he has resigned himself to this life; she seems so different from him."

"She is," said Thornton, gravely. "He is strong and firm in character, and she so trivial and vacillating. I never knew her firm but once, and that was in keeping poor La Guerita's secret. But, Adela, she is not the lost love that Fabean has buried in his heart. The night before we were married we walked together in the garden at Holmsford, talking of my future happiness, and I said: 'Fabean, may you soon know the like felicity. My friend, I pray thee take a wife.'"

"He smiled bitterly. 'No, no,' he said, 'such joys are not for me. I am a proscribed man; how could I ask one of a pure race to share my destiny? No, no; I must live alone. When Harold is a man there may be some woman like his mother to claim his love, but there is none for me.'"

"Poor fellow!" sighed Adela. "But can it be possible that he has never loved?"

"Alas, no," returned her husband, "for that night he laid in my hands a long, fair tress of hair. 'There, my friend,' he cried, 'is all that I may claim of earthly joy. That lock my dying Mysta gave me. She was a promised bride; thank God she faded from earth before my shame was hers. In Heaven, where no shame can enter, my bride awaits me.'"

"It is better so," sighed Adela. "His life will not have been passed utterly lovelessly. Ah, Thornton, love is so sweet that 'twere a lost life that knew not of it, even though it reached not its perfection in marriage."

They walked together in the twilight to their pleasant home, joined hand in hand and heart to heart, while the brother and sister at Enola spoke calmly together of the loved ones from whom, by the dark waves of Death they were divided.

CHAPTER XLIV.

CONCLUSION.

"It is a glorious occupation, vivifying and self-sustaining in its nature, to struggle with ignorance, and discover to the inquiring minds of the masses the clear cerulean blue of heavenly truth."

Gwint.

"I stand
On a sure ground, unshaken as a rock
That bears the force of storms, yet still remains
Firm on its base, and rears its lofty head
Above the clouds!"

Bushe.

A YEAR later all that La Guerita and her brother had set apart to do was well begun. Upon the grounds at Enola stood a large, plain building, and within it scores of homeless children found shelter, and young maidens learned the duties of life. La Guerita aspired to no high work ; she did not blindly strive to set the ignorant negroes on a par with the whites, but to fit them for lives of industry, that they might sooner gain the high destiny that God had set apart for them.

But, during that long year, La Guerita's pathway was not thornless. Oh, what random shots rankled in her heart! How every slighting word or look cut her to the quick! And there were many to laugh and sneer—to whisper of her origin, her insanity, and question lightly her purity of heart and mind.

But even the most thoughtless and most cruel could not withhold themselves from her long. Insensibly she charmed all hearts, as they saw how patiently she endured all things— how she combatted the evil tendencies of her child, and found solace for all her griefs in the great work she had undertaken.

And Fabean, too, in his native State, where scorn was showered upon him on all hands—where every white man was his enemy—triumphantly held his way. The most skeptical saw that his plan was good— that he comprehended perfectly the position of the freedmen, and how it was to be ameliorated, with profit to both the whites and blacks. He went as a missionary among them— as a teacher, not an autocrat ; and shortly he was both.

For a year he remained upon his plantation, toiling with and for the youths about him, and proving, in his daily life, that though love be dead, and only scorn be left on earth, that

the heart may still be happy which places itself above the things of the day and looks for its joys in heaven.

At Christmas-tide they met—the brother and sister ; and long they talked together of their toils. He told her of the youths he was training to become, in turn, the trainers of their race. How well they learned their tasks ; how they were casting off their ignorance and dependence of slavery, and learning, as men, to hold and use their freedom.

On Christmas-day their only guests were the friends who had known and shared their troubles—Mrs. DeGrey and Victor, and Colonel Leslie and his wife, with a little one they called Asenith, in tender remembrance of her whose life was a record of good deeds, without a single blot.

"To-day I have planned to show you my home and school," said La Guerita, as they drove from church ; "my children have a little festival to-day."

"I'll go before and tell them that you are coming," said Harold, stopping the carriage and springing to the ground.

"Harold loves his old companions still," remarked Mrs. Leslie.

"Yes," returned La Guerita, "and 'tis better so ; that time can never be forgot, and, thank God, it is not all dark to him ; and when I hear him speak of some of the happy hours he knew, his words seem like blessings to me ; yet I know he will live to reproach me."

"Let us think no more of that," said Fabean, gently, "but rather of the noble work you have begun. Look at the happy faces looking down upon us from those windows."

The carriage stopped at the door of the school, which was opened by an aged negro, who had belonged to Claude Leveredge's estate, and whom Fabean had sent from his own, to his sister's care. He welcomed them delightedly, but was silenced by Aunt Dilsey, the housekeeper, who, with all the dignity and importance warranted by her high position, conducted the visitors to the reception room, whence, after, warming themselves before the glowing fire, they went to inspect the different portions of the building.

Three large school-rooms were first visited, which were furnished with every convenience, and where well-thumbed primers and blotted copy-books showed the work of education had begun. The teachers spoke of the improvement of their scholars most encouragingly, and each had something to tell of a bright little creature, whose aptitude for music, or drawing, or figures, had made him or her appear a very genius. Then the work-rooms were visited, and the needle-work carefully examined by the ladies.

"This helps us much," said La Guerita ; "the ladies of the town have lost their first distrust, and send us more work than can be easily done. Already we have sent out two seamstresses, who are giving the greatest satisfaction. But come in here ; I will show you my nursery."

She opened a door, and conducted Adela into a large room, in which stood a number of little cots, the owners of which were disporting themselves upon the floor, while two young girls sat near them sewing.

"You see, I make practical nurse-maids," said La Guerita, smiling ; "and these will go into the world and give an example to others ; so, too, will the kitchen servants, whom you must see next."

They descended to the culinary department, where they were immediately overwhelmed with greetings from Aunt Dilsey and Roxy, who ruled there.

"I'se jest as happy as de day is long ! " cried the latter ; "though de Lord knows I didn't mind fur· myself, 'twas de chillun that used to fret me. Now dere ain't no more sorrow in dis worl' fur me. All de chillun is togeder, and no body kin part 'em but de blessed Lord. Heah, you, Seely ; you peel them taters ; Lizzie, is this a time to put cabbage a bilin' ? You'll never be a cook s'long s' you live, ef you don't 'tend to me better. Miss Rita, dere ain't anythin' in de word to be a done wid dat chile."

They went, lastly, to a large room, which had been fitted up as a chapel, and ringing a large bell, La Guerita seated herself with her friends upon the platform, and with glistening eyes looked upon her charges as they gathered in, casting upon her glances full of love and respect.

Colonel Leslie and his wife looked on in surprise. · Although they lived so near, they had not even conjectured that so large a number had been gathered in, so ostentatiously had the work progressed. Tears filled their eyes as they listened to the simple prayer offered by the old freedmen, and to the songs of praise and thanksgiving that ascended to God from the full hearts of those who were but beginning to know how great a boon was liberty.

Fabean spoke a few words to them, telling them how he was striving to lead their brothers to lives of useful toil, and encouraging them to pursue them for themselves. He spoke to them plainly, exhorting them to no ambitious goal, but telling them that minds long abased by slavery must struggle long, and cast off a thousand cerements of custom and ignorance, ere they can take upon them the work of those who have ever lived beneath the vivifying influences of freedom.

Adela—the happy wife, the joyous young mother—almost envied the lone widow as she stood among her charges, and they pressed around her for one word or kindly glance. There was about her an air of deepest tranquility and content, and in her sable weeds she looked more beautiful than when the bridal wreath rested upon her brow.

"Thank God!" whispered Thornton, "that tortured heart has found peace at last. In making the happiness of others, she has made her own."

They left the school then, and drove to Enola, where the day was passed in speaking of plans for the future. La Guerita's were simple enough; it was, through all her life, to continue what she had begun.

"I am not rich enough," she said, "to keep any one in idleness, and I love those poor creatures too well to wish to do so; and though now they sometimes repine, and often rebel, they will some day know that only by toil can their race be raised to the position of mankind—they were mere brutes so long."

"But they were made in God's own image," said Fabean, gravely; "and though they have been trodden under foot, yet will He raise them up; yet who will aid, who will guide them? Those that love them most will mislead them by their untimely counsels."

"That is true," said Thornton; "you alone do I know, who, in a practical way, demonstrate to them the path they must pursue, and strive to fit them for it."

"But others will arise," returned Fabean. "The Government has something of the spirit, as has been shown by the Freedmen's Bureau, and by other means, and private individuals are awakening to it. Your young brother, Mrs. Leslie, is with us heart and soul."

"We were much disappointed when he refused to go to college," said Adela; "we thought pride induced him to refuse Thornton's aid."

"No, no," replied Fabean; "it was not pride; but he rightly thought he would make but an indifferent professional man, while, as a practical farmer, his career of usefulness would be unlimited. He was correct; and already, from our example alone, agriculture has improved so greatly throughout the county that poverty must soon become unknown. Ah, I forgot; Will. Russell, too, since his return from Europe, has interested himself in our plans. But I forgot to tell you, and I know that for my remissness I shall never be forgiven—Will. Russell is about to be married!"

"To be married!" echoed La Guerita, in surprise, while Mrs. Leslie reddened, as her husband glanced at her ; "and pray who is he to be married to?"

"That is the most wonderful part of all ; it is to Mrs. Claude Lever-edge. It appears that when he first saw her, she reminded him of some one, who shall be nameless, and whom he had once loved, and that the most of his time in Europe was spent in inquiries concerning her, which, I presume, must have been satisfactory, for they are to be married within the month ; and all I regret is, that my engagements here will prevent me from witnessing the ceremony."

Victor reddened, and soon after bade them farewell, that he might spend the evening with his promised bride. His mother looked after him with a smile. He was to make no mesalliance; yet, as she lifted her Harold's child upon her knee, she thought : "Ah, my son, my son! if thou hadst but lived to know truly thy noble wife! God grant that in Heaven thou knowest how little cause thou hadst to have shame of her!"

And later when the guests had departed and Harold lay sleeping on his mother's arms, she sat with her brother looking upon the glowing fire, and talking of all the strange vicissitudes of her life, and Fabean, for the first time told her how their lives were twin by a common tie—the loved and lost.

Then bowing her head on his shoulder, she whispered :

"My brother, nought can darken our lives again ; all clouds of sorrow has swept over us, and should any return they cannot shut out the light, for we know that our sun shineth forever — that forever God liveth who hath led us and our people from bondage, and giving us the blessed work of guiding his helpless children."

"Thank God for that work," said Fabean ; "I feel my life a holy thing thus consecrated, knowing that though here I bear it in shame, God will account it worthy of honor in that day when he judgeth the quick and the dead."

His face sank upon his sister's shining hair, and his soul drank in comfort as she whispered the sweetest words of England's sweet singer :

"Only my heart to my heart shall show it
As I walk desolate day by day."

"For oh, Fabean, I know that my husband waits and longs for me ; that he has seen and pitied me in my bonds, even as the merciful Savior did. Yes—

"And yet I know, past all doubting, truly—
A knowledge greater than grief can dim—
I know, as he loved, he will love me duly,
Yea better, e'en better than I love him.

"And as I walk by the vast calm river,
The awful river so dread to see,
I say, ' thy breadth and thy depth forever,
Are bridged by his thoughts that cross to me.' "

And counting their work but just begun, and all their sorrows but preparations for it—the brother and sister —with steady faith, pursue their way, holding their loves precious, and hoping at last to yield them as jewels to the crown of Him who breaketh all bonds, and out of the depths of worldly scorn and shame, raiseth his loved ones to eternal glory.

MRS. C. COOK

FIRST PREMIUM

HAIR JEWELRY,

519 MONTGOMERY STREET,

Bet. Clay and Commercial,   San Francisco.

Boquets and Wreaths of Hair

Ear-Drops, Breast Pins, Finger Rings,

Vest Chains, Fob Chains, etc., made to order.